Edwin Hodder

John MacGregor

Rob Roy - With etched port. by H. Manesse

Edwin Hodder

John MacGregor
Rob Roy - With etched port. by H. Manesse

ISBN/EAN: 9783337399764

Printed in Europe, USA, Canada, Australia, Japan

Cover: Foto ©Andreas Hilbeck / pixelio.de

More available books at **www.hansebooks.com**

JOHN MACGREGOR

("ROB ROY")

BY

EDWIN HODDER

AUTHOR OF

THE "LIFE AND WORK OF THE SEVENTH EARL OF SHAFTESBURY, K.G.,"
"SAMUEL MORLEY," "SIR GEORGE BURNS, BART.,"
ETC. ETC.

WITH ETCHED PORTRAIT BY H. MANESSE

AND NUMEROUS ILLUSTRATIONS—

FACSIMILES OF SKETCHES, ETC.

LONDON

HODDER BROTHERS

18 NEW BRIDGE STREET, E.C.

1894

PREFACE

I GRATEFULLY acknowledge my obligation to Mrs. John
Mac Gregor for valuable assistance of various kinds,
and especially for placing at my disposal her late
husband's diaries, manuscripts, sketches, and correspondence, and for furnishing me with information
and explanations which could not otherwise have been
obtained. To other relatives, friends, and co-workers
of John Mac Gregor I am also deeply indebted.

My object throughout the following pages has been
to draw a true portrait of a Man who exercised a
wide and still-spreading influence by his courage, perseverance, reverence, and buoyant hopefulness; whose
character may be summed up in one word—Manliness, in the fullest, freest sense—physical, moral, and
spiritual.

Wherever possible I have left him to speak for
himself, quoting freely from his diaries, correspondence,
and writings.

E. H.

St. Aubyn's, Shortlands, Kent,
September 1894.

CONTENTS

CHAPTER I

1825

A STORY OF THE SEA

CHAPTER II

1825—1845

CHILDHOOD AND EARLY YEARS

CHAPTER III

1847—1850

SHAPING FOR A CAREER

CHAPTER IV

1851

SHOEBLACKS AND SLUMS

CHAPTER V

1851—1853

IN FULL CRY

CHAPTER VI

1852—1855

TRAVELS, STORIES AND ADVENTURES

CHAPTER X

1859—1868

THE LONDON SCOTTISH

CHAPTER XI

1858—1866

CONCERNING MEN, PLACES AND THINGS

CHAPTER XII

1865—1868

THE "ROB ROY" CANOE

CHAPTER XIII

1868—1869

ROB ROY ON THE JORDAN

CHAPTER XIV

1865—1869

ST. REMIGIUS, THE CANOEIST

CHAPTER XV

1869—1873

ON THE CREST OF THE WAVE

CHAPTER XVI

1870—1876

LONDON AND THE LONDON SCHOOL BOARD

CHAPTER XVII

1874—1886

FAMILY, SOCIAL, AND CITIZEN LIFE

CHAPTER XVIII

1888—1892

BY THE STILL WATERS

LIST OF ILLUSTRATIONS

THE LIFE OF

JOHN MAC GREGOR ("ROB ROY")

CHAPTER I

A STORY OF THE SEA

On the 1st of March, 1825, the *Kent*, East Indiaman, of 1350 tons burden, under the command of Captain Henry Cobb, was driving, close-reefed, in the Bay of Biscay before a south-west gale of unusual violence, bound for Bengal and China. She had on board 364 men and officers of the 31st Regiment, commanded by Colonel Fearon, 109 women and children, 20 private passengers, and a crew of 148 men, including officers— 641 persons in all.

About mid-day smoke was seen issuing from the hatchway and port-holes. The ship was on fire! Gallant and heroic efforts were made to stop the progress of the flames, but in vain, and recourse was had to the daring expedient of scuttling the ship.

As she was settling down a shout was raised, "A sail! A sail!" Boats were lowered to meet the brig

A

slowly coming to the rescue, and in one of these, tossing on a furious sea, under the leaping flames of the burning vessel, with

> the bubbling cry
> Of some strong swimmer in his agony,

mingling with sobs of grief and ravings of despair, a little child of five weeks old lay nestling in his mother's arms.

The perilous passage from the blazing ship to the brig was made in safety, and the first to be handed up from the frail boat into the strong arms of the brave Cornish miners on the brig *Cambria*, was that little child, John Mac Gregor, the hero of our story.

He was born at Gravesend on the 24th of January, 1825, his father, Major Mac Gregor, then in the 31st Regiment, being, at the time, under orders to proceed to India. His mother, formerly Miss Elizabeth Dick, was the youngest daughter and co-heiress of Sir William Dick, Baronet, of Prestonfield, near Edinburgh, a member of an old Scottish family, one of whom was a banker and lent money to the impecunious monarch Charles I., which was never regained, and who figures in Scott's "Heart of Midlothian." *

Mrs. Mac Gregor was a woman of great ability, of splendid character, and of as brave a spirit as ever woman possessed.

---

* See note "R" in Notes at end of "The Heart of Midlothian."

Major Mac Gregor was an altogether exceptional man, as we shall presently see. He possessed, and transmitted to his descendants, the spirit of daring courage which had come down to him from a long line of ancestors of the Clan Mac Gregor—famous in Scottish history as much for their misfortunes as for their indomitable pluck in maintaining themselves as a clan in spite of most severe laws, remorselessly passed, not only against them but against any clan which, when overborne by those more powerful, refused to assume the name of their conquerors. Tradition says, and Sir Walter Scott and family memorials are our authority for quoting it, that the sept of Mac Gregor claimed descent from Gregor or Gregorius, third son of Alpin, King of Scots, who flourished about 787. Their original patronymic was MacAlpine, one of the most ancient in the Highlands, of Celtic descent and occupying extensive possessions in Perthshire and Argyleshire.

For generation after generation the Mac Gregors were fighting men, holding their own with almost ferocious tenacity. So late as 1560 Queen Mary granted a commission to the most powerful nobles and chiefs of clans to pursue the Mac Gregors with fire and sword. Gradually they were deprived of their possessions and had recourse to predatory forages to procure the means of subsistence.

" Rob Roy " Mac Gregor Campbell—the latter name he was compelled by Act of Parliament to bear— one of Sir Walter Scott's finest characters, made

the clan famous for all ages, and, as we proceed
in our narrative, we shall find that not a few of the
splendid qualities which characterised the Scottish
hero are reproduced in the life of our "Rob Roy"
Mac Gregor. We may therefore quote Wordsworth,
who was quoted by Scott, and apply these words :

> Say then that he was wise and brave,
>   As wise in thought as bold in deed,
> For in the principles of things
>   He sought his moral creed.
>
> *   *   *   *
>
> All kinds and creatures stand and fall
>   By strength of prowess and of wit,
> 'Tis God's appointment who must sway
>   And who is to submit.

The mottoes of the Mac Gregors are " E'en do and
spair nocht," and the Gaelic, "Srioghal mo dhream"
("Royal is my tribe"); the crest, a lion's head crowned
with an antique crown with points.

Major Duncan Mac Gregor, the father of the " Rob
Roy" of this history, was born on the 16th of March,
1787, and was appointed to an ensigncy in the 72nd
Regiment at the early age of thirteen. At eighteen he
was commissioned as one of the captains of the second
battalion of the since famous regiment, the 78th, or
Ross-shire Highlanders. That battalion, when at
Shorncliffe, consisting as it did of six hundred Highland lads under twenty years of age, won the
admiration of the celebrated Sir John Moore, who
took a deep personal interest in it, intensified when,

in 1806, it embarked for the Mediterranean and conspicuously shared in the honours of the brilliant victory at Maida in Calabria, gained by less than six thousand British, under Sir John Stuart, over a superior force of Frenchmen commanded by General Regnier. In this action, out of 7000 men under Regnier, 1300 were left dead, and over 1100 were wounded, while the British only lost 44 killed and 275 wounded. Among the latter were Captain Duncan Mac Gregor, who was wounded in the right shoulder by a musket-shot, and his Major, David Stewart, afterwards the general who became the "historian of the Highland Regiments."

Busy years followed. In 1807 he was engaged with his regiment in Egypt in the sanguinary but fruitless attempt to occupy Alexandria, Rosetta, and the adjoining coast. In August 1809, his regiment joined the disastrous Walcheren expedition under Pitt's elder brother, the Earl of Chatham, in which the troops suffered severely from fever. After four years in Aberdeen, employed in recruiting, the regiment embarked for Holland, and, though not actually engaged at Bergen-op-Zoom, took part in several severe skirmishes, for one of which they drew forth this testimony in a despatch from General Sir Thomas Graham, afterwards Lord Lynedoch: "An immediate charge with the bayonet by the 78th decided the contest. No veterans ever behaved better than these men, who then met the enemy for the first time. The discipline and intrepidity of the Highland battalion reflect equal credit on the officers and men."

After this there came a long pause in active service ; Captain Mac Gregor became Major Mac Gregor, and while residing in Scotland he married, as we have seen, Miss Elizabeth Dick on the 19th of March, 1824. Not long after, he was under orders to leave with his regiment,. the 31st, for India, and in order to be near the ship by which he was to voyage, he proceeded with his wife to Gravesend. There, in lodgings at the Bathing Houses—the *Kent* being stationed immediately before the windows of the house, and not more than two hundred yards from the shore—John Mac Gregor was born on the 24th of January, 1825.

By the 3rd of February the excitement of leaving home and country in her weak condition so told upon the health of Mrs. Mac Gregor, that it would have become a question whether she could undertake the voyage had not her sister, Joanna Dick—whose name deserves to be enrolled permanently in the list of the world's heroines—resolved, almost at a moment's notice, to accompany her ; a resolution that brought back health and strength to the invalid. On the 18th of February, still weak, and almost helpless, Mrs. Mac Gregor was wrapped up, with her infant in her arms, and laid in a cot which was carefully carried on men's shoulders and placed in a small boat. Thence she was removed to the comfortable cabin of a yacht until finally placed on her sofa-bed on board the *Kent*,

By permission of Messrs. Henry Graves & Co.

[From the picture by Thomas M. Hemy

THE BURNING OF THE "KENT" EAST INDIAMAN

where her medical attendant, Dr. Beaumont, visited her, and her faithful nurse remained on board for the first night. Next day the ill-fated *Kent* left the Downs.

It is recorded of little " Rob Roy," as he was even then called, that in the early days of the voyage he " throve charmingly, but having a good strong voice rather annoyed the cabin passengers when at their morning and evening toilet."

Before the Bay of Biscay was entered, two infants had died on board and were committed to the deep, and Mrs. Mac Gregor having, unwittingly, gone on deck at the time, was much affected, thinking of what might perchance happen to her babe. Of the tragic disaster which befell the *Kent*, of the undaunted heroism of some of the *dramatis personæ* of this narrative, no words that can now be written will ever exceed in vividness the following extracts from a letter written by Major Mac Gregor to his father, amid scenes of unparalleled excitement and distress and within two days of his standing again on British soil, after being rescued from a hundred threatened deaths. The letter has never before been published and its length will therefore be pardoned.*

---

* " The Loss of the *Kent* "—another graphic description of the scenes described in this letter, and published by the Religious Tract Society, who sold it by tens of thousands—was written by Major MacGregor at a later date to an old and intimate friend, Mr. Evans. The last edition of this work, issued during the veteran's lifetime, bears this prefatory note: " The older I grow, and I am now in my ninety-fourth year, I am the more convinced of the special interposition of Divine Providence in the events recorded."

FALMOUTH, *7th March*, 1825.

MY DEAREST FATHER,

. . . . It will be impossible for me to give you more than a confused account of our miraculous deliverance. . . . . After the date
of my last letter, sent by the pilot off the Land's End, we continued
to proceed for a day or two with a favourable wind. But we had
hardly entered the Bay of Biscay when it veered round to the south-
west and forced us to beat about without making much way. After
encountering several days of bad weather, a tremendous gale from
the W. and by S. came on about 2 o'clock on the 1st inst. It
increased rapidly until the sea rose extremely high even for the Bay
of Biscay. We put in our deadlights—drove along under our
storm stay-sail and rolling our main-chains under the water. Indeed
the violence of our rolling was so great that the crew were lashed to
the deck, and all our young sailors, and even some of our old ones,
looked unusually grave. I had just quitted Elizabeth [his wife] and
Joanna [Miss Dick, his wife's sister] for a moment to go on deck
about noon, when an officer as pale as death met me, and wringing
his hands, said: 'Sir, the ship is on fire in the after hold!' I
hastened towards the spot, where I met Captain Cobb and others.
The smoke was slowly issuing from the hatchway, and all hands
immediately employed themselves in conveying water. I then returned to Colonel Fearon's * cabin, and, not to alarm his family, I
called him out, and in a whisper told him our awful condition. The
smoke, however, in a few minutes rolled forth in such volumes as
very soon to render secrecy unnecessary. The horror that was now
observable baffles all my powers of description. Elizabeth and
Joanna were comparatively composed, but the screams of some of
the other ladies and of the soldier's wives who came running from
the lower decks . . . . were piercing . . . . Our driblets of water

* Colonel Fearon was commanding the troops.

poured down from the buckets were absolutely useless. Wet sails, blankets, and other woollen articles were thrown down in the hope of their smothering the flames, but all to no purpose. The only means that now remained was to scuttle the lower ports and allow the sea to rush in. Some officers of the ship descended for this purpose, but the smoke below was so thick as to render a long stay there certain suffocation. Myself and one or two of our officers, however, were not driven from below until we had succeeded, and during the operation one of our people fell over three dead bodies of those who had been suffocated early in the business before they could gain the upper deck.

The sea now rushed in in torrents, but though it tended to keep under the flames, it appeared evident that the quantity of water which was now running into the hold was sinking the ship, which would scarcely obey her helm, and as it had all the appearance of settling, as it is called, previous to going down, we endeavoured to shut the ports again. The only thing that now remained was to close the hatches, and by the exclusion of the external air to prolong our existence, the speedy termination of which appeared certain. Some were now filled with terrible despair—others were very properly imploring the mercy of that God who alone could pardon and save us. Elizabeth and Joanna were the organs of prayer to as many females as could find access to their cabin. It is quite impossible for a human being to be nearer to death without tasting it, than we were, and believed ourselves to be at that tremendous hour. Notwithstanding that those whom I most loved were about to share with myself the same melancholy fate, I declare that I really felt as great a composure and collectedness of mind, as I do at this moment. I felt the nearness of my Redeemer . . . . I look back with utter amazement at the strength that was given me. It now occurred to me that to prevent to yourself, my dearest father, and to my brothers and sisters at home, the terrible years of anxiety which our fate would occasion to you, it would be well if I resorted to a plan which has often proved useful, of addressing a few parting lines to you—getting with some difficulty an empty bottle and corking it hard up, and afterwards throwing it into the deep.

Elizabeth and myself had determined to sink in each other's arms. She was wonderfully composed, but Joanna's conduct was magnanimous in the highest degree. . . . . Some of our old soldiers and sailors who dreaded death by drowning, ran to the forecastle, under which was the magazine, and there awaited the explosion which every moment they expected. But most providentially the fire travelled towards the stern. In this state it occurred to a gallant young townsman of ours, Mr. Thompson, the fourth mate, and son of the Rev. Mr. Thompson of Duddingstone, to desire a man to go aloft, and try whether anything was in sight. The sailor, after getting to the foretop, looked around, and a moment after, taking off his hat, he exclaimed with ecstasy, "A sail on the weather bow!" His announcement was received with three cheers upon deck. As the sail, however, appeared at a great distance—the fire had been making progress for some hours—the sea was tremendously high—and as no small vessel and few large ones could be expected in addition to their own crew, to take on board nearly 700 human beings—neither Captain Cobb, Colonel Fearon, nor myself entertained much hope. . . . . On a nearer approach she appeared to be a small merchant brig with English colours. A glimpse of hope, not for myself, but for the dear ones around, now shot across my mind. Seeing that some of the sailors were preparing to cut away our boats with a view to provide for their own safety only, Colonel Fearon, myself, and two other officers, stationed ourselves conveniently with our drawn swords to cut down the first man who should touch the boats without orders, or dare to enter them until the means of escape had been presented to the poor women. It was impossible notwithstanding, to prevent a rush into the first boat that was launched, which was in consequence instantly swamped, and the work of death was begun. The miserable men on board of it we saw struggle for a moment with the breakers, and then disappear for ever. On board the next boat Captain Cobb resolved on placing the ladies, and as many of the soldier's wives as it would contain. My dearest lassie implored for leave to remain with me, but on reasoning with her calmly for a moment she consented to proceed. At this instant shall I attempt to describe my agony of mind? The boat hung over the quarter, and we determined to fill it first from the cuddy window, and lower it down afterwards. The ladies proceeded one by one. I stood outside on the chains to lift them into the boat. When I had handed in my infant and saw the boat lowering down into an ocean so tempestuous that no sailor on board thought it would live for a moment, I grew blind. But my confidence was in the Lord my God. Twice the cry was that the boat was swamped. It at last was seen fairly clear of the ship, and encountering the billows. Sometimes it disappeared for several seconds. At last it reached the brig. I poured out my praises to the Lord, as well as did poor Fearon. Our hearts were comparatively light in consequence of their miraculous deliverance. It seems that on their passage to the brig, which prudently kept at a great distance from us lest they should be involved in the explosion of our ship, the boat was half filled with water, and Elizabeth and the other ladies who were obliged to sit at the bottom of the boat, were up to their waists in it. The other boats were now lowered down, but three out of the six that the *Kent* possessed were sunk, and almost all the soldiers and sailors in them perished, the others reached the brig. But on gaining it the cowardly seamen instead of returning for another supply, sought shelter in the rigging, and had it not been for the determined conduct of our deliverer, Captain Cook, an Ayrshire man, the master of the brig, and some blunt but honest-hearted Cornish miners (who were going as passengers in her to South America, in the employment of the Anglo-Mexican Company), who seized the poltroons by the neck and heels, and threatened to throw them into the water if they did not return to our assistance, all of us must inevitably have perished. On returning to us, however, the boats only hovered round the ship without coming near enough to allow any of the men to get on board. We looked round for some powder to fire into them to bring them to. Some of the women were now lowered down by slings contrived for the purpose, but the time (which was unutterably precious to us) required for saving one woman, might have preserved several men, and therefore while the one process was going on with regard to the former, many of the men, throwing themselves into the water, made

towards the boats ; some perished, the greater number were saved.
Nothing could exceed the composure and energy evinced by Colonel
Fearon and Captain Cobb ; and, with a few exceptions, the gallantry
and subordination of all the officers and men.   Seeing that the sun was
fast sinking under the horizon, and that the boats were slowly
carrying off our people, myself and other officers superintended the
construction of rafts formed of spars, hencoops, &c., but on
launching them they were dashed to pieces.   In the long absence of
the boats between their trips, I employed myself in sitting quietly,
first among one group and then another, of the soldiers, some of
whom were giving way to terrible despair.   And I endeavoured to
preach to them Christ crucified.   Never was preaching less eloquent
or studied, or more earnest.   Never was it more intently listened to.
Some of them begged me to pray with them.   It is impossible to
describe the scene.   These means, however, if they have not, as I
earnestly trust they have, been blessed permanently to some souls,
had at least the effect of composing those who were in the greatest
agony, and of moderating the noisy lamentations of the poor women.
The night was now closing in upon us, but our numbers were
diminishing, either by being carried off in the boats, or by their
perishing in the water.   The upper deck was becoming insufferably
hot, and our thirst excruciating.   About eight o'clock almost all the
officers and men of the 31st, and all the officers of the *Kent* (with
the exception of Cobb), as well as the sailors, had taken their
departure.   Shortly afterwards, as the boats did not and could not
approach so near as to endanger them by crowding, since the plan
latterly adopted for escape was either to throw themselves at once
into the water on any oar or piece of plank on which they held with
the chance of being picked up by the boats—or by dropping
themselves down from the spanker-boom, Colonel Fearon, who
could not be of any further use on board the *Kent*, and might be of
some service in the brig in hastening the boats, attempted his escape
by dropping from the boom in question, by a swinging rope, in
doing which he was so frequently dashed against the side of the boat
below, and by the heaving of the ship plunged so deeply into the
water, that all thought he was gone.   He was however preserved, but

with one leg so bruised as to require the greatest care to prevent the most serious consequences. Almost all had now escaped who were not prevented either by wild despair, or by brutal drunkenness caused by despair, from availing themselves of the means. In an early part of the day, however, I had pledged myself to the soldiers' wives who flocked around me for consolation, that I would not quit the ship so long as a single woman remained on board, the presence of a few of them still in the burning ship, kept me and two other officers on board for an hour after the time I now allude to. One of these, a noble little kind fellow, who was particularly active in saving the women, having received a terrible blow in the chest, I ordered on the boom, as I saw him still disposed to remain. I then directed our excellent serjeant-major to proceed, and, having seen the last woman fairly off, the officer and myself prepared to depart. The boom stretched a great many feet beyond the stern, and by the heaving of the ship was sometimes not less than forty feet above the surface of the water. A rope hung from its extremity, down which you slid to the boat beneath. But it was not only the danger of going creeping-ways along the boom, and of afterwards catching with dexterity the rope suspended from it, or of afterwards dropping hand under hand—but, from the tremendous swell of the sea, which in an instant would carry a boat which the one moment seemed directly beneath you, twenty yards off the next; if you let yourself too low, or even sometimes as low as fifteen feet from the surface, the next heave of the ship would carry you, supposing the boat to be removed, ten or twenty feet under the water, and this perhaps several times over. The consequence was that many men who dreaded this process, stood on the boom unable to go either backwards or forwards, and ultimately perished in the flames. The few that remained were either frantic or stupefied, but notwithstanding my comparative awkwardness at such feats, I had already encountered too much, and was too firmly convinced of the nearness of the awful closing scene, to be deterred for a moment from mounting the perilous boom, and having thrown my leg across, with a thankful heart that I had been enabled to perform honestly my temporal duty, I committed my spirit (for which I was incomparably more solicitous at that moment than for what should become of my frail body) into the keeping of my faithful Creator and Saviour, and slowly crept forward, feeling at every step the utmost difficulty to hold on. And watching the opportunity when the boat below had been carried away by the surf, I slid half-way down the rope, conceiving, very justly as it proved, that by the time I got there, the heaving of the wave would be bringing the boat back, when I should have time to slide down the other half of the rope, before the boat again retired. Thus by the mercy of the Lord, I believe I was the only officer and almost the only man, who got at once into the boat, without being frequently plunged in the water, or without some serious bruise. The night was now far advanced, and our boat was nearly broken up —one large hole at the bottom we stuffed with soldiers' jackets, &c. twisted into it—and after rowing for a considerable time, in which I assisted, expecting every instant to be engulphed—we came alongside the brig. But here the sailors told us the danger was as great as in getting from the ship, for the rise of the sea was so great that some of our men were either drowned or bruised to death against the side of the ship. I waited a favourable moment, made a spring upon the chains, and was caught by a friendly hand which pulled me, with a heart oppressed with joy and praise, into the ark of refuge. It seems that the agony of mind evinced by Elizabeth, the darling, during the many long hours she had for reflection on my account, on board the brig, was painful to all around her. As boat after boat arrived, with officers and passengers, her piteous inquiries for me were heartrending. Her cousin, David Pringle, on his arrival endeavoured to prepare her for the worst. But she says her hopes did not entirely die within her until the arrival of Colonel Fearon, who, from his manner more than his words, expressed but little hope. What greatly increased her horror was, that the arrival of each boat being announced, her spirits were buoyed up for a moment, and then to be broken, as the loud gratulation was given to the officers who successively arrived! At last however the Lord, who never tempts above that which we are able to bear, turned my darling's mourning into great gladness—the news of my arrival was scarcely conveyed to the cabin, when I had her and my dearest

Joanna in my arms. Poor dear lassie—she was stupefied—my cup ran over—we could not speak—but God knows our hearts were filled with the praises of the Lord. Shortly after my arrival, the boat, which was under the *Kent's* stern when Captain Cobb left it, returned empty, none of the few men who remained on board having been able to avail themselves of it. The flames had now ascended to the rigging and masts, and the blaze from the immense mass illumined the whole heavens. As the fire reached the guns which were loaded, they went off, and it required some manœuvring on the part of the brig to avoid the effects of them. The unhappy men who were still on board, were now seen climbing up the rigging, and their yells as the fire approached nearer became quite unearthly. A speedy termination was put to their suffering. The magazine, which was inundated early in the day, had at last been dried up—the fire reached—the explosion took place—the firmament was filled with the fragments of the once beautiful *Kent*—the sky was in a blaze for a moment, and the next all was darkness. On witnessing the fatal issue we put up our helm and bore away for the nearest port. We were four hundred miles from land. Our brig was crowded . . . . even in the cabin we had seventy individuals. There was no room for lying down, nor were many of us permitted to take up the room of sitting except by turns—and most of us, I believe, stood up for two days and three nights without closing an eye, and in a heavy gale of wind. Some children died of exhaustion on board, and I verily believe that had we remained twenty-four more hours longer in the brig, that many must have expired. Our situation in some respects was worse if possible than in the *Kent*. The baby's tongue and mouth were white as paper with the thrush, and since our arrival medical men say that he could not have lived many hours longer on board. Elizabeth had no milk for him, and from the crowded state of the vessel and the violence of the gale, no fire could be made to heat water. On the morning of Friday last we came to anchor in Falmouth. Our feelings, first on land being discovered from the mast-head, and afterwards on coming to anchor, no language can describe. And two hours afterwards the wind changed in such a direction, that had we not reached a port we must have been beating

B

about several days in the Atlantic. But the instances of the superintending care of Providence are so numerous, that I must make them the subject of a future letter. I came ashore, for Fearon was unable, to report the circumstances to the Governor here. All boats were immediately out and our people landed. The whole town turned out—and never have I seen or heard of such an outpouring of the feelings of humanity. This place is noted for possessing a large body of serious people and of Quakers. We were instantly taken to their houses, clothed, fed, comforted. With the exception of a few sovereigns which I put into Elizabeth's hand when she left me, as I thought for ever, we have not saved a single article, nor was ten pounds' worth preserved by any individual on board. We are therefore penniless—shirtless—but not comfortless. A most liberal subscription has been made for our women and men, who have all been clothed by the worthy inhabitants. But of all this more hereafter. We know not our movements, but to-morrow we shall hear from the Horse Guards. As I am employed among other things in drawing up letters to our deliverers in the name of the officers, &c., I have no time.

Ever most &c. &c.

DUN : MAC GREGOR.

The loss is sixty-eight men of the 31st, one woman suffocated in the smoke, and twenty-one children.

Five seamen only have been returned, but as no regular muster of them was made, it is supposed many more perished.

All this does not include those that died on board the brig since our arrival. Some of our officers and men badly bruised ; one must lose his leg.*

* In proof of the permanent interest in this historic wreck it may be mentioned that so recently as 1893 a large oil-painting by Thomas M. Hemy, was on view at the galleries of Messrs. Henry Graves & Co., 6, Pall Mall, London, representing "The Burning of the *Kent*" and the departure of the boat in which Mrs. Mac Gregor and her infant were sent off to the *Cambria*. By kind permission of Messrs. Henry Graves & Co., a reproduction of this picture from the engraving published by them is given on p. 6.

Hundreds of interesting anecdotes and exciting incidents cluster round the narrative of Major Mac Gregor. We can only refer briefly to one or two, and first we may note that frantic efforts were made to put Mrs. Mac Gregor and her baby, and Mrs. Fearon and her young children into the gig-boat, the first to leave. Happily these efforts were frustrated; the gig-boat sank, and all the occupants perished.

Safely on board the *Cambria*, Mrs. Mac Gregor and her infant were wrapped in dry blankets and placed in a cabin. Then as boat after boat arrived with rescued passengers, but not her husband, she was for a time in an agony of mind, but after a while she said calmly, " He is in the path of duty, and God's power can preserve him there."

When Colonel Fearon came on board the *Cambria* Miss Joanna Dick sought eagerly to speak to him but it was impossible; he went straight to Mrs. Fearon's cabin, and his first words were, "I fear poor Mac Gregor is gone!"

Certainly no man ran greater risks or bore himself with greater composure than he, and no one was more wonderfully preserved. At one time thinking his last chance was to construct a raft of hen-coops and lash himself to them, he calmly took his sash and some rope and set to work to this end, first of all placing an apple in a convenient pocket to enable him to preserve existence so long as it was possible!

Bravely through a stiff gale the overloaded *Cambria* ploughed her way. It was a terrible voyage. The

passengers were packed so closely together that the
atmosphere was intolerable, insomuch that the light of
a candle coming in contact with the impure air was
instantly extinguished.   It was almost impossible to
get either food or water and the suffering and exhaustion were intense.   Poor Mrs. Mac Gregor was unable
to give her babe its natural food any longer, and little
Rob Roy—who was fed only on sugar until arriving at
Falmouth—cried incessantly throughout the voyage.
The fact that so young a child should have survived
so many perils, such great exposure and discomfort, is
one of the most extraordinary events of that time of
trial and disaster.

On the safe arrival of the *Cambria* in Falmouth
Harbour on the 5th of March, Major and Mrs. Mac
Gregor and their party found a very hospitable reception in the house of Mr. William Crouch, an
excellent man and a member of the Society of Friends,
with whom and his wife and daughters a life-long
friendship was maintained.

It was a solemn day in Falmouth that Sunday
following the arrival of the saved ones from the *Kent*
and never had the Church there presented a stranger
or more interesting spectacle than when Colonel
Fearon, followed by all his officers and men, and
accompanied by Captain Cobb and the officers and
private passengers of his late ship, entered the Church
and joined in the expression of thanksgiving to
"Almighty God, Father of all mercies."   It was a
thrilling moment when all voices, some choking with

FAC-SIMILE OF LETTER WRITTEN AND PUT IN A BOTTLE BY THE FATHER
OF JOHN MAC GREGOR DURING THE BURNING OF THE "KENT" EAST INDIAMAN.
FOUND AT BARBADOES NINETEEN MONTHS AFTER.

emotion, uttered the words, " We bless Thee for our creation, *preservation*, and all the blessings of this life ! "

The Mac Gregors and their immediate friends left Falmouth on the 18th of March and what further adventures befell them thereafter will appear in the following chapters, but two curious coincidences may well be recorded here.

On the 30th of September, 1827, about nineteen months after the loss of the *Kent*, when Major Mac Gregor was at Barbados, a gentleman bathing from the Western shore of that island picked up a floating bottle. On breaking it he found within a folded paper bearing a signature with which he was familiar : " D. Mac Gregor, 1st March, 1825." It was the paper, of which we have given a facsimile, written, as it seemed then, almost in the hour of death ! A strange thrill must have passed through the frame of Colonel Mac Gregor as he looked once again on that paper handed to him personally by the finder.

Another curious circumstance may be mentioned here.

In the year 1856, when John Mac Gregor was over thirty years of age, he was one day on Lanark race-course in connection with the work of the Open-air Mission, when an old sailor was seen among the crowd selling doggerel verses relating to the burning of the *Kent*, at which he stated he had been present. Mr. Mac Gregor went up to the man and said that he too was on board the ship at the time of the catastrophe.

The sailor, seeing that the speaker was much younger than himself, curtly exclaimed, "That you were not unless you were the baby I helped into the boat!"

Surely a life thus miraculously spared from fire and wreck, and again from air—the foul and suffocating air of the overcrowded ship in which he was rescued —was to have some great mission before it. What that mission was we shall unfold in the succeeding chapters.

CHAPTER II

CHILDHOOD AND EARLY YEARS

AFTER leaving Falmouth the Mac Gregors went to Scotland for rest and recovery of strength.

Of course the strain on all had been tremendous ; and it is a never-ceasing wonder how much it is possible for women to bear and sometimes to forget. This was the experience of Mrs. Mac Gregor and also of Miss Joanna Dick who wrote : " For some weeks I was unable to write, and for part of the time even to read letters or anything to agitate the mind, but after being twice bled and carefully attended by many kind nurses I feel now quite as well and stout as ever."

Three or four months after the loss of the *Kent*, the child who had excited so much solicitude was stricken down with infantile illness, and his mother wrote to a friend : " I was too vain of him. I had so many friends who flocked to see him, and I did feel mortified to show my once noble boy reduced, as he then was, to one-third of his previous size." He pulled through, however, and his mother says : " A more engaging, lovely child, never blessed a mother's arms. I feel him a constant source for prayer and fondly hope he is indeed saved for the Lord's service,—perhaps he may be a minister of Christ yet."

After some months rest in Scotland, it was deemed necessary that Major MacGregor should be near the Horse Guards, and accordingly he, his wife, and the babe, sailed from Edinburgh in a steam-vessel for London. The weather was fine at starting, but within twelve hours a fearful hurricane was raging. The vessel lost her anchors and drifted during the night in the direction of Newcombe Sand Banks. When the morning dawned it was seen that the position was one of great peril. Within a mile and a half the breakers were dashing on those dangerous sands. The sea was so high that it broke over the deck, nearly extinguishing the fires, while the vessel was drifting almost helplessly towards speedy destruction. Then the gale suddenly fell, the wind veered completely round, and the rest of the journey was accomplished in safety.

"Poor little John has again been preserved in great danger," wrote Joanna Dick to her Falmouth friend, Miss Crouch; "he is now quite well and vigorous again, and uncommonly intelligent at his age, and is, I am told, looking joyful and rosy though his terrors and screams, poor infant, during the voyage up were truly distressing. Poor Elizabeth (Mrs. MacGregor) indeed says her nerves are so shaken with this last alarm that she looks forward with dread to another sea voyage." And no wonder!

An incident, very gratifying to Mrs. Mac Gregor at this time, was a visit to the celebrated Hannah More, then in her eighty-first year. On the following day she sent a present to "little Rob Roy" accompanied by the following lines :

To MASTER JOHN MAC GREGOR.

(With a pair of boots of my own knitting.)

Sweet babe *twice* rescued from the yawning grave,
The flames tremendous and the furious wave,
May a *third* better Life thy spirit meet,—
E'en Life Eternal at thy Saviour's feet.

BARLEYWOOD, *May* 23, 1825.   HANNAH MORE.

At the Horse Guards Major Mac Gregor's noble services were specially appreciated and were recognised by well-merited promotion. He was made Lieutenant-Colonel of that splendid regiment the 93rd, or Sutherland Highlanders. But—and the inevitable "but" is almost always as "the fly in the ointment"—his destination was the West Indies, and there was before him, almost immediately after the awful experiences through which he had passed on board the *Kent*, another sea voyage.

In August 1826, he sailed for Barbados, and after a perilous voyage arrived at his destination towards the end of September. At one time it was in contemplation that Mrs. Mac Gregor, "little Rob Roy" and Miss Dick should accompany him, but while they were staying in Edinburgh, on the 16th of

July, another son, William, was born, and it was decided that the Colonel should go out alone. During
his absence they went to a small but very pleasant
country-house in Fife, placed at their disposal by an
uncle of Mrs. MacGregor, and writing from that
house to her friends in Falmouth, she said : "You
would be pleased to see the talkative amusing little
John, and the rosy smiling sweet little William his
brother. They beguile the hours of long separation."

The separation came to an end in 1828. " I know
you will join in praising God with me," Mrs. Mac
Gregor wrote, "for the joyful tidings my last West
India letters brought me, that ere long my too much
loved husband is to be restored to me. . . . . My
two darling boys are in the highest health ; John
is really quite a companion to me now, a most intelligent dear child as it is possible for a mother to be
blessed with. . . . ."

The child is father to the man, and some of the
anecdotes of John's childhood illustrate the bent of his
mind and foreshadow his later experiences. One of his
earliest vivid recollections was the coronation day of
William IV. John was with his parents in a house at
Westminster, and at an open window of one of the lower
rooms he and his younger brother watched the carriages
passing to the Abbey, while their plates of porridge
were cooling on the window sill. Suddenly, on the
pavement close by them, a nobleman passed in court
dress wearing a coronet glistening with jewels. He
saw the two little boys at the window gazing with such

astonishment and curiosity that he stopped and spoke to them, and to their extreme delight took off his coronet and smilingly placed it on their heads.   It was an eccentric but a most kind action, and made a deep impression upon one who afterwards spent so much of his life in showing love and kindness to children.

Another of his earliest recollections was sitting on Dr. Chalmers's knee when a very little boy while the learned divine talked to him about a small piece of coal which he held in his hand.

In 1834, when he was nine years old, the 93rd Highlanders, under the command of his father, were stationed at Canterbury, and there John went to his first school—the King's school, within the precincts of the Cathedral.   Accompanied by his brother William, who was eighteen months younger than himself, and two other boys, also "Macs," sons of an officer of the regiment, he was taken to school each morning by a stalwart Highlander.   After a short time the Mac Gregor spirit rebelled against this infringement of the liberty of the subject, and the boys asserted their independence by making their attendant keep on the other side of the road.*

Owing to the constant removal of the regiment from one station to another, John Mac Gregor's education was varied.   At Weedon, Northamptonshire, in

---

* In after years John Mac Gregor used this incident in his addresses as an illustration of the saying, "The law is the 'child-leader,' to bring us to the great Schoolmaster (Christ)."   (Galatians iii. 24.)

1835, the two brothers were sent in a covered cart
with the other two " Macs " to a school some distance
off.   They received so much a day to buy their
dinners but after a short time it was found that the
boys were not in such good health as usual, and on
questioning them it was ascertained that they had
dined each day on candied peel in preference to more
wholesome and nourishing food.

There were merry, happy days at Weedon.   John
had always an intense love for the water, and from a
very early age he was allowed to manage a boat alone.
He often spoke of dangerous exploits and hairbreadth
'scapes on the canal at Weedon, and could tell stories
that would make the ears of boys tingle.

Brought up from babyhood with the constant recognition of God's wonderful love in sparing him from
fire and wreck, having always around him the prayers
and example of his saintly and heroic father and
mother, being in himself a good-tempered and loving
child, little John was easily susceptible to religious
influences, and the following incident made so deep
an impression on his mind, that even in the fulness of
manhood he looked back upon it with pleasure as his
first experience of "answered prayer."   We give the
story in his own words :—

At the age of eight I was staying with an uncle and aunt, Mr.
and Mrs. Smith-Cunningham, of Caprington Castle, Ayrshire.   I had
been fishing one morning for some time and had caught nothing,
when I suddenly thought ' I will ask God to let me catch a fish.'   I
prayed to God, and soon after I caught a fish.   Then the thought

flashed through my mind, 'If God can answer this prayer will He not take away my sins and give me a new heart if I ask Him?'

It was merely a child's thought, but it may perhaps be interpreted thus : "If God can give me the small things of life for which I daily pray, will He not give me the greatest gift of all for which I have never yet consciously asked Him in downright earnest."

Religion is not, as some erroneously suppose, a depressing influence, and it did not for a moment mar the full enjoyment of his boy-life or check the spirit of adventure, for, as we have seen, there were merry days at Weedon, and others followed close after, and the same spirit remained in him. At Belfast, when twelve years of age, he was with a number of sailors on the beach during a terrific storm watching a ship in distress. The life-boat was launched, and at the last moment John jumped into it and went off with the crew to assist in the work of rescue.

We have not been able to follow in detail the movements of Colonel Mac Gregor, and it will be enough for our present purpose to say that wherever he went he exercised a singular power for good and was almost worshipped by his men for his splendid manliness. One fact alone will give an idea of the extent of his influence.

When the 93rd, under his command, was stationed at Halifax, Nova Scotia, every one of the soldiers used to march to church with his Bible and Presbyterian psalm-book under his arm, and it is on record that on one occasion nearly 700 of them partook of the Sacrament.

In 1838 he was called home to occupy the lucrative and important office of Inspector-General of the constabulary force in Ireland—an office which he held for twenty years with great credit to himself and much advantage to the country in very perilous times. The establishment of a police force in Ireland had engaged the attention of the great Duke of Wellington, then Sir Arthur Wellesley, in 1808, and subsequently of Sir Robert Peel, when he too was Secretary for Ireland; but to no one does the organisation of that valuable force belong more than to Colonel Mac Gregor, and it is recorded of him that "by his superior and judicious arrangements in that establishment he gained for himself the confidence of the Government and the gratitude of every class of the people with whom he came in contact, not only in his official but also in his private capacity." During the time he held this post he resided at Belvedere House, Drumcondra, near Dublin, his family consisting of John and William; Duncan, born in 1830; Elizabeth Joanna Anne, born 1831; Douglas Alexander, born 1835; Henry Grey, born 1838.

At the age of fifteen, when boating was a passion and John MacGregor had the leisure, means, and opportunity of indulging it, he was wrecked in an iron boat, alone, outside Kingstown Harbour, near Dublin, and had a narrow escape of his life. We will let him

tell the story of what he calls his "Second Shipwreck," in his own words, as he told it to boys :—

There was a pretty little iron cutter for sale in the large harbour
of Kingstown, near Dublin, and I saved my pocket-money (as a boy
of fifteen ought to do) and hired the charming craft on Saturday
holidays several times, until the man let me go out alone—you
know the delicious feeling of that, my lads !

Sailing alone makes you understand the whims and fancies of a
boat, and how its boom *will* gibe and hit you under the left ear ;
and how much sheet is required for the jib.

I got bolder after practice—which was right ; but at last I got
rash—which was wrong ; so I ventured outside the harbour, just 'to
go a *little way* and then come back'—the usual intention which is so
difficult to fulfil.

The first few rollers in the great tide-way outside the piers were
perfectly delicious ; but at last a sudden billow gave us such a jerk
that the peak-halyard snapped, and at once my mainsail dropped
and hung dishevelled all in 'a mess.'

It was dangerous to 'wear her,' for the sea would come over the
stern, and it was impossible to 'go about' in the regular way. So I
had to jog on and thus get into smoother water ; and yet, somehow,
it didn't get smoother.

But eyes were upon me in this danger, and the skipper of a big
yacht, then at anchor in the harbour, kindly 'boused up' his crew
and gallantly came out to save the lonely mariner. Oh! how I
thanked him in my heart as I saw the fine schooner dashing through
the waves ; and then he whirled round my lee and dropped a sailor
boy on my bow with a strong rope to make fast to my sinking cutter.
But the boy took fright and failed to fasten the rope ; and, with a
shout of fear, he scrambled back on board the schooner, while
'oceans of water' poured into my lilliputian craft, and I was left
alone again. Not only alone, but sinking fast, because my iron
cutter had *no compartments ;* and an iron boat is sure to sink when
filled.

But see now, there are minutes still of hope; the schooner goes about to return, and here she is alongside again, in the whistling wind and the bursting surge—an anxious time indeed. They heaved a rope again to me, and I rushed forward, seized it, fastened it well round the 'bits' (for the anchor and bowsprit), and down she sank while I climbed on board the schooner—all in a few seconds.

Heavy work it was to tow the sunken iron yacht into the harbour, until at last she grounded, but when the tide left her dry she was got all right again.

Of the adventures in his boyhood—and they were far more than we can find space to record—he made ample use in after years. Thus, when he was engaged in an effort to organise agencies by which every boy in this " sea-girt isle " should be taught to swim, he spoke on one occasion to some successful prizewinners, and said :

Of the several cautions which ought to be observed in bathing, I shall mention only those that relate to chill, water too cold, time in it too long, diving when tired, or long fasting, or soon after a meal. Like many lads who forget or defy such cautions, I had a sharp lesson once which I never wanted again. As a youngster at Liverpool I used to bathe in the wide sea mouth of the Mersey, going out in a boat on the swift tide with a man to manage it while I was in the water. One day, after a long swim I got tired and cold, and tried to lay hold of a huge buoy which swung violently as the tide waves dashed it about. Missing my reach, I sunk under the buoy, and had to swim to the next buoy farther out to sea. Numbed and anxious I was swiftly carried near to this, and I leaped and caught the huge iron ring, but, alas! our boat had stuck fast on the beach and it was too heavy for the man to launch it. How I was rescued I never could find out. Beware of long swims in a tide-way.

One who knew John Mac Gregor in his early days better than any one now living, writes :

I don't remember any *important* event in John's boyhood. But I well remember our workshop where more than one boat was built by ourselves (and how we had various upsets in them) and how John, who showed a great aptitude for mechanics, made a little locomotive-engine which worked well, also a stationary one for pumping ; electrical machines, galvanic batteries, &c , and intolerable chemical mixtures which resulted in several rather serious explosions. John was a good tree climber, a very fair boxer and horseman, in fact he was a manly boy.

I know of no special distinction at school ; he was always a hard worker and fond of the society of those older than he was, and no doubt gained the usual prizes ; but I know of nothing special. I think he was at Dublin College for only a year or so and that he went direct from there to Dr. Tattersall's. He was very good at mathematics, and gained honours in these but not in classics—I think first-class honours. It must have been in 1839–1840 that he entered Trinity College, Dublin. He never was at a public school. That is to say he never was a boarder, he always lived at home, and he did so when at Dublin College. I think you may say he feared God from his youth and always wished—and that right earnestly— to be a missionary, but his mother dissuaded him, or rather begged him not, so he abandoned the idea. Then he very much wished to be a civil engineer, but Cambridge, I think, gave him a taste for the Bar, and owing to his scientific proclivities he associated himself with Patent Law, which then was practically monopolised by one man with whom he read and who thought very highly of him. There is no doubt whatever that he would have succeeded this man if money-grubbing had been his object."

This extract has carried us somewhat too far ahead, and we must go back to the year 1842 to tell one more story of his youthful adventures.

In company with six choice companions, Mac Gregor, then in his seventeenth year, started off in holiday time for a tour round the North of Ireland. One afternoon they went to see the hanging bridge at Carrick-a-rede, connecting a little island in the sea with the high cliffs, and formed of two ropes carrying a plank about seventy feet long and only a few inches wide, high in mid-air, over the dashing foam. As they drew near they were pressed by a crowd of men and women to take one for a guide, but they insisted upon being conducted only by their driver, a sharp little Irish lad. The men, disconcerted, followed them over the bridge, where the tourists inspected the island, the salmon nets, and the frowning cliffs, and then came back to the bridge to find all the men huddled together and the ropes of the bridge slackened. "Gintlemen," said one of the men, by name Corney Regan, "ye'll not cross till ye pay." The discussion lasted long, and after hours of wrangling—the wind meanwhile having risen to a gale—one of the tourists, Houldsher, a Cantab, gallantly volunteered to rush across the bridge if the others could draw it tight. He gained the other side in safety, ran to the car, and unharnessing a horse, rode off at full gallop towards the police-station.

The men were cowed by this bravery and offered to let the others go, but Mac Gregor said, "Not a bit of it, you are our prisoners, and we will not let you stir till we hand Corney over to the police." An hour of cold suspense followed, but at last the shouts of Houldsher were heard on the other side, and all he could say was in Latin, "*Non potui!*" ("I couldn't do it)"! His horse had fallen, his head was cut, he had lain insensible, his horse had disappeared, and, after

CARRICK-A-REDE.

vain efforts to ride a donkey, he had given it up in despair. The men, however, thinking that the police were coming, assisted in tightening the bridge, and in the darkness, with the bridge swaying and creaking in the wind, and the sea dashing wildly below, four of the tourists crossed one by one. Then the men made a rush for the bridge, but MacGregor had arranged the order in which they should pass, and he told them that the first who came to the other side out of that order should be hurled down the cliffs by his companions. It was one youth against twenty hulking and angry men, but "Horatius kept the bridge," the men gave in, and Corney prepared to cross with Mac Gregor close behind him. When they came to the middle of the bridge Corney plumped down, sat astride the plank, and vowed with dreadful oaths that he would never move until MacGregor had first passed. It was a moment of intense excitement, the scene was wild in the extreme, and in after years Mac Gregor said he never had been before in such peril. But his blood was up and, standing on that narrow plank with certain destruction before him if he over-balanced and fell, he buffeted the big bully with his knees, boxed him with his hands, kicked him with his feet, until at last he rose and scrambled over on all fours, followed quickly by MacGregor.

Once on the mainland seven pairs of hands were on Corney, who was now their prisoner, and they carried him off straight to a magistrate, although it was two o'clock in the morning. Corney Regan was sent for a year to gaol, and MacGregor and his friends proceeded with their Long Vacation tour.

When John was at Liverpool under the care of Dr. Tattersall, a tutor who took a few pupils to prepare for Cambridge, he was for some time in a somewhat delicate state of health, and suffered from bronchial attacks due, it was believed, to the exposure he experienced on board the *Kent* when an infant. So frequent had these become, that he was careful to avoid all occasions of catching cold ; a fire was always lighted in his room, and a "comforter"—falsely so-called—was wrapped round his neck. In course of time he threw aside the comforter, indulged freely in cold water and fresh cold air, and at length grew out of his tendency to throat complaints. At Dr. Tattersall's, among his companions were Lord Robert Montague and Lord Bangor, for whom, in after years, he entertained a great regard. From Dr. Tattersall's Mac Gregor proceeded direct to Cambridge.

It would be as superfluous to say that John took his religion with him to Cambridge, as it would be to say that he took his teeth or his hair or his clothes—his religion was woven, web and woof, into the whole texture of his character. Therefore by a spiritual law which works as surely as a natural law, like sought like, and he at once gravitated towards those persons and those things which he most cherished, and we find him from the first associated with the Jesus Lane Sunday School, and later on with one of the first small Bible Classes held in the University. In those days it was a bold and marked thing for a man to join such societies ; now, as they are comparatively common, no stigma attaches to membership. But stigma or no stigma, John had the courage of his opinions, and he no more sought to hide the fact that he was a Christian than he did to conceal the knowledge that he could handle an oar, or hold his own in a boxing bout, or skate, or swim. He stood up strongly for "muscular Christianity" so ably advocated by Charles Kingsley, and the robust men of his school, who brought upon themselves the wrath of the "unco' guid," who thought it was better to mortify the flesh than to train it to manly endurance. John soon distinguished himself at Cambridge in athletics, taking up boating with a wonderful zest, and winning his reputation as an oarsman in the Trinity eight. Of course even then he had to put up with a great deal of ridicule on account of his religious principles, but he could "give as good as he got," and he did so.

On his arrival at Cambridge some difficulty was experienced in obtaining suitable rooms for him outside the College, but eventually lodgings were found with some dressmakers named Abbott. When Mac Gregor threw himself with all a youth's vigour into Sunday school and other Christian work he was dubbed with the sobriquet "Abbott's young Christian." *

For the following interesting account of Mac Gregor's career at Cambridge we are indebted to the Bishop of Exeter (the Rev. E. H. Bickersteth) :

---

* Abbott's " Young Christian" was written by Jacob Abbott, an American Congregational minister, and was much in circulation in that day.

THE BISHOP OF EXETER *to* MRS. JOHN MAC GREGOR.

THE PALACE, EXETER, *April* 11, 1894.

DEAR MRS. MAC GREGOR,—

.... When we came up to Cambridge in October 1843, I was very soon drawn to your husband as one of a little band of five who were knit together for a weekly meeting in each other's rooms for the study of God's word. I remember at our first meeting it was discussed whether we should meet on Wednesday or Thursday, and Mac Gregor said, 'I vote for Thursday; Sunday is a good hoist, and carries you far into the week, but you want a little fillip to get you along to the end.' So we met every Thursday after service in hall (which was then at 4 P.M.), knelt down for a very short prayer, and fell to patient study of the Scriptures, referring to our Greek Testaments and using such helps as we could procure. We closed at 5 minutes before 6, the chapel hour—though I think most of us were morning chapel-goers at 7 A.M. The College law then was that we were to keep six week-day chapels and go twice on Sunday, and as the chapel door was locked as seven struck in the morning and six at night it allowed no coming in late.

It soon became known that we were always engaged on Thursday afternoons, and could not accept invitations to wine parties—very harmless desserts they were, and as we all had a large circle of friends we were constantly meeting in those friendly repasts on other days.

Then from time to time we had our breakfast parties, and I remember Mac Gregor one morning when we met at his rooms, pointing to a letter from his mother and saying, 'She writes every day to me, and my morning letter is as regular as my matutinal egg.' And another morning a letter came from the Editor of *Punch* to him at our breakfast-table, accepting his witty sarcasms on the newly ordered hats for the policemen in London with his diagram from Euclid, I. 5, showing how easily the *pons asinorum* was adaptable to the proposed head tiling of our custodians.

He was a very popular boating man in the Second Trinity Club, but if I recollect right did not keep his place in their first eight.

One day he had sprained and torn one of his hands, and so many friends crowded round to ask him how it was, that the next day he wrote 'Better, I thank you' on his shirt cuff, and to every questioner only presented his wrist.

I asked him to my father's house at Watton, where he was a universal favourite, and he was a guest at my marriage on February 24th, 1848, in Norwich, and soon found his way to my Norfolk home at Banningham, near Cromer, for the links which bound us together were many and strong, and when my first boy was born, who is now the Bishop of the Church in England in Japan, Mac Gregor was one of his godfathers, and when he came down another year and saw the boy and his elder sister playing together I cannot forget the deep earnestness with which he said to me, 'I don't think I could bear to have anything so beautiful as those children entrusted to me for my very own.' But God in His own time gave him this enduring heritage and gift that cometh from the Lord.

He was a life-long friend (though we were both too busy often to meet in London, as the opening of his letter to me on coming down to Exeter may testify), and I often take comfort in the words of another beloved friend of nearly forty years' standing (the present Bishop of Winchester), ' Earth is the place for making friendships ; heaven for enjoying them.'

Yours very sincerely,

E. H. EXON.

The letter from Mac Gregor, to which the Bishop refers, was as follows :

JOHN MAC GREGOR to the BISHOP OF EXETER.

7 VANBRUGH PARK ROAD EAST,
BLACKHEATH, May 10, 1885.

MY DEAR BICKERSTETH BISHOP,—

How it does recall old Trinity, and our Bible readings, and Watton, and Palestine ! Your father and my father, your children and my two girls !

I read your sermon with great delight.   Yes, 'the dove must settle on the Cross.'

Don't forget that I may claim to speak to you even when your mitre is on, for am I not your senior (by one day *) ?

My wife sends her best congratulations.

Yours ever,
J. Mac Gregor.

In the summer of 1845 John made a tour in Scotland with his cousin Sir George Mac Gregor,† and, so far as we can ascertain, entered, for the first time in his life, a few notes in the shape of a diary.   He records that he "walked from Loch Earn into Balquhidder and saw Rob Roy's grave."   In the pass of Killiecrankie "saw piper John Mac Gregor, an old man who had walked twenty miles with pipes, &c., and a violoncello made by himself, on his back."

Everybody and everything bearing the name of Mac Gregor had a fascination for him as the following rough notes testify :

The wearing of tartan was prohibited in 1745.   The Rob Roy tartan, improperly so called, is the true Mac Gregor pattern.   The play of 'Rob Roy,' being first acted by a man dressed in it, gave it this name.   The Mac Gregors are descended from Acharus, a king, A.D. 787.

O'Donoghue means grandson of Donoghue as Mac Gregor son of Gregor—so the country-people call a man's grandchild his O. Saw a cave where three Mac Gregors were hid many days. . . . . Passed an old castle built to keep Rob Roy in order but which he demolished.   Graves of soldiers he killed still to be seen. . . . Clan Gregor castle—unfortunately now not in the family.

* Mac Gregor was born January 24 ; Bickersteth, January 25, 1825.
† The late General Sir George Mac Gregor, K.C.B.

Although he was " Scotch to the backbone," he always kept a part of one eye open to the humours of his countrymen, and occasionally jotted down a note like this :

A man was whistling in Scotland on Sunday. 'Maun ye munnay whustle.' 'I am whustlin' to the doagie.' 'O ye may whustle to the doagie but ye maunna *whustle.*'

Mac Gregor used to relate that the most important event of the tour was when they visited the battle-field of Culloden, on the anniversary of the battle one hundred years after (1745).

John was always fond of a joke and especially when he shared it with his younger brother Douglas. Neither minded if the joke hit home—on the contrary, the harder the hit the better it was apparently liked. Here are some specimens aiming at the law and the army—the professions to which the brothers were in course of time to devote themselves.

A lawyer's likeness was taken in a favourite position with hand in his pocket. ''Tain't like.' 'Eh! not like?' 'No t'aint, 'taint— it would be twice as like again, if he had his hand in somebody else's pocket !'

In a retreat what ought to be the first movement? To extend the wings.

What kind of facings ought highland regiments to have? They should be bare-faced.

In night attacks what should invariably form the advanced guard? The light company.

And so on.

A few further extracts from the notebook will indicate in a small way the bent of his mind at this period :

There is an interesting book by Sandys, 1637. Paraphrases of Job, Psalms, and some of the New Testament, quaint, but beautiful poetry some of it is, and very true and literal in the version—he fails however in rendering into verse the description of the horse in Job xxxix.

Not satisfied with Sandy's paraphrase, Mac Gregor seems to have tried his hand at it, for the following bears his initials, and if the poem be his, it is probably the only attempt at poetry he ever made :

Job xxxix. vv. 19-25.

Hast thou bestowed upon the horse his might?
And clothed his neck with thunder ; hast thou made
Him, who has pawed the valley, at the sight
Of armed men and battle—be afraid?

The quiver rattles and the glittering spear
And sword and shield—for none of these he turns,
But, as he goeth forward, mocks at fear
Rejoicing in his strength, the foe he spurns.

With rage and fierceness swallowing the ground
Exulting 'mid the trumpets saith, ha ! ha !
The thunder of the captains and the sound
He smelleth all the battle from afar.

J. M. December 8, 1845.

Poetry and music ran in his mind at this period— the latter to be largely developed later on—and in the rough notebook to which we have referred there occur such entries as this :

Two strikingly beautiful pieces of sacred music are the following : Recitative beginning, " We called thro' the darkness," &c.—the wildness of a note coming in after the question, " Watchman, will the night soon pass ? " This is by Mendelssohn. The other is the air in Handel's *Messiah* beginning : " He shall feed his flock like a shepherd " (Alto), where the modulations in the last line are peculiarly beautiful.

J. M., December 1845, Dublin.

In 1845 Mac Gregor commenced writing for *Punch*, and continued his contributions for many years. For the first five articles he received a cheque which formed his earliest donation to the Ragged School Union. These appeared in vols. vi. and ix. of *Punch*; between 1845 and 1849 he contributed twenty-four articles, some half-page and some three-quarter page.*

During the same period he was indefatigable in his communications to the *Mechanic's Magazine*, and between 1845 and 1852 contributed no fewer than fifty-two papers. The subjects were so various that we give a few of the titles to show the nature of his studies : Jopling's Septenary Curve System—Frictionless Pendulum—Registering of Atmospheric Variations—On the Theory of Prismatic Colours—Railway Locomotion by Electricity—Improvements in Tile

---

* A writer in the *Pall Mall Gazette* in 1893 rashly denied that John Mac Gregor ever wrote for *Punch*. The present writer has in his possession a list of the articles referred to above, and also the receipts for some of the payments.

Draining—Decomposition of Water—New Flat One-fluked Anchor—Yachts and Yacht Sailing—Fire-engine Improvements—Railway Signals—New Printing Press—New Mode of Raising Water, &c. &c.

In 1846 Mac Gregor left Cambridge and came up to London to read for the bar.

CHAPTER III

SHAPING FOR A CAREER

In January 1847, John Mac Gregor obtained his B.A. degree with honours, being classed as a Wrangler (34th), in the Mathematical Tripos. Soon after this he took up his residence in London.

Among those with whom he was intimate at this time, and whose names occur most frequently in his diary were the Hon. and Rev. Baptist Wriothesley Noel and his family. Mr. Noel, who was one of the Queen's chaplains, occupied the pulpit of St. John's Chapel, Bedford Row, where he drew together a large congregation of the upper classes. In 1848, owing to the revelations in the " Gorham case "—an ecclesiastical suit which led to the secession of some of the Church of England clergy to the Church of Rome—Mr. Noel seceded to the Baptist body of Dissenters, his conviction being that the Church of England in her sacramental teaching approached too nearly to the Church of Rome. He still remained a staunch supporter of most of the leading evangelical societies. During the period of transition Mac Gregor was a constant attendant at his church and frequent allusion to the impending changes is made in his matter-of-fact diary :

Nov. 22.—Heard of Mr. Noel's intended secession from the Established Church. It will be of use to the congregation who have had too few difficulties to try them.

Dec. 3.—The sorrow of meeting Mr. Noel for the last time as our minister was increased by the tumult of the disgraceful crowd who took possession of the chapel. What a sermon on Eph. iii. 14–19 !

In a letter to his sister, he wrote :

Sunday morning saw a large number of us at the early sacrament, about 500, and in coming away we found the church doors even then besieged by people anxious to hear the parting sermon. Yet this was two hours before the time. We had to dismiss the school early, and with the greatest difficulty did any of us teachers get to our pews.

The scene was very disgraceful to numbers of strangers who filled the church and kept out its rightful congregation. I never saw a church so full before—ladies standing on the seats all along the pews so that two rows were in each pew standing—strangers sitting on the edge of the pew doors all along the aisles, the Communion rails full, and for a long time none of us could take off our hats. We hoped earnestly that the service would not proceed, but it did. The faintings and shrieks and bustle made the serious part of the congregation doubly grieved knowing how Mr. Noel hates such scenes. The police had no power, but in the evening everything was well arranged. The text was from Ephesians iii. 14 to 19, and it would be of no use to try to praise the sermon. How judicious to postpone even the very important reasons of his separation to the greater reasons for turning to God which each soul before him ought to consider.

He began : Neither on this occasion nor in the evening, shall I make any explanations or waste your time by speaking of myself.

Let us meditate rather on the Word of God. . . . . On analysing my feelings towards Mr. Noel it is not because he preaches exactly the doctrine I love to hear that I love to hear him, but because also he gives the precise importance to each part of it which in my most prayerful moments I should wish to do. . . . . In the evening I was asked to assist in the laborious duty of keeping the mob at the chapel door in order, and getting the pew-holders their proper accommodation.   I was quite done up by the work, and had my coat torn, and was very much knocked about.   John xvii. 24 was the text, and Mr. Noel . . . . began his wonderful discourse amidst the sobs of many a faithful follower.

Many a grey head seemed bowed with sorrow, and the majority were in tears.   It did not seem like a parting of an ordinary kind, but to me something of a martyr's farewell. . . . I thank God we are to have for a year Archdeacon Dealtry in our pulpit.

Mac Gregor remained a member of St. John's Chapel, and on the following Sunday noted, "a memorable day. Our first with our new minister.   Both his sermons energetic, simple, and fluent."

The year 1848 was remarkable in the career of Mac Gregor, as it was in the history of all thoughtful men.   Disaffection was abroad everywhere— Italy in open revolution, Austria falling to pieces, France in the throes of reform conflicts, Ireland in disorder, England harassed by Chartists and republican principles.   A revolutionary epidemic was spreading everywhere and broke out in all its virulence, with the third revolution in France, the proclamation of a Republic, the expulsion of the Orleans dynasty, and the election of a provisional Government and a National

Assembly. Although politics, as such, were never a strong point in Mac Gregor's studies, on the 1st of May, 1848, he commenced systematically to keep a diary. Unfortunately it is written for the first year or two mainly in cypher—not one system only but a conglomeration of several, and these were changed from time to time, so that the majority of the earlier entries are quite unintelligible. There are, however, a few in long-hand, and in the course of a year or two the notes in cypher practically disappear. A pencil note precedes the first entry :

I had visited Paris in 1848 before May 1st, and saw the Assembly in debate the day before they were dissolved and met Louis Napoleon on the steps of the Madeleine quite unattended and unnoticed.

It is greatly to be regretted that this is the only record extant, so far as we can ascertain, of what must have been a most exciting and therefore, to Mac Gregor, a most delightful time. Nor, owing to the cypher diary, are we any better off, with regard to his experiences in London during the period of the Chartist fiasco, except that he was one of the special constables during the Riot. In Ireland, however, where throughout the period of famine, and the subsequent mania for emigration his father had retained and successfully administered his difficult office as Head of the Constabulary, Mac Gregor found a fruitful field of discovery. The cry for Repeal raised by the believers in the policy of that consummate agitator, Daniel O'Connell, was giving place to the demands of the

D

Young Ireland party in whose ranks William Smith O'Brien had allied himself and soon became their leader, while Thomas Francis Meagher became the "Peter the Hermit" of the crusade—an orator of bolder and at the same time far more inspiring and poetic rhetoric than even the famous Grattan. It would be foreign to our purpose to tell the story of the attempted but abortive insurrection which, had it been allowed to ripen, might have been fraught with disastrous consequences, or even to record how Colonel Mac Gregor carried out with coolness and firmness his difficult and dangerous duties in baffling that conspiracy and maintaining the cause of loyalty, or how he won for himself universal admiration and respect. One or two incidents may, however, be recorded here.

At a meeting in Dublin, Colonel Mac Gregor was surprised and gratified when a gentleman, who asked to be introduced, was found to be the great agitator himself, Daniel O'Connell. The Irish patriot shook hands with the Colonel very warmly, and said that "he had always acted with great consideration and perfect fairness towards his countrymen," a very gratifying testimony to which he was wont to refer in after years with justifiable pride. It is a matter of history that the disturbances in Ireland, including the rebellion headed by Smith O'Brien, were put down chiefly by the armed Irish constabulary and for his eminent services in this connection, Colonel Mac Gregor received at the end of 1848, the honourable distinction of a civil K.C.B.

The following curious and old-fashioned letter was written about this time :

JOHN MAC GREGOR *to his Father*, SIR DUNCAN MAC GREGOR, K.C.B.

December 1848.

MY DEAREST FATHER,

It is not very easy to realise at first this new accession of honour, there being somewhat incorporeal in it. I can hardly decide which is greater, the sympathy of a parent in the advancement of his child, or the pleasure which a son feels in his father's promotion. It seems to me that we pervert the meaning of the text, "them that honour me I will honour" if we expect, much more if we demand, distinction amongst men as a necessary consequence of our right dispositions to God. It should rather be a matter of surprise and thankfulness if we may be suffered like Christ himself to increase in favour with God and man. It may savour too much of my pleader's education to discern in the mode of conferring this distinction more to congratulate you upon than if it had been given at once and yet I do see more—for the Government must have understood fully the merits of their servant in Ireland, the very focus of that crusade against order which all Europe had engaged in. If then they considered a Companionship as a fit reward for such services we see how highly they estimate the rank of C.B. Ergo, say I, how should we value the greater dignity of a Knight Commander?

Colonel Rowan has evidently profited by your refusal of the first step. No wonder that a government should delight to raise the status of a civil or demi-military arm of the Executive at a time when the powers on the Continent are lavish and hasty in rewarding the few purely military corps that were staunch to their respective crowns during the late trials. I remember when I was a little boy you were explaining what a K.H. was to me, and when I said, 'And what does K.C.B. mean?' 'Oh,' you said, 'that is quite a different thing, it is given only as a high honour to a few great men.'

Your most affectionate son,

JOHN.

The notes in the diary of John Mac Gregor relating
to his stay in Ireland at this time are meagre, but
they are sufficient to show that he followed the course
of events with keen interest and kept his eye open
for anything that might turn up.

Waterford.   Went round the barracks to see the preparations for
the rebels, who were expected to break out on the following day.

Arrived last night in Carlow.   The rebels in all the villages were
marching to join O'Brien and Meagher in the mountains.

He appears to have picked up a few stories on the
road, and records how a parish clerk, breaking forth
into a poetic oration, said :

To-night's the day, I speak it with great sorrow, that we were
to have been blown up to-morrow.

Another, declaiming against the oppression of the
times, said, with national fervour :

It's not the tenth part that these tyrants take from us but the
twentieth !

In another note is the following :

' How far is it there ? ' asked a half-tipsy Irishman.

'A mile if you go straight.' 'Oh, I don't so much mind how
long it is, but it's the breadth of the road that matters with me, for I
go from one side to the other so often.'

Another story, heard from the man himself, and
often quoted in later years by Mac Gregor in his " No
Popery " crusades, runs like this :

A priest in Ireland crossed a ford and arriving at an inn found his 'pyx,' containing the consecrated wafer, wet. He thought of the sin thus committed but found that provision was made by the fathers for such a case, and that if corruption had set in, then it was no longer the Body of Christ. He pondered and wondered and finally threw it into the fire, renounced popery, and is now a Protestant clergyman in the same parish.

Unimportant as it may seem in itself, the following note records one of those pivot-hours in life on which so many great events revolve.

Nov. 16. Found my article on 'Guy Fawkes' in *Punch*. Met Mr. Blackburn and went with him to the Ragged Schools in Westminster. Delighted.

This appears to have been the origin of his connection with Ragged Schools, and the proceeds from the article in *Punch* formed his first contribution to its funds.

Whatever Mac Gregor undertook he carried on with enthusiasm, and the energy with which he threw himself into Ragged School work, at a time, too, when he was reading for the Bar and was immersed in many important undertakings, is very noteworthy.

The Ragged School was then in its infancy—the Ragged School Union having only been founded in 1845—and it was struggling for existence. It greatly needed the aid of vigorous and able men like Mac Gregor, and the fact of his joining the movement was the signal for many of his friends, over whom his strong character exercised a powerful influence, to associate themselves with him. One of his oldest friends, Mr. Martin Ware, says: "His fearless confession of Christ, his frankness and good-humour towards all with whom he was brought into contact, and the charm of his conversation, full of life and originality, won many who were careless and wavering to a life of Christian usefulness; and not a few of those who have since done good service among the poor of London, trace their introduction to the work to the encouraging example of John Mac Gregor."

Ragged School work was no easy task in those early days. Sometimes the teachers could not reach the schools except under police protection; not infrequently a "rebellion" would occur when, in sheer wantonness, the whole school would, at a preconcerted signal, break out into laughing, talking, fighting, smoking and dancing. The present writer has a grateful and refreshing remembrance of addressing a ragged audience in Camberwell, many years later than the period to which we are now alluding. Having concluded with what he regarded as a stirring poem, he received five odorous bloaters on his head and face, because he declined to respond to an encore!

Mac Gregor's diary only gives very brief references to his Ragged School work, but the following will be read with interest.

Nov. 30, 1848.—At the Ragged Schools a little disturbance took place, when one of the boys went up to the master and said, 'I say, sir, why don't you go and hit those fellows in the eye, they're making such a noise!' They detect pickpockets by their manner of holding out the hand or turning round when ordered.

1849.

Jan. 4.—Went in the evening to the little Ragged School set up by some gentlemen under Mr. Maurice's * auspices—the girls were below with a schoolmistress, neat, clean and orderly, the boys and young men we had in two rooms above. An absence of scriptural or sanctified education was marked and affected me, but much is not to be expected at first. A lad learned addition very quickly from me, then I recited the story of Joseph. They ended by repeating the Lord's Prayer after one of their kind instructors. The cool nonchalance of the scholars amused me, sitting with their hats on and talking of such odd matters—subjects unaccustomed to be heard discussed in other society. But the evening had its effect, and may God bless the endeavours to teach wheresoever and by whomsoever conducted.

Feb. 7.—Ragged School Union Committee, Lord Ashley in the chair. Heard of my appointment to the committee.

March 2.—Went to committee meeting of Ragged School Union. Pleased with their business-like mode of proceeding. Glad to find they had £1300 in the bank.

May 15.—Meeting in Exeter Hall of Ragged School Union, where I stood as steward for six hours. Duke of Argyll's speech wordy, but clear and fluent. Fox Maule's rather involved. Mr. Corduroy's very eloquent;—a fine looking man with a splendid voice and perfect self-command. Mr. Shearin's, colloquial yet interesting. Lord Ashley's not forcible. Mr. Labouchere's too fast in delivery. The parliamentary speakers deliver very slowly, making each word tell.

Although Mac Gregor was an excellent "teacher," it was not in that direction that his chief power lay. He was an originator, an organiser, a teacher of teachers.

In the *Ragged School Union Magazine*, read at that

* The Rev. Professor Frederick Denison Maurice.

time by almost every Ragged School teacher in the land, he wrote a series of capital papers, full of suggestive hints as to the modes of imparting instruction, how to deliver an address, and how to use such language and imagery as should rivet the attention of the children. He felt the responsibility of his task ; thousands of young people were listening each week to addresses, many perhaps for the first time, and many, perchance, might drift away and never have the opportunity again. It was his ambition therefore, to attract and fascinate them, and it pained him to think how many good, true, and earnest teachers were, by lack of training or capacity, and not at all through want of heart, wasting their golden chances. The mere sermon, however excellent it might be, was useless among this class of hearers ; the religious essayist was as sounding brass and a tinkling cymbal ; the good but heavy gospeller who strung together passages of Scripture, incomprehensible except to those who had been educated in Biblical knowledge, was really exhorting in an unknown tongue. What the ragged children wanted was a speaker who would use language that they could thoroughly understand, full of sympathy that they could feel, attractive so that they could listen with pleasure, and above all that the words should spring from the heart of one who came to them not as a great preacher but as one of themselves, to whom they could speak without fear, and love for what he was to them.

In his printed and oral addresses to teachers therefore, he insisted strongly upon such points as these: Never to tell pointless stories, never to found discourses on "dry doctrines," never to come prepared with a good start and trust to the inspiration of the moment for the finish "which in such case," he says, "is generally weak and rambling; the refreshing wine being *drowned* not *mixed* with water, becomes vague, insipid, and cheerless"; never to continue speaking until your audience is wearied, but always to drive in one nail to a sticking place, to enforce one cardinal truth that shall be remembered. Excellent advice! would that teachers, other than those in Ragged Schools, would follow it! Among his strong points were these, that anecdote should never be employed for its own sake, never be dragged in by the heels, and never be used by those who do not know how to tell a story—and their name is legion though they know it not. In matters of style he urged, that if similes were used, at every stage of the simile the thing signified should be dilated upon; that, as far as possible, only Saxon words should be employed, and above all that no one should speak unless he had something to say, and was deeply in earnest in saying it.*

---

* When he read Hesba Stretton's beautiful little story, "Jessica's First Prayer," in the *Sunday at Home*, where it first appeared, he said "it was a capital story, and deserved being printed as a book and being *translated into English*." He prided himself on using plain, homely Anglo-Saxon in preference to long, sentimental and Latinised words. It was the *pathos* of "Jessica's First Prayer" that secured for it an enormous circulation in many forms, especially after its favourable launching into public favour by Lord Shaftesbury, whose remark was, "No one but a woman could have written such a story."

In his own addresses he chose such subjects as the wise and foolish men who built their houses on the rock and the sand respectively, and he would sustain the interest of his hearers until they seemed to hear the fall of the one house in the crash of the storm and to feel a sense of personal safety in gazing on the picture of the house on the rock.

He could tell a story well, and he could give it such tone, gesture, look, that the young people sat open-mouthed and spellbound. Here is a specimen of an illustration he often used :

One very dark night, no moon to be seen and no stars, I was in a steamboat with some hundred passengers. All of them were on deck, for the sea was smooth and the gentle air was warm, and the passengers chatted in Italian or in Greek, while the Captain told us we were nearing Cape Matapan, the most southerly point in Europe.

The noise of the steamer's paddle-wheels was like 'pitta-patta, pitta-patta,' but suddenly the paddles stopped.

The Captain had ordered them to stop because the night was so *very* dark, and he did not know the way, and perhaps we might be near some of the dangerous rocks in that part of the sea. So he was right to stop, and listen, and look, and all the passengers looked and listened in silence. At last some one called out, 'Oh, I see a light !' and all of us looked that way.

The light was very tiny, just like a little star, but it moved first down, and down, and down, and then it was steady a bit ; then it waved quietly right and left, then it went out altogether and everything was dark again.

All of us looked, and all were silent, but the Captain said, ' All right, go on ahead !' and the paddles again went 'pitta-patta,' and the vessel moved on in safety.

What was the light? Why did it move, and why was it put out? I will tell you now.

On these black rocks at Cape Matapan there was a little old man, a hermit monk, who lived in a hut of stones. He was too old and too feeble to do much work, but what he did was this. Whenever he heard a ship was near—by the sailors' voices or by the paddle-wheel's sound—he lighted a little candle, and stepped down slowly to the edge of the sea, and then he waved his light to the right and to the left, and then he blew it out and went back to bed in his stone hut. That was all he did, but it was enough to tell where the rocks were and safe water was ; and so the sailors knew where to go, and they thanked the old man, and sometimes (in the daylight) they took food to him and clothes. Now, you may remember that Jesus said, 'I am the light of the world,' and He came and lighted the way, and He went back to heaven, and He will come again to the world in brighter glory. Meantime He left us His word—the blessed Bible—to be 'a lamp to our feet and a light to our path,' like a candle in the dark to show us the danger, and to show the right way for going on our journey through a dark world to the bright heaven He has gone to prepare.

Every one can hold up the Bible as a light every day in the house, in the work-place, in the streets, in the school, and even in playtime, too.

His sympathy with children was intense, and some of his talks with them, whether as a young man of twenty-five, or later on in life, were models of what such expressions should be. There were oftentimes tears in his voice as he spoke to the poor little waifs and strays in the Ragged Schools and Refuges and Reformatories, and there were eager glances, tender sighs, sometimes tearful eyes when, "moved with compassion," he would address them in words like these :

Many of you have not a good father to shelter you and teach you ; many of you have not a loving mother to cherish you and kiss your tears away ; many of you have not brothers or sisters to play with you and love you. We have done our best to help, and the masters and matrons over you are very very kind, but they can never be the same to you as real father, real mother, and real brothers and sisters. But, dear lads, have you not heard of One who, better than any father on earth, loves you, One who is a Friend that sticketh closer than a brother ? He is the Good Shepherd. He will carry you like lambs in His bosom, and will gently lead you to His bright and beautiful Home !

Could any words express more womanly tenderness than these ?

In case any young men into whose hands this book may fall should think that we have drifted into a namby-pamby strain, we will turn now to an examination of his ordinary life and habits at this time. John MacGregor was no recluse, nor did he shut his eyes or ears to anything of genuine interest. He had a great passion for music and for the society of notable men—or at least with men who "had something in them," and he indulged his passion freely. We find his diary interspersed with many passages such as these :

1848.

July 7.—Carlyle, author of Cromwell's life, &c., came to dinner last night. A young Scotchman, clever and *outré*, designedly care-less, uses much strong language, but his epithets often twice over. Fond of fun and unaffected. Not happy looking.

July 13.—At Sir E. Buxton's. Met the poet Rogers.

Jan. 5.—Met Snape at the Cock and became acquainted with him.*

May 17.—Called on Snape and had a long and interesting conversation with him. It urges forward to hear the panting of a fellow pilgrim, so lately started on the path.

About this time he was paying considerable attention to music, and "took lessons in singing from Benson, three for a guinea." "Had some trios with Ebrington and Cane."

Pleasant concert last night. Sims Reeves's voice is very satisfactory. Thalberg's fantasia on *Masaniello* delighted me.

It is wise for a young man to give due place and proportion to things, and we find him, with a view to his future work at the bar, training himself in a variety of ways. One was by his frequent attendance at the "Grotto"—a debating society sustained for the most part, it would appear, by men in the legal profession. His references to the Grotto, so named from the Grotto Tavern in Southampton Buildings, are frequent, and, after attending many debates and other meetings, he was, to his great surprise, "elected Secretary to the Grotto by a large majority," and was present for the first time in his official capacity in February 1849. In the same month he began to write the "History of the Grotto," but what came of it this deponent sayeth not. That the meetings were

* This acquaintance ripened into a life-long friendship. Mr. Snape died April 18, 1894.

useful to him there is little doubt and we find occasional entries like this :

May 14, 1849.—At Grotto. Felt great improvement in fluency and delivery whilst speaking. An important rule seems to me to be this, to abstain from all diversions to parts of the subject not well prepared before rising, even though the connection between those considered may appear disjointed.

Mac Gregor, although he had many irons in the fire, was not neglecting his professional studies and the following entries in the diary for 1849 indicate what was to be the distinctive line he had marked out for himself.

1849.
Feb. 13.—Wrote home concerning the Patent Branch of a barrister's studies.

Feb. 24.—Called on Hindmarsh to speak about patent law and its bearings—it seems more attractive and exclusive than ever. Recommend me to become acquainted with the arts and manufactures of the country, and to read with some barrister practising in the line referred to.

John Mac Gregor's love of travel had early manifested itself, but hitherto his experiences had been mainly confined to Scotland, Ireland, Wales, France, and Holland. In July 1849 the great dream of his life came true, and he started on his first eastern tour comprising Paris, Geneva, Lyons, Malta, Athens, Marathon, Greece generally, Smyrna, Constantinople, Beyrout, Tripoli, Syria, Baalbec, Damascus, Tyre, Sidon, Carmel, Nazareth, Jerusalem, Dead Sea,

Jordan, Gaza, Cairo, Pyramids, Nile, Farshoot, Thebes, Cairo, Malta, Gibraltar, returning to London in March 1850—an eight months' tour. During the whole of this period he was indefatigable with his pen and his sketch-book, and we have before us enough material to form an interesting and a good-sized book—material that has never yet been published. We can only give in this place the briefest outline of the tour, with an occasional note of some of its leading incidents.

The start was a bad one.

July 19.—From Paris to Geneva by diligence, three days and two nights on the road. 23. To Lyons by diligence, all night again. 24. From Valence, again by diligence, to Avignon, making four nights spent in the baggage as a dormitory without sleep.

SELMONE

Then came a day's pause "to recover health."

At Malta, 'dined with the Governor and sailed in his yacht afterwards. Caught a small turtle lying on the top of the water.' 'Dined with White at the 44th mess. Bathed for a very long time by moonlight. Music on the coalscuttle and bellows, feats of strength, songs, pipes, &c.'

Aug. 8.—Started in the grey dawn in our sailing-boat to Gozo, fifteen miles. Stopped during the middle of the day at St. Paul's

Bay, landing on the island of Selmone on which his ship was wrecked.

Aug. 10.—Bathed, and swam to the mainland the same course which St. Paul and his company must have escaped by. Read the account of the wreck in the Acts. . . . .

Aug. 18.—Athens. Went in the evening to the Acropolis, where the ruins exceeded all I had imagined in the beauty and delicacy of proportions. The sensation of pleasure in beholding such refined

ST. PAUL'S MONUMENT

fulfilments of the longing for perfection of architecture quite over-came the mournful retrospect of what Athens once was.

Aug. 22.—Marathon. Much annoyed by donkeys, cocks, dogs, babies, swallows, flies, rats, mosquitoes, and bugs. Set off in the afternoon for Phyle to stop the night at Kephessia. Our cavalcade included five horses, Demetri, a Frenchman, as cook, and a man for the horses. These animals are astonishing for their endurance, strength, patience, and sure-footedness. Passed a solitary tortoise marching o'er the field of Marathon. Saw a lizard about a foot and a half long.

Aug. 23.—Kephessia afforded us as many bugs and as little sleep as Marathon. Thence to the ancient fortress Phyle guarding the old road from Athens to Thebes. The road in some parts still bears the marks of the Greek chariot wheels. Phyle is on a lofty rock, in beautiful scenery; the walls are built of marble, and the gate so constructed, as in the other old fortresses, as to compel those entering to expose their right sides unprotected by the shield.

At Athens, Mac Gregor and his companion (Frend) went on board a schooner, the *Isabel*, 100 tons, bound for Smyrna. Mac Gregor was not in good health, the fatigue at the start of the tour, the sleeplessness in

SMYRNA

Greece and a sharp attack of illness consequent upon eating over-ripe melons at Marathon, had done him some mischief and rendered him liable to further climatic ailments. But he was alert to see and do all that could be seen and done. Here is an incident of this part of the tour not recorded in the diary, but mentioned in a private letter.

In 1849 while among the Greek islands, becalmed in a little schooner, I heard the sharp rattle of musketry and the big boom of cannon behind a hill. To get at the cause of this, we entreated the Captain to lend us the boat. Pirates were at their work and had murdered the crew of a brig. This we told at Smyrna, and instantly

E

an English war-steamer started in pursuit of the sailor's common
enemy, the robbers of the sea. The pirates were captured, and seven
of them were hanged.

Some pleasant days were spent at Smyrna and then
arrangements were made to push forward to Constantinople. Just as Mac Gregor was about to leave
Smyrna he heard that an American gentleman, staying
at an hotel there, was taken seriously ill. Although
knowing nothing of him, Mac Gregor called, sat by his
bedside, read and prayed with him till the very last
moment that he could be away from the ship that was

ROAD THROUGH ROMAN AQUEDUCT, ACRE

to take him to Constantinople. In bidding the sufferer
farewell Mac Gregor turned down a page in a New
Testament and left it with him. On their way to
Constantinople Mac Gregor and his friend went ashore
at Gallipoli, and there it is believed they contracted
a fever which proved to be of a most malignant kind.

On arrival at their hotel in Constantinople they
immediately took to their beds, and a doctor was
called in who pronounced the disease to be local
intermittent fever.

For over a fortnight he was confined to his room, and, for a long time afterwards, he felt the ill effects of the dangerous malady, although with his indomitable pluck he went about as though nothing had happened. Every sight in Constantinople he seems to have visited, and, although he prosecuted his researches with unflagging zeal, the entries in the diary reveal how much he suffered during this period. Leaving the city he sailed again to Smyrna, and almost his first act on

STONE CARVINGS AT BEYROUT

arrival was to visit the hotel where, a month before, he had left the American traveller on his sick bed. He entered the room and found the traveller lying on the bed a corpse, his fingers gripping the open Testament that Mac Gregor had given to him, and the page upon which the dead hand rested was the third chapter of the Gospel of St. John, which Mac Gregor had turned down for his reading the moment when he left him.

From Smyrna he went to Cyprus, and from thence to Beyrout, where, health being now better established, many excursions were made, among them a visit to the stone sculptures on the rocks near Beibroun, and to Tripoli.

On the Lebanon Mac Gregor was again stricken down by illness and confined for a week to his

THE GATEWAY AT BAALBEC

room, but immediately after the words "Feeling better" occur in the diary, we find him visiting the cedars, passing over the ridge of Lebanon, sleeping at the foot of the mountain in a cornfield, encamped in the midst of the ruins of Baalbec, crossing the ridge of Hermon and finally settling down at the hotel in the street " which is called Straight." From Damascus the travellers proceeded to Tyre and Sidon, St. Jean d'Acre, and to the convent on Mount Carmel, and here he was kept for some days in confinement under the care of a doctor who talked only in Latin.

Nov. 7, 1849.—Started for Nazareth, I riding on the donkey in a most constrained position, and suffering great pain for three hours. Camped at night near a village where the jackals, dogs, camels, and donkeys prevented sleep. Frend observed a large scorpion crawling up the tent near me. We caught him, the second we have captured in the tent.

Another week of illness ensued at Nazareth, at the end of which this entry occurs :

1849.

Nazareth, Nov 14.—Thank God on this day may be said to end the illness which has oppressed me for nearly six weeks.

Nov. 15.—Got up and walked out, beholding Nazareth for the first time. Oh, the pleasure of being without pain !

Proceeding on their route the travellers appear to have visited every remarkable place and seen every remarkable sight in Palestine, but, as the notes are very condensed and matter-of-fact, it would not interest the general reader to insert them here.

Many years later, however, Mac Gregor contributed an incident of his tour to the readers of a magazine in connection with the School-boys' Scripture Union, edited by university men.   It was as follows :—

' The Bloody Way' was the name of the road from Jerusalem to Jericho, which Jesus described as you read it in Luke x. 25–37. I went along it five times with a guard of soldiers; but at last I went once quite alone. About the middle of the way, where it was very hot—for the Jordan Valley is the deepest spot in all the world—I thought I might stop for a rest. In dismounting from the saddle the handle of my thick umbrella struck a large boil on my face and burst it, and while I looked at the gush of blood, two strong arms clasped me from behind and a terrible struggle took place between an armed robber and myself. Both of us were strong men, and we wrestled and twisted and groaned, but neither would 'give in.' Suddenly the hilt of the rascal's sword came near my hand. I clutched it and drew the sword out, and at once the Arab 'gave in,' and I tossed the sword into 'the brook Kedron.'

I am not likely to forget the parable of the 'Good Samaritan,' because I have, even at this time, the scar on my cheek.

A journey was then made overland from Gaza to Cairo—a most fatiguing and somewhat uninteresting journey on camel-back.

In January 1850, a start was made up the Nile in a dahabeah and here adventures came thick and fast—thus :

Jan. 8, at Sooádee. Got out and walked, and saw a crocodile quite near me in the water. I had only my pistol with me, and he sank instantly on hearing me cock it.

Jan. 10.—A crocodile fell into our boat last night from the bank.

Jan. 13.—Girgeh. Took a long walk in the morning on the mountains and amongst the excavated caverns in the rocks. Last night five or six men rushed upon those of our crew who were on the bank tracking, and tried to overcome them, intending no doubt to rob the boat afterwards. Hany, the dragoman, fired shot and ball from my gun and they retreated. Though they called me often yet I slept through all the noise.

Jan. 21.—Thebes. The bats in tomb No. 35 nearly blinded me. The guides took me down a steep hole in mistake for a tomb.

Jan. 23.—Shot eleven birds for breakfast—four at one shot, three at another.

LIFE IN THE EAST—STRIKING CAMP

On the 28th Mac Gregor caught a severe cold, and two days afterwards, when walking with two men, Oxford and Cambridge, to Abydos, he felt that he had received a stroke of the sun on the back.

MY FIRST CROCODILE

Happily, however, some travellers were met with a day or two afterwards, including Lord Lincoln, Lord Robert Clinton, his brother Mr. Vernon, and Mr. Harcourt, who kindly offered him medicines.

Feb. 5.—Went in the small boat with Mustapha and Agedan to the crocodile rocks. After landing and waiting some time a crocodile appeared. Shot him in the head. He dived and returned, and I shot him in the spine, brought him to the boat, and he was skinned.

Some time was spent in Cairo and Alexandria, and the journey back to London was made *via* Malta, Gibraltar, and Southampton.

On his arrival, we find Mac Gregor taking up all the dropped skeins of his ordinary life, and the first entry in his diary, after he has noted a round of calls, is the following :

May 22.—Began to read with Chitty.

But almost immediately afterwards comes the entry :

Conceived the idea of writing a tract, 'Three Days in the East.'

Then follow many items respecting Ragged School work, prayer-meetings, studies in music, lectures, and so on, till one is surprised to meet, three months later than the announcement of "reading with Chitty," the solitary entry :

Aug. 19.—Read Archibald's 'Criminal Law'!

It was said of him by his friends that "he only wanted the spur of poverty to supplement a successful university career by a lucrative practice at the bar." It is not, therefore, in the line of his profession that Mac Gregor will stand out most conspicuously in these pages, for although what he undertook to do he did well, there were fresh paths of life opening up to him almost every year, and, at an early period of his history, he seems to have made up his mind that his life-work was not to be done in wig and gown.

Mac Gregor left two permanent memorials of his first Eastern tour. One was the little book entitled

" Three Days in the East," the peculiarity of which
was that it was written, with great industry and ingenuity, almost entirely in the words of Holy Scripture.   It was published by Seeley and all profits derived from the book were given to the Ragged Schools.

The second memorial was a more ambitious one.   It
was a valuable work on " Eastern Music," published
by Novello, giving in musical notation the characteristic and national songs of Greeks, Turks, Egyptians,
Nubians, Bedouins, Syrians, Jews.   These interesting
airs were caught by the ear, played on the flute, and
sung with a tuning-key at hand, and after many re-
hearsals with native orchestras they were written
unaltered precisely as they were performed.

In a review of the book Professor E. F. Rimbault,
LL.D., a musical critic of no mean order, says :
" The subject of Eastern music is one of very
great interest, not only as regards its antiquity as
the most ancient music in the world, but also in an
ethnological point of view, which is perhaps of more
importance.   The way in which sensations of thought
are expressed by modulations of the human voice is
one of the characteristics of races.   A great difficulty
exists in procuring copies of these ancient melodies.
Travellers are seldom experienced musicians enough
to write down a melody accurately.   An exception to
the general order of travellers in the East must be
made in favour of Mr. John MacGregor, whose volume
of ' Eastern Music ' shows us that he is not only able
to write down the melodies correctly, but to give us at

home a good idea of their effects when stripped of their surroundings."

Each song was preceded by amusing and descriptive letterpress, and the book was adorned with original sketches. As in the case of "Three Days in the East," the profits were devoted to the Ragged Schools.

We give a specimen of one chorus, which was a great favourite with John Mac Gregor:

BOATMEN'S CHORUS ON THE NILE

Towards the end of 1850 an event occurred, unimportant in itself, but of such far-reaching consequences to Mac Gregor and tens of thousands of his fellow-creatures, that we shall reserve the next chapter for the unfolding of our tale concerning it.

OUR CARAVAN

CHAPTER IV

SHOEBLACKS AND SLUMS

ON the 28th of November, 1850, some delegates from Ragged Schools met in the school-room at Field Lane, under the presidency of Lord Ashley, to consider by what means employment might be obtained for ragged boys when the "Great Exhibition of 1851" would draw all the world to London.

MacGregor was there, and among many others of his friends present was John R. Fowler, a student at the Inner Temple, who, when he was an under-graduate at Trinity College, Dublin, had known Mac Gregor and had visited his father's house at Drum-condra Castle. In 1850, when they were both attending the same church in London, Mac Gregor induced Fowler to visit Field Lane School, where he was then a teacher, and eventually to throw himself heartily into Ragged School work. A strong friendship subsisted between these two until death interrupted it.

Mr. J. R. Fowler has kindly written us some interesting notes of the commencement of a remarkable

movement in which the two friends were deeply interested. He says :

It was in the autumn of 1850 that Mac Gregor and I attended a
meeting of Ragged School Teachers at Field Lane, where the subject
of industrial employment for the ragged boys of London was
discussed, and various simple industries considered, such as wood-
chopping and mat-making. On leaving the meeting we were
accompanied by Robert James Snape and Francis S. Reilly
(afterwards Sir Francis Reilly, K.C.M.G., and now deceased), and all
four arm-in-arm walked up the middle of Holborn Hill on the way
home.

They continued the conversation about industries,
and in a pause the suggestion was made : " Why
should not we employ shoeblacks in the streets of
London as they do in Paris and Rotterdam and elsewhere ? "

All pronounced it to be a capital idea, and a rapid
calculation was made that a box, a set of brushes and
some kind of uniform would cost about 10s. each boy.
All four said they would give ten shillings each and
so start four Field Lane ragged boys.

Soon after when I went to Mac Gregor's chambers to pay my
money he said : 'Oh ! you're not going to get off in that way. We
must have a Society and form a Committee and you shall be the
Treasurer ; look here, the thing has grown,' and as he said so he
tossed across the table a letter for me to read. It was very short,
and ran thus :

'DEAR MAC GREGOR,—

    'Good idea, carry it out. I will give you £5.

                    'Yours sincerely,

                            'ASHLEY.'

He had evidently at once written to Lord Ashley who promptly responded with this encouraging note.*

I tried to back out of the responsibility. I was quite a novice in Christian work, whereas John Mac Gregor even then was on the Committee of the Ragged School Union where he had an opportunity of meeting Lord Ashley the President of the Union and Chairman of the Committee.

Mac Gregor's strong will overbore my reluctance, and not long after we held a public meeting at which he expounded the project of selecting the boys from all the Ragged Schools of London on the recommendation of their teachers, employing them during the day in the streets at fixed stations, having them overlooked by a paid superintendent, and in the evening required to attend the night school from which they were recommended, and live with their parents or relatives at their own homes. A resolution approving of the plan was adopted, and a committee was appointed, of which John Mac Gregor was Chairman, Robert James Snape was Honorary Secretary, John R. Fowler, Treasurer, and Lord Ashley, President, and the Shoeblack Society was launched. It was determined not to venture into the streets until the spring of 1851. Meanwhile the time was employed in completing the organisation, obtaining the goodwill of the police authorities, training the boys, and, by earnest prayer, committing the whole matter to the guidance and care of our Heavenly Father.

We will now take up the narrative from the notes of John Mac Gregor and other sources. On the 19th of · January, 1851, the Ragged School Shoeblack Society, being thoroughly organised, gave its first "demonstration," when a boy with a shoeblack box showed how the business was to be done. This first

---

* As a matter of fact, MacGregor rose at five o'clock on the morning after the meeting, carefully prepared a circular letter, superintended its printing, and sent out 500 copies by post. Lord Ashley's was the only response.

professor of the black art did his work well notwithstanding the fact that he had a bullet in his neck
which he got in a juvenile burglary. General approval having been expressed at the first attempt, a
small army was gathered in an alley off John Street in
the Strand, where they were taught the arts and

The original sketch for the front.
Circular of the Ragged school Shoeblack Society 1851

mysteries of polishing boots, chiefly on the feet of
committeemen, "who ran out now and then to get a
splash of mud in the street puddles."

The first out-of-door demonstration was made on
3rd of March, 1851, when two boys under the escort
of John Mac Gregor and Mr. Fowler, marched out to
take up their places, one at the corner of the National

F

Gallery and one in Leicester Square. Says John Mac
Gregor :

A crowd soon followed each of the red coats, and having planted
the first boy . . . . I placed my foot on the shoeblack's box, and
the people pressed round, and the boy began, and the police came
up, and then the whole arrangement was swept into space—a
complete *fiasco !*

Mr. Fowler continues :

We spent a great part of the day in standing by the boys and
encouraging them at their posts. It was amusing to watch the
passers by and listen to their remarks upon this new form of
industry. At times groups collected, but it was only a few at first
who had the courage to place their feet upon the box. I had my own
boots blacked many times during the day.

After this the police authorities were approached and gave a general
concurrence—that is to say, they promised not to interfere to send
away a boy from a stand unless valid objections were made by
occupiers of houses in the neighbourhood, or an obstruction was
made on the highway or a disturbance caused. In fact, as far as
they could, they gave their protection and approval to the employment
of the boys in this manner who were superintended and accredited
by the Ragged School Shoeblack Society officers.

By the time the Great Exhibition opened, May 1st,
further satisfactory arrangements were made with the
police by whom the "station" of each boy was
assigned, and this amicable co-operation continued
until Sir G. Cornewall Lewis, then Chancellor of the
Exchequer, obtained the insertion of a clause in an
Act of Parliament whereby street shoeblacks were
henceforth to be regarded as functionaries to be
regulated and protected by the police.

Few practical philanthropists ever worked harder than did John Mac Gregor and his band of helpers on that memorable 1st of May. The streets were thronged; everybody was gaping for novelty: crowds collected round the boys in their brilliant red uniforms, and some strong-minded people, who did not mind being stared at or jeered, ventured to put their feet on the boxes while a committeeman stood by and explained the objects of the Society. Not on that day, or for many succeeding days, was the life of a shoeblack an enviable one. They were for the most part boys who had been "picked up out of the gutter," used to the loafing habits of mudlarks or street thieves, and totally unaccustomed to habits of industry, cleanliness, or civility. Moreover, they were not allowed to blush unseen during the period of their reformation, but to be brought under the gaze of the public generally and the police particularly, and there was no love lost between the "Bobby" or "Peeler"* and the street Arab. Yet even this was tolerable in comparison with the jeers and tricks of their quondam associates, who would throw flour on their black boxes or otherwise torment them after the manner of their species.

From the first the scheme was a success. The press referred to it as a notable feature of the day, *Punch* made good-natured fun about it, and when one

* It may not be known by some that these names were almost invariably given to the police in those days, names derived from the founder of their order—Sir Robert Peel.

day Mac Gregor took thirty of the boys and marched
them in their blazing uniform through the Great
Exhibition, the boys not only had a treat but the
Society obtained a big advertisement.

During the time that the Exhibition was open,
between fifty and sixty boys were employed in this
industry, the old quarters occupied by them at the
start were abandoned, and new ones secured near
Temple Bar, on lease, while an "office" was opened
in a court off the Strand.　By-and-by this was out-
grown and branches were established in Southwark,
Paddington, Islington, Whitechapel, Westminster, and
elsewhere, and some hundreds of boys were permanently employed.

The system upon which the organisation was
worked was a very admirable one.　When the day's
work was done each boy made off for the "Home,"
deposited his box and uniform, and had a good wash
and brush-up.　Then he had to hand in his earnings,
"checked by a system never divulged."　To begin
the day he had sixpence down ; the earnings were
divided into three parts, one part went into the boy's
own pocket, one part to the Society's fund for working expenses, and one part to the boy's bank.　Fifty
pounds was not an unusual sum as the savings of one
boy, when, with the consent of the committee, he
wished to invest elsewhere.

After accounting for the cash, there was a hearty
meal of tea and coffee, eggs, sausages, bloaters, bread
and treacle—"all the luxuries of the season including,

occasionally, periwinkles." Then, the inner man refreshed, they addressed themselves to "pot-hooks and hangers," and the other elements of a polite education, concluding with games, family prayers, and bed.

"In the early years of the Shoeblack movement," says Mr. J. R. Fowler, "great individual interest in the boys was maintained by the gentlemen of the committee who attended at the office by rotation to regulate the details of the system and administer justice to the boys in the way of rewards and punishments, mark their attendance at night school, and advance the steady and intelligent boys into higher and better situations. No member of the committee was more assiduous or more sagacious than John Mac Gregor in attending to and controlling the management of the Society, and to his genius as the leader of the movement the success, under the blessing of God, of the Ragged School Shoeblack Society is mainly attributable."

Rarely has a happy idea borne better fruit than that which led to the organisation of the Shoeblack Brigade. Commenced in such quiet and humble circumstances, the philanthropic enterprise now extends to the whole kingdom. Thousands of boys have been trained under its auspices, but at their own cost, who, but for its instrumentality, would probably have drifted into the criminal classes. The wise forethought which prompted the founders of the Society to dispose of the earnings of the boys into equal proportions has been the rule to this day. Unlike many societies, which flourish for a season and then begin gradually to wither away, this has maintained its robust and healthy growth, and every year the earnings have steadily increased until in 1892 they reached, merely for shoe-blacking, the sum of £75,800. The present income of the Brigade in London alone is over £1000 a month. Nor have the boys benefited only while remaining members of the various brigades—the Society has endeavoured to train each one in good and useful habits, give him a fair amount of education, and eventually plant him out in some fitting station in life to make a living for himself. From the foundation of the Society to the close of his career Mac Gregor was its life and soul. It was his hobby, his pet idea ; he loved it and he loved every member of the Brigade, rough, uncouth, and almost brutal, as some of them were in their original state. Perhaps there is nothing shows this more vividly than the fact that for many years he left his chambers in the Temple early in the morning in order to reach the " Home " in Mac's place before 7 A.M. to conduct the morning service of the hundred boys stationed there, and to give them a word of cheery encouragement before they started at 8 A.M. in their bright red uniform, and with bright, well-polished faces, on their day's honest labour. If Mac Gregor had done no more than that, he would have deserved a place in the permanent records of the history of philanthropy. But, as we shall see, he did many other things with equal zeal, yet for the Shoeblack Society he was always willing to labour night and day, year in and year out.

At hundreds of meetings he pleaded the cause, and

everybody used to delight in hearing him tell stories
of the boys, and more so perhaps to hear him tell
stories *to* them.

A few illustrations may not be out of place here.
He liked to tell stories of the trade ; of the shabby
people who said, " I'll pay you another time," and did
not ; of the customer who gave a sovereign between
two halfpennies without noticing it, and, being
diligently searched for and found by the shoeblack,
simply said " Thank you ! " ; and of the old pensioner
on a wooden leg who gave a halfpenny as payment
for polishing his only boot! He told of a boy who
was dismissed, but who took his revenge by sending a
letter for " which the postman charged 2*d*., the only
contents being these words inscribed on his money
card, ' I of the Cumytee sarved out.' " And of another
who used to wash his shirt at the hot-water pipe of a
brewery and carry it to a lime-kiln to dry! This
ragged boy became a shoeblack chiefly on the ground,
" That he couldn't abide dirt."

Mac Gregor was delighted to watch the progress of
each individual boy, and especially of those who were
marking out a higher career for themselves. On wet
evenings the boys read aloud at the Society's rooms.
Once, in order to excite interest, the 9th chapter of
Joshua was chosen for reading, in which it is told how
the men of Gibeon approached the Israelites with
stratagem, wearing "old shoes and clouted upon their
feet." When a boy, who was "doing well" came to
the verse where the Gibeonites say craftily, "We be

come from a far country," the shoeblack, with a lofty
air, gave this delightful bit of criticism, "I suppose
they said 'we *be* come,' to make believe they were
country folk."

Of course as the Society was successful it had many
imitators, apart from the "Freebooters," as those who
"worked on an independent footing" were called;
separate societies took up the venture, among them
the Society of St. Vincent de Paul for Roman Catholic
boys. Their official badge "S. V. P." was perplexing
to the elder order of shoeblacks, who interpreted it as
meaning "Shoes Vell Polished."

When complaints were made that the scarlet
uniform was too glaring and conspicuous insomuch
that bulls on their way to Smithfield madly made for
it, Mac Gregor replied: "The uniform has survived
the sneers of early objectors and will blush only
deeper as they smile upon its ruddy glare. What!
shall we abandon the very symbol that has given us
the golden surplus? the coat that braved a thousand
boots, the bottle, and the brush!"

Speaking in after-years of the scheme generally,
he was wont to say that "it had been the means of
polishing the understandings of a generation of
cockneys." He even saw a good moral in the act of
having one's boots cleaned, for he said: "Not one of
the customers who is not a better Christian as he
walks off, cooled and rested, and proudly self-
conscious of respectability and a right footing in the
world."

From the first, a summer treat was given annually to the shoeblacks, and when they went to Herne Bay the simple rules which were to govern their conduct on this great day of freedom, were: "(1) That no boy may spend more than 2s. 6d. on donkey-riding, and (2) that not more than four boys may be on the same donkey at the same time."

Perhaps nothing shows more clearly the genius of Mac Gregor as a student of boy-life, or exhibits his hearty and manly sympathy with his *protégés*—and at the same time the privilege, rather than duty, it is for every one to do his best to raise the fallen, to care for the homeless, to see God's blessed image even in the most outcast and forsaken, than in a brief "Parliamentary Bill," from which we make a few extracts here in the hope that they may inspire those who read to follow up his work as it inspired many who heard "the Bill read for the first time."

At the annual session of the shoeblacks at St. Martin's, the Hon. Member for the Slums, Rob Roy, brought the Shoeblack's Reform Bill into "the House." It ran somewhat on this wise;

Whereas it is desirable that the shoeblacks and their societies and the public be made a great deal better than they are; Therefore be it enacted, with the consent of the boys and the red, yellow, blue, brown, purple, white, green and Union Jack societies, their teachers, masters, matrons, superintendents and the public:—

I. The said public who care for their own sons, with clean collars and watch chains, shall care also for the boys in dirty rags, with hunger in their stomachs, tears in their eyes and no homes.

And the said public shall try to help the societies that help these boys.

And the said public shall go to where the boys live and see how poor and dark and crowded the houses are and try to get light and air and water supplied.

And the public shall get good situations for the boys recommended by the society and help some to emigrate.

And the very same public shall also care for the black in Africa and the pig-tailed Chinaman and the bigoted Hindoo.

And the said public shall talk and think not only about balls, parties, dinners, politics . . . . tittle-tattle or fiddle-faddle—but also about the good of their fellow creatures.

And the public shall buy all their doormats at the Grotto Passage School and their printing at the London Reformatory and their baskets at the Cripples' Home.

II. And, regarding the Shoeblack Societies, be it enacted that they shall get good active gentlemen on their committee, not idle men, but those "perfectly overwhelmed with business" who always work the best.

[And so on through several clauses.]

III. And with regard to the Shoeblacks themselves, be it enacted that all of them shall be very good boys; and if they are ever bad boys, and get punished, suspended, fined, or degraded, they shall not get into the sulks, pets, or doldrums. . . . .

And they shall be steady at their stations, and not run away to look at the clock, or to see *Punch*, or the wise dogs, or white mice, or the hare that fires a pistol; nor shall any boy when at his station stand on his head for more than ten minutes at a time.

And they shall not spend much money in cakes, toffy, brandy-balls or any lollipops; and if they do spend they shall faithfully tell how much when they pay in at night. And for this they shall come home at the fixed time. . . . .

And that each boy may sleep sound at night he shall be honest with his pennies during the day, lest they trouble his conscience or make it hard to trouble. . . . .

And lastly be it enacted, that the charge shall be one penny to every customer with two legs except the three following, whose boots are to be always polished gratis, namely, Mr. Judge Payne * who gives poetry, Mr. Alderman Finnis who gives plum pudding, and the Earl of Shaftesbury who has always given patronage.

Success to the Shoeblacks. God save the Queen !

Printed by order of the Wellington Statue,† Royal Exchange. February 8th, 1859.

In this rapid sketch, although we have dealt mainly with the earlier history of the Shoeblack Society, we wish in this place to include the chief part of what we have to say with regard to Mac Gregor's activities on behalf of the Ragged Schools, of which the Shoeblack Brigade was an off-shoot. His ambition was to obtain honest, legitimate employment for *all* the waifs and strays of London, and we will take a glance at some of his schemes, noting, by the way, that in most of them he was much indebted to his old and well-tried friend, Mr. Martin Ware, for many years secretary of the Central Shoeblack Brigade, and one of Mac Gregor's staunchest co-workers.

A drizzling rain till noon, and brilliant sunshine till dark—that is the weather that turns mud into gold for the shoeblack. In November 1851, when bad weather set in and lowered the receipts — as on thoroughly wet days in London people put up with

---

* Judge Payne was a high-souled philanthropic curiosity and a delightful man, who in his day delivered thousands of humorous speeches at Ragged School and kindred meetings, and who always concluded with what he called a " tail-piece "—an impromptu set of verses more or less poetical.

† Wellington Statue was the chief station of the shoeblacks.

the inconvenience of bespattered boots—the boys were drafted into Regent Street and Bond Street to act as "broomers," or sweepers, tradesmen subscribing 6*d.* a week for the advantage of having the flags in front of their shops kept perfectly clean. But it was soon found that this employment was not anything like so remunerative as shoeblacking, and the experiment was not again tried.

Then a staff of boys was employed as "messengers," each being required to have at least £3 to his credit in the "bank"—the amount to which the Society was responsible in the event of the loss of a letter or parcel. But even this was not found to be so remunerative as "Clean your boots, sir?" and was discontinued. Nevertheless it was the precursor of the admirable corps of Commissionaires, and to the still more recent experiment of "call-boys," and "Express Messengers." It stands to the credit of John Mac Gregor that, forty years before the present movement, he had placed placards in prominent localities bearing this notice :

A messenger here to carry parcels and messages at 2*d.* for the first, and 1*d.* for every additional half-mile. The Ragged School Shoeblack Society is responsible for any booked parcel to the amount of £3. 1 Off-Alley, Strand.

When his hands were as full of work as they well could be, his mind was constantly on the stretch for developing new modes of employing the poor in work that should not make dishonesty a necessity. Perhaps the Salvation Army may like to take up an idea thrown out by Mac Gregor in 1852.

Steppers. A little girl in a neat frock and a straw bonnet could carry a pail of water to the doorstep of a gentleman's house, and having washed the flagstone, she might whiten it with pipeclay. A penny would repay her, and she could earn at least sixpence in this employment every morning before breakfast.

Who will start her?

He had in his mind at this time a knife and window brigade, a brigade of newspaper boys to be stationed at the railway stations, and many other philanthropic designs which have since been developed into successful commercial transactions, but without the inner meaning which he would have incorporated into them if time and opportunity had allowed.

All these schemes were in connection with Ragged School work, to which he remained devotedly attached although the department occupied by the shoeblacks claimed his special attention. Every Sunday he was in his place among the ragged boys to whom he seemed to have the special "knack" of speaking so that their attention was arrested, and their behaviour, as a rule, was good.

One very important part in Mac Gregor's work was the introduction of visitors to see the schools. Among them was that strange, meteoric, mysterious being whose after-life puts into the shade the stories of Munchausen and the brothers Grimm — Laurence Oliphant. He was taken first to Field Lane Ragged

School where Mac Gregor held his usual class, and subsequently to a school in Westminster for ragged adults.

Oliphant gives an animated description of his experiences when he made an expedition to this school in company with Lady Troubridge and a missionary, and we give the following extract as it shows graphically the class of people the teachers of that day had to deal with, the difficulties by which they were surrounded, and, in addition, a curious phase in the life and character of Laurence Oliphant who remained, despite his eccentricities and his divergence from all the recognised lines of religious thought and action, a friend of John Mac Gregor.

"Not altogether pleasant, addressing a group of thieves in old Pye Street," says Laurence Oliphant. "Lady Troubridge seemed to think it quite natural, so I could not help myself, and insinuated to the least brutal-looking of them that a meeting was going to be held in the next street which they might find interesting, upon which he laughed and asked 'Jim' if he heard that ; upon which Jim said that he did, and that he had other meetings to attend rather more to his taste than that, he'd be sworn to, 'not reflecting no ways on you, sir.' Whereupon, after a little chaffing among themselves, they decided it wasn't the sort of thing that would suit them, 'No offence to you, ye know, sir ;' and one man did me the honour to say that he'd no doubt I meant well. So I went unsuccessfully to the meeting, where I found congregated fifty or sixty fellows who had come in from curiosity, none of whom, to all appearance, had ever been in a church in their lives, and who either stared vacantly or chaffed and made jokes, while here and there a little sparring-match went on." On another occasion, when in the company of Mac Gregor, he says: "Some boys began to fight and had to be lugged out by their legs and arms, creating a great sensation. Some of the men seemed attentive, however, while others made jokes, and the boys who had been turned out, began throwing stones against the windows, so that by the time we got to the next hymn there was a considerable row, which increased as we began it, as everybody began to sing at the top of their voices a variety of airs, amid occasional bursts of laughter. When service was over, some promised to come back, while others went away amused ; but all through there was no absolute incivility shown, which, considering the men, was a great deal to say."

When Oliphant came periodically to London to "eat his terms," and later, when he was shaping his destiny, he always associated himself with Mac Gregor's work and with "the black-guards" his *protégés* in Westminister, and in his letters such passages as the following are of frequent occurrence ; "On Monday I have to deliver a lecture, to what is anticipated to be a crowded audience, upon reformatory institutions ; on Tuesday to make a speech at a public meeting for the Belgravian Ragged Schools ; on Wednesday to a large *soirée* to meet the swells who take an interest in these things. Last Sunday I gave an address to my black-guards at Westminster."

Years afterwards, when engaged in diplomatic service in America, his mind went back to the old days, never to return, and he wrote : " In my present capacity I am not engaged in any work of benevolence or charity by which I could, as it were, support myself, and though, no doubt, by my example I might glorify God, it is a much more difficult matter to do so in a ball-room at the French Ambassador's, surrounded by as unthinking a throng as ever tripped the light fantastic, than down in Westminster surrounded by Mac Gregor, Fowler & Co."

We shall come in contact again with Laurence Oliphant in the course of this work and find him, in his fantastic flights, often crossing the path of his friend Mac Gregor.

CHAPTER V

IN FULL CRY

A few notes from the diary of John Mac Gregor will help us to follow his movements in other paths than those we have already indicated. He returned to London, after his long tour in the East, in the spring of 1850. In the summer of that year he wrote :

June 29.—To Cambridge.

June 30.—Went to Carus's church and to the school. One boy only remembered me there.

July 1.—Incepted as M.A.

July 2.—Created Master of Arts.

1851.

Jan. 31.—Called to the Bar.

March 1.—Got my first brief.

March 8.—Another law case, No. 2, from Jones.

March 18.—Slept first time in my new rooms.

These entries look like business, but interspersed among them are others which show that his mind was occupied with many things foreign to a life of study and legal work. Thus :

July 27.—To Banningham, to see Bickersteth. Visited several

families and sick and dying. Taught in his Sunday School. He preaches well—is very happy.

July 28.—*Sunday.* His son Edward* was baptised, and I was one godfather to him. Miss C. Bickersteth being godmother.

Oct. 11.—Dined with Nolan, Dr. McNeile and Dr. Cumming. Dr. M. apprehended secret Bulls of Rome, advising conspiracies &c., and Dr. C. thinks we are in the seventh vial of Revelation !

Nov. 15.—Subject for Norrisian essay, 'The traces discernible in Holy Scripture of the influence exerted on the character of the Hebrews by their residence in Egypt,' to be sent to Whewell before the tenth day preceding the Sunday in Passion Week of 1851.

Nov. 23.—Called on Mr. Hamilton and was appointed Honorary Secretary of the Protestant Defence Committee.

This last brief entry stands for a great deal.   In the previous month a Papal Bull had been published abolishing the Administration of Roman Catholics in England by vicars apostolic and appointing instead two archbishops and twelve bishops with territorial districts.   Dr. Wiseman was raised to the dignity of a cardinal and was appointed the first Archbishop of Westminster.   He forthwith issued a pastoral, dating it, "From out of the Flaminian Gate at Rome," and this notorious letter, full of arrogant assumption, ignored the Church of England, and spoke as though England had been restored to the Roman Communion and would henceforth be ecclesiastically governed by the new hierarchy.

The Maynooth grant of 1845, the rise and spread of Puseyism and the Oxford movement, the secession of

* The present Bishop of Japan.

notable men to the Church of Rome, had all tended to stir up very strong feelings in the breasts of true Protestants, but the Papal Bull and the cardinal's letter created a sensation and an activity such as had never been known before and certainly will never be known again. The story of the Papal Aggression, as it was called, and the "No Popery" agitation, are matters of history and need not be even summarised here. But the attitude of Mac Gregor to the question and the important part he took in the controversy demand our careful attention. Many names stand out more prominently in the history of that controversy than his, but it is questionable whether any one exercised a more practical or abiding influence.

He was just the man for the work. As the reader will have guessed long ago, he was a very low Churchman—in fact, he would not have blushed had any one even called him a Nonconformist—he was a man of brilliant education, of ready if not fluent speech, of considerable social distinction, and he could wield his facile pen with marvellous energy and rapidity. He had watched with keen eyes every phase of the Oxford movement and he wrote :

The Greeks after ten years unsuccessful war with the Trojans pretended to raise the siege in despair, but in fact only retired to a near island and left a concealed garrison in the house within the walls. Thus the Tractarians are left in the church to work and prepare for the open attack of the enemy.

When that open attack came in the form of the

notorious Papal Bull, Mac Gregor accepted the duties
of Honorary Secretary of the Protestant Defence
Committee, which at once placed him at the very
heart of the controversy. From this date the daily
entries in the diary are : "Attended committee meeting, P. D. C.," until December 5th is reached when
he adds : "From this day to December 14th the
committee business was almost my sole occupation."

But the Protestant Defence Committee concerned
itself mainly with the political aspect of the controversy and eagerly promoted the issue of protests,
the suppression of Romish innovations in the Church
of England and especially the advancement of the
Ecclesiastical Titles Bill. Mac Gregor's heartiest
sympathies were on the spiritual side of the question,
how it affected the faith of the people rather than how
it affected the State, and it seemed to him that what
was wanted was, not so much to fight Roman Catholicism as to stir up in the hearts of the people of
England the spirit of true Protestantism.

We are not surprised to find therefore that when, in
June 1851, a great meeting was held to form an
association which should combine all classes of Protestants, whose object should be not merely to oppose
the recent aggression of the Pope, but to maintain and
defend, against *all* the encroachments of Popery, the
scriptural doctrines of the Reformation and the principles of religious liberty as the best security for
the temporal and spiritual welfare and prosperity
of the kingdom, Mac Gregor was not only present

but he accepted the arduous office of Honorary
Secretary of the new society, to be called the
Protestant Alliance. The record in his diary of
this great event which was to occupy an enormous amount of his time for the next twenty years
is simply this :

> June 25.—Protestant Alliance—great meeting.

To his sister, to whom he opened his heart perhaps
more than to any other being at this time, he wrote :

> A great meeting has been called at Manchester at which I must
> make my appearance, for it is solely on my account, and of course
> a speech is inevitable. You see we have yesterday finally established
> the new society to be called (I think) the Protestant Alliance. The
> last member whose name was put down was Goode (who wrote that
> excellent book 'The Better Covenant'). We shall have 3000
> members to start with, of all denominations.

It was stated to have been discovered that there
was an enormous conspiracy, ramified over the whole
of Europe, to rob the English people of their Bible,
their liberty, and all that was dear to them as Christians. The principal objects of the Alliance were to
establish union among Evangelical Protestants, and
to direct their combined efforts vigorously against
Popery—to arouse, enlighten, and organise the Protestants of Great Britain "to resist the machinations
of Rome in this country and to act with influence in
securing religious liberty abroad," and this was to be
done by sermons, lectures, public meetings, and abundance of literature. In the first year or two of their

history the Alliance took up such matters as the repeal of the Maynooth endowment, the inspection of nunneries, the appointment of " Popish " chaplains to prisons, the proposed alteration of oaths for Members of Parliament, the erection of a martyr's memorial at Smithfield, and a host of other questions at home ; while abroad they determined to stand by and succour persecuted Protestants everywhere and anywhere.

:One particular instance, known as the case of the Madiai, occurred at the outset of the existence of the Protestant Alliance and caused a sensation in religious circles to which we in these colder and less enthusiastic days are strangers. Two Tuscan shopkeepers, Francesco and Rosa Madiai, were brought under the influence of Protestant teachers and, as a consequence, renounced the errors of Rome. For the " offence " of reading the Scriptures and repeating to their neighbours what they had heard and seen, the Grand Duke of Tuscany condemned them to five years imprisonment with hard labour in the galleys. All Protestant Europe was up in arms—petitions were sent to Queen and Parliament ; the Prince Consort sent a personal appeal to the Grand Duke, a deputation headed by Lord Roden was sent to Italy to remonstrate with the Grand Duke ; eventually the British Government interfered and the Grand Duke, unable to withstand the storm his tyranny had provoked, set the prisoners free.

Referring to the agitation in a letter to his sister

Mac Gregor says : " It is a glorious symptom of the unity of the Church of Christ to see that when the humblest members suffer —all others feel in sympathy. . . . . I feel indeed as if a country must be blest in which such communion exists, even though it be mixed with much that is worldly."

From the same source we find that within a short time after the establishment of the Protestant Alliance he was so immersed in its work that from morning to night he was engaged exclusively in promoting its interests. He says :

Within the last few days these events have occurred : First, we, have appointed a first-rate man as travelling secretary at £300 per annum and travelling expenses to go over all the alliances and lecture, and put in the poker. Secondly, Miss Portal sent us £100 additional donation this morning. Thirdly, Our Monthly Letter, of which I send a copy, has a circulation of 1500 a month. Fourthly, I saw Chambers the other day who is arming himself for another campaign against convents. The Maynooth inquiry is proceeding, and in to-day's *Times* I see that it is a very searching one. Hopefully may it end ! Fifthly, I finished last night a memorial to Lord Palmerston about the appointment of Popish chaplains to gaols. Sixthly, I am to breakfast on Monday with twenty-five Protestant secretaries and to concert measures. Seventhly, On the same day we are to go to Lord Clarendon to bother him concerning the liberties of English Protestants resident abroad This will be a rarity in my work, for as I only run across the court to Hindmarsh's, and do not leave him until nearly six o'clock I am never now in the streets unless in the dark.

On the first General Committee of the Alliance there was enrolled almost every Evangelical of note in town and country, and Mac Gregor, to his great delight, was brought in contact with them all.   Within a year or two branch alliances were established throughout the length and breadth of the land.

So rapidly did the idea take hold that in 1853 it

Monthly letter
No. 15
Protestant Alliance
9 Serjeants Inn Fleet Street.
London. March 1. 1854

Dear Sir

229.   In the Christian Times of last Friday it is stated that two Englishmen have been imprisoned at Rome for having in their possession the Italian Bible. A lady at Florence was lately summoned before the Police & informed that she must leave the country on the ex- -piration of her present license for residence.

230. G. H. Davis Esq. the Travelling Sec. of the P. Alliance has attended the annual meetings of the York P. alliance

An old Pagan image is called a Statue of St. Peter. At Rome from Jupiter. This Clad in purple with a ring on the finger. The faithful worship it in St. Peter on this chair.

was found necessary to establish monthly communica- tion, not only with every branch, but with every individual member of each branch, and the first Monthly Letter dated January 1st, 1853, lithographed from the handwriting of Mac Gregor, is in the

possession of the present writer.   It is a full, yet crisp
and terse account of the doings and purposes of the
Alliance, and it was so well received, and so vastly
aided the spread of the work, that the letters were
continued not only so long as he was secretary of
the Alliance, but to the present day.   The first
twenty-five Monthly Letters were lithographed from
the handwriting of Mac Gregor—many of them being
ornamented by him with excellent pen-and-ink drawings.   No. 26, issued on February the 1st, 1855, was
the first Monthly Letter sent out in print.

No better man could have been found for the
arduous and responsible post of secretary to the
Alliance.   His early life and training in Ireland, and
his travels, to be extended as the years went on,
brought him in contact with the Romish system and
added to his experience.   When he spoke, he spoke
with authority, for when the Madiai excitement was at
its height he went over to Tuscany to make personal
inquiries.   He was in Spain when the feeling against
Protestantism was so strong that travellers were not
allowed to carry Spanish Testaments with them.   He
held a public discussion at King's Cross every
Sunday afternoon for eight months on Roman
Catholic Bibles, when he went thoroughly into
the differences among Roman Catholics as to the
various English editions of the Testaments and Bibles.
He made the assertion that "There is no English
edition of the Bible or Testament which the Roman
Catholics approve as a Church, but they allow some

seven or eight to be largely circulated and about twelve others, each of them greatly differing from one another." He was wont to produce many of these, some printed in Dublin, England, and America, certified by bishops, archbishops, and great authorities of the Roman Church, yet all differing materially.

It would be impossible to reproduce here even a tithe of what he wrote and said about Popery, but one or two specimens of his style may be briefly indicated.

" Popery in A.D. 1900" was the title of a pamphlet written by him in the interests of the Protestant Alliance. It had a large circulation and was much appreciated at the time, but it is now out of date. It is a supposed " Looking Back," from the Romanist standpoint on the progress of Romanism from the year 1870 to the close of the century. It reviewed the Oxford movement, the Maynooth question, the appointment of bishops "to rule over all baptised persons in this rebellious land," and the Papal Aggression—"which greatly alarmed the heretics of England although nothing more came of all the bluster but a paltry Act, long since repealed and hardly worth mentioning"—followed by the rise of "that vile conglomeration of our enemies, the Protestant Alliance, a mixture of all kinds and shades of bigotry, a sort of 'Evangelical Haggis,' as the Scotch would call it, with peers and M.P.'s to give it substance, as the standing paste of the Anglican Church, with the forced meat of Wesley, and spiced for raciness with Baptists and Independents."

Then the progress of Popery is traced in imagination until the *Tablet* becomes the organ of England instead of the *Times;* the "rampant braying" of the *Record* is suppressed by Act of Parliament; Ragged Schools and the lay teaching of religion are put down ; fasting is made a part of professional discipline in the army and navy ; the Bible is only issued in Latin ; Sunday *fêtes* for the people are organised ; and the pamphlet concludes thus : "O Bowyer, Lucas, and Wiseman, would that your righteous shades could see our triumph—the flowering of your hopes, and the fruit of your toils! England no longer a comet plunging in darkness, but nearer to the sun than Mercury, and revolving in its orbit round the see of Rome."

In all his writings and utterances on Roman Catholicism it was with the system, not with individuals, that Mac Gregor's contentions lay. After a visit to the East, where he had been brought into contact with the "scandalous impostures" in the holy places of Palestine, he wrote a word of warning to his countrymen in these terms :

Do we really know what Popery has been of old, and will be here and soon, and always—if dominant ? To the future England— the England that as yet is free—could you or I be true Papists, and yet be loyal ? Never ! It may be called 'indiscretion' to speak thus ; but I have seen too much abroad to be ignorant, and I fear too little and too much to be silent. For money, free trade, railways, anything you please that is earthly, you may hold meetings, write books, fight battles, make any din you like, and be 'earnest' and speak plain. But for the free Bible—the right to tell what

Popery was, is, and wants to be—you must hush to a whisper any voice you have. We must be 'charitable'—yea, and for whom our charity? Not for our women, our children, our herds of ignorant and weak, who are beguiled—but for the army of foreign priests who stream over the land and raise an alien name above our Queen.

To any individual finding difficulty as to what his relations to the Church of Rome should be, the style of MacGregor was altogether different, as the following letter written to one who was thinking of joining that communion will show :—

Our friend Ussher tells me you would not object to receive a letter from me and I venture to hope its frankness will not offend you. I think that when we believe Our Lord came to seek and to save lost sinners, His words spoken to sinners like ourselves will be found the very best and only certain truth on this subject. What he said to multitudes of common men and women, and what His Apostles wrote to multitudes by His command are no doubt for the whole world to hear. All Christian Churches agree to this, I think, and when we examine Christ's words we find them directed chiefly to bring each sinner as an individual to the Saviour, each being responsible for himself. Though men are not to be saved in 'bundles,' but individually, we find them encouraged to band together for mutual edification and comfort, and before the Apostles died, there were many groups of this sort, each of which was called a 'church.' Antioch and Jerusalem were the first of these Churches, in point of time ; Ephesus, Corinth, Rome, and other cities had their churches too. Soon one church claimed to be chief among these, and another opposed this claim and has always done so.

Now the question is, Has any one church a right to such a claim, and, if so, Has the Roman Church that right? and, if so, To what does this right extend? Though many churches existed in the Apostles' time, and many hard questions were debated among them,

I find only one occasion when one church was appealed to in settling a point of controversy. (Acts xv.) This was not the church at Rome, but at Jerusalem.

Precedent then is quite against the Romish Church being a judge of controversy for the world. However, as that church sets up this claim we must examine it again. Of course we are not to yield such a claim without being convinced. No Romanist ought to try to get our consent unless our judgment is persuaded by true arguments ; else *his* adhesion and that of all his fellow churchmen may be pronounced unreal, and against their own convictions, and only because of force or fear, or that they were taught one way, or born among Romanists. Well then, I find no one word in the Bible to say that the church at Rome is supreme—none by the earliest Christians, but protests from the first against this claim, and millions in the Greek church (older than the Roman), and all Protestant churches, who never allowed such a claim at all. The claim therefore is not scriptural, or of early Christian times, or generally allowed, far less is it self-evident.

It must therefore be rigidly proved.

Now I look at the doctrine of the Romish church and find it has changed from age to age, and is different in every country and almost in every diocese. St. Paul's Epistle to the Romans tells what was the true doctrine then. The Pope's last letter to his church is as different from this as possible. No wonder that the Romish church sees this difference, and while it publishes the Pope's letter, as if it could be plainly understood by all, refuses to publish Paul's letters, or Peter's letters, and forces meanings on them when it cannot prevent them from being read.

In Paul's, and Peter's and John's letters, I find that the churches of early times were often stated to be utterly wrong, to be much disunited, and often needed change. The Pope says his church is always right, always one and always the same—better than Christ's. In the Apostles' letters I find not one word about the Virgin Mary. The Pope's letters are crammed with talk about her. The Encyclical just issued in its last twenty lines implores her intercession as 'our Mediatrix,' and the prayers of Apostles and Saints, but entirely omits all mention whatever of Jesus Christ. The Bible says that there is only 'one mediator between God and man'—the Pope calls a woman 'our Mediatrix.'

In the creed of the Church of Rome, which is only just 300 years old, I find first the Nicene creed, which once the church of Rome had as enough, and which for 1500 years has been enough for other Christians. But added to this (only three centuries ago) she inserts twelve more articles necessary to salvation not one of which can I see in the Bible or in the early church—not one of these clears up a difficulty or gives new light or comfort, but all go to build up a vast scheme by which priests get power over men here, and claim to have power over them in another world. Where did Christ or Peter or Paul tell us to reverence images, or obey the Roman Church, or get indulgences, or pray to saints, or fear purgatory, or pray in a foreign tongue?

How then do so many join this Roman Church? Some because she promises salvation—some because she asserts antiquity—some because she assumes grandeur—some because she gives music to the ear and colour to please the eye and mystery to dazzle the brain. But chiefly men join Rome because she is a visible body seen by eyes, and heard by ears, and touched by hands; whereas Christ is not so seen or heard or handled, except by the eye, ear, and hand of faith given by God. So it is the want of faith and the wish to walk by sight, which makes the visible guide of Rome more welcome than the unseen but real and true guide, the Son of God. My dear friend, there are men who, to advance their church, will first puzzle you with questions and then terrify you with fears and so get you not to listen to Jesus who died for you and me, sinners, and who says to each sinner, 'Come unto me.'

Before yielding to such teachers ask them to put down in writing, or distinctly refer to some book, for the true reasons why you should hear a Church and not a Saviour and I undertake, God helping me, to give such an answer to every reason as will, if candidly read and considered, be thoroughly satisfactory in preventing you from being misled. May God by His Holy Spirit guide you into truth and keep you firm in the faith of the Lord Jesus.

We have seen that almost immediately after John Mac Gregor was called to the Bar, he was called to this work of Protestantism, which so largely occupied his time that he had little opportunity of making progress in his profession. He had a great regard for that profession, however, and he was revolving in his mind many schemes by which he hoped to make his mark in it, but it invariably happened that just at the moment when he fancied the right time had come, other, and as he thought better, things came in his way. Among his most intimate friends were many young barristers, and being like-minded to himself he enlisted their services in various kinds of religious and philanthropic work. He also sought to do some good to the profession at large and to this end on the 9th of February, 1852, he gathered together a number of friends, and started the Lawyers' Prayer Union, an association of those members of the legal profession who desired to unite their private prayers for the Divine Blessing upon all connected with the profession, and upon themselves individually, and who would agree to do this at stated times.

Similar prayer unions had already been established among members of the army, the navy, and each of the universities, and in all cases it had been found of spiritual benefit to concentrate prayer on the circumstances of each calling, and "men of prayer, otherwise unknown to one another, had derived mutual benefit from association for such objects, and had thus been

led to combine together for other holy purposes."
The subjects for special prayer suggested to the
members of the Lawyers' Prayer Union, were: The
Queen and "all that are in authority," the Chancellor,
Legislature and Government, and all persons in
judicial authority. For "right judgments and true
laws, good statutes and commandments."

Everything was done quietly and privately. There
was no flourish of trumpets. A few like-minded men
joined together and determined to ask only those who
they knew would sympathise with the object they had
in view, and not bring it into ridicule or contempt.
These again asked their friends, and thus from all
parts of the country there came requests to be enrolled
as members. All commnuications were marked
"private," so that no cause of offence should be given
to those into whose hands the circulars and papers
might inadvertently fall. That the institution answered
the end for which it was established ; that it brought
men into contact giving strength to the weak and
courage to the timid, there is ample known evidence,
that it supplied what was felt by many to be a
spiritual need is shown in the circumstance that the
Lawyers' Prayer Union exists to-day and is worked
on the identical lines laid down by John Mac Gregor
in 1852.

As this chapter is dealing mainly with religious
subjects, it may be well in this place to refer to a
common popular sneer often levelled at men engaged

in public religious work, namely, that it is, as a rule, at the expense of any such aid to their own household or kindred. In the case of John Mac Gregor, a more libellous statement could not have been made. His own spiritual life was intense, and in his earnestness he never left a stone unturned to help any one struggling after the higher life. About the time of which we now write his beloved sister Elizabeth—who in 1863 married Major Robert Wilmot Brooke,* of the 60th Rifles, and died in 1883—was in much perplexity of mind as to her spiritual state, and she found in him a wonderful counsellor and minister. Many letters passed between them, and some of those written by Mac Gregor lie before us. Several are too sacred to set before the public eye ; some are couched in language so dogmatic and theological that they would puzzle the general reader ; others are so old and wise that it seems almost impossible they could come from a young man full of life and energy, rising higher and higher on the tide of popular favour ; but all are so brimful of hearty affection, of burning desire that the happiness and rest of soul he himself enjoyed should be shared by one very dear to him, that we venture to give a few extracts :

It is not at all uncommon to feel the surprise you express at man's refusing salvation when it is simply the result of believing that salvation is already accomplished. You ask why then do not all accept it ? Surely the Bible gives a plain answer : our corrupt

* Now Lt.-Colonel Wilmot Brooke.

hearts, the devil, and our sinful desires all conspire against believing this simple truth.   But especially ask yourself why should you be astonished at few receiving this free gift if *you* have long refused it, or have resisted the conclusion that it is and has been within your grasp for twelve or fourteen years. . . . . Remember then that simple faith is all that is necessary to salvation, everything after it is only an evidence of its presence and its growth.

*   *   *   *   *

I hope you feel what an extremely interesting thing it is to watch a heart; quickly discerning the first assaults of Satan and summing up at night all the thoughts and actions of the day. . . . . It is a good plan to put down a list of things to pray for every day besides casual necessities.   If you can get a walk by yourself, no time is better for such prayer; but remember that the real spiritual struggling is to be on the knees in the quiet of your room. . . . . Such petitions as the following are useful for daily meditation :—greater earnestness in prayer, and faith that it will be answered in good time —remembrance of God all day, even when suddenly tempted—to be made somehow useful that day—spirituality, and cheerful holy joy and peace—energy in worldly occupations and duties.   Then be sure every day to pray for papa in this crisis—mamma so bound up in love to us all—for me and Duncan, Douglas and Harry by name. Now dearest Elizabeth, try to do all this to-day and then feel how enlarged you will be to pray for yourself after entreaty for others.

*   *   *   *   *

If you walk in the morning at seven o'clock, and are praying for me, think that I am then also praying for you and that some happy thoughts are sent to each of us from the prayers of the other.

*   *   *   *   *

How universal the same difficulty appears concerning faith.   I should recommend you to ask yourself some leading conscience questions: Are you not waiting to be converted whilst you ought at once to receive the mercy God is offering?   Are you not slightly relying on your repentance, prayers, or amount of faith as likely to bring about the state you desire rather than feeling it is already yours if you will but stretch out your hand? You mourn over sin and yet do not seem to really believe this truth that it is already washed away simply if you believe that it is so. It is not faith which saves. It is Christ through faith. There is ever a lurking dislike to be indebted to another for such a great boon. This keeps many a sinner from accepting what is freely given. Whose fault is it if you are not on the rock? Why should you not be firmly there to-night?

*　　*　　*　　*　　*

The fear of being thought to set up for holier than you really are is a favourite snare of the tempter. By this the Devil keeps you from speaking for God, reproving sin, combating wrong opinions, showing your colours and fighting boldly. He says, '*you* should not speak for you are just as bad yourself.' Now are we to wait until we don't sin before we try to spread God's Kingdom? If so we should not reprove a single man on earth.

*　　*　　*　　*　　*

The last letter in this special correspondence runs as follows :

MY DEAREST ELIZABETH,—

I can't be disappointed when I come back. I'll tell you what I expect to find. A sister who has felt the sand shaking on which we all naturally build our hopes for eternity, God's mercy, our works, all our prayers, all our faith—and has fled to the Rock. I can only expect to find a help to me in our common preparation for Heaven. I am really longing to get home and more than half the anticipation is for you. What nice rides we may have together and walks and talks! Often when I have walked with you I have yearned to hear some faint whispers of spiritual life and have abstained, too much perhaps, from speaking on godly subjects from the fear of appearing to force them, or of engendering hypocrisy. But I confess I am myself much changed since I came here. I see more than ever that *all* our business here is to get to Heaven and bring others there, and nothing bearing on these things should be left undone if possible. With greater grace I have far greater peace and happiness. I hope that you still pray for me; I do for you by name twice a day. Expect to find me far more zealous for God and more openly his servant. If this be boasting perhaps I shall be humbled before you, but let us both prepare for a joyful meeting.

JOHN.

Here we drop the curtain on a brotherly and sisterly love which was faithful unto death. We have only drawn that curtain aside to show the nature of the religion, and the interpretation MacGregor placed upon it, by which he was to carry on his spiritual life-work and gather together the forces which should ensure success to many noble enterprises. Whatever views may be held with regard to the dogmatic teaching of the school to which he belonged, it is a notable fact that almost every great religious, philanthropic, sanitary, and social movement of the earlier half of the present century was the work of men holding identical views. "By their fruits ye shall know them," and if, as some say, these views are narrow, nevertheless if they produce these fruits, who would not wish for a continuation of that narrowness, and that all were of the same mind?

A few years before his death, MacGregor, looking back upon his past life, wrote in pencil on a few sheets of note-paper a list of the "special events" that had marked his career. The first two pages run as follows:

Dec. 1848.—Went with Blackmore to a Ragged School. Sent to it £5 which *Punch* sent me for picture of Guy Fawkes.

1849.

March.—Attended Committee Ragged School Union.

April.—To Paris with 250 excursionists.

July.—Carlyle came to us at Drumcondra, Dublin.

July 17.—To Boulogne. Paris.

July 29.—Malta. Gozo.

Aug.—Piræus. Marathon.

Aug. 29.—Fought with water-buckets in ship—beginning of illness.

Sep. 30.—Smyrna.

Sep. 31.—Gallipoli.

Oct.—Beyrout, Damascus, Palestine.

Dec. 25.—On a camel by myself rode into Cairo.

1850.

Jan. 1.—Started up the Nile.

Feb. 5.—Shot my first crocodile in Nile.

March 15.—Started for home with hippopotamus for Zoological Gardens.

April.—Made Master of Arts, Cambridge.

April 28.—Godfather to Bickersteth's son.

Nov. 23.—Appointed hon. sec. to Protestant Defence Committee.

1851.

Jan. 1.—Called to the Bar. Temple.

July 7.—My first brief as a barrister.

Oct.—Manchester meeting of 85,000 Sunday School children and 10,000 teachers, when Queen came.

Dec.—Conference, Birmingham, which organised Reformatory and Refuge Union. Lord Lyttelton presiding.

1852.

Enlisted in Temple Volunteers.

Feb. 9.—Started Lawyers' Prayer Union.

July.—First proof of 'Popery in A.D. 1900.' With Ware and Oliphant to Ireland, visiting Achill and all west.

Nov. 6.—Slavery Committee. Duchess of Sutherland's.

To most of these events we have referred in the foregoing pages. One, however, to which he attached great importance remains to be touched upon—the "Birmingham Conference"—resulting in the Reformatories Act, the Industrial Schools Acts, and the Reformatory and Refuge Union. At the Conference, Mac Gregor acted as Honorary Secretary in conjunction with the Rev. Sydney Turner, afterwards Her Majesty's Inspector of Reformatories.

The main points discussed at the Conference and upon which all seemed agreed, were, that no agency at that time in existence was adequate to check the startling increase of juvenile crime; that voluntary agency was not equal to cope with it; that compulsory education and reformatory schools were needed rather than prisons; that legislative enactments were required in order to establish correctional and reformatory schools for those children who had been convicted of felony or such misdemeanours as involve dishonesty, and that magistrates should have power conferred upon them to commit juvenile offenders to such schools instead of to prison.

A committee, consisting of John Mac Gregor, D. Power, W. Locke, and Rev. S. Turner, was appointed to undertake the necessary preliminary steps in London.

The diary shows the progress of events.

Dec. 17, 1851.—First meeting of Preventive and Reformatory School Committee in my rooms.

Jan. 21.—Power came to settle Draft Bill. [This was after-wards the Industrial Schools Act.]

Feb. 6.—Preventive and Reformatory School Committee. House of Commons Committee appointed, went with deputations to Lord Granville. Took notes and published them in *Morning Herald* and *Times*.

May 11.—House of Commons Select Committee on Juvenile Crime.

May 15.—Conference with Sir John Pakington about Criminal Select Committee.

June 8.—Summoned by Baines to attend House of Commons Committee on Crime.

June 18.—Examined before House of Commons Committee from twelve to three o'clock about the Shoeblacks.

The result of the labours of the Parliamentary Committee was a "Bill for the Better Care and Reformation of Juvenile Offenders," brought in by Mr. Adderley. But it hung fire, and in 1853 another conference was held at Birmingham, when Joseph Sturge, the well-known Quaker philanthropist, invited Mac Gregor to be his guest.

JOSEPH STURGE *to* JOHN MAC GREGOR.

WHEELY LANE, EDGBASTON, BIRMINGHAM,
December 17, 1853.

ESTEEMED FRIEND,

I hope thou wilt favour me with thy company to lodge at my house on Monday and Tuesday night, as I understand thou art going to attend the conference, respecting juvenile delinquents, in this town on Tuesday. As a perfect stranger I have no apology for taking this freedom except a sympathy of feeling for these poor outcasts. It is right that I should say that I am such an ultra Teetotaler that I have for many years expelled all alcoholic beverages from my house, and that thy entertainment will be very simple in other respects. I rather hope that David Power, the Recorder of Ipswich, will also be our guest.

Very sincerely and respectfully,
J. STURGE.

For some years an agitation was carried on with regard to juvenile mendicity; a "Youthful Offenders Bill" received the Royal Assent in 1854, and as a result there was a marked decline in juvenile delinquency. In all these affairs Mac Gregor took a very active part and especially in assisting to inaugurate boys' refuges.

Perhaps the most valuable and laborious service he rendered was in attending committees to discuss the whole question of legislation with regard to further developments in relation to industrial schools and reformatories, and the powers that might be given to magistrates and managers. One entry from the diary will show the spirit in which he went to work.

May 3, 1856.—National Reformatory Association, Lord Brougham in chair. Adderley, R. Cecil, Northcote, &c. After their discussion of his Bill I proposed a clause which they all assented to, and it was inserted. I regard this as a remarkable answer to earnest prayer. In morning could not see how Bill improvable, and yet it had fatal objections. Prayed as I went along and at the rooms, but the idea was not suggested to me until after they had exhausted their plans, and therefore were less ready to cavil with mine. Such moments of success are to be hailed with joy and gratitude, and it is not easy to keep down pride and vanity.

Another important labour, which proved of invaluable assistance to legislators and others engaged in forwarding the movement, was the preparation of an elaborate work on the "Law of Reformatories."* It is now out of date but it was a task of much difficulty executed with great skill and for many years was the principal authority on the subject.

Mac Gregor's labours on behalf of reformatories and industrial schools continued throughout his life, and we shall return to the subject again.

* "The Law of Reformatories; containing—(1) A Compendium of the Law relating to Juvenile Criminals and to Reformatories and similar Institutions; the General Statutes at length . . . . and the Whole or Chief Parts of Special Acts for Particular Institutes; (2) Lists of Certified Reformatories; Information as to the Assistance given by the Privy Council to Industrial Institutes, &c. Intended for the use of Magistrates, Managers of Reformatories, and others interested in such Institutions." By John MacGregor, Esq., M.A., of the Inner Temple, barrister-at-law. London: Benning & Co., law publishers, 43 Fleet Street. 1856.

CHAPTER VI

TRAVELS: STORIES AND ADVENTURES

MAC GREGOR liked London—its life, activity, noise and bustle. In a letter to a friend, he says: "There is no place in the world like good old smoky towny London." He liked to see all that was going on, and, if possible, to take some part in it. Here, from the same source, is a record of a passing event :—

When I came home at eleven I saw the gleam of a great fire and put on some old clothes and set off to it. The blaze came from a hay store in Hungerford Market. I took a long spell at the engines and got the beer they served round to each. It is very cheering to see the earnest way in which Englishmen help to extinguish a fire wherever it may be. The sight was a curious one. Oceans of water flowing over our shoes. Children running naked in the stream, the firemen, with their helmets, on the roofs, women shrieking, and babies squalling, and the greatest noise and bustle. Then all the stout fellows at the engines—about forty to each, singing in chorus to keep time, and the smoke and flames waving about. We got it down about one o'clock, and this morning I went to see the ruins.

He greatly enjoyed the public position he occupied, and was gratified at the estimation in which he was held. It was quite pardonable pride that made him feel a little exultation when a letter from abroad addressed

MR. MACGREGOR,

Philanthropist,

London,

came direct to him without any delay in the post.

'I never can be sufficiently thankful for the society which I am thrown into in London,' he wrote, 'so Christian, so warm-hearted, so very kind to me. Only the drawback of its uplifting me with vanity is on the other side, and I believe no position whatever is without that evil. I feel sure that if I had been worshipping the world and were only ambitious of high position in it, my ideas are far too lofty ever to have been satisfied; perhaps I should be amongst the most discontented of men. But to be allowed to labour in such work as Protestantism and Ragged Schools is, I can truly say in my calm moments, far more honourable than any Government appointment—even the most exalted—and to be, if it be but for a year or two, thrust forward into the thickest of the fight in both regiments at once—what is it? surely it is a post rather to tremble in than in which to stand.'

He delighted in every kind of rational amusement and he "went at it" with vigour. The theatre, however, he tabooed all his life long. He said on one occasion in after years :

I was never in all my life so dull as to want to be made to laugh, and I always was near enough to real sorrow and sin and suffering to be made to cry if I were in that humour.

He took with him to every entertainment the

brightness, wonder, and vivacity of a boy, and all the energy of a man.

On visiting the Great Exhibition of 1851, he went characteristically to work. Writing to his sister, he says :

Every time I go to that place I am more amazed. After my second visit, when I had pored over its wonders for sixteen hours, I thought, well I certainly have a good general notion of the whole. Now I find that there were actually ten miles of counter which I had not touched.

A few extracts from the diary will show the kind of amusements in which he took delight.

1851.

Jan. 9.—To the Noels where about a hundred people were at a children's party. Dressed oriental and drummed. G. with a sham baby, and E. as Zuleika. G. acted the dwarf with A. Kinnaird. Everything went off capitally.

June 21.—My musical party with sixteen ladies and gentlemen.

July 1.—To Hampton Court with the Maudes. Then to Storey's Electro-Biology, where my character was delineated by phrenology by a man in a mesmeric state.

Dec. 3.—*Sunday*. Mr. Mac Grath preached a fine sermon. Walked fifteen miles afterwards.

1852.

Jan. 1.—Went with Mr. Bunting's party to Mrs. Bealey's party at Radcliffe where about fifty young people came. Eastern dress, music, charades, blindman's buff. Returned at 1 A.M.

Nov. 18.—Duke of Wellington's funeral. Went at 5.30 A.M. to Waterloo Place where I saw capitally. Was on my legs for six hours without any bad effects. Read Shakespeare at night.

May 17.—Dined Buxton's. Tried the table-turning experiment, but unsuccessfully. Tried to turn a hat and succeeded.*

May 23.—Visited Albert Smith's Mont Blanc Entertainment.

Mac Gregor could read character and understand the men he had to deal with. They were of all sorts and conditions, and it was an endless source of amusement and interest to study them. Writing to his sister he says : "A man called Hogg came this morning, an old soldier who was in the 23rd at Salamanca with Major Mac Gregor—nine clasps to his medal, and a Waterloo wound. My divination of features only permitted my purse to drop one shilling for him to go to Musselburgh (all begging people are always *going somewhere !*)."

One day he met a youth who had once been a member of the Ragged School. Mac Gregor accosted him with, " I'm very glad to find that you have left off going to church!" The youth looked at his quondam teacher in pious horror, while Mac Gregor gazed steadily into the boy's face until it blanched, and then the young fellow took to his heels. Mac Gregor knew that the young hypocrite's last conviction by the magistrates was for stealing the purses of old ladies in church, and the boy was shrewd enough to guess that his secret was out !

Much as Mac Gregor loved London, its work, its amusements, and its social life, he never lost an opportunity of getting away from it, and it was his

---

* It was old Mr. Gurney's hat, and probably had a good broad brim.

habit at least once or twice a year to break loose and wander away wherever fancy led him. We propose in this chapter to follow him in some of his home and foreign tours.

On the 10th of August, 1852, he set off to Liverpool for a run through Ireland with his friends, Martin Ware, Oliphant, and N. Bridges. Their route was Dublin, Malahide, Ballina, Ballindine, Belmullet, and thence by sailing-boat to Achill.

Aug. 17.—To Duagh school, met a priest, Father Henry, who entered into a warm discussion with me. He began about the crops—destitution—'soup schools'—the Bible; and then we disputed for about an hour—nearly 100 people gathered round. The priest was on a horse and became more curt as he was hard-pressed. He allowed that the Bible ought to be circulated, but with notes, and said the proper edition cost two guineas. He had spent forty-two hours on one text. His remedy for the evils of the poor was the workhouse and the old Catholic system of begging. He did not use the Bible in his own school, and appealed to a boy standing near as to his motives for attending the Protestant School, but the lad's answers did little service.

Aug. 18.—Visited the Orphan Refuge, the Infant School, and Girls' School. Bathed this morning and saw a shoal of mullet come into the little bay. About 60 people rushed into the water, some with baskets, pails, rods, sticks, and baled the fish into their hands. One put his fish into his mouth and another into his pocket. One girl caught fish in her apron. After all, not 50 out of thousands were caught. It was a sight quite new.

Of course he was not always well received. One Sunday the "boys became impudent and called us names. Some took the *Band of Hope* and tore it up, running after us and shouting." A very characteristic entry is made on September 21st : "Went to model farm attached to the Orphan Refuge. A new Scotch manager there; *pious but not agreeable.* There is good honest work doing there." This is excellent. Who has not met that man or his representative ?

Sep. 22.—Bridges and I went to Cong by Maam. Slept in the postmaster's house. A man whose bed I occupied came in at night, drunk, to dispossess me.

Sep. 23.—Saw the abbey and the pigeon-holes—a well-worth-seeing cavern through which the water rushes about 40 feet deep. Thence by boat, taking about three hours, to Oughterard. Met a convert who had been brought to the truth by seeing the heartlessness of the priest. On the chapel was posted a great placard against proselytism. By car to Galway (24th). Saw the old Spanish houses, the Queen's College, Bay, &c. On to Athlone, and thence to Malahide, where the tour ended.

This tour, taken mainly in the interests of Protestantism, gave Mac Gregor some good material for his Monthly Letter and other anti-popery literature, if the following diary notes may be taken as a specimen :

"Where was the Protestant religion before Luther ? Answer : Where was your face this morning before you washed it ? " The Bishop of London examined a National School and asked a child, " And who is your ghostly enemy ? " She answered, " The bishop, sir." A priest asked a girl why she did not pray to Mary to keep her safe. She said : " Mary could not find her own Son when He was lost, and how could she take care of me ? "

In 1853 Mac Gregor, again in company with Oliphant-Ferguson, made a grand tour on the Continent. The route was in its early stages, Strassburg, Mannheim, Frankfort, Homburg, Freiburg. From the last-named place he wrote to his sister the following :

FREIBURG IN BRESLAU, *August* 26, 1853.

I looked over the town this morning before dinner. The cathedral, higher than St. Paul's, appears an ordinary good height. Then the cooking ! When shall we learn to cook so neatly, nicely, cheaply, as these foreigners ? As I sat in the door of the hotel, smoking a cigar, listening to the bugles of Prussian soldiers with their pretty uniform and intelligent faces, and one eye on the kitchen, the other on countless vineyards and the distant Alps, I found that this was the first day I had been on the Continent among strangers quite alone, alone, alone ! One thing it profits—the speaking. You must, in such cases, speak, and with no English friend, must jabber German or murder French. I left Oliphant at Homburg. He goes to the Tyrol. Mamma's letter came all safe, which is the more wondrous because it was addressed to Hamburg instead of Homburg. The latter is the great gambling place, and in such a place to have a reunion of Protestants ! We dined first with Sir C. Eardley, next day with Lord Shaftesbury, and yesterday we seventeen gave them a dinner at the Kursaal. I had some confab with Lord S. and he told me that my name is so well known in Italy that all my letters will be opened, and I must use no religious expressions in them or in any way give an opportunity for their ejecting me. He cautioned me a great deal, for a policeman will be specially charged with my supervision as a suspicious character.

How very different this place is from England ! To go with the two Monods, the best preachers in France, and four others to take coffee at 1 P.M. in the open air, when all the reverend gentlemen light their cigars.

Although there are many notes of interest in the

diary on such well-known ·places as Basle, Baden, Zurich, and Schaffhausen, we content ourselves with one extract.

Aug. 30.—Constance. Sketched Council Hall where John Huss was tried. Saw door and window of his cell, and chair of Emperor Segismünd and bricks marked by J. H. in prison. In cathedral saw flag in middle where he stood to be sentenced. Also thigh-bone of St. Sebastian, flesh, and arrow he was killed by. Pillar with "To Mary, Queen of Angels, Terror of Devils, Refuge of Sinners."

Some of Mac Gregor's walks at this time were excellent training for feats he was to accomplish later on :

From Horgen to Zug in a thunderstorm. Up and down the Rigi. From Flüelen to Hospenthal. A walk of eight hours by the Ozpuzzia, looking over Italy and up Fibbia, snow and chamois track.

Sep. 5.—To Furka. At 1 started up Galenstock, 11,200 feet high, with guide. Soon got mist, ascended first and second top, guide refused to go on, crossed a glacier for half an hour, leaping crevasses. Began to rain, got to last peak. Darkness began, guide lay down in the snow and would not proceed, went on without him. He came, and we mounted to within a few feet of summit where a great crevasse made it utterly impracticable for man to go. Retraced steps, crossed two glaciers, but only one crevasse required alpenstock. Lost ourselves on last mountain in sleet and rain. Men with lanterns found us about 9 P.M. Had been out fourteen hours this day with two hours' rest. Got only one good view.

Sep. 6.—Furka, a foot and a half of snow and snowing fast. Started with three Germans at 1. Came slowly to Rhone Glacier, raining fiercely. Left Germans there, and started all wet up hill for Grimsel alone. Got on snow again, found tracks of one man who had come other way, snowing fast, marched quick as possible and got to Grimsel in less than one hour from Rhone Glacier.

I

Sep. 17.—To Chamounix, when I desired to go up Mont Blanc. Finest weather possible.

Sep. 19.—Albert Smith's party arrived. Went to the Flégère with Fanshawe, and settled to go up Mont Blanc next day.

Sep. 20.—Started for the Grands Mulets with Albert Smith, Captain De Bathe, Lord Killeen, W. H. Russell, P. Burrowes, Fanshawe, and Shuldham, and thirty-six guides. Slept in the little hut there, or rather nobody slept.

Sep. 21.—At 1 this morning aroused to go up to the summit. Lord Killeen and Fanshawe came part of the way with Shuldham and me, but one stopped after an hour's, and the other after three hours' walking. Shuldham was ill and sleepy. I got up to the top at about 10 A.M., and drank a bottle of champagne and ate breakfast. After staying about an hour set off down again, slid down the glissers with great rapidity. The view magnificent. Arrived at the Grands Mulets about 1, and stopped half an hour for Shuldham, then off again and arrived at Chamounix at 20 minutes past 4. Dined at table-d'hôte quite fresh, and stayed up till 11 P.M. Woke next day at 6 A.M.

Sep. 22.—Not fatigued, nor scorched, nor at all injured, thank God. In the evening a dinner to the guides and ourselves with toasts and punch, cannons, tar-barrels, &c. [Tissay was chief guide.]

Sep. 23.—Met Hindmarsh. In the six days including Mont Blanc spent £21. To the *Tête Noir* with A. Smith's party. The pass is the best I have seen.

Before leaving Chamounix Mac Gregor wrote to the *Times* the following account of his ascent of Mont Blanc:

The day before yesterday the ascent of Mont Blanc was accomplished by another Englishman and myself, under unusually favourable circumstances and without any accident, although nearly fifty persons were engaged in the work. On the evening of September 20th, I found that some gentlemen intended to go to the Grands

Mulets and to sleep in the hut lately erected there by the guides. The party consisted of Mr. Albert Smith, Lord Killeen, Captain de Bathe, Mr. W. Russell, and Mr. Burrowes. Another gentleman, Mr. Shuldham, had also arranged to commence the ascent to the summit on the same day, and, through the kindness of Mr. Albert Smith, I was permitted, with Mr. Fanshawe, a fellow-traveller, to accompany them. Mr. Albert Smith, whose popularity in Switzer-

THE ASCENT OF MONT BLANC

land is almost romantic, gave a breakfast on the opening to thirty-four guides who were engaged for the occasion, and at nine o'clock A.M. of September 21st, the long cavalcade left Chamounix. The weather was magnificent, not a cloud being visible, and after seven hours' walking we all reached the Grands Mulets—a place already familiarised to all who have seen Mr. Albert Smith's panorama in London. We dined on cold meat and punch made with melted snow; and then, when the setting sun left the last peak of the mountain, we made a hard struggle to find room for about fifty people in a hut constructed to hold twenty at the most. Gentlemen and guides, lying head and foot together, completely covered the floor, and one traveller occupied a board nine inches wide, which had served for a table. Presently some forty pipes and cigars were lighted, and the atmosphere of the little cabin became rapidly 'tobacconised.' It was, of course, impossible for any one to sleep, but the novelty of the situation and the incessant flow of good humour made the night pass tolerably well. On the preceding night I was unable to sleep from the excitement which the prospect of such an undertaking produces, and it is remarkable that several of the guides were prevented from sleeping from the same cause. However, after two sleepless nights, we who were to go on to the summit arose at one o'clock to continue the ascent. Mr. Shuldham suffered from toothache and was otherwise unwell, yet the indomitable perseverance of an Englishman enabled him to proceed and to finish the undertaking successfully. For myself, I felt perfectly well, and had, therefore, much less difficulty in accomplishing the work. As our party left the others, who were to return next morning to Chamounix, the solitudes of the snowy range were made to ring with three hearty British cheers; and, by the light of the moon, which at that altitude shines almost like the sun itself, our long string of twenty-three guides and travellers slowly marched over the snow. The cold had not been of sufficient intensity to freeze the snow into the proper consistency for supporting the feet. At each measured step, therefore, we sank nearly to the knees, and after about three hours of this tiring process we attained the Grand Plateau, where the effects of a rarefied atmosphere begin to be felt by the traveller. Two of the gentlemen, who had kindly accompanied us during part of the night, now returned to their companions, still jovially packed in the little hut, and Mr. Shuldham and myself with our guides continued the march. The night was so perfectly clear and the moonlight so bright as to make the aid of lanterns superfluous. A large number of stars became visible which could not be seen under other circumstances, and, when about four o'clock the east became rosy with the rays of a rising sun, the whole scene was at once awful and beautiful. The passage of the Mer de la Côte was somewhat tedious as nearly every step had to be cut by the axe in the ice. Here even the guides became overpowered by the sleepy air of the great dome above us. Out of thirteen persons only two did not succumb to this potent influence. At ten o'clock I sat down on the very summit, and soon afterwards Mr. Shuldham, whose unconquerable pluck had sustained him through all the difficulties, attained the same height, though compelled by indispo-

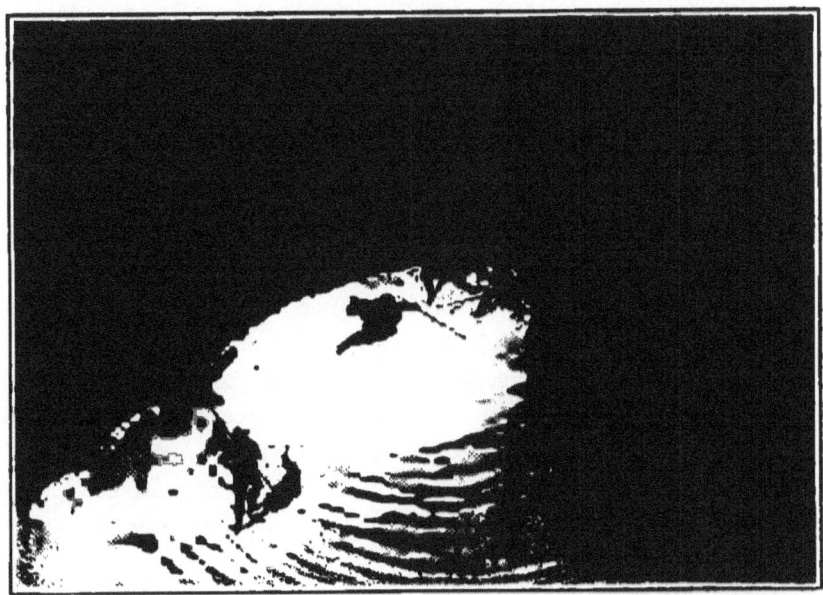

THE SUMMIT OF MONT BLANC

sition immediately to return. The Queen's health, and that of the King of Sardinia, were duly pledged in champagne, drunk out of a leathern drinking cup. We ate chocolate and prunes, the provisions most acceptable in those lofty places, but sleep rather than hunger seemed to prevail. The view was magnificent beyond description. From Lyons to Constance and Genoa all was clear. Beyond that a faint horizon could be distinguished, bounded by unknown mountains, but wholly obscured by clouds, or even fog. After spending nearly an hour on the summit, eating the icicles which, in the form of large cuttle-fish shells, constitute the great dome of Mont Blanc, the descent commenced. In five minutes, by sliding on the soft snow, we attained the spot which from below was an hour from the top, and thus passing rapidly over the ground, with the aid of our alpenstocks, we reached the Grands Mulets, and, finally, the valley below. The bells rung a merry peal—we were Nos. 33 and 34 of those who had ascended Mont Blanc—then the cannon boomed, and the damsels of Chamounix presented bouquets.

Seldom had there been so propitious an ascent, and with Mr. Albert Smith as chairman, the whole party sat down next day to an excellent dinner in the open air, with all the travellers then in Chamounix as admiring spectators of the very characteristic scene.

The bridge was illuminated, the guns were fired at intervals, the Englishmen made speeches and the guides sang lugubrious songs. The moon looked on too, brightly, but with a calm radiance, and an immense soup-tureen full of capital punch was distributed among the guests with an enlivening effect.

Thus ended the last ascent of the highest mountain in Europe, and I cannot conclude this account of the proceeding without the observation, that a repetition of the enjoyment is within the reach of every one who has good weather, good guides, a good head, and uffic ie nt energy for a walk of twenty-four hours chiefly over deep snow, and without sleep.

Yours &c.,

CHAMOUNIX, *September* 24.   JOHN MAC GREGOR.

Various other parts of Switzerland were visited; a night was spent with the monks of St. Bernard, and the traveller then proceeded to Italy, halting at Milan, Venice, and Ferrara.

Oct. 10.—Started at eight from Ferrara to Bolo gna and walked twenty-nine miles in seven hours. It rained heavily all the way Could not go out to see Bologna.

When at Naples it is needless to say that Mac Gregor ascended Vesuvius. Here is his account from the diary :

Nov. 4.—Went up Vesuvius. It takes about three hours. The last half-hour up the crater is tiring, but the view is magnificent. Two craters—that further inland more active ; ground hot, and different coloured lavas. Brimstone and sulphur in plenty, and smoke suffocating. Saw Pompeii well from the top. Went round the crater and boiled eggs at small blast holes. Wrote home from the top and burned edge of the letter to show the heat. Descended to the old crater and made sketches. Then our party, Macdonald, two Americans, one Canadian, two Scotchmen, one Frenchman, and one Irishman, took off our coats and had a trial at putting the stone. This day was one of the most interesting in my life.

The letter written in pencil on the top of Vesuvius ran as follows :

TOP OF VESUVIUS, *November* 4, 1853.

DEAREST E——

I am sitting on the edge of the crater, the smoke pouring forth, our eggs cooking at a hot blast, the awful chasm reeking with sulphur and three Americans and an Englishman eating pears. I have the shoes on which are now on the hottest, and were last month on the coldest ground in Europe. The clouds now and then open and the most glorious views are seen. A loud peal of thunder has just roared and my friends have started up quite frightened. Looking down, the smoke has cleared a little. Now I have nearly seen the bottom ; I have burned this paper at the fire as a curiosity, and send you three pieces of lava and sulphur.

JOHN.

After visiting Palermo, Mac Gregor made his way by diligence through Sicily to Catania : " Road dull, hills brown, people stolid and ugly ; no eatables

to be had. Two nights in diligence." The diary
continues :

Nov. 10.—Catania. Although without sleep for two nights I set
off alone to Nicolosi in the evening ; three hours' walk—rain stopped
me for two hours.

Nov. 11.—Rose at five, and started with guide, two mules and
muleteer for Etna. Rode for six hours, walked part ; first dreary

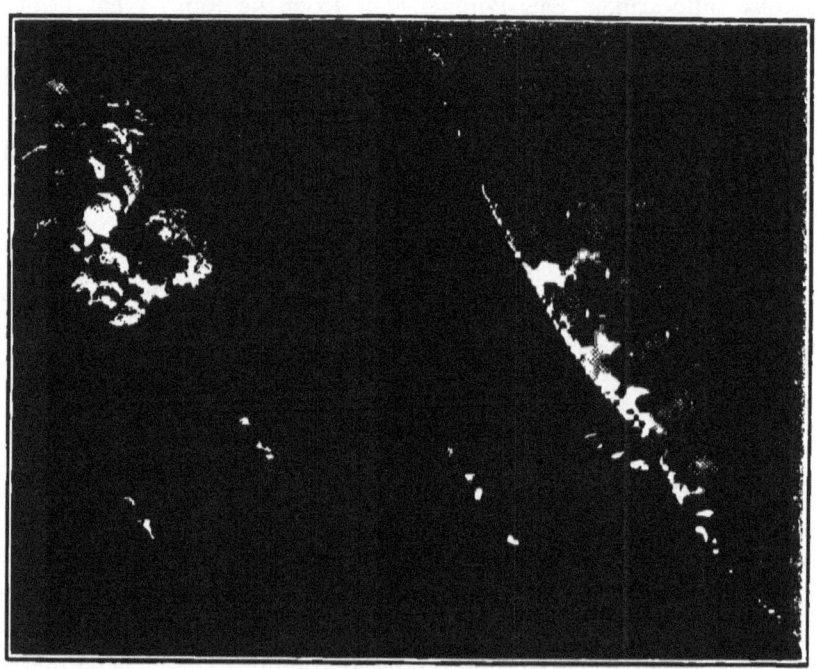

THE CRATER OF ETNA

as if all the walls in Galway had been heaped on side of hill. Mont
Rosa pretty, Casa Inglesi well built, good cottage. Day very fine.
Wood of oak-vineyards, then black lava dust for an hour. Stopped
at stone called Bosca for rest, halfway to Casa Inglesi. From Casa
Inglesi, mounted crater in an hour. Very steep, and sulphur extremely
strong. Only difficulty the mud on summit. Crater two English miles

round. See deep hole at bottom. Edge two feet broad, regular all round. Stayed half hour at top, walked with great difficulty to second summit. Snow in crevasses. Stones on crater covered with icicles on one side and on other smoking. My moustache frozen hard. Men digging snow near Bosca thirty feet deep, and carry by mules all over Sicily to make ices. Descended, after seeing all Sicily at our feet, and banks of clouds far below. Visited three other craters ; one very old, like a well. Threw down stones which took perhaps a minute before they stopped. Walked nearly whole way to Nicolosi ; dined on two eggs, and off at night to Catania alone.

MacGregor continued his tour by Syracuse, Messina, Reggio, Paolo, Naples, Toulon, Nice, Genoa, Turin, over Mont Cenis to Lyons, by diligence in three days and two nights, Paris and home—the tour lasting from the 18th of August to the 2nd of December.

During this tour he took many sketches, and soon after returning a series of his Mont Blanc views were published by Baxter with descriptive notes.

MacGregor kept up an acquaintance with Albert Smith for many years—the bond between them being Mont Blanc—and some of Smith's letters are curious. Thus :

MY DEAR MACGREGOR,—

Look here. If you will come any day and dine quietly with me at the Garrick at 5.30 you shall be treated delicately *en vrai malade,* put near the fire and made comfortable, and I will catch Billy to meet you.* We can't give way to the pleasures of the table too much as I must be at the Egyptian Hall by 7.30.

* Dr. William Russell, of the *Times,* who was one of the Mont Blanc party when MacGregor ascended

On other occasions the invitation would come on a lithographed form after the manner of a passport:

We, Albert Smith, one of Her Britannic Majesty's Representatives on the top of Mont Blanc, Knight of the Grand Crossing from Burlington Arcade to the Egyptian Hall, Secretary for his Own Affairs, &c. &c.

Request and require all those whom it may concern, and especially the police, to allow Mr. John MacGregor to pass freely in—to the Egyptian Hall—and to afford him every assistance in the way of oysters, stout, champagne, &c.

Given at the Box Office.   ALBERT SMITH.

Some of Albert Smith's quaint sayings greatly amused Mac Gregor, who duly noted them. We give one as a specimen.

Some one proposed to open oysters by smashing the shells by force. Albert Smith said, 'Yes, and they would have a taste something between a periwinkle and a gravel walk.'

Albert Smith's Egyptian Hall entertainment, " Mont Blanc," was not entirely of the kind that Mac Gregor most enjoyed, but there were points in it which he wished to adopt for a popular lecture to his ragged and other friends, and Smith obligingly replied to his request to pirate these by saying, "Any notion of mine is very heartily at your service."

Immediately on his return from this long tour Mac Gregor plunged into work with great vigour, and in our next chapter we shall unfold some of his new schemes. All his co-workers gathered about him, and one of the first was Lord Shaftesbury, who wrote:

December 5, 1853.

MY DEAR MAC GREGOR,—

We must have a thanksgiving that you are neither buried under the snows of the Grand Plateau, nor engulfed in the crater of Etna—though I take it that, if there, you would not be in greater darkness than we all are in London just now. To-morrow I cannot attend the Protestant Alliance; I have two chairs at Richmond for the Bible Society. My discourse at Freemason's Hall has brought on me such a swarm, that I shall well-nigh be stung to death. The ministers of Portugal and Spain are, I am told, quite in a state of Grand Inquisitors. An "auto da fe" would be a secondary punishment for me.

      Yours truly,

          SHAFTESBURY.

While the incidents of the Swiss and Italian tour were still fresh in memory, Mac Gregor prepared a popular lecture, or rather a series of lectures, on Mont Blanc, Vesuvius, and Etna, for which he drew a set of huge diagrams from the rough sketches he had taken abroad. It was characteristic of him that the first time he delivered his lecture on Mont Blanc it was to an assembly of shoeblacks and ragged children at the Field Lane Ragged School. Not long after, we find him in the full swing of lecturing and a note in the diary runs :

Lecture on Mont Blanc at Servants' Home School for Mr. Kinnaird. Have now lectured at Harrow, St. George's, Pimlico, Westbourne Schools, Redhill, Barnet, Hinton Martel, St. John's Wood Schools, Brampton, Home and Colonial, Barnet (second lecture), North-West Branch of Y.M.C.A., Fitzroy Square, Field Lane, Claydon, Brompton, Southwark, Gurneys, Villiers, Copestake and Moore's.

After the long tour in 1853 there came a pause in holiday making. A trip to Scotland, another to Ireland, and occasional runs to the sea-side, being all that was accomplished in 1854. It was a year of some change in the home relations of MacGregor, and it was a year of national trouble. He wrote early in the year :

As for a general war, I do not believe it will begin just yet, and for this reason, we are not in earnest about it. The *Times* is all *put on* belligerency, and that means the Government's. A new Government may perhaps begin treaties anew, but the good sense of Englishmen will require more cause for war than the protection of a false religion and a broken-down despotism in Turkey. Meanwhile things are horribly dear. My twopenny loaf is so small that I finish it every day—and could do more—whereas it used to beat me by a good crust.

The storm broke sooner than MacGregor anticipated, and the following brief entries in the diary indicate the changes that were coming over the home circle.

May 10.—Called on Hedley Vicars—a fine fellow.
May 12.—Ragged church and chapel meeting—Vicars was there.
May 13.—Douglas came up.*
May 19.—To Windsor, where prayed with darling Douglas previous to his departure with his regiment.
May 20.—Saw the regiment leave in two trains. Never was so moved. Douglas greatly affected. Wrote home. Returned to town.

Brief, characteristic entries. MacGregor never wore his heart upon his sleeve, and none save those

---

* Douglas was his younger brother, under orders for the seat of war.

who knew him very intimately ever guessed the storm of passionate feeling that the departure of his brilliant young brother—the companion of his youth and early manhood—to the war and all the uncertainties of military action, caused him. He felt as only the strong and robust in mind and body can feel, and in that parting the " bitterness of death was overpast."

Another incident of this year marked an epoch in Mac Gregor's life.

Sep. 30.—This the last entry I make in Belvedere House, Drum-condra, Dublin, where we have stayed sixteen years—since 1838.

In August of the following year, when Mac Gregor was on a tour in Norway with two very intimate friends, Mr. Martin Ware and Mr. Wilbraham Taylor, under date August 18th, he wrote :

Beautiful drive to Rodnaes, where we spelled out a Norway paper about Sebastopol, but I little thought what sad news was to come.

Aug. 22.—At 5 A.M. to Christiania by boat and rail. Arrived at 9, and then I read my darling brother's name among the killed in the attack on the Redan at Sebastopol. I did not realise this for two or three hours—God was present, and kindly broke this awful intelligence gradually to me.

Those who are familiar with Miss Marsh's bio-graphy of " Hedley Vicars," will remember reading of the splendid heroism, the Christian zeal, and the glowing example, of young Douglas Mac Gregor.

But nothing can exceed in tenderness and beauty the letters of his father, Sir Duncan Mac Gregor. Writing to his old friend, Mr. James Evans—to whom he wrote the letter which forms the material for the published volume " The Loss of the *Kent* "— immediately after the news had come from the seat of war, we have a glimpse of the character both of father and son.   He says :

> I forget whether you ever saw my darling, fair-headed, sunshiny boy Douglas ; never was there naturally a more joyous spirit.   He was the pet of his brothers and sister, and the light of our dwelling.

On the day before he was to join in the assault of the formidable Redan, Douglas wrote to his mother, and in concluding a touching letter, full of beautiful and simple religious faith, he said : " She would not be absent from his thought in the coming strife and were he to fall he felt certain they should be re-united in glory everlasting."

Sir Duncan in continuing his letter to his friend, says :

> The gallant boy accompanied the 160 volunteers who carried the ladders in front of the storming party, and were necessarily the very first to enter the Redan. . . . . He had penetrated to the centre of the Redan and was seen, with his cap on the point of his sword, cheering on his men, when he was killed by a minié ball.

The sorrowing father concluded his letter thus :

> Ample has been the testimony, borne from various quarters, not only to dearest Douglas's heroism, but to his consistency and boldness as a young follower of our blessed Lord.

Some years afterwards when writing to the same friend Sir Duncan said :

On receiving the fearful telegram announcing the fall of my darling boy, Douglas, at the storming of Sebastopol I became suddenly unable to sign my name, and for many years experienced the greatest difficulty in writing legibly—it may have been from a slight attack of paralysis.

As a matter of fact from that period the style and character of his handwriting totally changed. In that changed but firm handwriting there lies before us a "Morning Prayer" composed by the "Grand Old Patriarch"—as Lord Shaftesbury was wont to call him. One passage is so exquisitely tender that we venture to transcribe it here :

May it please Thee to make our beloved boy the means of drawing our souls closer to the Cross. I adore Thee for having called him in early life to the knowledge and the love of Jesus ; for having granted him grace to run—amidst much temptation—a consistent course, and given him to die in a manner honourable to his Christian profession, and translated him without pain from a world of sin and sorrow to the glory of the Upper Sanctuary. Though dead may he yet speak to us by his child-like faith and bright example, and may we more constantly dwell on his unspeakable gain than on our sad loss. I bless Thee for the lively hope that two of our beloved ones are already safely housed in heaven,* and the remaining four, through Thy grace, are on the road to it. . . . . Guide and encourage my dear John, direct him in all his ways, increase his faith, prudence, and humility, and continue to make him a blessing to us and to Thy people.

A tour in Norway in 1855 was, of course, a very different thing to one in that tourist-hunted country now.

* William died at the age of 13, and John Mac Gregor always spoke of this as his first sorrow.

Unfortunately for Mac Gregor, the one startling adventure of the journey fell to the share of Mr. Wilbraham Taylor, whose lot it was—the travellers having run short of money—to return alone from Lillehammer to Christiania to obtain some. On the way he was attacked by a pack of wolves and his escape was almost miraculous. It is on record that when John Mac Gregor heard of this adventure his countenance fell—he was distressed and mortified. If there was one thing more than another in Norway that he had sighed for, it was a ravenous pack of wolves, and he could not conceal his chagrin when he found that the yelping brutes had flashed their glittering eyes and breathed their hot breath in the face of Wilbraham Taylor and not in the face of John Mac Gregor.

But the tour was full of novelty and interest, and we append a few of his rough notes.

Soldiers, percussion breech-loading guns. Bad glass in windows at Christiansand. German came with 'two dead docks' in a parcel for cabin. We thought it 'dogs' and I ripped up the parcel. Found it was 'ducks.' King, Queen, and Maids of Honour at concert of Swedish music at Christiania. Women wear tartan. Boys at school don't play. Have not seen angry person, or drunk, or swearing. Hay and corn are made up on posts and rails, out of the wet. Spades used like axes for cutting tree roots. Barristers wear swords and walk about before the bench. Logs of all people float down river, and, being marked, are caught as they pass. Floors sprinkled with pine twigs. Bakers' shops have signs. Paid for a night for three of us 1/–. Angel hangs from roof in Church with font. Saw wedding. Præster blesses, laying hands on head. Travelling schoolmaster;

stays three weeks in a village and proceeds to another. Sunday begins on Saturday evening. Circus open on Sunday evening. Glissé on snow at Nystuen. Lapland colony near Nystuen. Aurora Borealis on the Sogne Ford, &c. &c.

This tour in Norway may be regarded as the last that John Mac Gregor ever took for pleasure pure and simple. In all the subsequent ones he had a fixed and definite purpose, and it is a point for travellers to decide whether a tour with an object is not really preferable to one without. One thing is certain, Mac Gregor's capacity for enjoyment grew as the years went on, and some of his later journeys were among the curiosities of travelling in the nineteenth century.

K

CHAPTER VII

IN THE OPEN AIR

WE must go back a few years in our narrative in order to trace Mac Gregor's connection with a work which he was apt to regard as the chief mission of his life. Although some may not agree with him in this estimate we must at least let him express his views, and then draw our own conclusions.

On the 17th of April, 1853, he was trudging to the East End to visit ragged schools and especially to have a friendly chat with the boys in Pultney's Home in Whitechapel. "On the way," he writes in his diary, "I found some groups listening to the Open-air Missionaries and one where a popish argument was going on. I joined the last and argued for an hour with some good."

This was the beginning of his interest in open air work—a work to which he remained true and faithful to the end of his days.

To "take an interest in a thing" was nothing in his estimation unless it were followed up by practical help and sympathy, and the following extracts point the current of his thought and action in this matter :

May 15.—Dined with Oliphant. Read at night Haldane's Life. This greatly enlivens one's thoughts and humbles pride to see so great a man with so little of self. In the end seeking God is seen to reward even with approval more than self-seeking which gives only temporary content.

May 27.—Corrected last sheet of Madiai pamphlet. Read "Girondists," by Lamartine. Mr. Jones called about the Open Air Mission. My attention has been directed to this by seeing the missionaries in Whitechapel and by reading Haldane's Life. I joined the committee and subscribed to the funds. Among the objects now claiming my best attention are, The Protestant Alliance, The Protestant Defence Society, The Ragged School Union, the Shoe-blacks, the Ragged School Shop, *The Band of Hope Review*, *The True Briton*, the Town Mission, the Open-air Mission, the Slavery Question, the Preventive and Reformatory School Society, the Lawyers' Prayer Union and the Mansfield Society.

June 3.—In the evening went to first committee meeting of the Open-air Mission. Only Jones and Joyce were present. Both men of God and with three we commenced. I see in this a small beginning of what may, yea will be, a great, a noble, a blessed undertaking. May the Lord give us wisdom, zeal and love to work unitedly, discreetly, vigorously.

From this time MacGregor was zealously employed in the technical details of organising the Society whose objects were to encourage, regulate, and improve open-air preaching, to create a bond of brotherhood between open-air preachers, to select those who should engage in the work, to assist them in their studies by lectures, conferences, meetings, and the circulation of suitable books, and to issue tracts and other publications relating to the Mission.

It was not, therefore, until nearly a year afterwards that we find this entry :

May 14, 1854.—Open-air preaching at New Cut, good service—after Church to James Street where found Cozens.   Men pelted us with dirt and cabbage-stalks—after Cozens had done I preached my first regular open-air sermon.

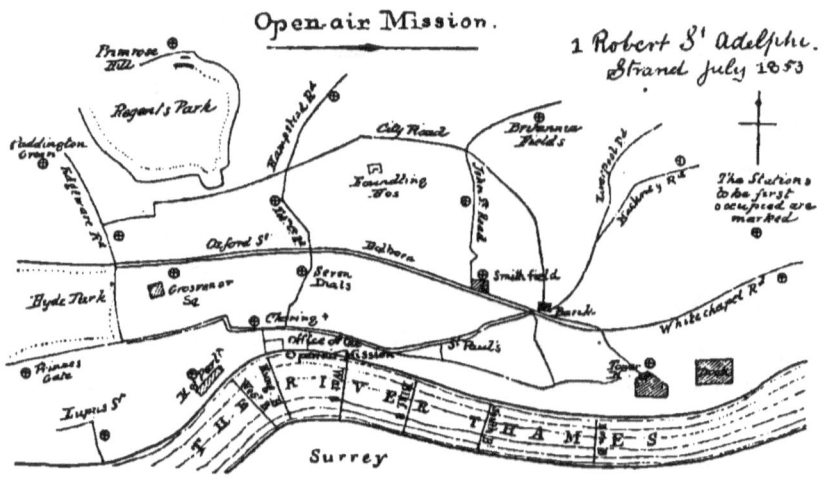

DIAGRAM OF MISSION STATIONS

Once launched out in the actual work of open-air preaching it became a passion with him, and for many years there are entries innumerable of his hopes, fears, prayers, struggles, and escapades.   Let one extract suffice for our present purpose :

June 24, 1855.—This was one of the most remarkable Sundays I have ever had.   Visited school, Bloomsbury, found boy beaten by H. Villiers.   Spoke to him, comforting, and after good sermon by Price spoke to H. Villiers about his beating the boy.   Walked with

Maunsell. He came at half-past two. Prayed, went to James Street where found city missionaries preaching, with pulpit. Few listened— many at windows. Found Oliphant and his sister. With Maunsell to Edward Street where I spoke to twenty men and women and they thanked us. Then to James Street; found Shaw and Cozens and Fowell; Shaw spoke on 'the wages of sin' but not in simple language. I spoke to them afterwards on the Good Shepherd when fifty attended well. With the others to Colonel Gray's yard school where found good rooms and few teachers and scholars, none of ragged class. Went out to top of Edward Street and spoke to one hundred on Sodom and Gomorrah. Oliphant and Maunsell engaged groups. Some at distance threw mud, cabbage-stalks, stones and oyster-shells. Hit my hat several times, my cheek and coat and waistcoat covered. Still many heard well and thanked us. Miss Oliphant went into a house. Many told us to leave as a disturbance was threatened. To Hyde Park where open-air meeting about Sunday Question had been announced. Found Cozens preaching, standing on seat under a tree. Two hundred heard. Several interrupted, mostly Papists. One said 'without money and without price' was nonsense as all preached for money, and nobody could get into church but with money. One answered, 'I'll give you £100 if you tell me any church where the Gospel is preached where you can go without money.' Another little man talked much, and after Cozens had given an excellent sermon I began with this man, and we had an hour's most interesting discussion. He said God punished in this world and therefore would not in the next. I said, 'If a thief said I have had so much trouble about my theft there will be no other punishment, he would find the law was not altered by that.' He said, 'Is it just for God to punish children for father's sins?' I told him, 'If a man was traitor, his goods were all forfeited and his children would be the sufferers.' He said he could not love a man he never saw. I told him he could love a good landlord and write to him and he to us if we got good from him, whether we had seen him or not. Another said, 'How could fishermen write books as they could not read nor write—was it not the Roman monks who wrote the Bible?' He said prayer must be fervent to be heard, and it

was impossible for working men who had been all the week strained
with work to be fervent, he must think of other things while
speaking to God.   I told him a man thus pressed could still ask,
like a child asking a father for bread, and as fathers would not give
stones so God would give only good things.   All the people thanked
me.   Went further down in the Park, heard a teetotaler, and
another afterwards speaking to the groups.   Thus I attended eight
open-air services to-day and thank God much was said and heard to
make men wise unto salvation.

Soon after this Mac Gregor entered upon a new
phase in his street-preaching career.   Instead of con-
fining himself, as at first, to the simple proclamation of
the Gospel, he undertook the difficult and dangerous
work of a street controversialist.   He had found in all
quarters that incipient infidelity was abounding, and
that just in proportion as men became "unsettled" in
their religious views, in that same proportion came
their zeal to expound the things they did not know.
Roman Catholics, elated by the strides their Church
had taken since the appointment of a Cardinal Archbishop of Westminster, had grown aggressive and
promulgated their doctrines through the agency of
street preachers ; spiritualists, Mormons, "rabid"
teetotalers, anarchists, socialists and sceptics followed
in the same course and had taken to the streets for
the ventilation of their views.

Mac Gregor placed himself in the midst of the
haunts of all these, listened to their arguments, and
came away with a great pain at his heart that hundreds
of discourses, based on what he believed to be false
doctrine, should be delivered, and not a word uttered

on behalf of the "good old Gospel." He determined, therefore, in future to devote himself mainly to the work of counteracting the effect of this erroneous teaching and to study every argument that could be employed to checkmate sceptics and Roman Catholic propagandists.

It used to be the fashion to dub any one who would not accept without cavil or remonstrance not only every statement of the Bible, but every interpretation put upon such statement, a "sceptic." Doubts were regarded as proofs of scepticism; inquiry, except under impracticable conditions for thoughtful men to accept, was called "a sceptical state of mind," discrepancies in the Bible narrative—and all honest-minded and well-read men are now agreed that they are numerous and in some instances irreconcilable at present—were not to be investigated; even the chronology at the headings of the chapters and the contents of each chapter, published in those days in nearly all Bibles, were regarded as "almost" inspired, and there is on record in the biography of a most excellent man, a story to the effect that when in reading the Psalms the word "Selah" occurred, he would bow his head reverently much as some Christians do now when the name of our Lord is mentioned. In no period of the world's history has the hackneyed saying been more fully realised than within the past half-century that "the heterodoxy of one generation is the orthodoxy of another."

John Mac Gregor was brought up in the old school

of Evangelicalism and he never altered his religious standpoint, although he took a much more liberal view of the opinions of others than many of his contemporaries.

And here, be it said, that without the grand old-fashioned fervour that characterised the Evangelicals of that day, Mac Gregor could not have accomplished a tithe of the good that he was permitted to bring to the ignorant and the unbelieving.

Of these and their tactics he had as good a knowledge as any man in London, and he knew how to manage them.

A mere babbler who jerks in an impudent remark to break the calm attention of a group listening to truth out of doors may usually be quieted by a solemn appeal, or an apt repartee, or a close fitting answer, but the well-tutored agents of Rome, Joe Smith, Tom Paine, or Teetotalism are fond of argument in stated places and at fixed hours.

He classified the opponents to his mission thus: Romanists, Mormonites, Communists, Sceptics, Infidels, Secularists, and Teetotalers. The Mormonites indulged in the most furious denunciation, and gave the most violent, but happily the shortest, resistance of any opposers of the truth. The Communists always had some new cure for every evil under the sun. The Free-thinkers generally showed a marvellous lack of originality in their attacks, always fastening upon such subjects as the "laziness of the clergy," "the paid agents of Christianity," or the stock objections about Jonah and the whale; David, "the man

after God's own heart"; the Trinity; eternal punishment; God hardening Pharaoh's heart, and so on. Of
such arguments Mac Gregor says :

Two people may discuss these for ever without any good until
they settle common ground of debate. They may tilt for ever over
such barriers without once coming really face to face. You must
dig underneath these outworks, march past these detached forts,
heeding not their fire, and you will find in nine cases out of ten that
the citadel is before you, and the devil reigning; then you know
what to do and with whom to deal.

When Mac Gregor speaks, as he often does, of teetotalers as "opposers," his remarks do not of course
apply to those who uphold abstinence as a virtue, but
to those who preach abstinence as *the* virtue, exalt it
to a grace, and build salvation on this ground—a class
that has largely increased since his day.

These are usually advocates of some other panacea in politics
to accompany their physical dogma for morals, and are seldom
met with except as very positive, irascible, and ignorant people,
whose audience speedily leaves them for a more smiling preacher,
if he holds out the whole truth clearly.

In course of time Mac Gregor and his colleagues
in the Open-air Mission became so efficient in their
work that they could judge of the season of the year,
of the day of the week, and the hour of the day most
suitable in each locality for preaching the Gospel out of
doors. They knew what sort of people might be
expected, what they would listen to, or laugh at, what
they would comprehend or cavil at, and how; the

questions likely to be put regarding particular doctrines; the arguments of Mormons, Infidels and
Romanists; the manner in which each class would
behave—the policeman, gentleman, tradesman, and
cabman—what each would be likely to say and do,
and what they the preachers, should do and say if
they desired to make good use of their time.

In a little pamphlet, entitled "Go Out Quickly," of
which within thirty years of its publication 111,000
were sold, Mac Gregor gave some wholesome counsel
to his less experienced fellow preachers.   Thus:

The whole operation (of street preaching) resolves itself into this
as the essence:—In a crowded alley, or thoroughfare, converse with
some idle men or careless children or gossiping loungers. Read the
Word and begin open-air *speaking*. Don't call it 'preaching'; and
if asked 'by what authority' say 'By *no* authority!' To use the
Parish fire-engine indeed you must have the keys but any one
seeing flames in the street may surely cry out 'Fire.'

The pamphlet concluded with a description of the
work and a call to participate in it.

No other duty or privilege need be neglected for this. It is a
variety and therefore little fatiguing. It is out of doors and thus
easily associated with healthy exercise. It calls forth the whole
power of the mind, and gives room for every talent and all kinds of
learning; therefore nobody can be above it. It may be effectually
done by simple words and simple knowledge of the Scriptures, and
therefore nobody need be below it. It is social for it is found well
that friends should join. It sends men to church, to school, to read,
to feel, to think and to pray, so it helps every other means of good.
Let those who will take part in such a blessed work burst through
the false shame which Satan ties up many hands with, cast aside the

slothful habit with which the flesh paralyses even active spirits, and brave the sneer of a world, which *must* sneer if both it and they are consistent. Once having begun they will not soon stop, for they are in a track well trodden by saints and martyrs, and sprinkled with the blood even of the Lord Jesus Christ Himself.

For himself Mac Gregor marked out a plain and unmistakable course. He would stand by the commandment, " Thou shalt not take the name of the Lord in vain," and he would, single-handed if need be, take his stand in the camp of the enemy. He collected and retained a number of circulars relating to the meetings of Secularists. One announced the acquisition of a room "where the lovers of anti-humbug may freely expatiate upon theology with a view to changing its baneful tendency upon society. The Clergy of all denominations and those in embryo, are invited to attend. Admission 1*d*." At another place a " Lecture by Iconoclast. Subject: The Bible, not a revelation; not reliable; neither true nor useful." Another by Iconoclast at a little later date; " Jesus Christ: his history fabulous; his teachings not calculated to promote the happiness of the human family." Later; " The Bible: immoral and degrading in its teachings and cruel and useless in its legislative enactments."

At meetings such as these Mac Gregor was in his element, and when the time for "discussion" came his ringing voice echoed through the hall the message of the Gospel. Consider the pluck, the manliness, the thorough fearlessness of it. Just as an honest schoolboy would plant his fist between the eyes of any bully in his school who said a treacherous word against father or mother, so the blood of MacGregor boiled when he heard the name and the love of his Heavenly Father blasphemed and he "went at them" with the schoolboy's honesty and the man's fidelity.

By-and-by we shall see him alone on his strange journeys in strange lands, surrounded by barbaric tribes, but we shall not find any stronger instances of magnificent courage than in his bold, heroic, single-handed encounters with his angry disputants in this field of controversy.

Year by year the Open-air Mission grew; competent laymen enrolled themselves under its banner; all London was marked out into districts and localities assigned to preachers; clergymen advocated the claims of the society, and Lord Shaftesbury gave it his sanction and assistance.   He wrote:

May 15, 1854.

My dear MacGregor,

　　I have no doubt of the value, nay necessity, of 'open-air preaching.' We must, and by God's blessing, we shall come to it.   My June labours are not much less than my May labours, but I will do my best for you.   I am for striking right and left, by day and by night, before and behind, wherever I can find the Devil; and that is at all times and everywhere.

Yours truly,

Shaftesbury.

Bishop Villiers approved the mission and remarked, "No one does good who does not now and then tread on the devil's tail!"   And this was regarded as no doubt an explanation of the rebuffs and trials, the rotten eggs of an unruly mob, and the "Move on!" of the policeman, experienced by the preachers.

Even the Archbishop of Canterbury (Tait) went in his robes with Mac Gregor and preached in the open air at Covent Garden.

In 1855 Mac Gregor wrote :

Truly this is a good and blessed work. The shame of it is passed away. The few short-sighted ones who were shocked at people baring their arms to save drowning souls are now silent. They are so ashamed that they are ashamed to be ashamed. . . . . God never gave greater blessings to any man on earth than to allow him to labour for sinners. How can I weigh *my* blessings of this kind?

Many years afterwards Lord Shaftesbury, speaking on behalf of the mission at the Mansion House, Lord Mayor Fowler presiding, said: "I think that it is singularly worthy of remark that we meet in the palace of the Chief Magistrate of London for the purpose of furthering the work of an institution which a few years ago was discredited to the widest possible extent. Let me say, however, that I look upon these open-air services as perfectly normal, as they are certainly primitive ; the very earliest preaching of the Gospel was in the open air, on the shores of the Lake of Galilee, by our blessed Lord Himself. And they are unquestionably ecclesiastical. In the days of the Reformation there was open-air preaching at Paul's Cross. All the worthiest of the bishops preached there ; there, too, the bishop of glorious memory, Bishop Latimer, preached the Gospel of the Kingdom of God, and hundreds heard these words of truth and brought forth fruit in after days. Thank God we have a noble band of true and faithful men who are still proclaiming the Gospel under the open canopy of heaven, and will continue to preach, in boldness and joy, the unsearchable riches of Christ."

We have before us a packet of twenty-five letters written by John MacGregor to his sister in 1858, giving details of his open-air mission work, chiefly at King's Cross and Rag Fair. Even if we had space to transcribe them—and they are full of interest to those concerned in this particular class of Christian work—they would not be cared for by the general reader. But we should fail in drawing a true portrait of MacGregor unless we availed ourselves of every possible sidelight on his character and a few brief extracts are therefore appended.

The first, written soon after a great bereavement, is dated March 28th, 1858.

Work of the Christian kind is a great soother. That is God's medicine for the heart-pains He sends us. . . . . So many good people warmly welcomed me back. . . . . I would not be taken away from this work for anything. It is one of the few things really worth living for, and it gives to London a great focus of interest in my eyes.

May 16, 1858.

With (Lord) Radstock, Oliphant, and Ogilvie to Rag Fair at half-past nine. It is in the Jews' quarter in Houndsditch, and one of the most amazing sights in the world. Many acres covered with low stalls or open-air booths, crowded with thousands buying old garments on Sunday mornings. Men and women selling, shouting, haggling, disputing; policemen guarding the public-houses, men and boys trying on clothes, huge bundles staggering up narrow alleys; mothers, wives, and sweethearts fitting out their friends.

We took about 500 tracts and got every one thankfully accepted except two—one, torn up by a drunken woman, the other cast on the ground by a Jew, but that was taken up for the sake of the picture by a little girl whose education for future womanhood is begun in this horrid sink of humanity.   Very many thanked me; ‘How good of you,’ ‘Glad to see people cares for us,’ ‘Our souls are cared for by somebody,’ ‘Many of us would give up this if we could,’ ‘Give us another, sir.’

I resolved to send twenty of our O.A.M. with 5000 tracts. . . . .

Found a crowd at King’s Cross. . . . . Called on an infidel, Dr. ——, to learn about poor Redburn.   The wife took to gin when her girl died.   This is the wretched solace for bereavement.   He said Redburn was honest and true, nervous and melancholy, affectionate and miserable.   My heart yearns over the poor infidels.   I hope far far more for them than for some so-called Christians.   They are so misunderstood, repulsed and bullied by men whose religion is the result only of the example of their parents and cannot stand either the test of argument or of experience.

Christ spoke most to the infidels.
May 30, 1858.

In reply to a man (not there to-day) who had some weeks ago demanded some contemporaneous writings of history, mentioning Christ, I have brought to-day several passages copied from Tacitus, Pliny, Suetonius, Trajan, Martial, Juvenal, Horace, Epictetus, and Josephus, and the Infidels seemed amazed at this, but no one would comply with my request for them to come and examine the very books with me.
July 11, 1858.

A large crowd, especially of infidels and well-known sceptics, heard my farewell address on the ‘Rock and the Sand,’ at King’s Cross. Many shook hands most cordially. . . . . Blackwood (the handsome fellow) spent an hour with me giving cards and tracts.*

* Afterwards Sir Arthur Blackwood, K.C.B.

July 13, 1858.

At two o'clock I did a bold thing, which I had screwed up my fortitude to attempt. Without anything to say to him, I called with Oliphant upon Holyoake, the clever editor of the *Reasoner*, the centre of the Anti-Christ of the world. We soon got into earnest talk and parted excellent friends though my name is unknown to him. He gave me two books to take to Horace Greeley, editor of the *New York Tribune*. I let Holyoake go on till he spoke of a certain thing as 'right,' and said I: 'I don't know what you can mean by "right." You give up the Bible standard, and what enables you then to divide into right and wrong?' He said: 'Universal conscience.' 'Then if you listen to that you cannot put it aside when it says everywhere, "there is Spirit," "there is God."' From this capital point we led off with a deeply interesting talk.

November 21, 1858.

At King's Cross found Mr. C. (Calnon) the Popish opponent. We had the most pleasant, orderly, and useful controversy I ever recollect. Three turns each, that is an hour and a half. I was to prove that 'the Old Testament was a rule of faith in the early Christian church,' and certainly it is a good thing to have to get up these points, and to pick out the weak parts and strengthen them, knowing that the other side will batter at these.

I found that Christ appealed only to it with Pagans, Sadducees, His followers, and the devil—that each Apostle used it, and then the people, as Bereans, &c. Calnon tried to show tradition was parallel. I answered, 'Christ never mentions any good tradition, only bad ones, and then denounces them.' Paul mentions only traditions from Apostles, and if Calnon could put any such before me I should accept them. This forced him to undertake to give a list next Sunday of what Rome actually counts as *good* traditions.

November 28, 1858.

We had four hours of very useful controversy at King's Cross. . . . . Many of the Romanists seemed much astonished by my offer to prove 'that out of sixty words said to be wrong in our

English New Testament, the later editions of the English Roman Testaments have adopted *more than thirty*, and thus their translations are getting nearer to ours every year.' No one would accept my offer to prove this in the British Museum and I think I shall buy the books and prove it out of doors.

December 5, 1858.

A very useful time at King's Cross. During the week Calnon has evidently been urged not to refuse the challenge about English translations, so he accepted it, and we are to go regularly through with the proper books. I am to prove that whereas we have an English translation 200 years old, they have issued several and all differing in hundreds of passages from one another; that the Popish Church has not decided upon any one of them; that the changes in their later translations adopt many important words from our version, which very words their authorities had condemned when used by us. I never knew before what a tremendous battery is here, and I have deemed it so important that I have written a tract upon it to-night giving twenty-four principal passages.

That was a good day's work; several hours of exciting discussion and then the composition of a scholarly tract or pamphlet to finish up the day. Mac Gregor, true to his word, never flinched from the arduous task he had undertaken, and single-handed against a host of Roman Catholic controversialists he continued the discussion for many months.

Perhaps the greatest reward of this laborious effort was in the fact that through all weathers the same audience came night after night to listen to the discussion. Of these "arrows shot into the air, which fell to earth he knew not where," it may be reasonably supposed that some pierced through the harness of his opponents, but whatever benefit may have been derived by his hearers, it is certain that this prolonged public controversy, often alluded to in the public press of the day, placed Mac Gregor in the forefront of religious controversialists.

December 12, 1858.

My opponent to-night would not shake hands at the end till I compelled him by good humour, and then he squeezed my hand warmly. I believe that man is convinced in his very heart. This is worth living for. Nothing can be more interesting than the intimate study of the Bible. How tremendous is the evidence when you come to weigh it ton by ton !

Mac Gregor certainly had the exact gifts which make a street preacher and a controversialist successful. He had a good strong voice which could at times tone down to great tenderness, a fund of anecdote and a knowledge of how to use it at the right time and place ; a perfect command of himself so that no interruption or insult ever made him lose his head or the thread of his argument, and what was an invaluable adjunct—a strong sense of humour. He enjoyed the saying of a youth at King's Cross, one of the ringleaders in trying to create a disturbance, " Don't he keep his temper beautiful with all that impudence from *those fellows*." Nor did he fail to see the joke when a youth asked one day, " Which is Mac Gregor ? " and his companion answered, " There he is ! " and pointed to an old woman in spectacles who was speaking to a small group of people !

Sometimes he would indulge in quiet sarcasm. Here is a specimen :

Those who are not convinced of the Truth of the Gospel must at any rate admit that Christianity exists. But (except as the Bible tells) how it came here, and how it works, more than all other energies, are questions that no man has solved without assuming far more unlikely things than the existence of a Christ such as the Scripture describes.

The phenomenon appeared, they must allow, some eighteen centuries ago, and among a few fishermen upon Bethsaida beach. These simple folk carved out the only God-like image ever seen. These crafty conspirators arrayed it with a glory that eclipsed first of all themselves hopelessly and for ever. They devised the most novel and successful scheme of moral conduct, and kept on preaching doctrines that convicted every day their own falsehood and deception. They invented the very best plan for benefiting other people, but they utterly failed to get anything out of it for themselves but weeping and loss. These simpletons that could not see through the flimsy veil of fable, saw deeper into human hearts than any other men, and they gave voice to yearnings that were felt everywhere, but were never understood before. These dupes exposed all other deceptions that had deceived the wisest of philosophers. These dullards conceived a system that outreached the loftiest fancies of the cleverest thinkers.

We, who are of course so much wiser, and cooler, and better altogether—we are the only fair and shrewd judges to try this case. A whirlwind of clashing thoughts is sweeping in thunder through the darkness above us, and an earthquake rends the rocks, but we are placid, and can sit unmoved, while we rake among the chaos and sift out grains of truth. We have not taken sides—we are only standing aloof from everything. It does not tell upon our verdict at all that, if these prisoners at the bar are in the right, then we are utterly in the wrong, and must lay our mouths in the dust and confess that we are miserable sinners, and give up our dearest idol—self, and change our whole course of life and labour, and suffer and die for the truths we are now judging. 'Tis true that we have ourselves no rival system that will bear five minutes comparison with theirs—that our advance towards any better truth from the beginning of mankind,

say fifty thousand years ago, is rather minute; but the day after
to-morrow we shall have explained all mysteries by our sun-like inner
light, without that dim candle of revelation—our existence in flesh
and spirit, right and wrong, happy and wretched, poverty, sickness,
death, and the illimitable past and future of it all. Oh! it is a delightful thing to live in an age so modest, impartial and serene, and to
trace back my pedigree with honest pride to the ancestral oyster in
a metamorphic rock, to feel a patronising regret that no light from
heaven could ever penetrate his thick shell, but that all truth is
revealed to my soul by me, and that my law of life is what I feel
right, and (for I am charitable as well as infallible) your law of life is
what you think right, and that nobody can say anything is more
right than anybody else, and yet we are all right together—and that's
the way to make things pleasant all round!

One who knew Mac Gregor intimately, the Rev.
John P. Hobson, writes :

With one sick man whom he visited on several occasions he was
able to hold a good deal of conversation as to the grounds of his
unbelief. At last John Mac Gregor said one day: 'Now, tell me,
what is your real objection to the Bible?' 'Oh,' said the other,
'I can hardly tell you, as I have so many.' 'Well, but tell me one,'
said John Mac Gregor. 'One thing I object to is this, the Bible speaks
of the sun rising and setting, when we know it does not.' Our friend
admitted that this was an objection—'but,' he continued, 'let me ask
you if you know a book called "White's Ephemeris"?' 'No, I don't.'
'Well will you take my word as to what kind of book it is?' Mr.
Mac Gregor then told him that it was an almanac of acknowledged
authority, giving the places of the old and new planets, the eclipses,
occultations, and other celestial phenomena, also the times of the
lunations, the rising and setting of the sun, moon, and planets,
adapted to the meridian and latitude of Greenwich; tables requisite
for the use of nautical men, astronomers and others, and was often
found bound with the 'Nautical Almanack.' 'In that volume it is
stated again and again,' proceeded Mr. Mac Gregor, 'that the sun

rises and sets,* and yet we know it does not. As this statement is no valid objection to the accuracy of "White's Ephemeris" so the same statement is no real objection to the truth of the Bible. This has, I think, disposed of your difficulty. But will you think over the matter, and when I come again tell me any words which, describing the phenomena of the sun appearing and disappearing, would have been understood when the Old Testament was written and would be equally well understood to-day?'

On the occasion of his next visit Mr. Mac Gregor asked the infidel if he would have any objection to prayer being offered in his room. 'Oh,' said the other, 'I don't believe in prayer.' 'Well, you won't have any objection to my praying here, will you?' 'No, you can do as you like,' was the reply. 'But you will not interrupt me will you, because I am going to talk to a personal Friend.' 'No, I won't.' So by the infidel's bedside he knelt down and offered up aloud, on behalf of his still unbelieving friend, a prayer to Him unto whom all hearts are open, and Who can, by His blessed Spirit, touch infidels as well as other men. And that prayer was not in vain.

Of many stories that could be told of Mac Gregor's conflicts with infidels in open-air discussion, of his visits to their own places of meeting as well as to their own homes, we select one which has been variously told and generally with much incorrectness.

In the present instance we can place the outlines of the narrative before the reader almost entirely in the words of the chief actors.

Mac Gregor wrote in his diary:

April 1, 1858. —With Snape to call on Mr. Redburn, 70 Great Titchfield Street, Oxford Street, once a great infidel and for whom subscriptions are asked in the *Reasoner*. Found him weak, sleepless,

---

* In the edition which Mr. Hobson has in his possession, "'Ἄτλας Οὐράνιος, White's Cœlestial Atlas; or, an improved Ephemeris, 1845," it is stated on every page of the calendar, "Sun Ri. Se."

full of thoughts, nervous, with a care-worn but kind wife, in great poverty but respectable. He said he had no fear of the future, God would do right with him and he could implicitly trust that all would be right. Philosophy he found was quite useless in hours of trial. Had tried his best to believe in Christ and wished to do so but could not help if the evidence did not convince him. Put faith as a believing things against reason, and seemed to think we, by faith, could believe in Bible, things contrary to reason. . . . We concealed our names and brought him some jelly and sponge-cakes.

This was the first of a series of visits broken by his absence in America. Before leaving he wrote an earnest impassioned letter to Redburn, and the following is his reply, written when he was in great agony of mind and body, and everything had gone wrong, in home, in business, and in health :

26 QUEEN'S ROAD, BAYSWATER,
July 17, 1858.

. . . . I agree with you, sir, that in all probability we may never meet again—also, that it is a solemn thought. I thought so when we parted and when I said to myself, ' May the great First Cause bless and protect you across the mighty Atlantic,' and although you have not succeeded at present in bringing me to your way of thinking (and I am exceedingly anxious to be convinced) still I hope to be able to reflect with pleasure when my last hour comes of the many kindnesses you have shown for my temporal and spiritual welfare. My own mind in regard to the future is perfectly calm and I feel a confidence in the immutable laws which govern this, and it may be for aught I know, myriads of other worlds, and in the justice and love of the great First Cause who knows I have made the best use I could of the powers with which He has endowed me . . . . Wishing you every happiness that you can wish yourself,

I remain,

Your grateful and obedient servant,

R. REDBURN.

A delightfully illogical letter! But is not all denial of God equally so, even though deduced by the most learned arguments? While Mac Gregor was away his ever faithful friend and colleague, Mr. Snape, looked after Redburn who, deserted by his wife, in pain and poverty, and removed to a cheaper dwelling, wrote:

34 NEW NORTH STREET, RED LION SQUARE,
July 29, 1858.

. . . . I most sincerely thank you for the kind supply you sent for my spiritual and physical wants . . . . I have not been able to read the book through, but I shall do so with care and with a sincere desire to understand it. I trust our dear friend begins to smell the Western Hemisphere and that he is in the enjoyment of every blessing which a gracious God can give him. If it is the Lord's will I do not know of anything (except the recovery of my dear wife) that will give me greater pleasure than that I may have my health restored to welcome him back to these shores and to thank him and you for your great kindness to a helpless stranger . . . . My heart bleeds for my poor dear wife whom I have neither seen nor heard of since I wrote you last, and although my struggles and sufferings by myself are great I shall not seek her but my prayers are that she may come to her senses and that we may be able to live together again in those pure and holy affections which first brought us together . . . .

Your grateful and obedient servant,

RICHARD REDBURN.

The reader will have observed that Redburn has advanced from appealing to a "Great First Cause" to "a gracious God"—a Lord who wills and a Being to whom he prays. Now let us advance to a further stage in the narrative. The following is from a letter written by Mac Gregor to his sister:

Each Sunday seems the most interesting until the next arrives. It will be a long time before I forget to-day.

Yesterday I read in the *Reasoner* another notice of Redburn. How little they know he has a Bible and has read my 'Three Days in the East' and knelt last Sunday to pray.

I went to hear the Rev. W. Brock, and a noble sermon we had upon 'Father, I will that they whom Thou hast given me be with me where I am.' Who could believe it, I saw Redburn at that sermon ! He read, he prayed, he sang, he listened. All the cases of conversion one reads in books are feeble to encourage compared with one actual case *seen* like this.

I lost a great deal of the sermon in seeing *this* sermon preached to me on the living text before me, a scoffer on his knees, an infidel believing, a despiser of the Word hearing, and a rebel praising God. I sought him after service, and, poor fellow, he seemed to have new strength to grasp my hand but little power to let it go. There will be some hands like this to be grasped for the first time in Heaven.

Entries similar in some respects to the following appear in the Diary from time to time :

Aug. 7, 1859.—To Redburn with whom a long conversation. He read xv. of 1st Corinthians with me and prayed. This remarkable after reading the *Reasoner* of this week. Poor fellow he was very much affected and so was I. These visits to Redburn are truly useful and do me very great good.

Towards the autumn the illness of Redburn increased, and as he needed some one to see after him constantly, Mac Gregor arranged with a Mr. W—— for this to be done.

From Mr. W—— *to* John Mac Gregor.

20 / 11 / 59.

Sir,—Agreeably to instructions it is my duty to inform you that Mr. Redburn departed this life at half-past eight this morning, completely worn out by protracted suffering. He desired me to convey his grateful feelings for your kindness continued so very long, and to say, were it not inconvenient, it was his wish you should see him to his final rest. It is not intended to make any formal procession through the streets, but to meet the hearse at 'Tower Hamlets' and 'Bow Cemetery' at 2 P.M. on Thursday next. One of the greatest horrors of our poor friend's life was the probability of a pauper grave. He wished to lie with that daughter whose memory he ever cherished. A few friends therefore are trying to raise the necessary funds to carry out his wishes.

Yours respectfully,

W——.

Notes from the diary :

1859.

Nov. 20.—Redburn died this morning at eight. When I called at 2.30 saw his body. On Sunday last I had read to him Psalm xxiii. and Revelation last chapter and prayed, when he was full of feeling and gratitude. Next day sent him arrowroot and jelly. I had taken him jelly the first day I met him (April 2, 1858) just nineteen months ago, and now he is dead, and it is a wonderful case of a true conversion of a thorough sceptic.

Nov. 24.—Buried Redburn. Only Mr. W—— with me. Put the coffin in a wrong grave and had to change it. No service of any kind was used. Walked home with W—— from the Tower Hamlets Cemetery. He had been an atheist with Redburn for twenty-five years and had been converted to a belief in spirits by spirit-rapping. He is a tailor, an Owenite, a clever man.

Took him over the Boys' Refuge and explained the Shoeblack Society.

What better thing could he have done? what better text could he have taken for a sermon? When John Baptist, alone, in prison, waiting his sentence in doubt and perplexity, sent to the Lord his despairing question, "Art Thou He that should come or look we for another?"—the answer came : "Go and show John again those things which ye do hear and see ; the blind receive their sight, the lame walk, the lepers are healed, and the poor have the Gospel preached to them."

This is the answer of Christianity to every form of doctrine opposed to the Gospel, "See what it has done!" and Mac Gregor did well not at that time to argue on Atheism or Spiritualism, but to take his companion from the grave of Redburn and show him the Boys' Refuge and the Shoeblack Brigade.

CHAPTER VIII

PERSONAL

It has always been a puzzle to people engaged in the
ordinary routine work of life, to know how a popular
philanthropist, who is here, there, and everywhere,
can get through the enormous amount of work that
falls to his lot and at the same time attend to his own
profession, if he has one, and give proper heed to the
claims of home, friends, and society. The solution of
the puzzle is easy : the business of a philanthropist
can only be performed satisfactorily when it is set about
in a businesslike fashion ; and it cannot be done at all
unless the individual possesses distinctive characteristics
and qualifications for his special work.

On the last day of each year Mac Gregor was in the
habit of recording in his diary some of the principal
things that had occupied his attention during the
year :

1855.

Dec. 31.—The time finds me at work on the Protestant Alliance,
Church of England Young Men's Society, Open-air Mission, Lawyers'
Prayer Union, C.T. Mission, Scripture Readers' Society, Ragged

School Union, Shoeblack Society, Pure Literature Society, Boys'
Refuge, Reformatory Committees, Protestant Defence Society, Field
Lane School, Scripture Museum, &c.

In the above extract the "et cetera" stands for a
very important and substantial amount of work, for it
is a trite but true saying, "If you want anything
done, always go to the man who has most to do,"
and the calls upon Mac Gregor's time, labour and
influence, were merciless and incessant. But he was
a man of marvellous energy, and the more he had
to do the happier he always seemed. He thought
quickly, wrote quickly, decided quickly, walked quickly
—every muscle of the body and every faculty of the
mind were always on the alert, and so soon as an idea
was conceived it was forthwith brought into action.
Many a weary secretary of a society knew this, and
would come with the plea, "I have my annual report
to write, and I really don't know what to say or how
to say it. May I beg your help? It will not take
you an hour—it will take me a week." Others wanted
some special subject ventilated in the public press, and
almost at random we find in his diaries entries such as
these, specimens of innumerable others :

1851.

Nov. 14.—Sent off my first article for the *Bulwark*. Appointed
to accompany Mr. Locke as deputation to Manchester to Conference on Ragged School system. Finished and made up article
for next month's number about shoeblacks and broomers. One
boy had bought a hoop to make him run to his work in the
morning.

1852.

Feb. 26.—Visited Maynooth College and wrote an account of it to the London papers.

Sep. 18.—Sent off article for *Sunday at Home.*

1853.

June 13.—Wrote first part of a new story for *M. Adv.*

July 10.—Prepared appeal of Boys' Refuge, which has the name I gave it.

Aug. 1.—My letter on 'Impostures' in the *Record.*

1854.

April 26.—Finished report of Protestant Alliance. Wrote articles in *Record* and *Morning Advertiser.*

1855.

April 4.—Wrote preface to Y. M. Lectures.

April 24.—Wrote article, *Sunday at Home,* 'Bread and Water,' &c. &c.

These extracts will suffice, but it must be borne in mind that they do not represent a period when a fit of writing was upon him, but the steady, persistent habit of his whole lifetime in addition to more important and elaborate literary work.

Another characteristic of Mac Gregor was that he was a man of method. For everything there was a time and season, and to everything he endeavoured to give due place and proportion. He rose early every morning, summer and winter, and every morning for many years at a little before seven he might be seen in the ¿Temple Gardens on his way to the Shoeblacks' Home to conduct "Family worship"; generally pausing to "pass the time of day" to his friend Faudell Phillips (afterwards Sir Faudell Phillips), who was equally punctual in his attendance at early

morning service in the Temple Church. Mac Gregor
found, as all men pressed with work must find
sooner or later, that nothing can be successfully done
without method. This included punctuality, and it
was notorious that although in his lifetime he attended
innumerable committee and other meetings, and
every day was booked deep for engagements, he was
never known to be five minutes late, unless from
some cause over which he had no control, such as the
breakdown of a locomotive. We have it on the
authority of one who knew him well for twenty-seven
years and worked with him constantly for a considerable
part of that time : *

His punctuality was a marked feature of his habits; he seemed
never to be in a hurry and yet never late—punctual himself, he could
not bear unpunctuality in others. A Ragged School teacher who
had been placed under his superintendence was given a trial, but a
week or ten days later Mac Gregor said: 'This won't do. He has
been late'—only a few minutes we found—'three times. I can't bear
waiting.'

Another phase of his method was the manner in
which he made careful preparation for what he had
undertaken to do. If it were to speak at a meeting
he invariably jotted down on a card or half-sheet of
note-paper the exact things he wished to say, never
trusting to that broken reed the "spur of the moment,"
or contenting himself with "saying a few words"—
which generally means the imbecile utterances of idle

* Mr. John Kirk, secretary of the Ragged School Union.

or incompetent men. And he took just as much pains upon his subject whether it were to speak before the Archbishop of Canterbury or to a few shoeblacks or ragged waifs and strays. It was not that his memory was bad—few men had better—but because he had a strong sense of honour, duty, and obligation, and " he would not offer to the Lord that which cost him nothing."

Although philanthropy was the great business of his life, he did not allow it to stand in the way of other just claims upon him. Thus we find him in constant correspondence with his family, interested in everything that interested those he loved ; frequently seizing opportunities to run over to Ireland to see his father, mother and sister ; and fulfilling faithfully his duties as son and brother. Nor did he in any way neglect his private friends, either those allied to him by spiritual ties or otherwise. His chambers in Mitre Court, Temple, were the rendezvous of all sorts and conditions of men, who always found a welcome and a companion "at leisure from himself" ; as ready for a joke with its accompaniment of loud ringing laughter, as he was for prayer if his visitor came with a sorrowful and burdened soul. Further, he did not neglect himself. He was a man of a robust type, strong, muscular, athletic, and wise enough to know that without fitting recreation the secret of his strength would vanish. The first day the ice bore, he would be out with his skates and would scud along with such surprising vigour that the wondering bystanders would ask who he was, and generally get the reply, " That's John Mac Gregor, the Ragged and Shoeblack man !" He was from his youth up an expert swimmer—in the gymnasium he could hold his own against all comers ; he understood the " noble art of self-defence," and was a formidable boxer,* and on the river he could pull a pair of sculls with greater skill and strength than when he rowed in the Trinity eight.

The Young Men's Christian Associations of all lands are greatly indebted to him for teaching in a practical way that the highest kinds of sport are not incompatible with holy living but, on the contrary, may be made to further it, and his whole life was a protest against those who at one time were pleased to speak of men as " crawling worms," and as " crushed before the moth," and a vindication of the statement of the Preacher, "the glory of a young man is his strength."

Mac Gregor was a man of amazing industry. He not only did what he felt morally bound to do, but he made time to compass things that should fit him for doing more in the future.   Here is an example :

1851.

Oct. 3.—Dined at Colonel Brown's to meet Abbott Lawrence, the American Minister.   Have inserted in commonplace book the ideas concerning Protestantism I heard from him.

---

* The following extract from the diary is amusing evidence of his muscular Christianity :—" May 22, 1852.—To-morrow we expect a regular row in the new thieves' school a young Scotchman and I are starting. Last Sunday I had a stick. One of the men gave me a great blow in the breast in anger, but we became the best friends afterwards when he saw how it was returned."

ἐξομολογήσηται ὅτι Κύριος Ἰησοῦς Χρι-
στὸς εἰς δόξαν Θεοῦ [a] πατρός.
12 Ὥστε, ἀγαπητοί μου, καθὼς πάν-
τοτε ὑπηκούσατε, μὴ ὡς ἐν τῇ παρουσίᾳ
μου μόνον, ἀλλὰ νῦν πολλῷ μᾶλλον ἐν
τῇ ἀπουσίᾳ μου, μετὰ φόβου καὶ τρόμου
τὴν ἑαυτῶν σωτηρίαν κατεργάζεσθε·
13 [b] ὁ Θεὸς γάρ ἐστιν ὁ ἐνεργῶν ἐν
ὑμῖν καὶ τὸ θέλειν καὶ τὸ ἐνεργεῖν ὑπὲρ
τῆς εὐδοκίας. 14 πάντα ποιεῖτε χωρὶς
γογγυσμῶν καὶ διαλογισμῶν, 15 ἵνα
γένησθε ἄμεμπτοι καὶ ἀκέραιοι, τέκνα
Θεοῦ ἀμώμητα [c] ἐν μέσῳ γενεᾶς σκο-
λιᾶς καὶ διεστραμμένης, ἐν οἷς φαίνεσθε
ὡς φωστῆρες ἐν κόσμῳ, 16 λόγον ζωῆς
ἐπέχοντες, εἰς καύχημα ἐμοὶ εἰς ἡμέραν
Χριστοῦ, ὅτι οὐκ εἰς κενὸν ἔδραμον, οὐδὲ
εἰς κενὸν ἐκοπίασα.
17 Ἀλλ' εἰ καὶ σπένδομαι ἐπὶ τῇ θυσίᾳ
καὶ λειτουργίᾳ τῆς πίστεως ὑμῶν, χαίρω
καὶ συγχαίρω πᾶσιν ὑμῖν· 18 τὸ δ' αὐ-
τὸ καὶ ὑμεῖς χαίρετε καὶ συγχαίρετέ
μοι. 19 ἐλπίζω δὲ ἐν Κυρίῳ Ἰησοῦ,
Τιμόθεον ταχέως πέμψαι ὑμῖν, ἵνα κἀγὼ
εὐψυχῶ, γνοὺς τὰ περὶ ὑμῶν· 20 οὐδένα
γὰρ ἔχω ἰσόψυχον, ὅστις γνησίως τὰ
περὶ ὑμῶν μεριμνήσει· 21 οἱ πάντες γὰρ
τὰ ἑαυτῶν ζητοῦσιν, οὐ [d] τὰ Ἰησοῦ Χρι-
στοῦ· 22 τὴν δὲ δοκιμὴν αὐτοῦ γινώ-
σκετε, ὅτι ὡς πατρὶ τέκνον, σὺν ἐμοὶ
ἐδούλευσεν εἰς τὸ εὐαγγέλιον. 23 τοῦτον
μὲν οὖν ἐλπίζω πέμψαι, ὡς ἂν ἀπίδω
τὰ περὶ ἐμέ, ἐξαυτῆς· 24 πέποιθα δὲ
ἐν Κυρίῳ, ὅτι καὶ αὐτὸς ταχέως ἐλεύ-
σομαι [e].
25 Ἀναγκαῖον δὲ ἡγησάμην Ἐπαφρό-
διτον τὸν ἀδελφὸν καὶ συνεργὸν καὶ
συστρατιώτην μου, ὑμῶν δὲ ἀπόστολον,
καὶ λειτουργὸν τῆς χρείας μου, πέμψαι
πρὸς ὑμᾶς· 26 ἐπειδὴ ἐπιποθῶν ἦν πάν-
τας ὑμᾶς, καὶ ἀδημονῶν, διότι ἠκούσατε

should confess, that Jesus Christ
is Lord, to the glory of God the
Father.
12 Wherefore, my beloved, as
ye have always obeyed, not as
in my presence only, but now
much more in my absence;
work out your own salvation
with fear, and trembling. 13 For
it is God which worketh in you,
both to will, and to do, of *his*
good pleasure. 14 Do all things
without murmurings, and dis-
putings: 15 that ye may be
blameless and [α] harmless, the
sons of God, without rebuke, in
the midst of a crooked and perverse nation, among whom [β] ye
shine as lights* in the world:
16 holding forth the word of life,
that I may rejoice in the day of
Christ, that I have not run in
vain, neither laboured in vain.

17 Yea, and if I be [γ] offered
upon the sacrifice and service
of your faith, I joy, and rejoice
with you all. 18 For the same
cause also do ye joy, and rejoice
with me. 19 [δ] But I trust in the
Lord Jesus, to send Timotheus
shortly unto you, that I also
may be of good comfort, when I
know your state. 20 For I have
no man [ε] likeminded, who will
naturally care for your state.
21 For all seek their own, not
the things which are Jesus
Christ's. 22 But ye know the proof
of him, that as a son with the
father, he hath served with me,
in the gospel. 23 Him therefore
I hope to send presently, so
soon as I shall see how it will
go with me. 24 But I trust in
the Lord, that I also myself
shall come shortly.
25 Yet I supposed it necessary, to send to you Epaphro-
ditus my brother & companion
in labour, and fellowsoldier,
but your messenger, and he that
ministered to my wants. 26 For
he longed after you all, and
was full of heaviness, because
that ye had heard that he had

[a] Ps. om. [b] ὁ Θεος. [c] ἐν μεσῳ. [d] Rec. τα του Χριστου Ιησου. [e] Bz. add προς υμας. [α] Or, sincere. [β] Or, shine ye. [γ] Gr. poured forth. [δ] Or, Moreover. [ε] Or, so dear unto me.

+A (See of page).

* Lights — The lifeboat is valuable as it saves the shipwrecked but the lighthouse is more valuable for it prevents the shipwreck. Nolan. 18/1/52.

φωστῆρες. may also signify the wardens of the [illegible] perhaps attending to the light house at Pharos. The Christian's light is not his own but committed to him. We must feel that this light has by our means been made useful in getting poor sinners out of a wrong track on the ocean of sin & steadily directing them to the haven of rest. Our business is to work though in a crooked & perverse generation, work we must. If we succeed, we ourselves will be honored, God will be glorified & the sinner saved will be benefitted. But succeed or not, we shall have exercised ourselves with spiritual difficulty & God will so overrule all as to benefit our souls. The strange appearance of our warning others or the disagreeable nature of the duty must not hinder us from it — neither must the remarks made on us turn us from our spiritual calling. If we went to visit a mad-house we should not feel insulted but pity for the remarks of the lunatics upon us, none are more mad than those under sin & the devil, let us pity them [illegible]

FAC-SIMILE PAGE OF MAC GREGOR'S ANNOTATED GREEK TESTAMENT.

This was a habit ; to fix in writing the thoughts
that influenced him ; to make live again in useful
form, words that would have been but "idle words"
had they floated upon the air and been lost.   Again :

Nov. 9.—Mr. Dallas preached a very remarkable sermon for the
Irish Church Missions and I have noted it on the text Acts
xvii. 1–5.

We have lying before us the "Bagster's Critical
New Testament, Greek and English," in which the
notes referred to in the above extract are made.   It is
a literary curiosity, a marvel of patience.   On nearly
every page the wide margin is covered with "notes,"
critical, philological, illustrative, devotional, valuable
for all future time for reference when preaching or
teaching, and written with great clearness, terseness
and painstaking.   The secret of all this industry
was a continuous enthusiasm.   He threw his whole
soul into everything he undertook.   It was said of
Lord Shaftesbury that he spoke on each of the
hundred subjects in which he was interested with so
much vigour and earnestness as to give the impression
that the matter occupying his thought at the moment
was the one hobby of his life.   This was equally true
of Mac Gregor.   To see him engaged upon any
apparently trivial work the observer would suppose it
was the one thing for which he lived.   An hour afterwards an equal zeal would be displayed on a totally
different object—one day or one year would be
devoted to herculean tasks which an on-looker would

M

prophesy must soon wear out the worker—but the next day or the next year would find him with the same enthusiasm not one whit abated. Heart never failed, and flesh but rarely. He wrote once in his diary :

1855.

Nov. 24.—Kept in by cold and neuralgia. Gave up. I was going too fast and recklessly at meetings. Here I am chequered to breathe. Stop doing and let me suffer. Worked at book.

But six days later the following entry occurs :

Nov. 30.—Never was harder worked than just now, but never felt in better spirits.

It may be well to glance at some of the many schemes and enterprises that engaged his attention about this time by giving a few extracts from the diary and from letters to his sister :

1851.

Dec. 8.—Liverpool Assizes. Met Liverpool deputation to establish Shoeblack Society there.

1852.

I have formed a Sunday morning class of shoeblacks from 9.30 to 10.30. It will be nice and quiet to take it myself.

Feb. 23.—Formed Irish Protestant Alliance.

Feb. 24.—Formed Dublin Shoeblack Society.

March 7.—Enlisted in Temple Volunteers.

March 8.—Sunday. Met Mr. Villiers. Became one of his congregation. Visited his Sunday School. Took leave of St. John's Chapel Sunday School. Visited Field Lane at night with Snape, Cane, Osburn, Day. Addressed the 170 persons in the Night Refuge.

1853.

April 17.—Went to Lord Palmerston in the morning with a deputation.

April 21.—Slave Committee. First since Lord Shaftesbury's return.

May 9.—Meeting at Lord Harrowby's about the *True Briton*.

Among other labours Mac Gregor took infinite pains to devise means to benefit the crossing-sweepers of London, but innumerable difficulties stood in the way of organising them into a body as in the case of the shoeblacks. To do this on the plan of importuning passers-by, would be to encourage mendicity; to disturb the vested rights of old sweepers would be to bring a prejudice against the scheme; a large number who were old, lame, or otherwise incapacitated for active work, paid so much per diem to a robust hand for sweeping the crossing once or twice a day, while they simply posed as sweepers for the remainder. He thought he might establish a kind of Labour Bureau, and send forth an army of men, women, and children at so much a day guaranteed; funds for their wages to be supplied by the public or out of the rates; or to organise a staff in uniform with secured boxes into which coppers might be dropped, the contents of such boxes to go to a general fund, and the sweepers to be paid 3*s.* a day and have the advantage of night schools.

Out of these suggestions grew up many more, but as the shoeblack movement was then all-absorbing, the matter was practically allowed to drop, as few men came forward to take up the new work.

Another suggestion, which shared a similar fate, was thrown out in a letter to the editor of the *Ragged School Magazine :*

Will any one assist in organising a corps of newspaper boys? Seven years ago a request like this was made through your magazine, in regard to the Shoeblack Movement and the results of united efforts have been largely blessed by God.

One good idea of Mac Gregor's which worked very successfully, was to open various shops for the sale of the products of the Industrial Classes connected with the ragged schools, and it was, in its way, a proud moment for him when he was able to announce that "Firewood at twenty-four bundles for one shilling may be had at the Ragged School Shop, No. 5 Crown Court, Chancery Lane."

Writing to his sister, he said :

July 27, 1853.

I have taken a splendid shop for the Ragged School Shop. Only two doors off the Strand. It is a great move and I trust will be useful. My colporteur sells away famously and I have just got him appointed at fifteen shillings a week under the British and Foreign Bible Society. We are to have the Shoeblack's fête, God willing, on Saturday week, the last day I shall be in town. I am making them the present (out of the wonderful £50) of a banner, scarlet and blue, with silk tassels, and blue and gold stick. On the top two blacking brushes crossed and a blacking bottle, with a nosegay of fresh flowers.

The same fund will enable me to give a tea and strawberries and cream to the open-air preachers, and some clergymen at my rooms will come to talk over our remarkably cheering prospects. I got £60 for it this morning. We have already more than £320—indeed more than we can spend, but it weighs heavily on me to see how people trust me with money thus readily.

My class of clerks is now fourteen in number, highly interesting. What a wondrous announcement, the Empire of China is divided in twain. Here is removed the last great barrier to the spread of the Gospel. When these things happen, what manner of persons ought *we* to be ?

JOHN.

Not at any period of his life did Mac Gregor confine his reading to one class of literature, and certainly not to "good" books. As a matter of fact he read some of the very worst he could find—but he did so either to refute their errors or to procure their suppression. About this time the reign of "penny dreadfuls" was supreme. Dick Turpin, Claude Duval and Jack Shepherd, were the heroes of the boy world, and the effect of such and other pernicious reading was only too patent. Judges on the Bench, and ministers in the pulpit, launched their thunderbolts against the demoralising influence of such books, but no one seemed to be able to prescribe an antidote.

Mac Gregor was always of a practical turn of mind .and when once he had investigated the matter and had found that the pernicious literature of the day was ruining thousands of young lives, it was not in his nature merely to sit still and lament the evil.

We find in the diary therefore the following entries :

1854.
Jan. 21.—Committee Purity of Press Society.
Jan. 27.—Formed Society for Pure Literature.

The efforts of the Pure Literature Society, in which he took the deepest interest throughout his life, were from the first in a positive direction. Its object was not to publish either books or periodicals, but to stimulate the circulation of the best reading among the people. To this end a catalogue of approved works was issued, libraries were supplied at half price, selections of books were made for schools and institutions at home and abroad, managers of publications were corresponded with, either in praise or blame, and at the society's offices thousands of books might be inspected by those who were seriously anxious to improve the reading of their households. An indefatigable committee of ladies and gentlemen carefully read and criticised every book that was to find a place in the catalogue. Referring to the class of works it was the object of the committee to eliminate, Lord Shaftesbury said :

Look at the immense efforts that are being made in various quarters and by various parties for the dissemination of literature the most insidious, the most attractive, the most foul in principle and design and yet the most deceptive that ever was composed by the hand of man, or that ever issued from man's foul heart. They are written with so much astutenesss, so much care, that I defy any lawyer that was, and I defy, moreover, any lawyer that ever shall be, to be able to draw up a clause in an Act of Parliament which should put down such literature as that.

By the means of magazine associations and other effective operations, the committee of the Pure Literature Society succeeded in bringing healthy periodicals to the homes of people of all classes, and over a hundred ladies and gentlemen in one district alone, were, in the early days of the society, acting gratuitously as canvassers.*

Although we have hitherto regarded Mac Gregor mainly in connection with religious and philanthropic work, it must not be supposed that there was not another side to his life. He was a man who thoroughly enjoyed society, mingled in it freely and was brought into contact with almost every notable person of his time. Moreover he was a man of many intimate friends.

Soon after coming to London he became acquainted with Lord Shaftesbury, first in connection with Ragged School work, afterwards with Reformatory and Refuge legislature, then in the crusade against the Papal aggression, and subsequently in almost every form of labour in which the "Good Earl" was engaged. Platform and committee acquaintanceship soon ripened into friendship, and that friendship was continued almost without interruption till death severed it. Although in the course of years a vast number of letters passed between them, they were chiefly brief and businesslike, as they were in the habit of seeing one another so frequently. Each admired the work of the other; in cases of difficulty

---

* The Pure Literature Society not only exists, but continues in a flourishing condition. The offices are No. 11 Buckingham Street, Strand, and the valuable and energetic secretary is Mr. Richard Turner, who has held the office for thirty-eight years. The Society owes much to his zeal and energy.

or doubt they almost invariably consulted together, and in each there was the consuming desire to better the world, to raise the fallen, and to fight against ignorance, poverty, and crime among the lowest of the people. In Mac Gregor's diary the name and deeds of Lord Shaftesbury are recorded with great frequency, and a few extracts here may not be uninteresting.

1851.

July 23.—Lord Shaftesbury, Chevalier Bunsen, Hon. William Cowper visited the shoeblacks with me.

Oct. 28.—Wrote to propose myself for the National Club * asking Mr. Napier to propose and Mr. Colquhoun to second.

1853.

May 11.—Evening at Lord Shaftesbury's. Met Mrs. Beecher Stowe and asked her to go to the Ragged Schools †—also the Archbishop of Canterbury, &c.

1855.

Dec. 24.—By Southampton to visit Lord Shaftesbury at St. Giles. Found there Lord Ashley and his three brothers and four sisters, Marquess D'Azeglio, Mr. and Mrs. W. Ashley, and A. Kinnaird. A very pleasant time.

Dec. 26.—Long walk with Lord S. and his sons in the rain conversing on very deeply interesting subjects and again after dinner.

Dec. 27.—Shooting hares, rabbits and pheasants with his three sons, drew caricatures and played billiards. Lord A. most entertaining and interesting.

When Lord Shaftesbury safely brought through the House of Lords his "Common Lodging House"

---

* In March 1856 MacGregor was elected a member of the Athenæum Club.

† Mrs. Stowe refers to MacGregor in her "Sunny Memories."

Bills—"the first successful efforts that had been made to reach the very dregs of society—the first to penetrate to the deepest dens of vice, filth, and misery—" Mac Gregor, who knew the slums of London and the manners and customs of the denizens so well, was able to render him most important services. The personal interest that he took in the matter may be gathered from the following :

1856.

Jan. 13.—Morrison with me to seven lodging-houses at night with Jackson and Joyce. In one fifty people were waiting for us. Went into the Pie House on Holborn Hill and found thirty boys and gave them reading. A crowd collected.

Feb. 24.—Spoke in two lodging houses. This is a heavenly work. It brings the best news to the lowest people.

Another life-long friend was one whose name can never be forgotten in the philanthropic history of this country, the Hon. Arthur Kinnaird (afterwards Lord Kinnaird), a genial, generous, and delightful companion—one of the best-hearted and most right-minded men of his generation, whose name, like that of Lord Shaftesbury, will frequently be mentioned in the course of this narrative.

A third friend, with whom at the time of which we write Mac Gregor was intimate, was Mr. Alexander Haldane, a barrister-at-law of the Inner Temple—one of the proprietors of the *Record* newspaper—and the friend and confidante of Lord Shaftesbury. Mr. Haldane has been described as "an active, energetic man, strong in body and mind, of great intellectual

force and tenacity of purpose, full of keen and warm-
hearted sympathies, lively in temperament, with a
strong sense of humour and an inexhaustible fund of
anecdote." In this case "like sought like," for the
description of Mr. Haldane might have been applied
in identical terms to John Mac Gregor.

But Mac Gregor's friends were legion and we only
refer to these three typical ones in passing. It was
his nature to be staunch and true—one friend never
thrust aside another—and though as the years went
on new names were almost daily added to his list of
friends, the old ones, Snape, Fowler, Martin Ware,
Wilbraham Taylor, Nathaniel Bridges, and a host of
others were constantly recurring and were always
mentioned with generous affection. In the same way
that the names of friends stood in his memory as
landmarks of his personal history, so did certain
events, and it is interesting to note that almost every
year on the 1st of March he makes a special entry in
his journal in grateful remembrance of the fact that
on that day he was rescued from the burning ship,
the *Kent*. Thus :

March 1, 1856.—Remarkable day for me. For, thirty-one years
ago, the Lord saved me on the 1st of March from the flames and
waves, in the *Kent*.

In that same year he wrote :

Sep. 25.—Saw Lanark Mills with Mr. Miller, and Falls of Clyde,
and went to the annual races and preached to eleven groups of
people. Met the sweep, thimble-rigger, hard-headed cosmopolite,
old elder, and Jack Collins of the *Kent*. All this sent to *Record*.

The man, Jack Collins, was selling a broadsheet with doggerel verses giving harrowing details and a glaring picture of the "Burning of the *Kent*." Mac Gregor bought some copies, and one he had framed. It is still in Mrs. Mac Gregor's possession, and bears this note :

In returning from the race-course at Lanark, in September 1856, when I had spoken to several groups of people upon 'better things,' I overtook J. Collins, a fine-looking sailor, whose feet having been burned he had to push himself in a go-cart. He is one of six who were on the maintop of the *Kent* and were burned. He sold this paper to a crowd of persons, listening to the conversation between two men who thus met thirty-one years after they had been both so wonderfully saved from fire and water. J.M., 1856.

It is impossible to paint a faithful biographical portrait of a man and not draw aside the curtains which conceal his inner thoughts and spiritual life. Mac Gregor was not guilty of the bad habit of morbid introspection ; and he rarely wrote in his diary, still less to his dearest and most intimate friends, the hopes, fears, aspirations, and regrets that all must experience and that some express so freely as to destroy the fineness and purity of the feelings. Nevertheless, here and there in his diary—which, be it remembered, was mainly a note-book containing memoranda of things done—there are a few charming passages of self-revelation, and we make no apology for quoting some of them.

1855.

May 1.—Read part of Bradford's life and felt that the highest grace of humility is that which feels deeply and shows much, but speaks little. Even the world knows that professions of humility, when with any show of truth, do in fact raise instead of lowering, and it is possible to be proudly humble.

May 6.—We are between two dangers always—exultation and vanity at being instruments in God's hands, and disgust leading to despair at being such feeble and sinful instruments. Lord preserve me from both dangers.

March 16, *Sunday.*—I had a most pleasant dream this morning early. The vivid impression of music beyond idea beautiful and yet only a few notes, made me awake suddenly. The only other recollection was that at the moment of hearing these tones I thought they never could be surpassed or heard again. Strangely enough I read afterwards of some cases of ecstatic glimpses. Gradually it becomes a truly pleasant habit to awake with thoughts of God. The first few movements of the mind are more connected than at first we see, with the line of thought throughout the day.

After entering many details of places visited and engagements fulfilled on a certain Sunday, he adds :

I never had a more delightful Sunday, yet here I go writing all *I* have done. So full is self of self.

At another time :

If one were perfect for an hour what a misery would the next minute be, crammed with sin as before. The continual intercession is needed like the perfect redemption.

Dec. 28.—Last Sunday of 1856. Not conscious of one single act not covered with selfishness. Cannot even imagine the feeling of labour for God purely. It must be half heaven to get rid wholly of self.

Surely much importance is to be attached to expressions such as these and others that follow. Do they not explain much of ordinary philanthropic life, of conscious and unconscious motive, and of religious routine? Accept the confession as true—and if it were not true it would be miserable cant—it is repeated year after year—and what does it show? That he was a real man, true to himself and therefore, in the main, true to God. There is no shadow of mock humility in the expressions but honest manliness and godliness. He could not be a humbug and he could not ignore, what so many do, that politics are not wholly for the good of the people, that scientific discovery is not wholly for the assistance of the world's progress, and that so-called Christian activity is not always for the glory of Christ.

The entry in the diary continues :

Valuable lesson this, to reflect on difference between means of grace and end of religion ; machinery and products. Hardest work, sanctification of one's own soul. Often must be silent to hear God speak to one's self. Hundreds of times we add to labour when we ought to redirect it. Put on more wheels and noise when the spring of motive ought to be purified and intensified. Never in more honour with man or more mean to myself than now. Sin not that grace may abound, is a very needful maxim after we feel grace. Security begets forwardness.

Feb. 22, 1857.—A very happy useful Sunday. Noble sermon from Bayley, 'Except your righteousness exceed the righteousness, &c.' He rightly says it means our inherent righteousness, not imputed. When I think that their righteousness was to be seen of men in their good deeds, and that unless mine exceeds that I shall in no wise enter the Kingdom of Heaven, full and unconquerable despair would close on me. I am not sensible of ever doing a thing of good except in some way or other to be glad of it to myself

or others. I cannot imagine the grandeur of Paul's or John's working good, unless alloyed with miserable human motives. Still I *wish*
the best motive and *strive* after it and really love and trust, and hope
and pray.

In reviewing some of the main features in the character of John MacGregor we must not omit to mention
one with which all who knew him well are familiar.
He was a man who never hesitated to express his
opinion. As a rule he did so modestly but firmly as
became a man who had made up his mind ; at other
times he was brusque and dogmatic, in which case he
did not give a fair representation of himself. In
illustration of our point we cannot perhaps do better
than let him speak for himself by giving in his own
words an account of an interview he had with Bishop
Wilberforce. It will assist the reader to understand
the " notes " more fully if we recall to his mind that
Convocation which had been extinguished in the last
century (1717) was revived in 1852, and that the
revival, taking place concurrently with the introduction
of the confessional into the high churches, was the
occasion of considerable public controversy in which
Lord Shaftesbury took a leading part. The occasion
of the interview was that MacGregor had sent to
Bishop Wilberforce a copy of his tract on the Open-
air Mission entitled "Go out Quickly," which was
acknowledged as follows :

February 6, 1855.

My Dear Sir,—

I thank you greatly for your deeply interesting
publication. I regret in it your sneer at Convocation which I

believe I could show was actively engaged in your own work. I should be very glad if on some occasion within the next ten days I can have a conversation with you on the subject.

I am, ever yours,

S. OXON.

An appointment was made, and, on the day before his visit, Mac Gregor wrote to his sister :—

How very funny it will be to go to see the Bishop of Oxford to-morrow. You know he is a very great gun.

We give the notes exactly as they were written.

*Notes of Interview with Bishop Wilberforce,
at 26 Pall Mall, February 13, 1855.*

Bishop Wilberforce. Writing letter went on and directed it.
Mac Gregor. Silent.

W. Praised tract 'Go out quickly,' would gladly do what he could to help anything to bring people to Christ, ought to be a missionary work, but, to bring to fold of church.

M. People ask if we are 'touting for the Rector' and any visible connection with a system or congregation would be a barrier. On this people most sensitive, would not cross a chalk line. Will not come on 'kerbstone,' tents at Chobham not frequented, but services outside crowded.

W. Should Bishop of London preach himself out of doors?

M. No, but if he went to ten others preaching, and standing by each for five minutes were to say, 'I rejoice to hear the truth preached here, you will hear the same in that church,' he would in fact preach ten open-air services in fifty minutes, and without exhaustion.

W. Who ought the preachers to be?

M. Not the clergy who work hard in their pulpits, for they have enough to do; not those who are lazy in their pulpits, for they will not do enough.

W. Ah, you would have laymen. Ought the Bishop of Winchester to get clergy and laymen together and organise?

M. He should speak to ten of his best clergy and each of them choose two laymen and say, 'Go to the worst places in my parish and do your best with the Bible, out of doors, and tell me this day three months how you get on; they are doing the same in ten other parishes, we are not singular, we shall interchange and compare our accounts of success.'

W. But clergy have preached in the open air.

M. Yes.

W. How are they received?

M. Very well; they go in clerical dress and this mostly 'draws.' It would soon cease to do so. The groups must not be too large for any one to be otherwise than personally near the speakers.

W. You don't make a difference between appointed ministers and all laymen?

M. A great difference. The clergy ought to be exalted. I would put them on the pedestal God has made for them. You would place them on man's pedestal. Yet mine would be higher and on firmer basis. Where lay-agency is most honoured by the minister, clerical influence is most cherished by the people.

W. In Convocation we want to get lay agents.

M. Nominally.

W. How do you mean? What do you think I want Convocation for? Surely it is unfair to charge these motives. Why sneer at Convocation? What do I want it for?

M. It is more unfair for you to ask me to divine your motives.

W. I daresay you would rejoice to see me burned in Smithfield; people malign and abuse and threaten me. Don't those who look from your side of the heavens imagine all evil against us?

M. First 'pure, then peaceable.'

W. Yes, but peaceable then pure, and pure then peaceable. Why can't we agree to work together? In ninety-nine points out of a hundred we are united.

M. But the hundredth may be *the* point, and if distinct opposition is felt upon that, it indicates the agreement in the others to be only skin-deep.

W. If we had Convocation there would be more union.

M. Convocation, even last week, more effectively than before, ranged the two parties of the Church in opposition.

W. Why do you call them *parties ?* There are no parties mentioned in the Bible. We ought to get on together and not speak of parties.

M. That might be a wise saying in A.D. 2, or A.D. 3. I question if in A.D. 4, it was not proved doubtful, but in 1855 it is utterly absurd. We differ in essentials, men died, three hundred years ago, for these differences.

W. No! but for the absurdities, the bestialities of Romanism. You don't think there is any danger of our falling into these?

M. Men believe in the 'real presence,'—as ghastly a doctrine as any Popery ever had.

W. Well but don't make it a 'Shibboleth;' we need not all hiss together.

M. No, but it is known as a mark of far more serious errors, and scarcely ever found without them. It is known on one side, and acknowledged on the other, to be a badge, just as the cross in a church is itself nothing, but may yet become the very 'mark of the beast.'

W. But you don't define 'the real presence.'

M. In this way. Do you believe that when you eat the bread after consecration and all the rest is rightly performed, the bread is at that moment mere flour and water?

W. Yes; but do you believe that Christ is not specially present in certain means?

M. He is, but that is jumping from the bread to the Saviour. The heresy about the 'real presence' has got to do with the 'bread,' and Denison does not say as you have done about that. His party would not, and he has many in it.

W. Oh, no! not many supporters.

M. Not many friends, but many supporters.

W. Your party does not run down this doctrine for its own sake, but making it a pretext for opposing those who advocate other modes of teaching than yours.

M. I have more knowledge by correspondence and communication with the Evangelical party than it is possible for your lordship to have, and I do believe we oppose for a far different reason.

W. Why malign, and abuse, and oppose? The sleeping Church, long in a trance, awakes. The man becomes conscious. He sneezes and coughs, and you say, 'No, he may not rise.' He gives signs of life, and you oppose those who would quicken him to live and move and vivify all things—why do you smother his first returning breathings?

M. Because his first sign of life is to stretch his hand along the ground to reach his *cudgel*, and in olden times with that he sadly belaboured those who have now laid him low. If he wants to live it must be as a brother, not as a master.

W. Why do you impute such motives? Do I want Convocation to live for this? How can you judge of the aim of Convocation? Those who are most anxious for it are the same who most eagerly desire that the Church should reach the people.

M. The Bishop of Exeter is one of two Bishops who will not subscribe to the Scripture Readers' Association, yet he is anxious for Convocation.

W. Don't judge men by any Society.

M. No; but if a man does not support even that mode of reaching the masses which the whole bench, but himself and another, support, and if he does not allow any other means, how is it possible that he wishes for Convocation so as to make the Church reach the people?

W. He is an old man now, and was bred in other views than those we have.

M. Men older than he have been burned rather than allow clerical supremacy. But there is the other Bishop.

(I did not know this was Bishop W. himself. He rose, stood by the fire as if he wanted me to leave, but I stuck on!)

W. He may have other reasons.

M. Yes; but to speak plainly—if Convocation had to vote

to-morrow about lay-agents, even the Scripture Readers' Association being as the type, these two prelates would be in the minority.

W. I like speaking plainly—I never like mystical words. I like exactly to see a man's meaning and to make mine known.

M. I fear I have been only too plain-spoken.

W. Not a bit.

M. Well I will be plainer still, shall I ?

W. (Sitting down.)   Do pray.

(I began to suspect that Bishop W. was the other of the two prelates who reject the Scripture Readers' Association, for he got very bitter.)

M. What should you say to this ?   We—a few laymen—keep a layman in a clergyman's parish against his will and protest, because while he gives Popish books with his name to his people, our layman is afraid to get more than nineteen people together to hear the Word of Life.*

W. That's your parable, and here is mine. A worthy minister works with his curates and agents in his parish, and teaches them all he can and ought, and one of your Societies sends a man to him who creates dissension and comes without any need of him, and for no purpose but to quarrel.   This is *the other side.*

M. And put both sides together, what do they show we want ?   A body large enough to settle when, where, how, by whom, additional teaching may be sent to a parish. Convocation cannot do this unless the full body of the laity is its major part.

W. That's your view.   You want Convocation to have the laity as part ?

* The reference is to an enactment then in force prohibiting the teaching of the Gospel and the worship of God in private houses where more than twenty persons besides the family were assembled. Although the law was practically a dead letter, Lord Shaftesbury thought it would be wise to have it repealed, and brought in a Bill accordingly. This was strenuously and bitterly opposed by the Bishop of Oxford, Earl Derby, and others, but after a sharp struggle Lord Shaftesbury carried the day. It is a curious phase of ecclesiastical history that not until August 1855 were religious meetings in private houses " lawful assemblies."—(See " Life' and Work of the Seventh Earl of Shaftes-bury," vol. ii. pp. 511–521.)

M. Yes; as Jewel says, 'Where there are three laymen there is a church.'

W. Yet to get the laity is my object in Convocation, and we cannot have them unless a united voice is heard asking for them.

M. The voice of Convocation never was less united than last week. The Upper and Lower Houses are quite disagreed.

W. I believe the opposite.

M. I know persons in both Houses, and being only a spectator I can see the quarrel more easily.

W. That goes back to our former subject. How do you know our object in bringing Convocation together? Why do you think it is not for the very purpose of organising lay-agency?

M. We judge in two ways. First, by reading the reports in the papers of the words used and resolutions passed. Second, by looking to the dioceses and parishes of those who constitute the House of Convocation and seeing there what they do in the matter to encourage it.

W. That's hardly fair. The church has established such rules. We ought to be like the leaves of a tree of every form and colour and turned every way, but all giving health and receiving nourishment from the same root, not being all of the same tree.

M. We ought to bear one fruit too.

W. But the tree is nailed to a wall, and when one tree or another sprouts or looks alive the gardener prunes it off at once. . . . . How can we help you in Convocation?

M. If that now sitting only plays, it will show that no Convocation is needed; if it works it will infallibly cause a real Convocation to be asked for. Our laity were represented by Parliament until that was un-Protestantised—then some assembly without Romanists became necessary.

W. We are powerless at present.

M. If we repeal the Acts of Uniformity we shall be at least free, if not strong, and this can be done without Convocation.

W. There are two great extremes. On one side Individualism, man's soul communicating with God's Spirit, and not by sacraments or ordinances or appointed means ; the other, making Romish ritual the only means. Surely truth lies in the centre.

M. It is the oldest and most dangerous of all fallacies to set two opposing errors as extremes, and to say 'truth lies equally distant from both' in the point of indifference or neutrality.

W. I did not say 'equally distant from both.'

M. Yes, the centre.

W. It may be like the foci of an ellipse.

M. It lies between.

W. Yes.

M. Truth may lie much nearer one extreme than the other, and here I believe it does so. Man's spirit communes with God directly and without ordinances, but also with ordinances. The ordinances are only helps to facilitate the direct personal communication, and that the main object is so overwhelmingly more noble and important than any other, or than the means for it, that the means are quite subordinate.

W. We differ in words, perhaps, but maybe we have the same object in view.

M. If that be the conversion of every living man and his sanctification by the Spirit our object is one.

W. I shall be delighted to aid you in any way I can.

(I left him a list of our stations, report of services, &c., and talked a good deal about the committee directing the Open-air Mission.)

In the " Life of Bishop Wilberforce," the following reference to the interview with Mac Gregor is made in an extract from the Bishop's diary :—

Feb. 13, 1855.—Met ————————[6] a curious specimen of earnest, evangelical, Protestant men, very narrow and earnest, ready to burn a Tractarian or spend himself in preaching the Gospel to the

[6] A clergyman.

poor. A lawyer in the Temple, a bishop of Exeter on that side. Thought ill of Convocation because the Bishop of Exeter supported it.

In 1883 there is a note in Mac Gregor's diary :—

"Feb. 20, 1883. 'Bishop Wilberforce's Life' contains a reference under Feb. 13th, 1855, to my private meeting with the Bishop by appointment. But the editor put in a note that it was 'a clergyman' who is referred to. I wrote to the editor to correct this important error and to offer him the perusal of my notes of it as written by myself."

CHAPTER IX

IN SPAIN, AMERICA, RUSSIA, AND ELSEWHERE

FROM his youth up John Mac Gregor had a strong predilection for science. His early ambition was to excel as a civil engineer, and his first contributions to periodical literature consisted, as we have seen, in a series of articles to the *Mechanics' Magazine* on scientific subjects. Cambridge, however, gave him a taste for the Bar, and he had not long entered upon the duties of his profession before he cast about in his mind how he could combine them with his scientific proclivities. There was one man, Hindmarsh, who practically monopolised patent law, and it was into this department of investigation that Mac Gregor made up his mind to enter.

It would not interest the general reader to follow him through all the stages of one or two gigantic tasks he set himself to perform. It will be enough to say that he threw himself into this apparently dry and hard work with all the vigorous energy he had shown in other spheres, with the result that he produced several valuable books — " Specifications for Patents," a "Digest of Patent Laws," and an exhaustive work on "Marine Propulsion." He was also engaged by the Government to prepare the official Blue Book for the Patent Office.

Had he been a man of worldly ambition, had the pursuit of "filthy lucre" been the object of his life-quest, there can be no doubt that he would have taken a very high place, if not the highest, in this important department of law. As it was he made a very definite mark and his works were received with the warm appreciation of all the best authorities on the subjects he dealt with. A few notes from the diary will speak for themselves as to the force he threw into his work and the spirit in which it was undertaken, but the reader must bear in mind that concurrently with these labours he had the care of all the philanthropic enterprises described in the previous chapters of this narrative.

1852.

April 15.—Began to read with Hindmarsh. Read Patent Law.

April 15.—Worked well at Patents.

Feb. 14, 1853.—Thought of writing a book on 'Specifications for Patents.'

1854.

Jan. 19.—Began to collect cases for my work on 'Infringement of Patents.'

Oct. 30.—Began to write my book on 'Language of Specifications.'

Oct. 28, 1855.—My book on Specifications came out to-day.

1857.

Nov. 27.—Conceived the idea of writing a supplement to Webster's 'Digest of Patent Cases.'

1858.

Jan. 9.—Yesterday began my Digest of Patent Laws in the Library, hoping that God would give me strength to finish it for good.

June 7.—Finished my 'Patent Law,' book and index.

1859.

Feb. 6.—Woodcroft finally arranged with me as to beginning to write for him the two volumes on 'Marine Propulsion.'

Feb. 7.—Got columns of specifications from Patent Office and asked strength from above for this large work.

July 4.—Finished my book ('Marine Propulsion'*) begun February 6th with much satisfaction.

The compilation of this work was a most laborious task. Part I. was an exhaustive summary, with elaborate historical notes, of the principal British and early foreign inventions relating to the propulsion of vessels arranged chronologically with Abridgments of the Specifications of British Patents; in Part II. Abridgments of the Specifications of all the British Patents on the subject were given from 1831 to 1847, with notices of unpatented inventions and of experiments, and in Part III. the Abridgments to the end of 1857. The name of Mac Gregor does not appear in connection with the publication, the preface bearing the signature of " B. Woodcroft " (of the Great Seal Patent Office), and the date, June 1858.

It was no little gratification to Mac Gregor to

---

* "Abridgments of the Specifications relating to Marine Propulsion (excluding sail)." In three parts. With indices of names and subject-matter. Printed by order of the Commissioners of Patents. London: Published at the Great Seal Patent Office. 1858. Price 4s.

receive from such men as Sir Joseph Napier and J.
Scott Russell, warm encomiums on the "marvellous
research" and "conspicuous ability" he had shown in
the preparation of the work.

Two passages from "Marine Propulsion" we must
quote here.

In A.D. 1543, Blasco de Garay, a Spaniard, is related to have
propelled the vessel *Trinidad* at Barcelona, by an engine which
'consisted of a large cauldron or vessel of boiling water and a
movable wheel attached to each side of the ship,' that is to say,
propelled by steam and paddle wheels.

Although Mac Gregor quoted eight authorities giving
credence to this tradition his own opinion was that it
was not trustworthy and he determined to test the
matter.

The other passage relates to Denys Papin, natural
philosopher.

There are drawings still in the King's Library at Hanover, left by
Papin and Leibnitz, but not examined.

Soon after completing "Marine Propulsion" Mac
Gregor commenced collecting materials for a new
work on the steam-engine, projected by Mr. Scott
Russell, and in prosecuting his researches he visited
the Royal Library at Hanover and at great sacrifice
of time and labour succeeded in establishing the
claims of Papin to be the first who used a steamboat.

To investigate the Spanish claims he determined to

visit Spain. His first step was to enlist the sympathy and practical aid of Loftus C. Otway who wrote in reply to his application:

MADRID, *July* 25, 1857.

. . . . On receipt of your favour of 20th inst., I called on the Under Secretary of State for Foreign Affairs and fully explained to him your wishes and enlisted his good offices and interest in your behalf. He is shortly to send me a letter from the Minister of Instruction and public works with whom it rests to give the authorisation to visit the Archives of Simanchas. Senor Cueto (the Under Secretary) thought there would be no difficulty or objection whatever in giving you this permission, and said that Blasco de Garay's first experiment of a steamboat took place at Barcelona before the Emperor Charles V., and that an account of it has been published in some official Madrid Gazette, and thought if you made Barcelona your road to Simanchas, or returned home by it, you might probably fish up some valuable information in the archives of that city. . . .

L. C. OTWAY.

In due course a "copy of the Royal Order sent to the Archives of Simanchas to authorise John Mac Gregor to examine the books and papers on the subject in question" was received, and on the 10th of September 1857 he left for Spain.

Shortly before doing so he noted in his diary:

Dublin: Read my paper at the Section G of the British Association on 'Early modes of propelling ships.' Livingstone dined and stopped with us. Russell, Napier, Woodcroft, Moffat, Larcom and many others in the evening.

The tour in Spain was one of great interest to Mac Gregor. Paris, Tours, Bordeaux, Biarritz, and Burgos were visited. At the latter place he wrote:

Sep. 20.—Read Lucille with delight. In quiet walk saw from the hill the bull-fight with thousands shrieking delighted as the horses were gored and their bowels trailed on the ground.

Thence to Valladolid and Segovia, the Escurial, Madrid, Valencia, and on the 7th he arrived at Palma, Majorca, where he wrote to his sister as follows :

PALMA, MAJORCA, *October* 7.

. . The steamer to Algeria sailed on Sunday and thus after a good struggle to secure it I was baffled in my attempt again to mount the

IN THE MARKET PLACE, PALMA

delightful old camel and to rush, as I meant to do, to the Bedouins over the French Kabyles to inspect their enemies. Then I betook me to the Balearic Isles . . . . I like men and manners rather than the *thing* of the place to see. After stopping at Iviza, one of the Islands, and inspecting the Roman remains I came here to a capital hotel, far the best I have seen in Spain. At Iviza came on board two Spaniards who I saw at once were clever men. They turned out to be engineers searching for coal and when I mentioned my mission to Simanchas and my search about Blasco de Garay, one said: 'That is very curious indeed, I have just finished a volume of collections for the Engineer School of Spain on the same subject.' So we agreed to meet at Barcelona on Saturday week that I may inspect his productions and thus add a superlative gratuitous postscript to my present valuable information . . .

The streets are clean here. The women wear white lace on their heads instead of that universal mourning, black mantillas worn by the Spanish women—the ugliest dress on the ugliest women. Dear me, how a real English lady rivets the table d'hote and peers above these shrivelled, mincing, yellow-tanned Spanish women !

I am in rude health with a violent attack of moustache far more vigorous after one month here than it was after nine months on my Syrian Tour.   J.

PALMA, *October* 12.

The mosquitoes are the only drawback to Majorca. They were indeed most cruel to me. Though I tied my handkerchief double in

MOSQUITO PRECAUTIONS

a bag round my face and put the sheet over my head and panted inside, yet these extraordinary plaguers found their way in—dived their probosces into my cheeks through double silk. Sleep was impossible. In the morning, however, with healthy stomach and fresh mountain breeze one forgets such trifles and in a pour of rain I shouldered my knapsack for a ten miles' walk before breakfast.

I like all this a thousand times more than the beaten track.   Best
of all I like after breakfast in a new town to smoke a cigar in the
market and just stand and look on.   What a tide of new life one
sees.   Then meander down the street.   Here a man tinkers a pot in
quite a new fashion, there a woman with peacock feathers in her hat
sells forty-eight large plants for a penny, or 100 figs for the same and
the jabber and the talk, the guitar man singing the while and the
rosaries cried for a halfpenny and the priest with fat face eyeing me
askance.   Then I eat six peaches, twenty figs and five bunches of
grapes a day, and sketch a funny car with two poles and eight oxen
passing the chocolate man, with whom I chat and stare into the
barber's where fifteen men are talking their highest political themes
about how Spain will be ruled right well—some day.

All this will clear the cobwebs away for a right good hard working
winter, please God.

I find only one Englishman has been here for five years.   Dear
me! how that child is screaming.   I never heard such squalling
babies as in Palma . . . . In an hour I am off to Barcelona.

JOHN.

In continuation of his tour Mac Gregor visited
Barcelona, Perpignan, Cette, Nimes, Lyons, and
Paris, arriving in London in October.   He sums up
the journey in the diary by a page or two headed,
"Spanish Notes":

Boys play and whistle much more than the Italians.   Streets of
small towns more lively and noisy.   Basques speak much to horses,
saying, 'Arriva! Macho!' and all say 'Ida' for go on.   They whistle
to moderate the pace and say 'Wo-o.'   Very many dishes in no
precise order.   Music with very delicate turns.   Spanish ladies
accent with a drawl and persuasive lisp.   Servants proud and quarrel
with each other.   Great interest in knowing English terms.   Beat
the mules, though they show they understand words.   Lancer's
uniform red.   Officers great airs.   A bugle call turns out guard at

even and the officers stand with hats off for part of it—perhaps a National anthem. Priests chant and sing with bassoon and trombone to a lively air. Old and young men in church confess and are extremely devout. Space nailed down aisle for priests to go from altar to altar. Mules larger as you go south. Women with yellow petticoats over head, or red, like Galway peasants. Forty-four priests and acolytes servicing in Segovia and fourteen persons to hear them.

Sep. 23.—Walked from Valladolid to Simanchas with Mr. J. Ussher, presented Royal letter, but principal keeper absent. After five hours got admission, and with much persuasion allowed to inspect the two letters signed Blasco de Garay which Don Manuel Garcia, the gentleman in charge, said were the only ones he knew of. He said that there was no mention of steam or steam-engine, and that it was *un mensonge historique* to say Blasco de Garay invented steamboat.

The "notes" then proceed to give an exhaustive account of his further researches not only at Simanchas, but also at Barcelona and Paris, and how he ascertained beyond doubt that the Spanish claims to the invention of the first steamboat were without any foundation.

Soon after his return from Spain (April 14, 1858) Mac Gregor read a paper at the Society of Arts on "The Paddle and the Screw from the Earliest Times," illustrated by fifty-eight elaborate diagrams drawn and mounted by himself, as well as by numerous models lent from the museum of the Commissioners of Patents. In thanking him, Mr. Scott Russell, the chairman, said his admirable paper was calculated to promote the advancement of manufactures and mechanical inventions, and that his laborious researches on this subject and his judicious elucidation of the relation of these inventions to one another had conferred a lasting benefit upon mechanics in general.

An incident on the return journey from Spain was a visit to La Salette, a celebrated place of pilgrimage at that day, where it was alleged a notable miracle had been performed. Mac Gregor fully satisfied himself that the whole affair was a clumsy and silly fraud, and on his return prepared a lecture on La Salette which he delivered frequently for many years in the interests of the Protestant Alliance. It was a matter of great gratification to him when in 1879 a clerical organ at Toulouse announced that the Pope had pronounced against the alleged miracle of La Salette, and all representations therefore of the appearance of the Virgin in peasant costume to two children were no longer to be objects of adoration but were to be removed and destroyed. It transpired that Melanie Giraud, one of the heroines of the affair, had lived for some years on the coast near Naples and had professed to receive revelations and visions, which found many believers. The Pope eventually summoned her to Rome, subjected her to a severe cross-examination, and at last extracted an admission that she and her brother had played a concocted *rôle*. The latter was at one time a Papal Zouave and addicted to drunkenness ; but as even in that condition he always told the same story as to the "apparition," this was considered an additional proof of its genuineness. As a resort for pilgrims La Salette has long been thrown into the shade by Lourdes.

A few days before going on his Spanish tour, Mac Gregor, it will be remembered,* met at the house of his father in Dublin, the world-famous explorer, Dr. David Livingstone.   Livingstone had at that time travelled over no fewer than 11,000 miles of African territory, having, in his latest expedition, traversed South Africa from the Cape of Good Hope by Lake Ngami to Linganti, and thence to the Western Coast in ten degrees south latitude.   Then, retracing his steps eastward as far as Linganti, he had followed the Zambesi down to its mouths upon the shore of the Indian Ocean, thus completing the entire journey across South Africa.   He returned to England in 1856 to propound his views on the question of African civilisation by recommending the growth of cotton upon an extensive scale in the interior of the continent, and the opening up of commercial relations between this country and the South African tribes as a means of abolishing the slave trade and advancing the interests of European civilisation.

It could not be otherwise than that the heart of John Mac Gregor should go out towards the great heroic pioneer of Christianity in Africa, but it is not generally known that he was able to render him important services.   Not the least of these was that Mac Gregor placed his pencil at the disposal of Dr. Livingstone and illustrated for him his celebrated book, "Travels and Researches in South Africa," and

* See p. 203.

O

also arranged a reception for him at Cambridge which led to such important ulterior results.

We give a few extracts from the diary and from letters relating to these circumstances :—

1857.

June 4.—Conversed with Dr. Livingstone.

Dined at W. Taylor's and met Dr. Livingstone and made some sketches for his new book.

Nov. 18.—Wrote Whewell suggesting he should ask Livingstone to Cambridge. Yesterday, planted seeds in flower-pot from Crimean grave of darling Douglas, kindly brought by William Russell.

To his sister :

13,800 of Livingstone's book sold on Saturday, and so large a sale is only the beginning. When people hear of it they will ask for three times that number.

I am amused at your 'substantial and permanent gift' of £50, but hammer away, my lass. He is here still but soon starts for Portugal, and he will come back, please God, before he goes away with all his machinery. I hope to see the good man in a day or two. I went to Barnet on Saturday and found Wilbraham Taylor had a magnificent portrait of the Doctor, with his stick and cap, and Taylor sitting by him on a table. It is the very life-look of both of these excellent fellows. I went because Dr. Faa (queer name), a pope man, was actually to preach there out of doors. We found 200 people in the misty evening on the grass, and I got up in the chair and gave a quarter of an hour on La Salette which opened the eyes and mouths of the faces staring up at the lamp over my head. It was my first speech for nearly three months, and the bottled-up Protestantism was uncorked !

In March 1858 Livingstone returned to Africa to follow up the Zambesi expedition. Before doing so he wrote to Mac Gregor :—

18 Mart Street, Bloomsbury Square,
February 5, 1858.

In following out my plans for opening Africa to Christian civilisation, I intend to try and make the Zambesi a path of lawful commerce by stimulating the tribes inhabiting its banks to engage in collecting and cultivating the raw materials of English manufactures. Success in this will demand that the first efforts the natives may make should be encouraged even at a pecuniary loss as, if a man cultivates half a pound of cotton, unless he gets something like a shilling for it he will not feel inclined to proceed with what may seem so unprofitable a speculation. Mr. Clegg gave as much as half a crown a pound at first for cotton which brought him only sixpence at home, but now he gets hundreds of bales at about twopence or threepence. The loss which must be incurred I have resolved to bear until the sale is profitable, then retire for ever from anything like trade, for this employment I abominate. Now it did not occur to me till after you left, that Christian men might wish to bear a part in this which to worldly men may appear only Quixotic want of regard for the main chance. If the idea appears feasible to you, would it be well to ask your friends to raise a sum which might at your discretion be applied to sustaining a part of the loss I contemplate. I don't like to appear greedy and after all my countrymen have done I am sure my heart overflows with gratitude to them and to Him who put it into their hearts. This plan would assist me indirectly and at the same time aid the cause we all hold dear. The development of the African trade is not the whole object in view. We have our own population crowding on us in misery, and it seems absolutely necessary that free-labour-loving Englishmen should form a counterpoise to the slave-holding across the Atlantic. If we can have a healthy stand-up point, our enterprise and our Christianity may push its way thence to the unhealthy cotton districts beyond. To this my first efforts will be directed and it is of great importance that the interest which has been excited should be sustained and that is often done by people feeling themselves actually engaged in the work. This they will feel if they give of their substance for its promotion.

I say this though I really have a strong aversion to appearing greedy. My views reach a little farther than appears on the face of the exploration; the members of the expedition have each a practical object in view, and are expected to give a full report of the vegetable and mineral resources of the country. I mention these things in confidence and am,   Affectionately yours,

DAVID LIVINGSTONE.

In 1858 one of the saddest events in the history of Mac Gregor occurred. His brave and heroic mother, who had shielded him in the burning *Kent*, who had made so much of the brightness and beauty of his home, and had watched every phase of his career with tender solicitude, passed away from earth.

1858.

March 8.—Got a delightful letter from home. One end began from dearest E., and the other from beloved mother, with their blessed words meeting in the middle. This was the only letter I ever got of this kind though often both wrote on the same paper, one ending, the other beginning. Sorry I burned this letter.

March 9.—Day of eternal remembrance. Got telegraphic message to come home. 'Mother unconscious!' Left by train through Oxford and overtook Henry at Chester, and with him by Holyhead arriving at home at seven on the next day, when I found our dear one died on the 9th. On the 8th she was writing to Duncan, and at four God stopped her hand when in the middle of a word of love, so that she left the earth in the midst of her maternal duties. She was insensible all next day, and then peacefully left us.

March 16.—My father is 71 years old. My mother was 10 years younger.

The loss of his mother was a great blow to Mac Gregor and it was not for many a year that he could venture to breathe her hallowed name without a tear in his eye.

In July of that year Mac Gregor, whose fame as a philanthropist had gone forth to the ends of the world, made a visit to the United States and Canada, and even before he set out he was booked deep in engagements to preach and lecture. He was faithful to his diary throughout the tour, sent home a number of letters to his family, wrote a series of articles for the weekly issue of the *Record*, and in 1859, soon after his return, wrote "Our Brothers and Cousins: a Summer Tour in Canada and the States," which was published by Seeley, Jackson, and Halliday. The idea in the title is that "the American citizen is our cousin by nationality, but the American Christian is our brother at once and for ever." From these sources we cull a few particulars of his journey.

His remarks on men and things in the America of that day are graphic and amusing. At Halifax for example:

Five sedate judges are sitting out a five days' cause in the Courthouse and the eloquence of the Attorney-General and five other counsel is listened to with profound attention by the audience, consisting of one man. The good people of Halifax are too sensible to waste time in hearing arguments; and no doubt they will be content when the Chief Justice pronounces the decision next November.

Referring to the restless activity and constant hurry of the Americans, he says:

A quiet half-hour after every meal would be a specific for much of that restlessness which every American seems born to, and hence, perhaps, the thin-limbed men and pale women of the great Republic. One of these voracious citizens said: 'I tell you what it is, sir, I guess I have a good appetite and can finish my dinner any day in

INDIAN TENT

seven minutes.' 'Oh, that's nothing,' answered a sarcastic Briton; 'I have a hound that can bolt his dinner in three!' In another place two Yankees tried a race at dinner; but one pushed the pepper castor under the other's nose. He gave one cough and lost the race.

Mac Gregor's visit to America was before the glorious days when slavery was abolished. He speaks of the "darkies" on the American side of Niagara who would be free for ever if they could cross the river.

And they do cross it constantly. Only a few days ago two runaway slaves made good their liberty; and, as they left the other side, no doubt they hummed the tune of 'the land of the brave and the free,' as it is foolishly called by our good friends, whose flag has 'stars' for the white and 'stripes' for the black.

It happened to be Mac Gregor's luck to visit America at the time of "cable-joy" or "telegraph ecstasy," that is to say, just after the laying of the Atlantic cable. He made a few extracts from newspaper articles thereon :

A Chicago paper says, 'The world is finished, its spinal cord is laid, and now it begins to think!' Another: 'A cable it is indeed! To it is attached the best bower anchor let down deep in the hearts of two great nations, and its flukes are embedded among their living fibres.' A Philadelphia paper announces: 'Unless we have a national Jubilee, the pressure (of excitement) will burst the boiler of the American Republic and lay out the American Eagle dead as a wedge!'

He describes the wonderful illuminations and decorations in New York in honour of the occasion. One that seems to have arrested his attention more than any other, was a device over Niblo's Theatre bearing a single text of Scripture : "When the multitudes saw it they marvelled, and gave glory to God which had given so great power unto men."

As an expert "slummer" he kept his eyes open to observe the characteristics of the poor and he says :

I am once more forced to remark that the true type of London ragged boyism is never to be seen but in London.

In Washington he of course saw the monument to George Washington, and remarks : "If ever it is completed it will be like a great milestone to show how far the designers are from taste."

In the slave States it afforded Mac Gregor a great pleasure to take part in the worship of the negro congregations and to hear the darkie preachers.

Jim Hamly gave a sermon that was far better than any of the three white sermons I heard next Sunday. After my evening address the negro hymns and prayers went on for two hours. They sing and pray with a hearty vigour, that rouses in a sober mind the question, Does not our propriety often suppress our earnestness? Jim Hamly commenced his sermon by reading the verse 'Comfort ye,' and shutting the book he said, 'Perhaps you will wonder why I don't tell where the text is to be found; but I'm not yet arrived at the proper standing in the ministry for that.' Imagine the little blackie in light-coloured shooting coat ending his discourse thus, 'I may not have been just as eloquent as Volteer, or learned, like Cicero, or Cato or the other scientific theologians!' He often alluded to 'Calvary's rugged rock,' and one of his expressions was 'God will blow out the king of day that gilds the eastery horizings with his magnificent meridion ray!' but there were small and few grammatical blemishes compared with the insufferable ignorance and stilted pretentiousness that some of the illiterate white preachers begin their service by, and painfully continue till they warm up to naturalness.

In visiting schools and churches in the American cities, he says :

I was introduced as a 'friend of Captain Vicars' and no more was needed to ensure a most cordial Christian welcome ; for the lives and deaths of Vicars, Hammond and Green have been read as much here as in England. How little did those brave heroes think that their names would illuminate both hemispheres of the earth when their souls were shining in Heaven!

He found much pleasure in talking to the negroes whether in church, street, or hotel.

After a long talk with a negro in my bedroom he suddenly said, 'Sir, how far is your station from Ayshy?' meaning, how far is England from Asia, and he was sure we went always by railway. He added, 'Is England anywheres near Liberia? for there's a very pertickler friend of mine there !'

He did not always relish the company he had to mingle with on the river steamers, especially at meal-time. He seems to have met with some exceptionally bad specimens, and says :

I do not object to 'roughing' it. Few people like more than I do to consort with all classes ; but I do object to forcing those people to an apparent equality whose habits and tastes are different, and who clearly indicate that they are not at ease, by preserving a dead silence, and then rushing away as soon as possible from one another. It must never be forgotten that there are some people who do use salt-spoons and butter-knives, nail-brushes and pocket-handkerchiefs.

At Chicago he listened "with very great delight to a black preacher, in a 'coloured man's church' where almost all the congregation were fugitive slaves," and he adds "it was with the heartiest good will that I partook of the Lord's supper with the poor fugitives."

Writing to his sister he says :

BOSTON, *October* 16, 1858.

. . . . I wrote last to you from the middle of the Mississippi and nailed it on a bit of wood and threw it on board a steamer that had got stuck on the same bank with us and quite near. I got 2100 miles up the river. Well, haven't I had a wondrous tour ? Only four hours unwell and that a slight chill, nothing lost but the handle of an Indian pipe and a penny pencil !

Every minute of my three days here is all laid out for me by my friend Greenough and I must cram tight to do half of it.

To-morrow I shall hear Theodore Parker and go to a Quakers' meeting and a school at night.

I shall send one more letter to the *Record* to-night telling of my falling in for a Convention of Ministers on the Mississippi, 400 of them, and meeting Lady Head and Lord Radstock at Magasa.

At Chatham visited the nigger free settlement. How I do pitch it into the slave men ! 'I find quite as many gentlemanly minded negroes as whites,' and sincerely I really do. There will one day be a Civil War here about these slaves. This hotel is almost like dear dear old England. It has the first open fireplace I have seen for three months.   J.

Of course he went the "round of the churches," and some of his criticisms are smart and incisive, others somewhat caustic.

I tried to hear the Rev. Theodore Parker, so as at least to make one effort to ascertain his views (if, indeed, he knows them himself) and thus be prepared the better to combat his followers in England ! A Mr. Higginson of Worcester preached in his place to a congregation of about 1500. The preacher prayed in a strange mysterious manner as if he approached the Almighty with his hand over his face, and complained he could not see Him even dimly. His text was, 'They laded us with such things as were necessary' (Acts xxviii. 10), and putting the Bible carefully aside, forthwith left it and the text as a starting-post to run away from.

Mac Gregor made good use of the whole of the time he was with his "cousins and brothers" and tried to see every detail in the great picture that unrolls, as a panorama, before the traveller every day. But he left the vast continent with this question constantly in his mind: "Is this progress or is it only movement? Is it going ahead, or is it only spinning round?"

The final entry in the diary relating to his journey is: "Never had a more useful or happy tour, which for health and gladness could not be surpassed."

On his return from Canada his interest in emigration revived. While there he had met with several boys and girls who had been sent out under Ragged School auspices and he made exhaustive inquiries concerning them. He found that only one had failed and one was going on indifferently. Thus encouraged he put himself into communication with the gentlemen officially employed by Government to assist and direct emigrants from England, and was able from his recent experiences to give many useful hints, and above all to tell of the success of those who had gone out and to furnish the gratifying news that there was room for thousands upon thousands more.

In the summer of 1859 Mac Gregor set forth on

another long tour, joining at Antwerp the flood of
English travellers that spreads over Europe every
year and leaves its golden track behind. Passing
through Hanover, Hamburg, and Lubeck, he took
ship to Cronstadt, and arrived in St. Petersburg in
time for the fête of the assumption of the Virgin Mary.
The ceremonies of the Greek church did not shock
him as did those of the Roman Church, while the
music fairly captivated him.

The music from well-tuned voices subdued into a blandishing
minor key fills the dome from an invisible source, so unlike the
Pope's plan that enables you to see the grimaces of the flute player
and the wagging of twenty fiddlesticks. All this is so much better
managed by the Greek that I cannot but wonder how it is our High
Church friends in England do not follow the Czar rather than the
Pope when they seek for new or old crotchets on religion under the
name of proprieties.

A short stay in Russia, however, brought out all his
strong Protestant feelings, and he tars with the same
brush both Greek and Latin churches :—

The Papist exalts one woman above all mankind and debases ten
thousand in the forced celibacy of the Convent. The Greek
worship forbids our sisters to stand near the place where God is
supposed to reside, though His Son, when on earth in veritable
presence, suffered a Magdalene to bathe his sacred feet with tears.

From St. Petersburg he struck off for a journey of
a thousand miles to visit the Great Fair of Nijni
Novgorod, where Chinese and Tartars and all nations
meet on the Volga. Quitting the railway about five

hours short of Moscow, he determined to push his
way on by boat, and· persuaded an Englishman, a
fellow traveller, to accompany him.   It was a new
excitement to get out of a railway carriage at a town
where inquiries were to be made about steamboats,
to find them, and to take berths without the knowledge
of a word of Russ, and without any courier or interpreter.

Once on board the river, navigable for 3000 miles
or more, he found plenty of work for pen and pencil;
shoals, rocks, and sands abounding on all sides;
entangled trees, rafts, and countless barges and boats
clogging up the widest channels.   He describes
graphically the national tea-drinking habits of the
Russians :—

At all times, and in all parts of this mighty empire he can get it
good, and drinks it without stint.   A little tray is brought in with a
glass tumbler and saucer, and a tea-pot of very small size, and a large
one full of hot water.   No milk is to be used.   The tea is poured
into the saucer of glass, and the Russian, taking a lump of sugar
between his teeth, holds the saucer in both hands, with the elbows
resting on the table, as he sucks the genial beverage through the
sugar, and thus glass after glass disappears between his beard and
moustache, while the little tea-pot is drenched over and over again
from the large water vessel, and the oftener the water is renewed the
Russian seems more decidedly to think the tea is better than before.

The boats on the Volga greatly interested him.

There is a train of them ascending with 10,000 good tons of
goods, several of the largest being 400 feet long, and bearing 1500
tons on one keel.   They are pulled up by a huge vessel carrying 150

horse, which work, by fifty at a time, a great wheel that winds up an enormous cable attached to an anchor carried out in advance from time to time.

He was much struck with the punctilious courtesy of the Russians, exceeding any code of manners with which he was acquainted, even the lowest carter taking off his hat to his equal friend; but "when two

FAIR OF NIJNI NOVGOROD

great hairy fellows," he says, "set to work energetically kissing each other, it becomes ridiculous, and one is almost reminded of the hugging of two bears."

The great Fair of Nijni Novgorod, held in a large tongue of land formed by the confluence of the Oka river with the mighty Volga, he describes as "one of the grandest sights in the world for modern travellers to see."

Probably no Englishman ever saw more of the

Fair in the same space of time than Mac Gregor. He was here, there and everywhere, simply revelling in the enjoyment of the scene; now driving amongst a hundred Kalmucks, bargaining for apples at the women's stalls, tasting the milk in little jars of bark, jumping from stage to stage over the mass of floating houses, rafts, boats, and barges; mingling

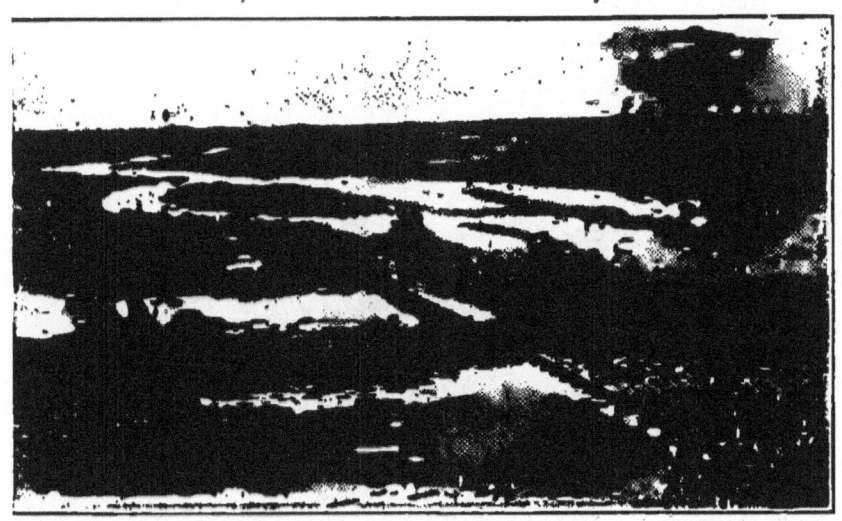

FAIR OF NIJNI NOVGOROD

with the dense mass of human beings eating, drinking, laughing, sleeping, shouting, and doing everything except business; or joining the money changers with their scales and weights, and scores of silver pieces lying under glass cases.

He visited the Chinese Quarter, and drank tea inordinately. He went into eating houses for curious fare, into the dreary wooden buildings where the scant amusements were offered, into clothing bazaars, and

into the Iron Quarter, where whole miles of streets
were filled with iron in every shape and stage of
manufacture; and throughout his stay he had the
pleasure of knowing that he was the gazing-stock of
every one he passed, that his Glengarry cap was the
novelty of that season's Fair, and that he was the only
Englishman then at Nijni for the sole purpose of
seeing the Fair.

TARANTAS TO MOSCOW

Nijni was the farthest point in his journey, and he
summed up his experience of the Great Fair thus :—

It is a wondrous sight to see—a crowd without the usual con-
comitants we Englishmen expect in all crowds—a multitude without
confusion—an intensity of traffic without a deadlock—an improvised
city without the evils of a town—a Babel of languages which nobody
but the English stranger has a difficulty in understanding.

To reach Moscow MacGregor had to travel night
after night by tedious stages, "without any excitement

except that of fifty bumps a minute ;" and getting tired of this mode of travelling, he and a young officer of engineers straight from the war with Schamyl, started off in a country cart with a bundle of hay, a string of biscuits, and a bushel of apples, under a contract with the driver to take them a hundred miles in twelve hours ; and how the journey ended he tells in the following letter to his sister :—

Moscow, *September* 17, 1859.

Charming, and well, and browned to any mahogany. I've had rather hard work, too, and last night, arriving here, got between the sheets again the first time for very nearly three weeks. The description of the Fair I will send to the *Record*, and my three days of additional waiting, because I would not start on Sunday, enabled me to get some additional walks there, to see the thing very thoroughly, to make a careful sketch, and to write a careful description. So, as usual, one does not lose at all by keeping the fourth commandment.

It was a curious feeling to be left alone in the middle of Russia. We had three days, villainous days, on a most uninteresting road, and at last a fine young Russian engineer officer from the Caucasus and myself took a common cart and set off at a tremendous pace to finish the last hundred miles, and save a night's wretched half-sleep. Our last three horses did forty miles in five and a half hours with much horrible bumping. However, it's all over, and one forgets it.

Moscow, utterly different to any other town, a fairy scene that can never be described or forgotten, with its domes and minarets of brilliant colours, its green-roofed houses embedded in trees beside the winding river, and above all the solemn tones of a thousand bells blended into one mighty swelling ceaseless sound, made the soul of Mac Gregor rejoice ; and again we

P

find him speaking a good but guarded word for the Greek church :—

The constant bowing, and crossing, and kneeling till the forehead touches the ground, or, with a step aside, till the lips kiss the frame of some sacred picture—these constant and various physical acts, repeated on all sides of you, and seemingly at the will of the worshipper, without any order—give to the Greek form of worship a peculiar interest, not altogether unpleasing, for there is, apparently at least, much of devout adoration mingled with the ignorant idolatry.

It was almost always Mac Gregor's good fortune to visit particularly interesting places at particularly interesting periods, and while he was in Russia he had the advantage of witnessing the great imperial displays in St. Petersburg in honour of the heir of the Czars who had come of age to reign, and of being present at the entry of the conquered Schamyl, who was said to have cost the Russians 20,000 men annually for many years.*

The former event nearly cost him his life. At one particular corner he posted himself among a seething crowd to witness the passing by of the Emperor and his suite, and perhaps for the first time in his life he felt frightened.

The shrieks of women were loud and piercing, and, finding I was being carried towards a canal, I made a desperate effort, and was only just able to rescue myself, when the iron rail gave way,

---

* Mac Gregor says, " Few that went down to the Caucasus ever came back. We met one soldier who had been nine months walking back from this distant seat of war."

and, amid fearful screams and shouts in a hoarse key, more than thirty people fell over into the water, deep down below. A scene of much sorrow and little bravery then occurred, and several people were killed in my sight, and large numbers wounded.

In a letter to his sister written from St. Petersburg, he sketches the outline of his return journey to London :

PETERSBURG, *September* 20.

Think how delicious to find your letter and one from Hany my worthy dragoman in Palestine—sent home by Mr. Taylor, to whom I had recommended Hany in Toronto. What odd events. Glorious weather, and all the place astir, to prepare for the evening's grand event, the coming of age of the future Emperor —and a letter from my clerk showing (so far) no need to rush back for the American business, but I expect his and your next letters at Stockholm, and as I may never be in this place again, I hope to take a look at one or two towns in Finland—Sweaborg, Helsingfors, and Abo, so as to start from this next Friday (this is Tuesday), and come back across Sweden.

Nice sermon on Sunday, and Sacrament. I have caught up my friend W. here, having stopped my two Sundays, and yet have seen more than he has.

How many mercies to be enjoyed ; perfect health, good news from you, delicious travel and fine weather, and no call to business for at least a fortnight, by which time I may be nearer you.

And now farewell for a little. J.

We shall only refer to one more incident of this tour—an incident which causes him to chronicle a new experience :

With my French friend I set off to Dannemora where we inspected the oldest iron mine in Sweden, and the richest iron ore in the world. Our horses did not complain after eighty-four English miles in one day, but it is a sight that is better divided when you

DESCENT OF THE DANNEMORA MINE

have so much walking, at least four hours of it besides. The sight, however, is worth all the trouble. Conceive an enormous chasm, 500 feet deep, with an area of several acres, and perpendicular, black, rocky sides, not unlike the crater of Mount Etna, especially when the blastings of the rock beneath fill the bottom with a languid floating whitish smoke.

Here and there, far, far below you, are the miners labouring away and looking like specks of brown dust. At twelve o'clock their preparations are complete and they move towards the various buckets, lowered to the bottom from engines at the top worked by oxen turning great wheels that wind up the thin wire rope, not at all larger than a bell-rope for a bedroom. A long-drawn musical shout from the dark gulf below tells that the men are ready, and the oxen soon begin their slow-paced, weary rounds. The explosions that follow are among the grandest sounds that one can ever hear. Nothing but this ever seemed to me more awful than thunder, even when the voice of the skies is heard over the cauldron of Niagara, or deep down in the centre of Vesuvius.

We determined to make a descent into this wonderful place, and a large bucket was attached to the rope. It was an exciting thing enough to be one instant safe on *terra firma*, and a moment afterwards to be launched out over the brink, three of us standing together clinging to each other, and suspended over a yawning cavern of which we could not see the bottom, but where St. Paul's, if it stood there, would be far, far below us. The sensation was certainly more powerful because of the ample width of the sides, the complete dependence upon your holding on, and the very thin rope that kept ever slowly unwinding from above. The descent into a coal-mine is far less impressive because the shaft is so narrow that you retain at least the impression of being near the sides and cannot realise the depth below. As we swung round and round the grandeur of the scene was displayed to perfection. Here was a mighty rock projecting some hundred feet into the smoky nothingness, and there a magnificent arch, under which the Monument could stand with ease. Some of these arches opened into other mines and were 'tinted with the light of day, while others led to endless galleries, all cut out by human hands. The smoke at the bottom was as white as milk, and the water was frozen as we 'landed.' The scene beheld in looking upward I cannot even attempt to describe. It was very interesting to compare the feelings experienced here with those I had last summer in the cave of Kentucky, said to be the largest in the world. The iron mine at Dannemora is far the better sight of the two. Next there was a deep, dark hole to descend, about 400 feet of iron ladders, but this is more like what one can see in England, and I need not, therefore, describe the place.

The experiences of Mac Gregor in the deep places of the earth formed the subject of one of his most interesting lectures, which he entitled "Rob Roy Underground."

CHAPTER X

THE LONDON SCOTTISH

THERE was never a more peace-loving man than John MacGregor, and yet few ever believed more firmly than he in the doctrine that the "best way to ensure peace is to be prepared for war." He would not for the world harm a fellow creature if he could help it ; but if he could not help it he knew exactly where to plant his fist with the greatest advantage.

He felt that the safety of the individual depended in large measure upon being able to defend himself, and that the safety of the nation depended upon the strength and courage of trained men who, in the event of the "regulars" being called away into active service, should be able and willing to take their place in protecting the country.

In May 1856 the great National Thanksgiving for the restoration of peace, after the horrors and terrors of the Crimean War, was celebrated in London and throughout the country. Within a year a feeling of insecurity began to manifest itself in consequence of persistent allegations that the national defences were insufficient and, in consequence, the Victoria Rifles, and one or two other corps, were formed.

In May 1859 notice was issued from the War Office sanctioning the formation of Volunteer Rifle Corps, as well as of Artillery Corps in towns where there were forts or batteries. The movement spread with great rapidity throughout England and Scotland, and within a year or two, many thousands of volunteer riflemen were enrolled.

On the 4th of July 1859, a great public meeting of Scotsmen was held in London, the outcome of which was the "crack" regiment, the London Scottish.

It would be out of place to give anything like a history of the Volunteer movement in general, and the London Scottish in particular, in these pages, but a few brief notes may perhaps assist some readers to get a clearer understanding of the matter now under treatment.

In 1860 the whole volunteer force of the country numbered 133,342 men, and in that year the National Rifle Association was formed, which inaugurated those great yearly meetings held till 1889 at Wimbledon (and since removed to Bisley near Woking), where many thousands annually competed for prizes.

In January 1860, the London Scottish was accepted by the military authorities as a battalion of six companies of 100 men each. The kilt was worn at first by only one company, later by four companies. until in 1866 the whole of the regiment was put into that dress.

Field-Marshal Lord Clyde, G.C.B., was honorary Colonel from 1861 to 1863, Lieutenant-General Sir J. Hope Grant, G.C.B., from 1864 to 1875, the Earl of Wemyss, A.D.C. (formerly Lord Elcho) now holds the appointment. Lord Elcho was the first acting-Colonel of the corps, and he was succeeded by Major (afterwards Colonel) Lumsden.

The writer of a series of well-written papers on "Our Battalions" says :—

"The London Scottish Rifle Volunteers enjoy the distinction of being the only corps on this side of the Tweed clothed in the kilt, and perhaps more interest is taken in their welfare on this account. To the metropolitan mind the skirl of the pipes, the swing of the kilt, and the light jaunty step which appears to be begotten of the pipes, on all occasions and in all climes, have many attractions. Other corps may come and go, and the British tradesman observes them not, but let the 7th Middlesex (London Scottish) march down Piccadilly and he is at his door in a trice. Everybody seems to take more interest in them than in either of the thirty odd soberly clad battalions to be found within a very few miles of Bow Bells." . . . . "The members of the corps are as fine a set of fellows physically, socially, and from a strictly military point of view, as it would be possible to band together anywhere in the civilised world for any purpose. . . . I do not say that there is not as good a body in the volunteer service but I do say that there is no better. *Nulli secundus* might truthfully be adopted by them as their motto." *

Although it does not appear that Mac Gregor was present at the great meeting in London which led to the formation of the London Scottish (he was, as a matter of fact, absorbed in clearing up a mass of work prior to his tour in Russia), nevertheless we know that from the first his full sympathies were with the volunteer movement ; he was a firm believer in its motto " Defence not Defiance," and, naturally enough, his sympathies were deepest with the London Scottish.

Almost immediately after his return therefore we find these entries in his diary :

1859.
    Oct. 31.—Joined London Scottish Volunteers.
    Nov. 1.—First drill, with Snape and Girdlestone.
1860.
    Jan. 18.—Rifle general meeting when I was nominated bugler.
    Jan. 21.—First bugle blown. Westminster Hall.
    Feb. 4.—Rifle general meeting. Certainly my popularity in the corps is very dangerous to my modesty.
    Feb. 17.— With E. and A. to Westminster Hall where I acted as officer of No. 2 and at night Mac Kenzie actually said they were thinking of me for Major.
    Feb. 19, *Sunday*.—King's Cross, good sermon and then a discussion ; 100 at class at night. Could scarce keep out of my thought all day the idea of being a Major.
    Feb. 25.—Appointed Captain of East Company.

* *Volunteer Service Review*, May 1892.

Feb. 29.—Assembled my Company for the first time, 29 present, 44 names.

March 1.—To Millbank to form the East Company and met the Committee.

March 2.—Got name of company changed to 'Central Company' by Lord Elcho and Committee.

March 3.—First drill of my Company at Westminster Hall.

At the heading of the page in the diary in which the last of the above entries appears there is a note in MacGregor's handwriting, evidently written many years afterwards but with the same honest pride that characterised the days of his vigour, "My Company, L.S.R.V.!"

Whatever he took up after mature deliberation he carried on with enthusiasm and henceforth for some years there is scarcely a page in his diary that has not some reference to volunteering :—

March 16.—My Company which was twelve in number on Feb. 25 has increased until on this day, three weeks afterwards, it is eighty; of these seventy were present to-night.   I feel this to be a very great honour.

July 27.—Went to Wimbledon to fire, supped with Carlisle and told him of the kilt. [This was the first idea of a kilted company.]

Nov. 19.—Lord Elcho spoke to me at drill to-night asking me to act as Adjutant.   This high honour is certainly appreciated.

Nov. 20.—With Company at Sterlings.   First broached to them my kilt Company.

Dec. 4.—To Hythe and at mess.   Here Phillips whom I met in the train proposed me as chairman for a night and next night I was proposed as permanent chairman.

Dec. 19.—Finished shooting at Hythe, got fifteen in 1st class and went straight off to London where serenaded Lady Elcho.

CAPTAIN JOHN MAC GREGOR, LONDON SCOTTISH RIFLE VOLUNTEERS.

Dec. 20.—Back to Hythe to be congratulated as winner of a prize. My hits 28, Hoare 27, Saunders 26, Frost 25.

1861.

Jan. 15.—Began musketry class.

Feb. 20.—First meeting of the new kilt company No. 10 at the Westminster Hall.

April 24.—The Central Company presented me with a sword. Lord Elcho spoke.

June 4.—Wimbledon ; where I won the first prize of the Regiment, making 24 points at 200, 500, 600 in 15 rounds.

Aug. 14–17.—To Paris. In the kilt to Vincennes to visit the Tir Nationale for the National Rifle Association.

Up to this time nothing had ever taken the fancy of Mac Gregor so much as volunteering and in nothing else had he won so much popularity. He was master of every detail connected with drill, firing, and the hundred and one matters that are of interest in the career of a volunteer ; he threw his whole heart and soul into what he did, and his enthusiasm grew contagious. It is a fact within the knowledge of many that not undistinguished men * sought to join his company, many having for their main object, intercourse and perhaps friendship with him. And it is also a fact that wherever he went, he came in for applause, and that in whatever he proposed he had a following.

"Comrades of his in those times have told us," says Dr. Macaulay, "that often after a long and fatiguing day at Wimbledon, when many preferred returning to London on foot, John Mac Gregor was in the front,

---

* The Marquis of Lorne was in his Company.

followed by an orderly array, not of the London Scottish only, but by men of many regiments, the leader singing a cheery song in the chorus of which all heartily joined.   This joyous spirit not only lightened the weary way, but helped to keep up the patriotic and enthusiastic feeling of the early volunteer times."

The same spirit that animated Mac Gregor when his mind was occupied in finding out all that could be known about the Law of Patents and Steam Propulsion is to be traced in his activity as a volunteer.   For example :—On May 17, 1861, he read a paper, before the members of the Society of Arts, "On the Hythe School of Musketry Instruction in Rifle Shooting," a paper over which he took as much pains as if he were writing an elaborate book on the subject.   He traced the history and development of gun-firing, from the year 1430, and then entered exhaustively into the construction of the implements of modern warfare, and the best training for their use, mind, eye and limbs needing to be exercised and educated; the mind, to understand the reason for rules and their application so as to load, fire and clean the rifle with speed, precision and safety; the eye, to judge the distance of an object and to aim at it; the limbs, to assume readily a position that should be steady during fire; the limbs and eyes being tutored to act in unison with the mind, so that the finger presses the trigger during a short instant while the body steadies the rifle and the eye brings three points into one line.

Much of what he wrote concerning the Hythe

School, and the rifles then in use, is now out of date ; moreover the discourse was highly technical and would not be of general interest to quote from largely but it was applauded in the press as being exactly what such a review of the subject should be.

In like manner at a great Rifle Conference of volunteers, he read an excellent paper on "Card Targets, and a system of Foil Screens," founding his remarks upon what he had observed at the Tir Nationale at Vincennes in 1861, where targets of light pasteboard were in use which he believed to be better in many respects than iron ones. Although in practice the card target did not turn out to be the success he anticipated, the pains he took in experiments, in tabulating results and in preparing diagrams and models were as great as if he intended the suggestion to be a life-study.

Perhaps the thoroughness of his work on behalf of the volunteers is shown even more strikingly in the following circumstance. He was invited by the National Association for the Promotion of Social Science to read a paper at their great meeting in the Guildhall in 1862, on the "Moral, Social and Hygienic Effects of the Volunteer Movement." Few men were better qualified than he to sit down and write an excellent paper straight away ; but this was not his method. He would make his paper valuable as the expression of the opinion of every volunteer of position and experience, and to this end he sent out the following letter broadcast :—

1 Mitre Buildings, Temple, London,
May 6, 1862,

Dear Sir,

At the request of the National Association for the Promotion of Social Science, I have agreed to read a paper at their meeting in London this summer on the 'Moral, Social and Hygienic Effects of the Volunteer Movement.'

The testimony of volunteers qualified to judge will be of the greatest value for this purpose. I venture therefore to request you to have the kindness to give me information from your experience under the following heads as soon as is convenient,

(1) Names of various corps to which your experience relates.

(2) Are the men improved in manner, character, or conduct by becoming volunteers?

(3) What are the results in general as to idleness, dissipation and vice?

(4) How is the movement regarded by the families, relations, and friends of Volunteers, with respect to Social life?

(5) What effects has the movement upon health and strength, activity, diligence and fitness for business, and as a manly exercise and recreation?

(6) Pray state probable reasons for exceptions to general conclusions under the previous heads.

Yours faithfully,
J. MacGregor,
Captain, London Scottish Volunteers.

The result of this appeal was a mass of correspondence involving the most patient care to tabulate and arrange so as to make it of practical value, but he succeeded, and the London and provincial press bore unequivocal testimony to its abiding worth. We cannot give even a precis of the paper here, but a few notes on MacGregor's opinion of volunteering, taken from it and from other sources, may be useful to present and prospective volunteers. He held that the mere fact of wearing a uniform has as good a moral effect on a soldier as the academic costume of the universities has on a man of letters, and that habits of control formed in uniform are sure to affect the same man in plain clothes. He considered that it is a good thing for a man to be drilled, to keep silence when he wishes to talk, to give a loud and prompt command in public when shyness would keep him silent, to be ordered this way when he would like to go that way, to have in fact another's will as his rule; and to engage in all this, not as a pastime, but for a serious purpose and under the law. Moreover the volunteer makes new acquaintances, especially with his superiors, and at a time when he is observant and when they also are on their good behaviour. He is exercised in temper, patience, promptitude, obedience, punctuality and smartness, and he finds that success is attained on the old principles of right and wrong and these are thereby strengthened within him. Again, the volunteer learns to consort with other men, to persuade or agree to differ; to manage, or take part in, public business; to read with attention the directions of others; to speak with accuracy in giving his own orders; to write with clearness, and to rely with confidence on his memory. He becomes more patriotic, loves Queen and country better than he ever did before, and his respect for the regular army warms to admiration, for now he is half a soldier and can appreciate those who are soldiers indeed. He is rich, perhaps; but he finds a tradesman beats him at the target. He is poor, it may be; but he finds that true gentlemen are most courteous to him. He is a deep scholar; but he may be the dunce of a squad in the new school. He blamed law and the constitution for all his ills; but he soon finds that all large bodies must have heads and must have defects. He was, perhaps, a Chartist before; but his charter now is order, love and liberty. The moral effect of all this upon a man's character soon becomes apparent, and one aspect of it is well summed up in a note by an experienced officer: "The check is in the mixture of classes, producing (1) a dislike, which gradually becomes habitual, to do that which conscience or the decencies of society forbid in the presence of a superior; (2) the reflection that what is evidently objectionable, if committed by inferiors under our eyes, must be unbecoming and 'low' in ourselves."

The opinion of Mac Gregor, from which he never wavered, was that the minds and habits of young men were greatly improved by volunteering, and that the movement was the deadly enemy to idleness, dissipation and vice.

Although, of course, there was then, and is now, considerable difference of opinion as to the moral effects of the volunteer movement, there was and is much less as to its hygienic effects. The health of a young man is almost always improved when he is a volunteer. He learns to stand erect; he is taller when he is drilled; he becomes more supple as he

learns to wield a sword, to handle a rifle, to box, to
fence, to sing, to walk, to leap, to run.   He goes out
on breezy hills to shoot, and he never had so many
country walks before.   He cannot make "bull's eyes"
at the target if he takes much beer or tobacco, or any
spirits; nor will he win a prize in shooting if he sits
long nights in music-halls or enervates his heart and
brain by dissipation.   There is, no doubt, another and
a dangerous side to the question, but this has to do
more with the physical constitution of the men themselves.   There have been deaths innumerable and
chronic invalidism produced by exposure to heat and
cold, to night air, to over-fatigue, and such like, but
the blame for this rests more with the individual than
with the system.

With regard to the social aspect of the question
there is also, and always has been, considerable diversity of opinion.   Complaints were made on the one
hand that it broke up home life, and on the other that
it made every home a barrack, as so many volunteers
brought home other volunteers.   But the social aspect
has changed at different periods in the history of the
movement.   MacGregor in his paper to which we
have referred, sums up his remarks on this phase of
the subject thus:

The volunteers never can repay the debt they owe to the ladies,
to the mothers who permit, and the sisters who encourage, and the
fair friends who smile on the very system which abstracts those they
love from many hours of home society.   It is true that 'the Ledger
must support the Volunteer's rifle,' but the rifle would fall to the

ground if the women of England were to frown on it.   They will not frown on such a movement. . . . . They will still follow in this the noble example of the highest lady in the land and she will still befriend the volunteer.   The Government will approve them ; parliament will help them ; the army will teach them ; the press will encourage them ; the clergy will sanction ; employers will assist ; the rich will give gold ; the great will give influence : the wise will give counsel ; and, above all, God will give His blessing upon this great work, a pledge of peace, a living bulwark to keep Britain safe.

It must not be supposed that because Mac Gregor threw himself with such consuming vigour into the volunteer movement, he was less earnest in his philanthropic and religious work in consequence.   On the contrary he took that work with him and opened up a new sphere of Christian activity.   He was willing to share in all the manly exercise, the joyousness, the hilarity, of a volunteer's life, but he would only do so within proper bounds.   Here is an absolutely true story sent to me by one who knew him intimately :

" Many years ago a captain of volunteers, whom I knew very well, was one day in the office, when Mr. Mac Gregor entered.   After a little conversation together, and Mr. Mac Gregor had left, Captain W. said to me : 'What a fine fellow he is.'   He then said : ' I will tell you something that occurred down at Wimbledon.   We were a number of officers assembled together, Mr. Mac Gregor joined us. Some of the men were indulging in very loose conversation.   At once Mr. Mac Gregor said : ' Gentlemen, we are met here to serve our Queen ; let us not dishonour our King of Kings.' He then left the group. One officer asked afterwards, 'Who is he?' and the reply given by some one was: 'John Mac Gregor; one of the finest men that treads God's earth!' Captain W. then added: 'I can tell you that no one dared after that to indulge in loose language in his presence. The cry went forth, 'Here's John Mac Gregor,' and all unseemly language immediately ceased.'"

Such was his influence among the volunteers.

In an old book, printed in 1579, and called "Stratioticos," the author, in describing the qualities of a general of volunteers,* says: "Above all things let him love and feare God, and cause true Christian religion in his armie to be had in due reverence, in such sorte that his soldiers may perceive he is indeede religious."

And such a man was John Mac Gregor. In May 1860, almost immediately after he had joined the London Scottish, he formed the Volunteers' Prayer Union, on lines almost identical with the Lawyers' Prayer Union, to which we have referred elsewhere; on long marches he never lost the opportunity of speaking on topics which he held to be not only more important but more interesting than any others; and in his rooms there was always a welcome and an overture of brotherly confidence to any who came to him to speak on higher things.

---

* Volunteering is not the modern movement some suppose. The Honourable Artillery Company—the oldest volunteer force in Great Britain—received its charter of incorporation from Henry VIII. in 1537.

Among many testimonies to his usefulness found among his papers, I select the following :

My Dear Sir,

I hope you will not think me intrusive as a stranger addressing a few lines to you, but as the mother of three sons in the Scottish Corps, I cannot but express my deep thankfulness that it has pleased God to set over our own dear sons a captain whom *they so respect and esteem* as they do yourself. I earnestly desire the influence He has given you over them may lead on to a far higher, holier blessing than they thought of when they were led to join that corps.

But when I heard there was to be a meeting for prayer on the 1st of every month, especially for the volunteers, I felt so thankful, and though perhaps my own sons may not yet personally join in it, I trust their mother, in spirit at any rate, may unite her fervent desires for the outpouring of the Spirit upon all those who have so nobly and energetically come forward to fit themselves, if need be, to help in the defence of their country.

I am the mother of five sons, one is in Heaven, and my earnest desire and effort has ever been to train our dear children up in the fear of the Lord. . . . .

I have much, very much, I know, to be thankful for in God's restraining grace over all our dear boys, keeping them from the immoralities and follies which many young men indulge in, but a Christian mother's heart can never be at rest till she sees the fulfilment in those so dear to her of that blessed promise, ' I will pour my Spirit upon thy seed and my blessing upon thine offspring.' I cannot tell you how thankful I have felt for all our dear boys have told me of the influence you had gained over them. Beside the privilege of being a ' living epistle known and read of all men,' God has given you wisdom to understand young men thoroughly. I feel so thankful, for all can appreciate if they do not seek to imitate such an example. . . . . I should like personally to thank you for all your kindness, which I trust I well know as a mother how to appreciate. May you be blessed, and a blessing in all your undertakings. I can wish you in return for all the kindness our boys have received from you no higher blessing.

Believe me to be, yours gratefully,

———

If we have failed hitherto in making the reader understand the character and motives of the man who could win such gratitude as this, or if we have incurred the suspicion that our portrait has been too highly coloured, it will be well to let Mac Gregor tell us himself what he was in his own eyes at this period of his life. We repeat that he was not guilty of a habit of introspection. It was rarely that he wrote about his most private thoughts and feelings; he was too honest, too upright, too manly to pose in a diary as a sentimentalist, but he knew his capabilities, the estimation in which he was held, the snares that lay around his path, the failings in his own character; and so one Sunday night in August 1862, he fell a-musing and wrote down one of the most remarkable pieces of self-analysis that it has ever been our lot to read.

In a pondering state. How is it I have so few trials if I be a child of God? In the very prime of life now with every possible thing I can enjoy, and enjoying everything. No anxiety whatever, no care, no want, no pain. It is dangerous but useful to catalogue my good things. A high part in Protestant work, in preaching, in Ragged School work, in literature for the people, among the Christian barristers and among volunteers. I don't care for money, but ambition has made me wish for things that mere money could not purchase. To be a traveller; and I have seen nearly all I wished and have enjoyed twelve foreign tours. To be a good shot; and I have won a first prize in 1860, 1861, and 1862. To have health and strength; and God has given me both. I suppose that by working harder at law I could be rich, by working harder in societies I could be important, by working harder at books I could be a more learned man, certainly by praying more I could be more holy. I have less worry and anxiety about any earthly object than I ever had, and I really think this is not caused by any failure in reaching points I have started for. Humility would perhaps keep me from feeling all this, and mock humility would certainly keep me from saying it or writing it. But I have neither enough of real or mock humility to affect me. A very great yoke has been cast off that bound me now and then for the past three years when I always craved for distinction among my friends. The most careful, thoughtful, and deliberate conviction about this is that quiet, unobtrusive, gentle, humble piety—never once speaking of oneself—is the true way to be admired. I am perfectly well aware of this, and I know if I wished most of all to be thus prominent I should rigidly guard myself against what I am very, very remarkable for; boastfulness, rude pride with vain self-praise, and a yielding to the quick impulse of exercising authority, telling of every success and omitting no chance of promoting myself before my friends, not to say before the public. The rapid and frequent pleasure of doing this is more enjoyed than the deep calm sensation of being great, which a humble self-negation in these things would entail. Like other fields, this is one in which we distinctly go against the road that leads to happiness and belie our best convictions of the best way of attaining the most of it. I have gained vastly by coming to the conclusion that my present position in various circles—shooting, travelling, learning, profession, religion—is more pleasant than the attainment of higher posts if the strength for each, with all its anxiety, trouble, and failure, is taken into account. This is a very curious position to be in. With respect to religion it is a wrong one. There seems to be a level in all these points I have got to;

At this point A, and the supposition that there may be some great fall for me in one or all lines, makes it worth while to write down now and here this off-hand account of myself.

We do not propose to follow step by step the career of Mac Gregor as a volunteer, but his diary marks its progressive stages :

1862.

July 1.—Wimbledon shooting meeting. Fired for Queen's Prize. Started off with a bull's-eye, made 8 + 5 in 15 marks.

July 24.—Lady Elcho's cup and Regiment prizes.

July 25.—Won the cup. Score at 200 yards, 32. Score at 500 yards, 31. Ten shots at each.

July 30.—Found I had won the honour of being highest score, at 200, 500, 600 yards in the competition for Lord Elcho's challenge cup on the 26th, viz., 38 marks, which entitles me to have my name engraved on the shield.

1863.

Jan. 28.—To the range where I made

At 200 yards (10 rounds)		19 points
At 300 „ („) .		15 „
At 500 „ (5 „)		18 marks
At 500 „ („) . . .		20 „

In this last I made five bull's-eyes in succession, Hythe position, which I never did before ; yet this is the first practice of the season after five months of cessation.

Feb. 18.—With Lord and Lady Elcho to Mrs. Barnes's table-turning physical exhibition.

Oct. 7.—Wimbledon, where put up frame for cardboard target and walked back to London.

1864.

June 29.—London Scottish prizes. Fired for Lady Elcho's cup and won it.

1865.

Feb. 27.—The row about the targets began.

July 21.—International small bore match. Helped Ross and his men. In afternoon intelligence came of Cooper shot.

July 23.—Saw Cooper and wife again. It seems an age since they first knew me. Review. Had no heart to go and receive our shield.

Nov. 26.—With Inns of Court to see them inspected, which was useful and good. First meeting for the year of London Scottish in Westminster Hall when Lady Elcho gave our prizes and I took away her cup for the second time.

1866.

Feb. 2.—My company supper was most successful. The plate and music and dancing and speeches all much above ordinary times.

March 25.—Dublin. Boy to Highlander soldier. "Souldier you're cold with the kilt. And I am kilt with the cold!"

A few months later and there comes an entry which touches upon a matter to which we shall refer at length later on. From the day Mac Gregor wrote it, some of the old ardour for volunteering began to die away. It was a case of "off with the old love and on with the new."

July 21.—Wimbledon Review. Returned fully persuaded that the Canoe Club, of which prospectus is out to-day, is far better for fun, exercise and real amusement.

1867.

Nov. 22.—Mentioned to Lord Elcho about my retirement from L.S.R.V.

Dec. 17.—Meeting of my Company when I addressed them explaining reasons for retiring from command. All most kind.

1868.

Feb. 14.—Dined with my Company at Freemasons' Hall. This is the end of a useful, pleasant and intimate connection with volunteering as an officer.

Of John Mac Gregor as a volunteer, no one is more competent to speak than the Earl of Wemyss and March who, as Lord Elcho, was associated with the London Scottish from its formation, and did not retire from active connection with the corps till 1880 on which occasion he was presented with a fac-simile of the celebrated Elcho Shield in oxydised silver picked out in gold, the presentation being made by Mac Gregor on behalf of the corps.

The following extract from a letter from the Earl of Wemyss to the present writer will be read with interest, especially by volunteers :

"Of himself I can only say that he was a very dear and valued friend, a most able man, and one of our most zealous and efficient officers—none more so in the regiment."

CHAPTER XI.

CONCERNING MEN, PLACES AND THINGS

IT is somewhat difficult in recording a career so meteoric as that of John Mac Gregor's to give in anything like proper sequence and due proportion the full story of his many-sided activities—to see him at one and the same time as lawyer, philanthropist, athlete, preacher, traveller, author, volunteer, controversialist. In this chapter, therefore, we propose to gather up some of our dropped threads and so make our narrative as consecutive as we can.

The year 1859, the same year in which he joined the London Scottish, found him in the heat of controversy with many leading men connected with the *Reasoner* and similar publications. This was no child's-play with such opponents as the late Mr. Charles Bradlaugh and Mr. George Jacob Holyoake. A little episode relating to the latter will be read with interest. Mac Gregor wrote in his diary in 1858, "Called on Holyoake and had a most wonderful conversation with him, which I shall remember not only to my dying day, but for Ever and Ever and

Ever;" and at the end of the following year, in summing up what he considered its most important occurrences, he includes "Interviews with Holyoake,' of whom, as a man and a controversialist, it may be said here he always spoke in the warmest terms. In reply to a letter from the present writer, Mr. Holyoake says :—

EASTERN LODGE, BRIGHTON, *December* 16, 1893.

I remember Mr. Mac Gregor very well. He was in the habit of coming to my house in Fleet Street and next to Mr. Logan (a Town missionary of Bradford and afterwards of Glasgow, for whom I had much regard) I thought Mr. Mac Gregor the pleasantest-minded Christian controversalist who, in those days, gave us the advantage of explaining his views to us.

Mr. Mac Gregor had a frank, gentlemanly vivacity, always engaging to me. Indeed he had a love of controversy which only those manifest who believe they have the truth, and that it is strong enough to bear any ordeal of fair examination. He was at once inquirer and advocate—in my experience a rare combination. He wished to know and was not afraid to know. He had a dash of that boldness in disputation which we associate with Rob Roy—whose name he adopted. Though he had the full persistence of his countrymen in argument, he had little, if any, of that imputation in which Scotch controversialists often excel. I am pleased to hear he made friendly records of intercourse with me, but I think he must sometimes have confused as mine what I may have said to him of my mother, by supposing that I said it of myself.

To my mother the belief in a personal providence was an indispensable consolation.*

---

* This has reference to some notes of a conversation recorded by Mac Gregor, in which he states that " Holyoake when he was ill said to me that he felt the want of a person for his soul's sympathy, just as his wife was a personal comfort to his social life."

It was probably his fame as a controversialist more than any expression of his political opinions—for in this respect he was singularly reticent—that marked Mac Gregor out in the estimation of his friends as a suitable man for Parliament. Although on many occasions he was urged to stand, he invariably declined. Here is his comment upon one such invitation :

1859.

April 16.—Waldegrave came to me at the club and said he had sent my name to Birmingham as a fit candidate to stand against Bright.   Strange honour !

Honours of other kinds, and more to his taste, came to him year after year, and in 1859 he records with satisfaction his election on the Council of the Society of Arts, and his appointment as Lay Consulter of Sion College.

While each year added to his toilsome engagements —and apparently to his strange capacity to deal with them—there was nevertheless a certain hunger and thirst after adventurous travel which increased as the years advanced, and no schoolboy ever flung his cap higher in the air at the sound of " Dulce Domum," than did Mac Gregor when opportunity enabled him to "pack up his traps " and rush off to some foreign land.

In August 1861 he broke away from drills and firings, controversies and committees, and started off for the Danube, sending home from time to time, as had now become his habit, a weekly letter to the *Record*, giving an account of his travels, besides his usual interesting and chatty letters home. The voyage down the Danube "in a splendid steamer," past "fine old hills crowned by proud castles," greatly pleased him, and scarcely less so the towns of Pesth and Buda, centres of civilisation in striking contrast to the wild wastes beside the mighty river.

In the early stage of his tour nothing gratified him more than a visit to the cave at Adelsberg—the finest cavern in Europe. He says :—

It is never easy to describe a mountain, or a cave, or a waterfall, and the grotto at Adelsberg is not to be painted in words. The entrance is a mere hole in a rock, but almost at once you dive into a cluster of chambers pillared, domed and walled with magnificent stalactites. An excellent path, made by the Emperor Ferdinand, conducts us down, down and still down, into colder air until the river is found at the bottom quiet and clear. This is crossed by a bridge which the guides had lighted up before we came with candles, lamps and torches, so that the water glistens as if a starry sky were above it. I have seen the river in the Mammoth Cave of Kentucky, and the winding passages of the cavern of Montserrat, and the clustered crystals of the Cave of Arta in Majorca, but none of them are so fine as this of Adelsberg. The Cave of Adullam surpasses it in interest because there once dwelt 'in a hold' the Psalmist of Israel. But Adelsberg may rightly be called the finest cave to be seen anywhere. From hall to hall you advance for about four miles, and an unknown distance beyond is open if you choose to tire your feet and eyes. For it is no easy thing to keep looking at an endless variety of shapes and figures for three hours at a stretch. Here the pillars form as it were an organ ; there we find a throne ; next a cemetery with a hundred mocking monuments, all moulded grotesquely by the mere dropping of water. Many pieces are like most beautiful thin drapery with varied patterns of red, blue and white. Others sound, when struck, like bells, gongs or organs. The candles are placed by hundreds in one part to lighten up a noble chamber 160 feet high, called Calvary, and lamps, cleverly introduced in little alcoves, recesses, or hidden galleries, surprise the amazed traveller with new effects where everything is new.

Proceeding on his journey, MacGregor next visited the Isles of Greece. "The beautiful harbour of Patras," he notes, "is studded with English vessels, all filling up with currants."

I visited the gardens where these grew. They are in huge bunches like small grapes and the women carry them in baskets to flat floors where the sun dries them into the small black specks that we buy in London. Carried in sacks on donkeys' backs you find them next in piles in the cool dark warehouses and then they are stamped tight down into casks by men treading upon them with naked feet.

As a volunteer he kept his eyes open to observe the soldiering of the lands he passed through. He says :

The soldiers of Greece are a strange set. Here (Patras) there are far more officers than soldiers and they never move without sword and spurs. As for parade there is absolutely none and their drill consists in individual strutting about, which sort of independent manœuvre they certainly execute to perfection.

He describes the mingling of the bustle of Western commerce and the quiet, easy, dreamy life of an Eastern clime shown in the Greek ports, and concludes a long letter with this charming word-picture :

The evening sun gives a rosy hue to the bare mountains and warms the top of old Parnassus reared behind above them all. From the calm sky a most magnificent meteor suddenly shoots brightly towards the water and leaves a smoky tail that rests for some minutes visible in the heavens. The soft music of Greek singing is overcome by a louder and more solemn strain as a band plays the 'Dead March in Saul' at an English sailor's funeral. On the coffin is the clasp-knife of the dead man—a simple token. How his mother and sisters in England will weep when they hear he has been buried so far away! As the procession slowly wends by the calm water, you see the other sailors looking on, and even that boy, going to plunge from the mainyard into the water for a swim, waits motionless for his dead comrade to be carried past. The waves wash quietly on the shore, the moon silvering them. The red light of the pharos shines over the water, while a soft cooing of doves seems to win rest for a busy world, weary on a summer eve.

After re-visiting Malta, MacGregor managed to catch a little screw-steamer belonging to a Greek Company—"a steamer that bobbed up and down in the blue waves like a cork, so light was she"—bound for Tunis with a hundred passengers huddled on deck.

The weather changes far more rapidly in the Mediterranean than in other seas, and no one who is not a good sailor should risk a voyage upon a small steamer or a native vessel. MacGregor was, fortunately, a capital sailor, and this was his experience of the voyage:

A cloud passes over the sun and then a whiff from the breezy north and the captain reefs the sails and down comes a regular gale at once upon us. The sea-birds scream so soon, one wonders where they were an hour ago. With loosened sheet the little white-sailed vessels scud past us that we noticed fishing for coral, picturesquely quiet, but a few minutes since. The wind is dead in our teeth, and the angry sea washing that cape ahead, shows plainly what must be expected when we labour up to that point. Still we held on, and splash came the rising wave over and over, wetting the sails and drenching the hotch-potch of human life that encumbered the deck.   We kept on till dark—more dark because the white sea could be seen in it—but at last our captain turned the ship's head back again and ran before the storm.   [Thus I was just a week passing from Malta to Bona in Algeria which could easily have been done in two days by a well-found steamer.]

We anchored for the night under a high headland, and the forked lightning played around it for many hours, but I could not hear the thunder for the wind.   As suddenly as the gale rose the sea calmed, the air stilled, the stars gleamed forth, the clouds disappeared, and then the splendid moon came brightly into the heavens.

The "fiery, hot, and filthy town" of Tunis did not please Mac Gregor, but its surroundings did.   The sandlarks twittering on the beach, long rows of Turks groping for shell-fish some miles out in the shallows of the lake that divides Tunis from old Carthage, lines of camels winding through the olive groves and under the grand aqueduct that carried glittering water, in days gone by, to slake the thirst of Hannibal.

He was charmed with Algeria, the climate, the scenery, the people, and the mode of travelling, and prophesied that it would soon become a common part of the holiday rambles of the wandering cockney.

In one important respect he found the country unique.

You can breakfast in the hotel, furnished with all the luxuries of France, and you can dine the same day on a dreary mountain on the *Kus-Kus* served by an Arab in a wooden bowl, and sleep, if you have a leathern skin, under his black tent at night.   Now this is a manner of colonising thoroughly French ; to push their cook to the front and let trade follow.

Of course Mac Gregor made himself at home wherever he went. At Quelma, the old Roman Calma, he says :

It was a great fact for the little front shop, called an hotel, to have an English traveller, and I had to talk for hours to the neat little French madame, explaining British manners while I helped to unravel her worsted !

At Quelma he made up his mind " to plunge right into the heart of the country and go straight to the

MY SLEEPING PLACE WITH THE ARAB CHIEF

hills of the lions." With one Achmet for a guide, a horse without saddle or bridle to ride, and a mule with a cornsack to carry the luggage, he set off towards Constantine, over the mountains and down by the hills, threading the myrtle groves, climbing the rocks and steering right across the weary arid plains. After sunset he came to an Arab encampment where

R

he found accommodation in a hut of bamboo and straw just six feet long, eight feet wide, and two feet in height. The furniture consisted of a sack and a wooden pitchfork, and he tried to find comfort in the reflection, "What a gala day it must be for the commonwealth of fleas when a well-fed Englishman suddenly becomes their prey!"

But the hope of a lion encounter was not to be gratified.

The panthers here are numerous, and the hyenas come even to the farmers' doors; as for the lions, I did everything I could to see one, but I only heard the roar, and that is indeed worth hearing. . . . . I passed through the centre of the lion country, and felt all the time that there was a grand and new feature, albeit invisible, added to the scene.

He visited the remarkable springs at a place called Muskuteen ("Waters Bewitched") where—

In a deep valley, luscious with figs and melons, you find a mass of tumbled rocks all crusted with salt and sulphur and exactly resembling the interior of the crater of Mount Etna. A hundred little cones rise from the hollow-sounding ground to the height of ten or twenty feet, and water, bubbling, boiling hot, gushes from every one. The steam rises like the mist about Niagara, and the little rivulets of pure, clear, but scalding water rush together, circle round in eddies, burst here and there into pools, and then fall in cascades over a mass of lime, white as snow and ever increasing in size and changing in form, pillared, domed, crystallised, or as stalactites—the whole forming one of the most curious, interesting, and mysterious places in the world.

At the close of his description, he adds :—

Much as I like the snow-peaked mountains and the crags of the desert, I always find a deeper thrill in visiting caves and volcanoes and everything that takes one's thoughts down to that unknown centre of the earth where darkness reigns, or fire abounds, or the roaring waters boil with fierce heat, reserved for the future purifying of the crust we live upon.

That he "worked well" at his travels in Algeria there is abundant evidence. One extract, in illustration, from his notes will suffice : "My wretched horse was so tired, it was plain I could not finish the fifty-four miles still remaining for the day's work—this, be it remembered, after a few hours' riding already in the morning."

On his return journey he travelled from Marseilles to Lyons with Lord Frederick Cavendish and Sir Henry Holland, and with the latter from Lyons to Paris and London, and this was the beginning of an important friendship. He noted in his diary on the way home :

P. of Wales very strongly likes smoking, which the Queen disapproves. Used to ask Sir H. H. if he smoked. Once P., speaking to another, Sir H., speaking to D. of N., mentioned smoking with the President. P. turned; 'I've caught you, Sir Henry!' P. likes 'ten pins' very much and played with coat and waistcoat off at nights, glad to get away from the fuss and ceremony. Bishop of Ohio delighted with P. and came to several places to meet him again. Once P. heard Bp. of O. was one of the best players at 'ten pins,' so said, 'Oh, let us get him to have a game.' Sent to Bp., who was in bed, but at once got up and came and played. Delighted !

London thirty years ago was in a thousand particulars in a worse case than it is in to-day in relation

to its criminal classes. Then, crime was striding
rampant through the land, and the mind of every
philanthropist was on the stretch to know how to
grapple with it. At last, in 1862 or thereabouts,
when garotting had come into fashion, people aroused
themselves to consider the British criminal generally,
and Mac Gregor circulated pamphlets widely, asking
why violent criminals like garotters, most of whom
were returned convicts who had been transported or
imprisoned long ago, should again prowl the streets, a
terror to every one? How was it that crime, instead
of diminishing, seemed ever on the increase? This
was his answer, and in it he looked forward to what
was needed, and we can look back to see what has
been accomplished :

All the people in England are bound to consider the criminal.
Over and over they have been told, and they know it well, that without prevention criminals will multiply beyond bounds ; that prevention is better than cure ; that refuges are cheaper than prisons ; that
thieves cost less in reformatories than at large ; that the hand you
refuse work for in an industrial class may next year rob your economy
of a threefold amount ; that the homes and houses of the people
must be bettered if your own house and home is to be safe ; that the
children must be taught good or they will learn evil ; that sober
recreation must be provided or men and women will be driven to
drunken crime ; that the destitute must be relieved with discriminate
care, and the depraved reclaimed, and crime be punished with cer-
tainty and promptitude, as well as in justice and mercy ; and that sin
in its guilt and power can only be dealt with in the heart by following
the Way God has revealed, believing the Truth of Christ, and living
the Life born again of the Spirit.

Is that all you can say while we are being robbed and strangled?

Have you no new general principle to provide for all cases, no special method to stop all crime, no particular body to undertake the whole subject and rid us of its care? We reply, We have no new principle for dealing with evil, but we are daily improving the application and concentrating the action of the old principles. Crime is the result of a moral disease, which we cannot expel by a specific, though precaution can narrow its contagious spread, and treatment can mitigate its violent spasms.

Crime is the blaze of a moral fire. We can try to get houses more fire-proof, give the soonest alarm, bring fire-engines to assuage the flames, and fire-escapes to save, and the insurance company to console the loser; but fires there will be, and crime there will be always.

In devising, improving, and applying means, however, we may vastly progress. Indeed, we cannot sit still. The criminal himself in his own rough way, has fully awakened us to his case. The study of it is new, not fifty years old, but it is a hard study, and much has yet to be learned.

It was a peculiarity of Mac Gregor's work among the poor, as well as among the criminal classes, that he would never take his information at second hand but would himself personally investigate matters so that of his own knowledge he might speak with authority. And in these investigations he was rarely alone. So many men were interested in him that they became interested in his work, and thus his influence spread. The following long but typical extract from his diary will show the thoroughness of his inquiries:

Jan. 16, 1864.—With Drummond, Leslie,* Gibbs,† and Inspectors Rean and Power to East of London to inspect the low haunts of vice

---

* The Hon. Mr. Waldegrave Leslie, who married the Countess of Rothes.
† Mr. Gibbs was the Prince of Wales's tutor.

there. (1) Largest theatre, 1/- best, 3d. worst seats. Great stage. Jew proprietor. Crowded by men and boys. Dark in distance, and many evils there perpetrated. (2) Boys' penny gaff—all lads, 10 to 16. Wretched dresses and acting; nuts and oranges ate. Actor openly denounced boy for throwing nut at him, and pointed out offender saying he threatened him outside. Pantomime and comedy. (3) Music and acting saloon. Loft, with tables and forms, men and women drinking and smoking, and loud talking. Man dressed as Punch. Three German musicians, Punch, with hammer on seats for order, too-i-too-i. Boy sang of 'Gingham umbrella, name was Isabella, father kept barber shop at Islington!' (4) Great dancing saloon, hot, stuffy. Twelve women dressed jewels, red hats, short dresses. Sea captains smoking. (5) Another lower style of place. Comic Irish song and dance. Of six boys asked, only one went to school. Sole music here a harp. (6) Another great hall, with galleries. 600 people. Girl, badly dressed, sang stupid song. Nearly all audience sea captains. (7) Drinking saloon. Girls dressed in kilts moved among customers. Drunken man had a fight with the proprietor in our presence. (8) Common lodging house. Twenty present in common room. Beds and upper rooms miserable, but clean and orderly. (9) A house of ill-fame. (10) A lower kind of ditto, where negroes and the veriest beggars come. Wretched Hindoo lived there two years. Came from Singapore. (11) Another, same sort, where a murder was lately committed. (12) Music saloon, where man fought lately with spectator in pit who abused him before public. (13) Thieves' lodging-house. 99 in house. (14) New pork-shop being opened. A brass band in front with lights and windows open, and playing loudly to attract a crowd. (15) Public house. Old English jig danced to a fiddle. All through streets music of every kind. The missionaries from West End come here at night. (16, 17) Lodging-houses, in good order. (18) Sailors' lodging-house, most comfortable and clean. Sixteen beds, all separate. Good light, air, water, linen, and diet. Master once a sailor. In parlour, pictures of Great Eastern and Yankee clipper, a parrot, a dog, coral shells, &c. (19) Another somewhat like it, and equally good. Man from Ely once dismissed from police now a Christian. Swede there and open Swedish Bible. On Sundays has hymns and piano, and prefers Swedes to Englishmen. In yard a little alcove for laboratory, clean and lighted. (20) Fighting saloon. Two lads had a spar. Squared raised platform with ropes round, in room holding about 100 people. Master proclaimed, 'Young Jones and a friend,' and they shook hands and pummelled away. (21) Rat-pit, the largest in London. In a room holding about fifty people, a square 10 feet each side and 4 feet high. The rats in cages. Several dogs in the house, others brought for matches, sometimes twenty dozen of rats killed at once. The best dog would kill twelve in a minute. One little dog, two and a half pounds weight, kills five in a minute. The dogs bred in the potteries. The master, from Norwich, a fine, hearty, good-looking man. The rats are got from ships or sewers. At first they are so shy they will not eat in public, but soon get better. The man pitched the dead rats on a fire so that no smell is produced.

The last place we were to go to was the opium-eaters' saloon, but this had to be given up as one of our party had to start soon after one o'clock. As we came to each district, the police sergeant of the place was in attendance by private arrangement, and walked on the other side of the street to see 'all right.' In the dark alleys a bull's-eye lamp had to be used, and in one case a boy warned his thief companions of an approach. But deference and civility were universal except from some of the unfortunate women in the thieves' lanes. In one of these there were 200, all thieves.

To the theatres and saloons access was had by private doors leading behind the scenes, whence we could see the audience, and the strange hobgoblins, sprites, and fairies clothed with masks and wings or huge heads and beasts' bodies, all mingled in a crowd in the dressing-room, eating sausages and drinking porter through their masks. Lord Shaftesbury's Act now appreciated even by the thieves' who find their rooms made more comfortable.

It will be remembered that early in Mac Gregor's

philanthropic career he had laboured hard to procure proper legislation for dealing with the neglected children who congregated in arches and dark alleys or ran wild and uncontrolled in the large thoroughfares. It was a source of great satisfaction to him therefore when the Industrial Schools Act of 1866 (29 and 30 Vic. cap. 118) came into force.

That Act related, however, only to Industrial schools certified by the Home Office and under its control. It dealt with children under the age of 14, found to be begging, wandering, destitute, orphan, having parents in prison, in thieves' company, too bad for parents, too bad for workhouse, charged with offence (if under 12 years of age).

In itself it was an excellent measure, but it had one serious defect—its chief power was left to be set in action by anybody or everybody ; that is to say, by nobody. A clause—the pivot on which the whole scheme turned—enacted that "any person may bring before two justices or a magistrate any child found begging, &c." The power thus given to "all people" was employed now and then by a few active men, sometimes by an enthusiastic philanthropist, and for a brief season by the police.

If, however, any busy man, such as the master of a school, brought a homeless lad before the magistrate under this Act, he had to brave the question, "Why does this man capture a strange child?" He would have to spend days in inquiries, attendance and correspondence, to get the consent of some institution to receive the child, and, after all, the case might be dismissed and then the "any person" had the costs to pay.

The Act had provided for homes and teachers, and had conferred authority on Courts, and there were thousands of hapless ones in the streets who ought to have been in the schools, but there was no one appointed to put them in. It was, as Mac Gregor said, "as if children were struggling in deep water, and a receiving house was on the shore, and a boat, but there was no sailor told off to work it."

When he was in Sweden he found that the compulsory education scheme there was made operative, without being oppressive, by an agent in each district called a "Persuader," whose business was precisely what was wanted in England to make the Industrial Schools Act effective, namely, to take up the case of the neglected child, to lead with gentleness those who would not go unasked to school, and to bring under quiet authority those who must be compelled.

Mac Gregor determined to appoint a "Boy's Beadle" to exercise similar functions, and his idea received the ready approval of the Council of the Reformatory and Refuge Union.

After much difficulty in finding an ideal beadle the selection of a right man was at length made, and the oversight of his work fell to the lot of Mac Gregor and two other members of the Council. The beadle had no more authority than "any person" to deal with the neglected children ; he was neither constable

nor parish officer, he wore no uniform, but was simply
a man acting under a self-constituted society which
employed him to do systematically what any other
person was at liberty to do if he had felt so disposed.

The scheme worked admirably. Within a few
weeks the effect of the beadle's visits was appreciated by some, while they had a deterrent effect on
others. Magistrates welcomed him, and every institution for the poor throughout the metropolis perceived
the advantage of having such an agent. On January
1, 1868, a similar agent was appointed by the "Birmingham Neglected Children's Aid Society," for the
same purpose as the boy's beadle in London.

When Mr. Forster's Elementary Education Bill
passed into law, School Boards were empowered to
contribute to Industrial Schools, and to employ and
pay officers to do part of the work of the boy's
beadle.

With regard to the children amenable to the Industrial Schools Act, they divided themselves into two
classes—the visible and the invisible, the former being
the obtrusive sellers of newspapers, matches, and such
like ; "freebooters," and all undisciplined street-sellers,
loafers, and crossing-sweepers. For this large class
MacGregor pleaded that a few earnest business-like
men with large hearts should organise employment
and at the same time secure some education for the
children ; in short, should do for them what he had
done for the shoeblacks. If no such men could be

found, he urged that at least they should refrain from adding to the number of their classes by indiscriminate charity, falsely so-called. "I am glad to think," he said, "that I never gave a beggar child in London even a penny."

The children unseen, but who were amenable to the Act, were those in courts and alleys who, after school hours, were totally neglected — lively, wretched, smiling, dirty children, who at night ran in everybody's way, while they themselves ran on the road to ruin.

In dealing with these waifs and strays Mac Gregor ventured to prophesy that in a few years' time the School Board would become the most unpopular body in London—a prophecy that was amply and literally fulfilled.

For a time Mac Gregor in prosecuting his inquiries and carrying out his schemes became unpopular even with the Ragged School Union, inasmuch as he urged the committee to confer with the School Board so that all the voluntary refuges in connection with the Union might vigorously co-operate for the reception of children, and that the subscribers to Ragged Schools might be re-assured who were withholding their contributions in the hope that rate-paid free schools would at once do Ragged School work. But the unpopularity was only for a time, and in the end his judgment was fully vindicated.

In carrying out his innumerable philanthropies it could not be otherwise than that Mac Gregor should have to draw largely upon his private resources. These were fortunately ample, although he could not by any means be called a man of great wealth. But, like Lord Shaftesbury, he was made the almoner of others who could not themselves engage in active work, and we find in his diary a great number of entries such as this : "Miss Portal gave me £200." This was the same lady who, year after year, sent to Lord Shaftesbury a cheque for £1000 "to be devoted in whatever manner he pleased, to the welfare of the poor." Such acts of generosity and sympathetic co-operation in good and useful work, deserve to be had in remembrance.

If MacGregor expended his money freely he drew as freely on his store of health by working late and early. But the "cruse of oil was not impoverished." He wrote once at a very busy time :

Feb. 24, 1862.—Not quite well, consulted Dr. Ware. This, with one visit to Dr. Chapman when I had quinsey, and one to Ferguson on arm hurt by rifle, are the only occasions I have needed a doctor during fourteen years in London.

Turning now from the laborious to the more playful side of his life we may note that he always found time to keep abreast with the literature and science of the day. Even in the wilds of Algeria, we find him "lying down under a rock while the sun scorches the other side of it, and flies buzz, and lizards peep out, and a tortoise creeps slowly by, and a jackal steathily prowls from his hole," reading "Adam Bede."

Of adventure, and of national sight-seeing, he came in for his full share. He made a tour to the North, almost solely for the purpose of exploring mines, and one day he went to the Crystal Palace for the purpose of going up in a balloon. He purchased his ticket, and took his place in the car. But when the preliminary trial was made, it was found that the balloon was too heavily weighted, and MacGregor, greatly to his mortification, had to get out, he having been the last to buy his ticket.

For a time of real jollity and merriment, a cruise in the *Beagle*, a yacht of Mr. (now Sir) John Burns—will furnish a good illustration.

FROM THE LOG OF THE *BEAGLE*

John Burns, of Castle Wemyss on the Clyde, chairman of the Cunard Company, president of the Gaiter Club, and one of the heartiest, most genial and most hospitable of the Sons of Scotia, delighted to get together a company of kindred souls, and sail away with them in one of his magnificent yachts.

Castle Wemyss was, and is, the happy hunting-ground of princes and peers, of men of business and men of letters, of distinguished men in army and navy, of bishops and deacons, philanthropists, and good men and true, of all sorts and conditions, who have the good of the world, or of any special department of it, at heart. It was under this roof that Lord Shaftesbury spent a long summer holiday for fourteen consecutive years, and always spoke of it as "his home in the North," where "the place is beautiful, the house supremely comfortable, and the people of it kind, hospitable and pleasant beyond description."

It was here that John Mac Gregor loved to come, for his friend "J. B." as it was the custom of intimate friends to call Sir John Burns, was in full sympathy with his philanthropic labours. Being himself a well-known philanthropist and being also an open-hearted man, Mac Gregor found in him a very special friend to whom, as we shall see later on, he could confide in the most critical and important period of his life. And besides were they not both members of the far-famed "Gaiter Club?" a club organised

The Mann's dream after "a necht la Burns"

FROM THE LOG OF THE *BEAGLE*

for social purposes, such as walking tours in Scotland, in gaiters, and an annual dinner at which only humorous speeches were to be made, and where the rule was enforced "that at a 'Gaiter' there shall be no upright speaking!" It was alone worth a visit to Scotland to come in contact with the Gaiter Club, among whose officers were John Burns president, Cleland Burns secretary, Norman Macleod chaplain; while the membership was composed of such men as Sir Daniel Macnee, the painter, Laurence Oliphant, Anthony Trollope, John

Mac Gregor, Hon. Evelyn Ashley, Admiral Sir James Hope, Lord Kinnaird, Lord Kinnear, Sir William Thomson (now Lord Kelvin) and a host of others famous in literature, science, and art.

On the particular occasion to which we now refer, Mac Gregor was invited to make one of a small party for a cruise through the western isles of Scotland in the screw-steam yacht, the *Beagle*, 500 tons. The Beagles, as the shipmates were called, were John and Cleland Burns, Hon. Evelyn Ashley, R. O. Cogan, Captain Colquhoun, 15th Regt., Major Hay, Hon. C. Hanbury Lennox, M.P., Col. Lockhart, C.B., 92nd Regt., Col. Ross, C.B., 93rd Regt., R. Stewart Shaw and John Mac Gregor. Eleven men in a boat, for eleven days, "with good health and weather, good appetite and fare, good temper, and good company."

It fell to the lot of Mac Gregor to keep a log—not *the* log—of the *Beagle*, and it was written with such rollicking humour and in such a whimsical style, "taking off" in pen-and-pencil caricatures every person and incident on board, that the book was afterwards published by Sir John Burns, "for private circulation only," and some of the sketches were reproduced by photography.

The title was,

THE

TAIL OF THE BEAGLE

SHIP AHOY!

WAGGED IN THE DOGWATCH

BY ROB ROY

WITH SOL'S PICTURES OF THE PACK
CHUCKED TO THE KENNEL
BY THE WHIPPER-IN

MDCCCLXV

The book bristled with jokes that have now lost their point, but we reproduce a page of the log, and a few of the sketches.

Although when MacGregor had a special chance of thorough enjoyment, he went into it with tremendous gusto, he never forgot for a moment the true ends and aims of life. More than a quarter of a century after the Beagles had finished their cruise with all its pleasant accompaniments of fun and nonsense, and not long before MacGregor had passed away to his final home, one of the Beagles wrote to Mrs. Mac Gregor, a letter of condolence, and referring to his long friendship with her husband, said :—

I often think of our happy days together, and never forget our first really *knowing* each other. It was on board the good ship *Beagle* in one of the sixties, and we cruised on the West Coast for some eight or ten days—such a happy party. On getting to Stornoway, Sir James Matheson hospitably rigged up a ball and invited all the Beagles. Rob Roy and I elected to take a moonlight turn on the island while the others danced, and that lovely long moonlight night's walk passed like a Midsummer Night's Dream ; the beauty of the scene and the charm of my companion's conversation left a *deep* mark. I had not then realised the power I was wasting, and his earnest, cheery talk gave me a new view of the Higher Life.

We close this chapter concerning men, places and things, with a few selected passages from the diaries

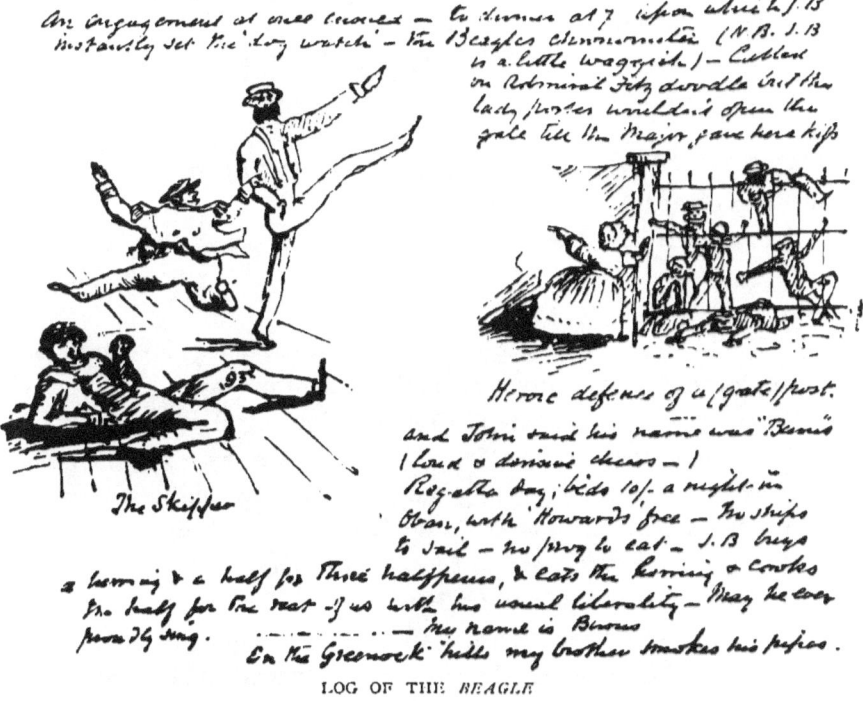

LOG OF THE *BEAGLE*

of Mac Gregor, which point the current of his thoughts, give an insight into his manner of life, and introduce us to some of the people he met.

1863.

June 14.—To Westminster Abbey where Hoare, Dean of Waterford, preached a plain thorough Gospel sermon in manly English, his fine voice filling the crowded, vaulted and noble space. Middle class congregation, with good church service and hymns sung by all.

Verses of it printed in large type or sheets suspended on the dear old pillars. The whole air and circumstance of this special service most deeply impressive. Cathedrals thus used are not in vain. Sermons like this, in places like that, are bonds of love between the church and the middle class of old England. There was nothing Popish in the service and nothing at all maudlin. Lord Dudley sat next some common man, no pew, each man on plain chair and at least 1500 listeners. A splendid sight.

Sept.—Wrote several articles for *Punch* about this time—one a dictionary of ladies' dress.

1864.

April 13.—To Duchess of Sutherland's splendid party where introduced to Garibaldi.

Dec. 22.—Dined Lord W. Russell to eat a swan. Walked with Snape.

1865.

Jan. 7.—Wrote to *Mechanics' Magazine* claiming invention of electro-locomotive by current along the rails of railway.

March 13.—At the House of Commons looking at the buzzing of business round the door, just like a beehive. On my return found a letter from Mr. Baxter offering me Parliamentary business—which offer will I hope be an episode in my life.

March 14.—Saw Baxter and accepted his offer.

March 15.—First retained for Parliament.

March 21.—First appearance in Committee of House of Commons.

April 30.—Met Vambéry the Hungarian traveller, and had intensely curious confab with him. For years he travelled as Dervish in Central Asia. For three months in the sun as a beggar picking vermin and without shoes. Found it hard to sleep without fez cap and so cut a hole each night. Found MS. 1500 years old about tea.

May 15.—To shoot and in the wind, made 39 at Queen's ranges. Charles being ill I hurried back by 5.10 train which at Nine Elms ran violently into a goods train and wounded twenty persons and some dangerously. The sudden sensation was, 'Death now—good-bye world—what shall I see first in Heaven?' then a tableau of my past life spread at once before me. Thrown violently on my head protected by my hat and then got out and attended to the fainting and bleeding and off to a cab and to the Agricultural Hall where worked till late at the Exhibition.

May 16.—Thankfulness for yesterday's preservation. Could not sleep with pain in head and heart. At the Exhibition again.

May 19.—A grand day indeed. The opening of our International Reformatory Exhibition at the Agricultural Hall by the Prince of Wales. Early there and got all finally in order. The whole passed off splendidly. I was presented to the Prince by Lord Shaftesbury with Hanbury and Cave.

May 22.—Wet day. Laurence Oliphant told me he was now a firm believer, and his mother says he reads and prays. We had a useful conversation.

June 13.—First stone laid of our new Field Lane School after 23 years' work at the old.

Oct. 23.—Officer of Sherman's called on him. 'Wal, general, how are you? don't know me?' 'No.' 'Wal I was one of your bummers' (commissariat). 'And how did you get on?' 'Wal, I guess you and me bummed away pretty considerable social.'

Dec. 18.—Temple Lending Library here, 1st committee meeting. These rooms have been the birthplace of Open-air Mission, Refuge and Reformatory Union, Volunteers' Prayer Union, Lawyers' Prayer Union, Pure Literature Society.
1866.

Jan. 24.—Birthday, 41 years of age. I feel quite as buoyant as ten years ago. Mercy and truth have followed me and the trial of prosperity is still continued.

Feb. 3.—My father on his way to serve on the Royal Commission in Dublin about Constabulary called to see me. Dear, dear man.

Feb. 20.—Dined Lord Ducies. Met Sir H. Havelock.

March 17.—Ware told me a good story. A friend examining youths in spelling for Electric Telegraph Company rejected one because he often spelt *is* with an h. Next day the father wrote to say he was much disappointed his son failed but he had since looked in the newspapers and found that the word *is* was spelled just as often with an h as without it !

April 3.—With Mr. Gladstone and daughter on board Lawton's yacht *Lenore* and then Mrs. Warren asked me to meet them at dinner. Here had most intensely interesting confab with Chancellor of Exchequer on following subjects among others—shoeblacks ; crossing-sweepers ; Refuge Field Lane ; translation of Bible ; Syria and Palestine Fund ; Return of the Jews ; Iron, brass and stone age ; Copper ore, Canada ; bridges in streets ; arching over whole Thames ; ventilation of London ; *Ecce Homo ;* Gladstone's letter to author and his reply in clerk's hand to keep unknown ; speculation as to his being a young man who wrote it ; Language of Sound at Society of Arts ; Dr. Wolff's Travels ; Vambéry and his travels ; poster with Reform resolutions at Norwich ; use of the word 'unscrupulously ; ' marginal notes on Scripture. Took leave deeply impressed with the talent, courtesy, and boundless suppleness of Gladstone's intellect and of his deep reverence for God and the Bible and firm hold of Christ.

April 25.—Called on Gladstone.

April 29.—With Wood to Gladstone's refuge ; service intoned by man in white.

July 16.—Palestine Committee. They put me on sub-committee for Exhibition.

July 18.—Paris Exhibition Committee at South Kensington. They made me work the boat-builders.

Nov. 5.—Palestine Committee and launched the Biblical Museum. The suggestion of this I made to Mr. Edwards several years ago. I then brought it before the Palestine Exploration Fund Committee where it was warmly seconded and now seems likely to be carried out.

Nov. 6.—Dined F. Pollock, met Tyndall, Froude, Merivale, Lord Houghton.

Nov. 8.—Duke of Edinburgh presided at meeting Paris Exhibition Committee. Convinced that whole affair is a complete jumble of grand names and cumbrous machinery, useless for action.

Nov. 12.—Dined Lord Elcho and met Delane, Editor of *Times*, and Bob Lowe. The latter chiefly notable as a detractor of every person mentioned in conversation.

CHAPTER XII

THE "ROB ROY" CANOE

IN the early spring of 1865, while at the height of his popularity in the London Scottish, and while diligent in every thing that related to his Company, Mac Gregor seems to have taken more kindly than ever before to boating, and there are frequent references in his diary to pleasant pulls on the river. One day towards the end of May, he noted, "Idea about canoe voyage was in germ to-day," and ten days later, "Canoe project hatched." On June 21 he wrote, "Went to see my canoe the *Rob Roy*," and on the 27th, "Saw the *Rob Roy* completed." A month after that he started on his first famous tour.

But the germ of the idea was really of much older date, for in the last journal he ever wrote, when his adventurous tours were over, and all his honours in the world of sport had been won, he wrote :

Canoe. The idea of this occurred to me on May 22, 1848, when Archibald Smith showed me an india-rubber cloak which could be expanded by air, and I wrote ! 'perhaps I shall go to the Lakes next year.' The first wooden canoe I designed and had built in 1865, after seeing the canoes in North America and the Kamschatka with double paddles.

On turning to his diary, the actual entry to which he refers, stands thus :

May 22, 1848.—Met Archibald Smith and saw his india-rubber boat which forms a cloak, tent, boat and bed—perhaps I shall go to the Lakes next year.

The first *Rob Roy* canoe was fifteen feet long, two feet six broad, built of oak, and weighed, with mast and sails and a two-bladed Indian paddle, about ninety pounds. The boat was covered fore and aft with cedar, leaving an elliptic opening about four feet long where the rower could sit facing the bow. A bag held all necessary luggage, a silk Union Jack fluttered its nationality and the name *Rob Roy* was painted in blue letters on the stern.

Starting on the Thames to Sheerness on July 9, 1865, and then by Dover to Ostend, Mac Gregor had a few days on the Meuse and the Rhine. The boat being taken by railway from Mainz to Aschaffenburg, gave opportunity for two pleasant days down the Main. Thence he went up the Rhine to Freiburg, and carted the canoe to the Titisee, in the heart of the Black Forest. He had a paddle on this lake, which is about three miles long and 3000 feet above the sea, notwithstanding that the people there protested against the proceeding, and said that Pontius Pilate, who, it seems, is at the bottom of the lake, would assuredly drag the boat down.

Again carting the boat to Donaueschingen, he

THE FIRST *ROB ROY* CANOE

reached the source of the Danube, and travelled down through Sigmaringen, past the romantic monastery of Beuron and amid splendid rocks, woods, and rapids for a whole week.

The Germans were astonished to see a boat on this untraversed part of the river where Mac Gregor only saw three boats, and these only for short ferries.

SHOOTING THE RAPIDS IN FULL SAIL IN THE GALE NEAR EKENGEN
ON THE DANUBE, SEPT. 1865

Every morning, hundreds of people, and in one case more than a thousand persons, assembled to see the canoe start. In several places, guns were fired, and the bells were rung for the event. At Ulm the navigation of the Danube begins, and it becomes like any other river, so he left it by railway for Lake Constance, the canoe travelling as baggage.

Paddling through this lake and the Zeller Zee he descended the Rhine to Schaffhausen, and then went to the Lakes of Zurich, Zug, and Lucerne, sailing and rowing every day.   From Lucerne he descended the river Reuss, and passed the somewhat dangerous rapids of Bremgarten without injury, and so got into the Aar, and by it again into the Rhine, which he followed to the falls of Laufenburg, round which the boat was taken in a cart drawn at first by a milch cow. Both rapids at Rheinfelden were also successfully passed by the canoe (though many larger boats have been lost there), and so he reached Bale, and by the Mulhouse Canal got into the river Ill ; but it was so dry and the scenery so dull, that he took the boat by cart over the Vosges mountains to the source of the Moselle, commencing the descent of that river as high up as Reinoremont, following it to Epinal, Chalet and Charmes.   He then left the Moselle and came down the river Meurthe, but that being also rather uninteresting, he went to the Marne which took him to Paris.

This journey of about a thousand miles was one of surprising interest, and of great variety of scene and character.   Week by week, an account of his tour appeared in the columns of the *Record* newspaper, and extracts from these, with editorial notes and comments, were transferred to the whole newspaper press, at home and abroad.

When, therefore, on the 7th of October, on a flowing tide, he paddled the *Rob Roy* under Westminster Bridge, and deposited her again at Searle's, the builders, he was the hero of the hour, and all the world talked of him and his exploits.

In January 1866, his first canoe book made its appearance under the title of "A Thousand Miles in the *Rob Roy* Canoe on Twenty Rivers and Lakes of Europe," * illustrated by twenty woodcuts from the author's drawings, and accompanied by a note on the title-page that all profits derived from the sale of the work would be devoted to the Shipwrecked Mariners' Society and the National Lifeboat Institution.

Some idea of the popularity of this book may be gathered from the following notes :—

1866.

Feb. 17.—Low told me new edition of canoe book was needed.

March 22.—Read paper on *Rob Roy* canoe before Institute of Naval Architects. Sir John Hay in chair and full attendance. Showed sails, paddle, &c., and put on dress.

April 5.—Review of my book in *Times*—a splendid 2¼ cols. of unmixed praise.

April 16.—Second edition of my canoe book came out to-day.

April 18.—Went to Mrs. Gladstone's assembly.

April 20.—Found that 2000 of my second edition sold in five days. Grove said the Emperor of the French had read the book and decreed an exhibition of pleasure-boats in 1867.

April 21.—God has given me remarkable blessing and honour lately—the election as a member of Athenæum Committee, success of the canoe book and favour of society and of individuals.

May 12.—Sent copy of canoe book and photograph to Emperor Napoleon (specially bound).

May 16.—Laid keel of *Rob Roy the Second*.

May 17.—Third edition of book came out to-day.

* Published by Sampson Low, Marston & Co.

May 21.—Wrote to E. about my design to go round the world on
a missonary tour, an idea I may expect God to bless.

A new set of friends and circumstances now began
to environ the life of John Mac Gregor. Nothing is
ever really done well without enthusiasm, or, as an
Irish orator expressed it, "Nobody is really sane
unless he is a little bit mad on some subjects," and
it must be confessed that Mac Gregor got a "little bit
mad" on every subject into which he threw his whole
heart. But surrounding circumstances never moved
his heart from its right place, or diverted him from the
real plans and purposes of his life. He fully recognised the danger of his new enterprise both to life
and character, but he never questioned his own right
motive in the least degree. In a note relating to his
first voyage he says :

It cannot be concealed that continuous physical enjoyment, such
as this tour presented, is dangerous luxury if it be not properly used.
When I thought of the hospitals of London, of the herds of squalid
poor in fetid alleys, of the palefaced ragged boys, and the vice, sad-
ness, pain, and poverty we are sent to do battle with, if we be
true Christian soldiers, I could not help asking, 'Am I right in thus
enjoying such comfort, such scenery, and such health?' Certainly,
not right, unless to get vigour of thought and hand, and renewed
energy of mind, and larger thankfulness, and wider love, and so,
with all the powers recruited, to enter the field again more eager and
able to be useful.

Canoes and canoeing having now become the
popular rage, we are not surprised to find that in the
summer of 1866, while rowing at Kew with his friend

Mr. J. Inwards, he "formed the idea of a Canoe Club;" nor is the inevitable sequel long delayed, for within a week he adds, "Formed the Canoe Club at the Star and Garter." The objects of the club were to improve canoes, promote canoeing, and unite canoeists, and the means for attaining these objects were to hold meetings for business and bivouac, for

RAPIDS OF VRANG'S ELV

paddling and sailing, and for racing and chasing in canoes over land and water. The idea took hold of the popular taste, and the first list of members included a number of distinguished oarsmen, travellers, alpine climbers, and athletes. In less than a month after the club was formed, Mac Gregor was off on his second adventurous tour.

1866.

Aug. 2.—Started from Simmons' in the *Rob Roy* and paddled down river to steamer for Christiania below London Bridge. Got under way with early tide next day and off.

Sep. 29.—Arrived at Thames Haven in steamer from Bremenhagen after the most delightful tour of three weeks in Norway, Sweden, Denmark to Baltic and North Sea. This being in my album and described in my new book to come out at Christmas, I pass over here.

The second *Rob Roy* in which this tour was made was

SPYING OUT THE CHANNEL—LAKE VENERN

an improvement on the first. It was fourteen feet long, twenty-six inches wide, was, like the former one, built of oak, and decked with cedar and had a double-bladed paddle and a lug and foresail. The boat weighed sixty pounds, luggage nine pounds, cooking apparatus and stores three pounds.

Beginning his tour at Kongsvinger on the beautiful Glommen river in Norway, Mac Gregor proceeded to a small lake whence the water overflows in winter both

westward into the North Sea and eastward, after a
long route, into the Baltic ; then, by the Vingen See
and the Okranger Lake and a chain of waters, he
entered the Vrang's Elv, "a river most varied in
character, fast and slow, deep and shallow, winding
under dense woods and through open lawns," until he
reached the Hugen See and by the Glava and a
variety of other lakes, entered lake Venern, an inland
sea about 100 miles in length. Traversing this for
some days, amid countless islands and in stiff gales,
when a compass was nearly useless and the navigation
at some places very intricate, he went up a branch of
the Great Klar River to the cholera-stricken Carlstadt
and steamed to Lake Vettern, nearly as long as the
other sea, but with brilliantly clear water, sudden
squalls and rocky shores. He then sailed down the
Motala River, and passing through the pretty lakes
Bosen and Roxen, came by the lake Glan to Nonköp-
ing, where he took steamer for ten miles to the Baltic,
and dropped the canoe in the open sea for a three
days' cruise. After a thorough exploration of the
lakes and seas near Stockholm, he proceeded west
through the many-isled Malar Lake to Hjelman,
some fifty miles long, and then on the Orebo River
and by rail back again to Vernern.

Such is a bald outline of a tour marked by many
exciting incidents and adventures. Sometimes he had
to wade, dragging the boat in the shallows, or, when
the rivers were choked with logs of timber, pulling the
boat through the forests, and carrying the luggage and

fittings separately to lighten the task. Once a horse ran away with a cart in which was the canoe, and dashed the cart to pieces, the wheels running one way while the canoe was upset in the opposite direction, and came down on a paling with a crash but without injury except to the flagstaff and one rib of the boat. Eight times he had to reach steamboats in open water and haul the boat on board, and twice this happened in the night. On one occasion, in a fierce gale, the canoe was blown away, even off the ground, and had to be held down by both hands for a long time on shore. Crowds came to witness the *Rob Roy* pass the whirlpool some miles below Trolhatta, a feat he " should scarcely be induced to perform again."

Reaching Helsingborg, at the end of Sweden, by steamer, he paddled across the Sound to Denmark, coasted along to Copenhagen, and having crossed Seeland to Korsor by rail, traversed some large fjords, and then launched on the Great Belt and inland lake. From this point the route was to Sleswig and Austenburg, where Mac Gregor put his boat on a little steamer, but during the voyage the cylinder of the engine exploded, "and in a rough sea, without mast, or sail, or food, or an oar, or a boat, (except the canoe) we drifted to a reef of rocks, but were rescued, after many hours, by another steamer, itself disabled at the time."

At Hamburg the *Rob Roy* penetrated the inmost canals even through the Jews' quarter and sometimes by tunnels. Then she started for a four days' cruise on the Elbe and next ascended the river Rhyn which goes forty miles into Holstein. Villagers turned out, *en masse*, to see the boat; schools were dismissed with shouts, and men at drill were disbanded. At one place a lad ran off and returned to the sight with his grandmother on his back, carrying the poor old lady by her wrists like a sack. Mac Gregor had often to take the canoe upstairs and lock it in a room for safety, and once the people reported that he had brought a large violoncello with him. In a letter to the *Times*, he says :

I had now to attempt the hazardous feat of catching a steamer near the bank of the Elbe, with a heavy sea on. After an hour's work I landed for a rest at a bleak island with a pilot boat (chartered by me to signal the steamer) and which had sailed alongside with two reefs in. The natives who watched our approach were told I was 'a wild Chinaman being chased,' and they came with bludgeons and axes and pursued me for half an hour until the steamer was in sight, and the *Rob Roy* was taken to Heligoland.

He circumnavigated the little island-rock and then paddled to the island of Dune. From Bremen he went up the Gesta River and then sailed along the Weser to Nordenham, tossing about in the swell among a fine shoal of porpoises. Thence by steamer to Thames Haven, and then—

The *Rob Roy* paddled up the river until from the Temple Pier she was carried upstairs into my chambers safe and sound, and with all her crew in radiant health after travelling over a thousand miles, of which about a third was done under sail. In addition to this nearly a thousand miles of travelling was accomplished in twenty-five

T

steamers and five hundred miles on six railways.   The time occupied was from the 2nd of August to the 29th of September, and the total cost of the trip was £45.

Week by week, under the title of "Rovings of the *Rob Roy*," an account again appeared in the *Record* of his daily experiences, and immediately upon his return he devoted every leisure moment to re-writing these in literary form, with the result that on the 20th of December there appeared the charming book "The *Rob Roy* on the Baltic." *

A quite phenomenal success attended the publication of this book, and revived the sale of the former one. High and low, rich and poor, princes and peasants, read and talked about canoes and canoeing in general, and of John Mac Gregor and the *Rob Roy* in particular.   Every newspaper had its article; those devoted to the chronicle of sports, such as the *Field*, had several, and from these there arose much amusing criticism and controversy.   By some exception was taken to coasting trips in canoes, not so much on account of the danger, but simply because *le jeu ne vaut pas la chandelle*.   "It is a mistake to paddle where you can go in a steamboat," said some.   "A canoe is only meant for water impracticable for other kinds of boats," said others.

Some in advocating the claims of ordinary kinds of

* "The *Rob Roy* on the Baltic.   A Canoe Cruise through Norway, Sweden, Denmark, Sleswig-Holstein, the North Sea, and the Baltic."   By J. Mac Gregor, M.A. Trinity College, Cambridge; author of "A Thousand Miles in the *Rob Roy* Canoe."   With numerous illustrations, maps and music.   Sampson Low, Son & Marston.

rowing boats felt it a duty "to utter a word of warning or of protest against the claims of an upstart
phenomenon of our days to share in the unapproach-
able merit really possessed by the gig as a boat of
pleasure. We denounce, abhor, scout, and scorn the
notion that the canoe is anything of the kind. That
article has its proper uses, and is highly commendable
in its own sphere—that is, where nothing else can
navigate. It is the invention of savages, dwellers on
savage waters whose shallowness and rapidity would
be destruction to regular craft. It is necessity, not
choice or pleasure, which justifies recourse to such an
imperfect, unscientific, uncomfortable imitation of the
true boat. We say it is a species of mockery of boating to go on expeditions of length and cost in a craft
whose only method of propulsion is based on the most
wasteful expenditure of man's powers ever invented."

Another critic described the canoe as "a broad,
clumsy, flat-bottomed, 'funny,' with the outriggers
removed." The propeller is likened to the king com-
memorated in the "Arabian Nights," who was turned
to stone from the waist downwards. MacGregor was
described as having gradually become a kind of
aquatic centaur, his lower part being a boat, and his
upper a wandering Englishman! A suggestion was
made that "as the constrained position of the legs
produces continual cramps, it would be an improvement to have the legs amputated," and a fear was
expressed that "mortals of less buoyant spirits
might get tired of sitting in a damp tub, paddling in

a confined attitude, and being confined to watercourses as the only available routes."

One steady-going paper, in giving an account of these "unique tours," considered that "they must have given to the Continental peoples amongst whom they lay, confirmation strong of the constitutional eccentricity, not to say madness, of Britons. Imagine a gentleman traversing rapid rivers, stormy firths, and unknown lakes in a vessel that he could carry on his shoulder. It seems impossible that a man could venture his life in such a frail toy; but the author did it, and was utterly insensible to his peril."

Another enlightened organ felt that it dared not recommend Mac Gregor's example to athletes generally: "The traditional John Bull would have been shot at, arrested, stoned, cut down by scythes, or burnt as a wizard before he had accomplished the smallest part of Mr. Mac Gregor's journey. He would have quarrelled with the railway officials for refusing to take his canoe in the luggage van. When asked on a French canal to show his pass for the locks he would have knocked down the querist. He would certainly not have received the curiosity of whole towns as a compliment, or have delayed his start to accommodate a bedridden old man who particularly wished to see it. He must have lost his temper at having to paddle through a forest of grass four feet high, and would probably have remained there to this day. For a canoe voyage has its drawbacks, and paddling through a jungle is one of them. When Mr. Mac Gregor gets soused in a rapid, or tumbles sideways over a weir, he does not mind, because it is all in the day's work."

Not from newspapers only, but from grave and reverend .seigniors at home and abroad, from Mrs. Grundy and her relatives, and from many others who should have known better, protests and objections came. Among his fellow countrymen abroad, he met with certain fine gentlemen who remonstrated with him on his mode of travel. One, for example, said : "Don't you think it would have been better to have had an attendant with you to look after your luggage and things?" The most obvious answer to this was probably that which Mac Gregor gave : "Not for me, if he was to be in the boat : and not for him, if he had to run on the bank." Another Englishman asked in all seriousness about the canoe voyage : "Was it not a great waste of time?" And when Mac Gregor inquired how *he* had spent his vacation, he said: "Oh, I was all the time at Brighton!" One English gentleman, who smiled at "the extremely odd notion," was found to have himself wandered over the Continent upon a velocipede ; a second was travelling with a four-in-hand and two spare horses ; and a third was making a tour in a road locomotive, which had cost him £700 !

To all his objectors, and they were but an infinitesimal fraction of the number of his applauders, Mac Gregor had a ready answer. Asked by a reviewer whether, in his heart, he did not think that rowing was really preferable to canoeing, Rob Roy replied: "As the reformed convict told his master who quoted the proverb about honesty being the best policy, 'I have tried them both,' and infinitely prefer the canoe. It is the spine on which fatigue tells—the one bone that supports the whole fabric—and it is precisely the spine which cannot be rested in rowing. What is the restful attitude of an oarsman? Cowering over his oar—about as comfortless a kind of repose as you can imagine.* In the canoe, on the contrary, one is perfectly at ease all the while, and the low position in the boat gives immense comfort and power."

To his armchair critics Mac Gregor appealed to experience, and would reply: "Has he travelled in other ways so as to know their several pleasures? Has he climbed glaciers and volcanoes, dived into caves and catacombs, trotted in the Norway carriole, ambled on an Arab donkey and galloped on the Russian steppes? Does he know the charm of a Nile boat, or a Trinity eight, or a sail in the Ægean, or a mule in Spain? Has he swung upon a camel, or glided in a sleigh, or trundled in a Rantoone?" Mac Gregor could answer that he had done all these things, but the pleasure of canoeing was greater than them all.

Making all allowances for his rare and fine enthusiasm, here is his deliberate opinion of the canoe:

The canoeist looks forward and not backward as he sits in his

---

* What would he have said to the "crumpled-up" cyclists of to-day who ride safeties—falsely so called—with their chins not much higher than their knees?

little bark. He sees all his course and the scenery besides. With one powerful sweep of his paddle he can instantly turn the canoe, when only a foot distant from fatal destruction. He can steer within an inch in a narrow place, or press through reeds and weeds, branches and grass ; can hoist and lower his sail without changing his seat ; can shove with his paddle when aground or jump out in good time to prevent a decided smash. He can wade and haul the light craft over shallows, or on dry ground, through fields and hedges, over dykes, barriers, and walls ; can carry it by hand up ladders and stairs, and can transport his boat over high mountains and broad plains in a cart drawn by a horse, a bullock, or a cow. Nay, more than this, the covered canoe is far stronger than an open boat, and may be fearlessly dropped head foremost into a deep pool, or a lock, or a millrace ; and yet when the breakers are high, in the open sea or fresh water rapids, they can only wash over the covered deck, while it is always dry within. Again a canoe is safer than a rowing-boat, because you sit so low in it and never require to shift your place or lose hold of the paddle ; while for comfort during long hours, for days and weeks of hard work, it is evidently the best, because you lean all the time against a back-board, and the moment you rest the paddle on your lap you are as much at ease as in an armchair ; so that while drifting along with the current or the wind you can gaze around, and eat or read, or chat with the starers on the banks, and yet, in a moment of sudden danger the hands are at once on the faithful paddle ready for action. Finally, you can lie at full length in the canoe, with the sail as an awning for the sun, or a shelter for rain, and you can sleep in it thus at night, under cover, with an opening for air to leeward and at least as much room for turning in your bed as sufficed for the great Duke of Wellington ; or, if you are tired of the water for a time, you can leave your boat at an inn—it will not be 'eating its head off' like a horse ; or you can send it home or sell it, and take to the road yourself, or sink into the dull old cushions of the 'Première Classe' and dream you are seeing the world.

In 1867, the same year in which "Rob Roy on

the Baltic" was under review, the Canoe Club, John Mac Gregor captain, and James Inwards mate, was attracting much attention, and adding daily to its membership. Soon after it started a caustic evening paper said, "This club, uniting as it does a maximum of discomfort and danger, with a minimum of utility is said to be fast obtaining a hold on the mind of the muscular Christianity of the day."

Another journal, however, said that the captain of the Canoe Club, deserved the gratitude of our athletic youth for having found a new mode of enjoyment tending to develop "that poetic perception, that imaginative faculty which is crushed and stunted by the stern monotony of our social life."

But perhaps the happy medium was struck by the American who said: "I guess that darned Canoe Club is a big fact."

At its first annual meeting rules were drawn up requiring that each member should send his portrait, full description of his canoe and a brief account of his voyages and, if possible, a map with his routes marked clearly on it. At that meeting, several voyages, canoe wrecks, and adventures were detailed, including the total loss of one canoe and one dog.

In the early days of the club, canoe-chasing was a favourite pastime and we borrow from a sporting paper, an account of the canoe-chase in 1867.

The great event of the day was the canoe-chase over land and water. Four flags were arranged at the angles of a square, and the starting-point was fixed midway between them. Mr. Inwards, the mate, was selected as chevy, and had two minutes law, after which the remaining canoes rushed after him. The course was diagonally across, round all the flags, and back to the starting-point. The excitement was very great when Mr. Kinnaird and the purser (Col. Wright) went for the same flag, and finally emerged from behind a tree, 'heads and tails' to the water side. The purser was in first with the head of his boat in the right direction, so away he went to the next flag. Kinnaird's boat, however, had its nose the wrong way, so he bucketed across, jumped on land, and tore away to the next flag ; here the purser rounded the flag together with the owner of the *Rossie*. In the end Mr. Kinnaird won, the purser being 2nd, and the chevy 3rd.

More important work was however in store for the club. The Emperor Napoleon III., whose fancy for imitating everything English led him with alacrity to patronise the introduction into France of English sports in particular, having read of Rob Roy's exploits as told in his books, was anxious to have an exhibition of pleasure boats, including canoes, at the Exposition Universelle, "and would be glad to encourage a taste for the exploration of solitary streams and lonely currents among the youth of France." The Boat exhibition was decided upon, followed by a new thing in the boating world : the announcement of a Regatta on the Seine with the sanction of the Emperor of the French, under the presidency of the Duke of Edinburgh, and whipped in by John MacGregor—with prizes amounting to £1100 in value, to be competed for by rowing boats. Of course all this, while it entailed much labour, brought with it much honour to Mac Gregor who notes some of the events of this time in his diary thus :

1867.

March 18.—Designed cooking canoe.

March 30.—Committee meeting Stafford House, where met P. of Wales, D. of Sutherland, Rev. J. Rogers, Captain Donnelly, C. Wylde, for two and a half hours. Prince most affable, shook hands with me first and last. P. spoke to me of canoe—London Scottish—Belgians—Sailing voyage. We settled programme of British Regatta in Paris (originally drawn up by me, and agreed to in my rooms, and then discussed by the Royal Commission). Felt quite charmed by the Prince—business-like too in his committee work and amusing in his criticisms. They call him ‘Sir’ invariably.

April 9.—Wrote Gen. Knollys, asking P. of Wales to be commodore of the Canoe Club.

April 11.—Heard from Gen. Knollys, P. of Wales pleased to become commodore C. C.

April 13.—The health, honour, joy, granted to me day after day year after year. How shall I be enough thankful and workful for all this?

May 10.—Paris regatta committee met Marlborough House, P. of Wales in chair. I sat next to him and he was most kind.

May 17.—Last night and to-night found poor boys in streets and helped them. Heard of Cambridge branch of Canoe Club. SAW YAWL.

May 26.—Sir F. Faudell Phillips died. My dear friend who walked with me every day in Temple Gardens before breakfast, he going to the Temple Church early service, and I to the Shoeblacks' morning prayers.

May 29.—Presented at the levée held by the P. of Wales for the Queen, by Lord Elcho: the Prince graciously shook hands, and turned to the Duke of Cambridge and said, ‘You know who that was—the canoe man.’

June 7.—Started from Forrester's in my yawl *Rob Roy*, and on Sep. 21 proudly brought her back after three months and a half. Record of this in my book ‘The Voyage Alone.’ *

From this to Nov. 2 occupied in writing this book.

---

* "The Voyage Alone in the Yawl *Rob Roy*," by John MacGregor, M.A. Sampson Low, Son & Marston.

The yawl *Rob Roy* was a little yacht of three tons, twenty-one feet long between perpendiculars, seven feet beam, and three feet deep. She was a life-boat, with a cabin nine feet by three feet and a sliding hatch four feet long which in harbour could be raised to form a roof five feet high ; astern of this was a well, three feet square, which could be covered with macin-

THE YAWL *ROB ROY*

tosh in bad weather. She was built of two skins of plank—the inner of yellow pine, and the outer of mahogany—varnished, and without paint. The rig was a yawl with a bumpkin bowsprit of two feet giving a jib of nine feet in the foot. The mizen carried a lug and, for gales, a storm sail. A small "dingey" went inside the yacht, and could speedily be hauled out and launched. Mac Gregor's idea was "to have a thoroughly good sailing-boat, the largest that could be well managed in rough weather by one strong man, and with every bolt, cleat, sheave, and rope well considered in relation to the questions: How will this work in a squall? on a rock? in the dark? or in a rushing tide? a crowded lock; not to say in a storm?"

It may be said here that the "cargo" consisted chiefly of tracts, periodicals, books, Bibles, and Testaments for distribution among the sailors of all nations, gathered in French and English waters, during the time of the Paris Exhibition.

"The Voyage Alone" was a cruise of about a thousand miles, across the Channel in its narrowest part, along the dangerous French coast, up the Seine to Paris—where he stayed on board a fortnight for the Exhibition and the English Regatta—back again across the Channel in its broadest part and in and about the Medway and Thames. The book, which we do not propose to describe more fully, met with as warm a reception as its predecessors, and the profits were given year by year in prizes to the boys of the training-ships, the *Chichester* (on the Thames), the *Indefatigable* (on the Mersey), and the *Havannah* (on the Severn)—the best "Refuges" for destitute lads ever known.

It was almost immediately after the publication of "The Voyage Alone" that Mac Gregor retired from the command of his Company in the London Scottish. He had revolved in his mind how he could best employ the time he allowed himself for "hobby work" and recreation, and he came, as we think wisely, to the conclusion that the canoe was better than the kilt for purposes of practical philanthropy which included popularity and influence, for, as Lord Shaftesbury once said, "Applause is the daily bread of the philanthropist."

A few extracts from the diary will now bridge over the interval between "The Voyage Alone," and "Rob Roy on the Jordan," the enterprise and the book on which his greatest fame as a traveller and an author rests.

1867.

Dec. 6.—Finished last correction of last revise of book 'The Voyage Alone.'

Dec. 14.—My book came out.

Dec. 17.—Meeting of my Company when I addressed them explaining reasons for retiring from command. All most kind.

1868.

Jan. 3.—Met Lifeboat inspectors about my improvements in compass.

Jan. 5, *Sunday.*—With D. of Sutherland, Kinnaird and D. Miller (American) to Boys' Refuge and Field Lane. He came in a cab and I would not go in it. He recognised the consistency.

Jan. 6.—Lunched at Marlborough House with Prince of Wales. He took me into his private rooms and settled letter to Prince Imperial.

Jan. 8.—Lunch Holland's. With children to American Circus.

Feb. 9.—Dined at Moore's. A. K. (?Arthur Kinnaird), Spurgeon Punshon, &c. Big parties are not good.

March 3.—First lecture on 'Voyage Alone' at Whitechapel. Large attendance.

March 27.—To Cambridge. Lecture 'Voyage Alone' in Town Hall.

April 4.—University boat-race. With eight men in canoes.

April 8.—O. A. M. Committee. Asked by Hamilton to stand for Marylebone against T. Chambers.

May 9.—Second edition 'Voyage Alone' came out.

June 4.—Launched *Rob Roy* Yawl and on 5th went down to Erith with her.

June 6.—Sailing match of Canoe Club. Charming breeze. Great fun. At night five canoes off by moon like ducks with wings, soon like specks on flowing tide.

June 10.—In yawl Erith to Hungerford. London by night. 12.—To Putney. 16.—By Wey River. Adventures in Locks. 18.—Entered Arun. 19.—Littlehampton. 20.—Bognor. 23.—Portsmouth. 27.—To London after broken bowsprit.

June 30.—Declined proposal of Constitutional Association of Finsbury to stand at next election for the Borough.

July 8.—Presented Rob Roy prizes to boys on board *Chichester*. Splendid sight, addressed them afterwards.

July 11.—Finally resolved this week to take canoe to Palestine and Egypt.

Sep. 2.—Inspected new *Rob Roy*.

Sep. 3.—My two letters in the *Times* about Marine Propulsion. My paper on the compass published.

Sep. 12.—Sold the Norway *Rob Roy* canoe to Callaway for £12.

Sep. 13.—Read Angus's 'Handbook of the Bible' again. The evidences look stronger and stronger every time one reads them. My memory of their minute particulars is bad but the gush of conviction comes afresh on every systematic perusal. Took leave of many friends in a serious anticipation of difficult voyaging.

Sep. 15.—Macaulay about boys' newspaper.

Sep. 16.—Delightful letter from Lifeboat Institution approving my new binnacle.

Sep. 29.—Brought the *Rob Roy* to London Bridge in heavy gale. Crowd at Temple pier to cheer her start.

The start was for Egypt and Palestine.

CHAPTER XIII

ROB ROY ON THE JORDAN

THE cruise of the *Rob Roy* in Egypt and Palestine, comprehending the Nile, the Red Sea, the Jordan, the Lake of Gennesareth, and the Waters of Damascus, was, without doubt, the greatest tour that John Mac Gregor ever made, while his book on the subject, "Rob Roy on the Jordan," * is equally, without doubt, the best book he ever wrote. Hitherto in referring to his tours, we have mainly quoted from his correspondence to the public press and his diary. In this chapter we propose to give a few extracts from some of his charmingly fresh and natural letters sent by every available means to friends at home, and our selection will relate principally to the beginning and the end of his really wonderful journey.

The canoe in which the cruise was made, was the fifth *Rob Roy* and was specially built for the voyage. She was 14 feet long, 26 inches wide, and one foot deep outside ; built of oak below and covered with cedar, with a waterproof apron for protection from

* Published by John Murray.

waves and rain.   Her topmast was the second joint
of a fishing-rod; the sails were dyed deep blue to
temper the glare of the sun, and her blue-bladed
paddle was the same that MacGregor used in Sweden
minus an inch of its edge, broken off when a runaway
horse upset the canoe in a Norwegian forest.   She was
the smallest vessel ever launched for such a voyage,
and withal "strong and light, portable and safe, a
good sailer, and graceful to behold."   Moreover she
carried material to form a little cabin less than 5 feet
high, more than 6 feet long, covered by a strong white
waterproof sheet, six feet square.   As so much depended
upon the comfort of the sleeping accommodation,
the canoe was built round him reclining, as his first one
had been built round him sitting, "in each case recog-
nising the one great principle, far too often forgotten,
that a comfortable boat, like a shoe or a coat, must be
built for the wearer and not worn down to his shape."

MacGregor and his canoe travelled from England
to Alexandria in the good ship *Tanjore* and after a
few days' run he was at Port Said at the mouth of
the Suez Canal, from which place he wrote, presum-
ably, the first letter, from which we quote :

I have had such a good breakfast (N.B.—Forgive 'eaty' notices,
they mean health, and without that this Eastern life would be very
different). The accordion is playing sleepily over at the debit de Tabac.
Women with their thick veils carry a gourd in each hand and one on
their head. The face must be concealed ; as for other portions of their
humanity it is little matter. However, nothing can beat our chignon—
dead slaves' hair on ladies' necks.

Colonel Stanton presented to me the most beautiful little traveller's lamp, the bijou of the Exposition at Paris, and I will certainly try it. It needs oil, but is such a pretty thing and so completely in accord with the canoe. All sorts of money pass here. I paid the Nubian in rupees! To-day I put *Rob Roy* to rights, and to-morrow hope to sleep out the first time. The water here comes from the Nile by a small canal; it is filtered then and is healthy. Collars and razors retire to-day into private life for ever so long. I bought a *Times* of October 17, and will use it by bits up to Suez. Later I will tell you to be good enough to buy them for me to send to Tiberias, where they will be invaluable. I am making decided progress in Arabic. Alone is the best way to travel. One sees, hears, and feels more in a day thus than in a week with others. It is a strange, poetic, pensive, and solemn feeling alone. Two Yankees were on the steamer. They had heard of the *Rob Roy* in America. I got well bored by mosquitoes the first night at Alexandria. Some ammonia relieved the pain, but my hands are mottled. My grey flannel things are invaluable. The very dress for this. I have my old Norfolk on —its fourth tour—the new one is for 'swell times!'

PORT SAID (ENTRANCE OF SUEZ CANAL),
October 28.

Everything most capital, and all safe here. My first paddle in Africa was truly amusing. The officers and sailors of the *Tanjore* were, of course, interested. I launched the *Rob Roy* down the ladder and hoisted the canoe flag, and then went the whole evening skimming about. The Egyptians instead of being languid were most excited, and all very kind. They rushed to the wharves, peered over the vessel's decks, ran into the water, followed me in boats, and when I hauled up the blue sail and ran out to the *Crocodile* it was a sight of the largest and smallest vessels in Africa—both English. Next day I visited the *Crocodile* and saw the admirable arrangements. The officers, who had read of Rob Roy, expressed a wish to be introduced, and the whole came up in a body to shake hands and chat.

We had a nice church service but no sermon—my little pocket 'St. John' was the only resource. I am learning the Gospel by heart.

U

Colonel Staunton, the Consul-General, a most agreeable man, asked me to dinner, where I met Capt. McKillop, R.N., who has begun a naval college for the Egyptian government. Next day I went over it with him at the Arsenal. Thirty youths received us, playing 'God Save the Queen.' The Minister of Marine came up and shook hands. He knew about the canoe. Certainly it is a splendid introduction. The French steamer charged *nil* for it when I showed the P. Imperial's name on our list, and so we landed here at this wonderful place. A negro and a very tall Nubian carried R. to a summer-house (cool and shady), and I am in the little hotel.

After one day of languor my best health came, and eating, drinking, and sleeping well I never enjoyed anything more.

This place has been raised from the sand in two years. It is quite like an American town, crowded with people of all nations and numerous ships. My window looks on illimitable desert, and this afternoon I will take a paddle for two hours. I have written to Hany, the dragoman, to join me at Suez on November 10. The pros and cons about Sinai by sea must be settled there. At any rate I hope to go by camel. I had to bribe the douane by 4*s.* not to search my boat or boxes—the most open corruption, the head man looking on. It is in fact a tax. This 4*s.* is the only thing my luggage has cost yet !

PORT SAID, *October* 29.

I fall upon my legs wonderfully and always.

Nothing could be better than my reception here. When I got a Nubian to help me down with R. for her first paddle on the canal, after two hours of work in overhauling her to perfection in a garden, the whole populace was agog.

Turks, Greeks, and Egyptians, but all so *very* kind, and how they did laugh to see me glide away. Then I went out to sea for a burst in the salt waves, and hoisting blue 'lug' sailed splendidly back up among the shipping, the wharves, the wondrous dredging machines, the shores of Lake Menzaleh, covered with red and white flamingoes exactly like armies marching.

I visited the steamer that had brought me, and everybody cheered. The captain, a nice fellow who had much talk the night before, and his officers taking off their hats and ' bravo ! bravo !' Then I went to the Transit company. They were enchanted : hauled my boat on their ship for the night; asked me to their ' cercle' for the evening, and we had fine fun by the full moon. To-day a Maltese clerk who could speak English took me in a boat to see all the machinery, which is on a gigantic scale.

The canal is 100 miles long, 300 feet broad; one half is finished. The other half is passable on fresh water conducted from the Nile. This town has 6000 people. Six years ago it was sand. They 'treated' me at their club with excellent beer and billiards, but could not comprehend my distinct refusal to go afterwards to the casino. Lots of dogs here just as in Cairo. They made an atrocious noise. Just now I looked out and saw a man leading two little bears over the sand. Every morning a screw launch starts down the canal with the post. To-morrow I will send my luggage by it to Ismailia, the healthiest and most beautiful town here, not far from Ramses the first journey of the Israelites. In the evening I will sail off with fair wind, and sleep in my boat half-way into the land of Goshen ! Next day I go to Ismailia. From all I can gather it is likely I will not canoe it to Sinai. You may be *certain* I will not if it is dangerous. I am the most cautious man in the club ! Besides, it is not proper canoeing 240 miles on sea, and already I *love* the R. too much to risk her uselessly. In that case, if Hany comes I will go on a camel to Sinai the right way. Every article I have got or made is just right. This is the reward of good preparation.

KANTARA, *November* 2.

Here I am in a little wooden shed, very comfortable, but can't get on because a furious storm rages over the desert and the sand whirls across the canal like sleet. This is a station in the desert route from Syria to Egypt, which I recollect coming to in 1849, but now how changed ! From the tiny inn door one sees the illimitable sand joined without any horizon to the sand-sky, and betimes a few camels appear like phantoms in this yellow mist, or lie down with their backs to the gale, groaning. But I never felt better in my life, and the food is good and what I like. Water brought by pipes a hundred miles from the Nile.

Huge dredges, cranes, elevators, and other immense engines ply by steam day and night (all yesterday, too, though Sunday) scooping out the sand and mud and piling it on either hand in mimic mountains.

Thousands of tons are whisked away by the wind, but still the work goes on. Ten years have been consumed, but it is to be done next October. On Friday I sent my heavy luggage by the mail boat (like a big omnibus in a steam launch) on to this place, and with a crowd to see, I hoisted my flag and with both sails filled, off went the R. The day before I had a paddle on Lake Menzaleh which stretches shoreless (to the eye) and resonant with ducks. It was at last so shallow that a crowd of naked black boys came wading to me and at last shoved the boat over mud and sand, but I had finally to get out and drag her through. On the canal, however, the water is twenty feet deep.

The sun set over the glorious desert, and I went on by the light of the full moon still sailing. My big cloak was needful, for at sunset the air chills unless I am paddling.

Stopped near a village Ras el Esch ('beginning of bread'), and selected a flat sandy beach for night quarters. The cabin plan did admirably, but the mosquitoes were innumerable, and even the flies. Next morning I found I had placed myself six feet from a heap of dust, rubbish, and filth of all kind. Moonlight, however bright, gives no colour to objects, and hence my grievous mistake. I cooked some Liebig soup famously, with bread and wine to match. Oh! the strange thoughts! they were better than any book, and more and more assured me that *alone* is the way to enjoy nature. Lots of people passed now and then and all were astonished at the white covered boat. Some peered in. The jackals yelled, a wild dog stood on the bank half an hour grumbling. I could see all these things through a window two inches square. My loaded pistol, capped and cocked, was put handy, but the worthy folks, except Greeks, won't harm one. For these last, I am advised to fire at their boat, and they being cowards will not come near.

At 4 I rose and smoked, and at 6 had coffee in a tumbler brought by a boy. O, *when*, when shall we English learn to make coffee! The worst coffee here is as good (positively) as our best. An engineers' boat gave me a tow for a few miles, and then I paddled on. The canal here is perfectly straight for thirty miles, and it is 300 feet broad. Plenty of Egyptian boats are on it sailing, and steamers of all sizes, for the works. The early morn showed hundreds of wild geese were over head on the wing to the new-day feeding place on the lake. At 11 I drew up, rigged my sail and awning for a shade, cooked delicious tea, and put my mosquito net over my head, and lay down for a charming doze after reading *Punch* and the *Times*. I have enough to do for every instant of the day, and it is extremely interesting and so novel. The canal examined thus becomes well worth investigation. The hydraulic engines are perfectly astounding! There are fifty of these, and each costs £40,000! They move on slowly and the expenses per month just now are *five millions of francs*—*i.e.*, £200,000. I shall never regret seeing thus the grandest engineering work ever attempted. Whether it will pay is another question.

I sailed again in the cool evening. The moon rose most lurid with torn and shredded clouds hustling about aloft; the wind in my teeth so I furled all sail and paddled. One good thing is the wind contrary gives coolness. Three men passed me, each leading a bear. One got into the water. The fish are by millions. Two minutes after starting the day before, a fish leaped right over my boat. Their splashing at night was continuous.

I stopped ten minutes to observe a big spider, one of the hundred on my window, manœuvring with a very big fly. How splendidly they hunt to be sure. My Levinge apparatus is perfect and I sleep inside quite sound. Oh it is a comfort indeed! This of course I cannot rear in my boat but if I choose a good place to-night on the lee side of the canal so that the water is between me and the bank whence wind blows, that will do. Well it was strange enough sailing in the dark—no danger, I had the sheet in my hand (and one sail only) and with so much luggage on board, yet I skimmed along for the two lights far far ahead.

How difficult to realise that in an hour I should be there and my luggage found and an hotel (!), the padrone a Milanese and Andrew the waiter one of Garibaldi's men. He adores English (so do the Arabs). I went last night to a fire in the desert (here it is real desert —150 yards from where I sit) and found three Arabs baking their bread on the red ashes and they said, 'English and Arab ever good friends.'

Yesterday I visited the Arab camp. A little Greek church is there and telegraph posts near it ; how curiously mingled science and savagery.

One may readily see how a fortnight of this sort of work would get materials for a little book—what will it be if I am privileged to have a winter of it ? However when Hany, the dragoman, meets me next Saturday it will even be better (in one sense—less work about luggage ; he will take that and get ready for me and I will merely canoe it to him instead of riding alongside. N.B.—They charged nothing yet for my R. since it left Southampton except three porters, who would have to be paid even for one's canoe luggage). Have I not invented a new mode of seeing old lands ? The R. is in the 'Directors'' garden shaded by big gourds ! The man is 6 feet 7½, a tremendous fellow. I bought a French book to read—an abridged account of Speke and Grant's journey, but as yet I have not had a minute to spare to read it. On Saturday next (Nov. 7) I hope to be in Suez. From Ismailia, where I expect to be to-morrow, there is a railway to Suez so Hany may come by that. The gale is very high, it is called the Khamsin and is from S.W. As this would be impossible to stand in the Red Sea, I may now say that I give up the idea of canoeing it to Sinai and at Suez will decide whether or not to camel it there with Holland, &c. This will please you. It is the only Quixotic part of my tour and formed no part of the original scope and plan.

ISMAILIA, *November* 4.

Such fun, and here I am half-way through the canal. The rest of it I go on the freshwater canal. The gale at Kantara detained me till yesterday. As it wouldn't stop I set off against it and hard work it was. I had to tow the R. with a long string round my waist. She tows wonderfully light but walking against the wind and on sand and in sand was no joke. How you would laugh to see me with a double gauze right over my pith helmet, and yet sand came in. Glorious desert all round and in the hot midday I sketched beside R. and ate my breakfast. Wind veered. Thunder came on and I got in and skimmed along under sail. My hotel bill at Kantara for three days with all accessories was £1. Wind again opposing I had a hard paddle in the dark to El Guisr. There the banks are high hills and the hyenas live in them. At last I asked how far to it (Italian passes best—Greeks, Maltese and Italians are more numerous than French here) and found I had passed it in the dark, so retracing the way I found two houses, the village being half a mile off on the hills. A man who offered to get me a bed was so ill looking I would not leave my boat; so on again till in a quiet spot I pitched my quarters. Rain came. I had most foolishly not brought a second coat and only half a loaf of bread and no Liebig. I felt if ever I am to get ill now's the time, but I turned in. The cabin kept out the rain perfectly and my new lamp warmed it up and I wound my second trousers round my waist! putting off the wet coat at all hazards—of course I had my big cloak (invaluable) and slept like a top. This morning I bought a pennyworth of bread from a Greek boat, and a nice man brought me two cups of coffee from his house and so I paddled on here, perfectly well thank God. Here is an excellent hotel and a most beautiful place. From my window I see the real Arabs and their camels and tents 300 yards away. I mean to stop here till Monday the 9th, and have written to Suez to tell Hany to come. Here is lots to see. The first man who met me here was a gentleman (French) who saw me leave Havre in the yawl, and who now thanked me for a tract I then gave him.

RAMESES, *November* 8.

Here am I in Hany's splendid tent. He lies outside and I have just read to him Exodus xii., wherein this place is mentioned. So funny to have an unseen congregation. I wrote last from Ismailia. That night I spent on the lake Timsah (Crocodile lake) about two miles each way. I paddled and sailed and fished till dark, then dined, and, when the moon rose, fixed on a graceful bend of purest sand, and lit my lamp. It was very cold and I lost my fishing rod, the one I had in Norway and used also for a topmast. So next day at early sunrise I ran up a high sand-hill exactly like snow, and only marked by cats and jackals of the past night some of which I traced to their holes. Wonderful view with the mountain Attaka at the place in the Red Sea where the Jews crossed, standing high and bold on the horizon, and sand, gravel, shrubs, marshes full of ducks, and game dotting the foreground. I revisited every spot I had fished in, and at the very last, found it again, the rod and line and fly all safe, floating on the water.

One wild walker of the night had evidently come within a few yards of the R. by moonlight, and then his paws turned away. . . . . At night I was fairly puzzled what to do with my luggage in prospect of four days more on the canal, for it is grinding work to look after all oneself and a canoe too. In my cogitations the waiter brought in a card inscribed 'Michael Hany, Dragoman.' How truly delightful it was to see this. When he came up he rushed into my arms and kissed me over each shoulder in true Eastern fashion.

He has greatly prospered in dragoman work, and it must be real attachment to me that makes him give up chances so much more lucrative, to come with a single traveller. . . . . But there is no disguising that Hany's scale of doing things has advanced in style, and of course in price. It is however a charming relief to have such a man seeing after everything, and his new servant Seliman, a handsome youth who waits very quietly. The barking of dogs in Ismailia was so terrific at night that I could not sleep, and I resolved that this is my last night here, so we hired a boat with two Egyptians, and put the tent and things in it, and sailed and towed four hours out to the real good desert to stop the Sunday at this place only lately settled to be Rameses. To-day, walked for three hours over the grand old plain where the Israelites undoubtedly lived, and from whence they made their first start 'from Ramses to Succoth.'

SUEZ, *November* 12.

Most curious, interesting, and amusing journey from Ismailia.

Seliman is always getting into scrapes or into the water and meekly suffering while Hany abuses him terribly as a 'dog of a Jew,' and then pats him on the back. . . . . Hany will break his heart if I reduce his grandeur. He is proud of his traveller, and I am proud of him. A capital, splendid fellow indeed, and both of us with nineteen years of travel-experience since we went out before. . . . . Camels on all sides, lovely-eyed baby camels, with little black boy-Arabs from Sinai clinging to the hump. Hundreds bathing, washing clothes, and other things in the water, our drinking beverage, mind you, but it subsides into a pale, thin, and nice soft, palatable fluid after all this commotion. Universal delight at seeing the R. . . . . As evening falls, and it is cold enough (three blankets at 10 P.M. and panting for breath at 10 A.M.) the murmuring of ' Alla-a-a-a-h ' and the whole jabberation of the ritualistic churchmen of the desert who will repeat things over and over a hundred and fifty times. . . . . The villages are quite unique. The French begin, the Greeks and Italians come next, the people from far-away Nubia are packed off to work, 'forced work but good pay,' and all is in extreme bustle—the heyday of a scheme which will have another day of sad prosaic reckoning.

As I swept into Shalouf yesterday with my topsail swelled by the breeze, two persons called out that they had a letter for me, and just as I took it, and was putting it into my breast-pocket, the most beautiful little fish, two inches long, leaped out of the water into the pocket ! Hany hurrahed loud and long as it is a sign of the highest luck for an odd fish of this kind to come forward and give his advice. . . . . Instead of going to Sinai I intend to spend four or five days in the Red Sea with the tent ashore, and then while luggage and tent go with Hany in a boat on the Nile, I canoe into Damietta and Port Said, and then steam to Beyrout. Thence by a cart I take the R. to Damascus, and launch upon the Abana and Pharpar. This is perfectly new as an idea, H. says it is quite feasible. It is far more interesting too than the lower Jordan which has been done twice, and nobody knows what is in the lakes at Damascus simply because there is no boat there. Then south to Banias, the source of the Jordan—the lake Huleh (the main object

of the whole voyage) and so to Tiberias. . . . . Hany doats on
the canoe, and keeps steering into the bank or turning round so
often to look at it. . . . . Hany was dragoman to the Prince of
Wales.

To-day two eagles kept soaring about but scorned to come near
enough for a hit. I don't like firing at birds merely because they are
birds. I feel no scruple in fishing for mere fish, but the poor bird is
so happy-looking, that, unless it would give some more benefit than
killing it, I will let it live. The Eastern says Englishmen, when they
have nothing to do, say, ' Come and let us kill something.' This is
a blunt way of putting it, but really it is too true.

Now began one of the most charming paddles I ever had in my
life along the edge of the Red Sea. Fresh morn with lively breeze
in my face, and the sun not yet too strong on my back. The
beauteous sand glancing with light under the clearest sparkling
water, red and blue rocks, varying the pretty painted floor I seemed
to skim over, and patches of coral and gaudy shells every here and
three. Before me the grand red mountains of Attaka ; wild screaming sea-birds circling round my head, and ever and anon shoals of
darting flying-fish, little bigger than minnows, which sprang out
of the tiny waves, and, glancing through two or three wave-tops with
a flash of silver light, dropped again into the clear water, until
another and another bright, living cloud of the same kind rose, broke
and fell. The troopship and English, French, and Egyptian men-
of-war at anchor in Suez Roads seemed to rise and fall on the glassy
surface, but this was the mirage, and my eyes being close to the
water, very wonderful effects passed in half an hour, but so silently,
and with such solemn pomp of colour that there was a weird feeling
of life cast over the mind quite indescribable. Oh ! it was a curious,
poetic, enchanted feeling to see these bright visions as my canoe
steadily advanced with gentle ripples beating on her bow. I soon
felt this was the best of all modes of travelling for true enjoyment,
exercise and sight-seeing at the same time.

MOSES' WELLS, RED SEA,
November 17.

The place where the Israelites crossed the sea seems clearly to be north of Suez near a part now fordable at low water. Long ago the sea must have been 20 feet deeper than now—*i.e.*, the land has risen. North of the end of the Red Sea there are dry beds of bitter lakes which are to be filled with water for the purposes of the Suez Canal in four months from now. Many many miles have thus to be covered, so the water will pour in for months before it does that.

But anciently the sea extended some miles to the north. The place often assigned for the passage is that opposite where my tent now is. But the water, between this and the other shore, could be in places about 70 feet deep even now, and a 100 feet long ago. The Bible speaks of the water over and over as a *wall* on each hand. A *mountain* would have been the word to describe it by if it was so deep as 100 feet. It is curious how we avoid taking just the exact description of the Bible but insist upon adding to it and making out our own story.

A wall would truly describe water seven or eight feet high, and this depth would be quite enough to cover all the Egyptians. The bend of the mountains, the lay of the plain, and the distance of only five or six miles instead of twelve miles across, are all in favour of the idea that the children of Israel passed over very near to the present ford where the camels cross at low water now, to get fresh water on the other side.

My canoe has been the wonder of the town. I had to show her off at the hotel. She was on the pier and a great crowd assembled. The balcony was full of English ladies and children with their ayahs from the Indian mail. Officers of the *Malabar* (like the *Crocodile*) and the *Fenze* (here to take Lord Mayo to India) and other ships in the foreground. Numerous Hindoo servants of the hotel with their silken locks, Greek and Egyptian sailors, Englishmen from the P. & O., officers, Scotchmen from the railway, Arabs from the desert (here to take a German to Sinai), and three Chinese sailors, all jabbered at once as I set up my cabin, inflated my air bed, drew my mosquito curtains, fixed my lamp and showed my cooking apparatus, the compass, the chart, the pistol, waterbottle, fishing rod, landing net. One of the *Malabar* officers had bought a *Rob Roy* after reading my book—another officer here is going to order one. There is no need to disguise the fact that the canoe is regarded as a very great wonder indeed, and I have an amount of consideration as a 'distinguished traveller' far beyond what belongs to me.

Hany put the tent and luggage into a large sailing boat preparing to follow me, and I launched the R. and hoisting the blue lug soon skimmed over the long waves out to sea. The wind was quite favourable but I had about sixteen miles of sailing along the coast and a most charming though rather adventurous trip. The water was beautifully clear, brilliant coloured sand and patches of coral whisked past me and the wind increased to a gale, so I put in a reef but still sailed merrily. Hany by some mistake never hoisted the large English ensign he had strict orders to put up, so that in vain, hour after hour, I looked to see his boat coming.

The white goose-winged sails of many boats swelled up on the horizon and glided past me at three or four miles distance, but I never made out which was his. I went ashore to stretch my limbs— oh how lonely that spot of yellow sand and clear crystal ripples and no one to hear if you shouted ever so loud! I could just discern some Bedouins and camels like black pin-heads on the illimitable desert. I got in again and could now see the palm-trees near Moses Wells. The air here is so excessively clear that you can see easily fifty miles. The mountains in sight of my tent door are much further off than that, but the rocks and crannies on them are quite distinct. At last I thought I saw our boat hopelessly ashore some five or six miles dead to leeward. It would never do to run down there and find it *not* my boat for I could never get up against this furious wind. Then I had only some water on board and no bread, nor my bed, nor my tent sheet for the night. At length I resolved to run ashore and chance it at Moses Wells (which are two miles from the sea though they positively look 500 yards!) and just as I did so Hany appeared over the bank. He had come unperceived by me and was putting up the tent, so it was all right. We had a cold night of it and I slept in my clothes but that doesn't make the very least matter, of course.

A camel was got and we took the luggage out of the boat now left nearly dry by the receding tide—a camel in the water looks very funny. This morning I have been quiet after the exertion of yesterday and I will go and see the Wells in the cool afternoon and to-morrow hope to have less adverse wind to get back to Suez with. This little trip, however, will amply justify the title of my book if I live to write it : " The *Rob Roy* on the Red Sea."

It is an expensive mode of journeying—*not* the canoe but the Eastern plan altogether, it will however be the leading journey of my life and it would be a hundred pities to omit this or that particular while I am so near each, and with a little exertion and outlay can add them to my catalogue of sights.

My tent is now close by the sea. Hany has put a carpet over the R. and is throwing water upon it now and then, which persists in drying up five minutes after.

The R. is in perfect health and has given me infinite satisfaction. She sails splendidly, and nothing has yielded, or cracked, or failed yet in her gear. My plans are to start by rail for Cairo on the 18th or 20th, and after three days there to descend the Nile ; this will be easy work, and I see that there are a few antiquities and ruined temples on the route I have chosen very rarely visited and very grand to see. I will just keep on telling you my story and imagine how delightful must be my picture—lying on a bed in a yellow tent, with the canoe alongside, and the dragoman cooking in a ruined limekiln ; the sea in front and the desert of Sinai behind ; a few palms and trees by the fountain of Moses—but stay, I will go and see them before writing any more.

I forgot to mention a Mr. Stanley at the Suez hotel, the special correspondent of the *New York Herald*. He was for them in the Prussian war and the Abyssinian campaign. Oddly enough, a week before I left you I wrote a long letter to that very paper, strongly urging the claims of the Palestine Fund upon the Americans.

I soon worked up Stanley to see the importance, and he got so interested about the R. that I lent him a copy of the ' Voyage Alone.' He sat up at night till he read the book right through ! He said he would write a regular ' stunner ' to his paper about canoes and my present voyage, and to give it point would telegraph about my being here to the Associated Press, which would be in five hundred American papers, and put people on tip-toe to hear more! What a sensational set these Yankees are! In return I gave him a short letter of introduction to Dr. Livingstone, and he went off to Aden to meet him and to get the first news for America from his own lips—that is to hear if he went round Lake Tanganyika, and so solved the problem of the Nile's source.

I went to see some negro dancers. Exactly like a book picture. One had a harp hung about with ostrich feathers and skins, five others sat about like monkeys, with drums little and big which they thumped with the flat of one hand, and with a big stick in the other. Another had a girdle with some dozen of goats' hoofs tied in bundles to it, and as he danced he shook his loins to make music. The grave Arab smiled—the Nubians and negroes laughed outright. Two of these danced together with languishing looks, the perfection of humour.

Hany is quite in his element here. He adores me; he says he will travel with me in Egypt merely for expenses, but in Syria I shall have to pay very high.

I see I cannot do without a horse for each of us when we go to the east of the country as it *might* be necessary to *get away* quickly. So I must make up my mind to do this tour well, and for health and for safety a good many pounds must be cheerfully paid. My expedition is regarded as a regular exploration and by no means a holiday picnic and my name and fame may be gained or lost in it. If it adds a line of help to the Bible student it will be money well laid out, and the materials I am getting fast, ought to form the staple of a very curious book.

I have been up to see the Wells of Moses. They are certainly most curious. About a mile from the present beach but on the *very highest* point of what must have once been the sea-shore, fresh water bubbles up through the sand and runs about twenty yards and loses itself in the sand. About fifty feet from it is one palm-tree, lonely and tall, and at its foot a round basin, about three yards wide, of clear fresh water. People have, a little way off, dug about a dozen pits, and in all water bubbles up in a pond more or less dirty-looking. It is then lifted by a rod and leather bucket to irrigate little patches of ground where numerous palm-trees and vegetables grow.

Port Said again, all well, charmed and safe. What wonderful enjoyment I have had since I left this place. We are too apt to call God 'gracious' when His ways are pleasant to our natural tastes. He is ever gracious. 'I love them that love me,' He says, and I feel I can say with Peter, 'Lord Thou knowest all things, Thou knowest that I love Thee.'

But it really is unusual to have so long, so varied, so unique a voyage without one accident to the boat, or myself, or Hany, or Seliman. Nothing broken, nothing lost, nothing failing, nothing omitted of the programme I sketched out.

I suppose I am at the age when travel of this kind is most enjoyable. Old enough to be sobered from the mere skin of outer sights and to feel sentiment and inner joy, yet young enough to bear the fatigue without the slightest trouble, to be buoyant all day and eager for the next day's unknown toils.

How much better it is to be alone. How much more I hear, see, feel, and think, of all that is around than if half one's time were mere chat with a companion. I really have not a moment unoccupied all day. I finish my reading at night at ten, only by forcing myself to go early to bed. The others, Hany, Seliman, Regis (captain), two sailors, boy (baby brother besides), have been long since snoring, and two guards—must have them at every village—snoring the hardest. Poor Hany has had to sleep in the cold fortuitous shelter of each place as we have only one tent, and though it is meant for three, nothing would persuade him to sleep with the master. But from this time forth we shall be in different state. His larger tent (given by Robert Hanbury) we left here and we shall put it up and have a tent-warming of a dinner to which I have invited Mr. Chatelis, the Director of Works here, who has been most kind, and has allowed us to pitch our tent in the company's yard (with R. under our eaves and ten feet from the sea) and Mr. Leduc, a nice young Englishman (the interpreter here) and Dr. Jacob, the Vice-Consul. As I don't take wine with me (and how little one misses it in this climate), I must get some for them from the hotel. Hany quite relishes having a party, being a

truly good cook. The first duck I shot from the R. he served up
with 'preserved green peas' on Lake Menzaleh, rice pudding,
oranges, apples, nuts, raisins, and dates and Arab bread (which I
consider a luxury), and then coffee. I intend to stop here for the
French steamer leaving here for Beyrout on the 8th.

Strange sight to see us in the luggage-boat with a smiling sun and
a gladsome breeze. The crew aft. The captain kneeling on his
cloak saying his prayers with face to Mecca. Hany and I in the boat's
waist and when the Mahomedan is done I say to Hany, 'We are
going to read now if you like Hany.' I never ask him or force him
but I do believe he has become deeply interested. Yesterday at
Zoan I read several chapters of all the plagues of Egypt. To-day I
read the last part of John I.—what a marvellous chapter it is ; it is
all kernel, meat, and drink, most wholesome for the soul.

The roar of the Mediterranean seems quite a new sound to hear.
We are just out of Egypt now. I shall always look back on that old
land with very great reverence, almost awe, and with most pleasant
associations of both my tours in it.

No wonder people come for climate here—cool at night, but from
6 to 6 in the day the air *just* right and the sun only for two hours too
hot to be neglected, but not a languid heat—nay, I have worked
harder this week than on the Danube, and they say I am very brown.
N.B.—I don't even take out my mirror at all. I can (in a way!)
divide my hair without seeing it in the morning.

You see I am in quite a gossipy mood as I feel so happy that the
first and most anxious part of my voyage has been so successfully
accomplished. But the three days' rest here will do us all good, and
I have lots of little perfectionments to my canoe which, having her
alongside and my tool box (sent with all our heavy luggage a month
ago here) I can do neatly at leisure to-morrow. I wrote yesterday
from Zoan to congratulate my friend W. H. Smith, now M.P.,
especially for his beating the philosopher Mill. I had five shots at
pelicans to-day with ball and missed all. It was a *great* omission not
bringing my rifle with me. Six pelicans at once in a bunch is not infrequent, and their beaks all so very 'Zoological Gardens.' But another
duck I shot is, I see, hanging in our larder—a tall peg in the ground.

Dec. 5.—Hey presto! I am in another tent this morning. H. is so proud of being able to show off both his tents on French ground,

ON THE ABANA

with his beautiful English ensign, red on the clean white. This is a large double tent which gives an eave of shade all round. French, Greeks, and Moslems, are all looking on. I meant to have sent you my letter to the *Record*, but I have only half an hour to write as the steamer has just come in, so I must ask you to wait for my next letter (next week) for all the curious history of this week's travel.

PORT SAID, *Tuesday, December* 8.

The steamer to take us to Beyrout is in port, and I start at 5, to arrive, we hope, on the 10th.

My dinner last night went off splendidly—a lady came, too. Really, H. is a capital cook. I shall ever look back on Egypt with most happy thoughts. If my boat is smashed to-day, I have plenty already for a curious book, and whatever happens is, of course, for the best.

MOUTH OF THE ABANA, LAKE ATEIBEH,
Christmas Day.

Happy Christmas to one and all! I write this after the tent and fire scene described within and which really is like a book. This is the furthest point I propose to take the R. to. From this we turn back, having fully accomplished all I desired, and with infinitely more pleasure and satisfaction than I could have imagined. The men are still talking with wonder and gratitude for the speech I made. I spoke first of our journey and condoled with them for their mishaps. They answered they felt none of these as they did when they saw me start alone on this lake. Then I spoke of Christmas and told the story of the world, the creation, prophecy, advent, and with the moon over us and shepherds actually around keeping their flocks from panthers and hyenas, the effect was powerful. This was indeed an 'open-air sermon' and it will never be forgotten by *me*.

Hany interpreted admirably, and I feel that this Christmas day has been perhaps the most useful I ever spent.

But fancy a stuffed turkey, to-day and here, too, and wine and a huge plum-pudding exceedingly good and all flaming in brandy! Hany is a splendid fellow indeed.

I am now going to have a good glass of punch, saving your presence, and here comes the hot water.

MOUTH OF THE PHARPAR, LAKE HIJANEH,
December 28.

Briefly let me sum up since my last—came down the Abana to

Damascus—opened the new school there. Dined with Mr. Digby. On Tuesday last started below Damascus in the R. on the Abana and thus got down to the wonderful marsh, or Lake Ateibeh, in the dreary desert. The consul sent two soldiers with me for ten days as my present path is not safe without. Passed a wondrous day on the lake. Prepared for

THE ISLAND, LAKE HIJANEH

danger because there are panthers and hyenas, and worst of all wild boars. Many natives are lost in the deep holes and the only boat that ever came here was three years ago when the three men in it, missed for five days, were all found drowned after twelve days' search. Then I mounted R. on a frame of poles on a very good pony's back which has so far answered admirably. After wonderful adventures brought her safe to this lake Hijaneh and my tent looks out on Hermon snowed above the clouds. The sheikh of the village has just been sitting with me. To-day was my *grand* day—to go out on lake Hijaneh nearly all covered with reeds ten feet high—the highest twelve feet—and to steer through them by compass. Thus I got to the other side and with breathless excitement landed alone in the Hauran—that marvellous waste where are the 'giant cities' of Porter. I *ran* up the nearest hill, though the sun was fearfully hot, and behold the bleak Argob—the hills of Bashan—the wide plains of King Og! No one can understand my feelings in looking over this wilderness with five lakes and three rivers below me, and my canoe (dearer than ever, and now my only way of getting back safely) quite uninjured, dry, still, resting on that ancient shore!

Thence, and with delight, I spied the island in the lake where are the ruins seen from the hill, but which the R. is the first to visit. I carefully took all the compass bearings and dashed into the reeds. Myriads of ducks, of course, and so stupidly impudent. *They* are never bothered by guns. Of course once in the reeds you can see nothing but them except in a few open pools, and by standing up in the boat—which I can always do. She is so dry, I wear two pairs of *socks* and keep my shoes off (for steadiness in standing, to 'punt' with a pole I carry) with one foot on the deck which I find is quite strong enough. At last I got near the black ruins, entered one of the hundred boars' tracks all leading to it. I went cautiously round before landing, for a wild boar, if he smashed my R., would leave me helpless. At length with pole and cocked pistol I landed! the first traveller ever there! I shall tell it all again through the *Record* for next mail, so no more at present.

After four hours found Hany and the horses and all singing. With success crossed the Pharpar and safe in my tent crowded by con-gratulators. My health still magnificent. If the R. now is broken I have enough for my next book, but to-morrow I mean to paddle *up* the Pharpar—quite easy—it is all in a level plain—to Neja whence this letter is to be sent to Damascus to catch the mail. From Neja I hope to go to Burak in the Hauran, the nearest of the 'giant cities' (doors and windows all of stone—all deserted), which it would be too bad not to see when only one day off. We shall leave our tents and men and watchers and canoe, &c., at Neja, and only have three guards and nothing to be robbed of! Then I hope to be at Damascus on Friday, Jan 1, and to get your letter on 2nd or 3rd there and start for Jordan on Jan. 4.

I have said so often how delicious this tour is that I fear to say it *too* often as being wearisome to you—therefore once for all! It has been one unbroken delight—except the little fever day—and wonder and surprise to me.

Never can I expect to write such things again as boating antiquities, and sacred travel. Positively it is a new invention this canoe which can be carried on a pony and opens up all the lakes and rivers while you ride and walk the land. My anxiety has of course been great as to her safety sometimes. Once in a marsh mule after mule went down and at last a donkey went literally out of sight over head in a hole—only its tail was caught by a muleteer! In such cases we put the R. on the water and mount her again on better land.

But I am over all that sort of work now. The glorious weather is cold at night but Hanbury's double tent is pretty warm with five blankets. Still this *is* the weather for J. In the day it is bright sun and hot as fire.

BEYROUT, February 10.

. . . . Here ends my glorious and charming tour. I came in a Russian steamer. Such crowds on this beautiful beach to see me paddle in on a magnificent swell. . . . . After Tiberias I went to Carmel and to the place of the sacrifice—a most interesting church. Then I launched on the Kishon—a dull river, very hard to get to, over a wide plain of soft mud, where Sisera and his host were engulphed, and many odd things happened. Once in it, I was away from all, till I emerged in the sea! After two hours I thought it so lonely floating down, I would lunch, so I went easy and stopped, and was taking water in a tin can (sitting in my boat), when I heard a curious gurgling sound near me and looked round carelessly. Near my paddle end what did I see but the nose and open mouth of a crocodile! For an instant I was paralysed, but kept cool and dipped my paddle blade.

He was sniffing at me as they do in the Nile. The water was

too muddy to see more of him, and he was not big [Here an attempt at a sketch].   I find I cannot draw it, but I never, never, can forget it.   Soon I noticed on several sand-banks many traces of crocs' feet and tails, and going near to examine (for the thing is utterly unknown, but then nobody has ever been down the river), when I stopped, a thing came *under* my boat, and his head or nose went bump, bump, bump, all along the keel.   Then I confess I was a good deal frightened, and set off at a good pace.   When the croc knows human beings he is afraid and keeps away, but never having seen one he might have snapped at my hands, so near the water.   At any rate, I kept on the move, and got safely to Caipha.   What makes it quite likely that crocs are in the Kishon is that Mr. Zillah showed me at Nazareth a croc, killed three months ago in the Zerka, a river not far off.   However, I am the first to see one on the Kishon.

Next I went to the river Belus.   Its name in Greek means ' glass ' and it was there that glass was discovered when men made a fire on the sand.   It may be what is alluded to in the Bible, where the blessing is given to the tribe that possessed that district, ' and treasures hid in the sand.'

Out of the Belus I paddled across the sea to Acre.

It was an anxious time for all Mac Gregor's friends while he was in Palestine.   The unsettled state of the country, the ignorance and superstition of the people amongst whom he passed ; the unknown and unsuspected dangers that beset him on every hand ; his propensity to explore alone wild and almost inaccessible places ; the frailty of the tiny boat in which his hazardous excursions were made ; his own strong will which could not brook let or hindrance ; each of these constituted a source of anxiety.

We can sympathise with his good old father, Sir Duncan Mac Gregor, when he wrote to his friend, Mr. Evans :

My Rob Roy son was, thank God, quite well a few days ago, after having, by the goodness of God, made several hair-breadth escapes. He had, in reality, finished his expedition, and was, when he wrote last, at Beyrout, whence he was going to Jerusalem to assist Warren in his explorations there. . . . . I think John's next book will be interesting, but I earnestly wish the fellow were at home.

MacGregor tarried for a month at Jerusalem, rendering very important services to Captain Warren in connection with the Palestine Exploration Fund in which, to the end of his days, MacGregor took an absorbing interest.

Writing to Mr. Gawin Kirkham, his coadjutor in the Open-air Mission, MacGregor sums up the spiritual aspects of his great tour thus :

. . . . Everything I have seen and probed to the bottom has always turned out at last to be in *complete* accordance with the Bible. . . . . It is *not* a cunningly devised fable that we are living by. Christ's religion is a reality—a dreadful reality—dreadful to many, but sweet and charming to some . . . .

I shall soon have finished this tour; but I can never, never forget its sacred delights. Nor is it other than pleasing to God that we should be thankful for such sights as I have witnessed. When the two disciples of John followed Jesus, He turned and asked, 'What seek ye?' They said, 'Where dwellest Thou?' He said, 'Come and see!' Gracious words these! I, too, wished to know where He dwelt, and He says to me, 'Come and see!' Yes, and where He dwells *now* I shall also see; nor can I suppose that even in Heaven the redeemed followers of Jesus will cease to remember or to speak of with interest, the very hills, and rivers, and plains, and cities, which, during this very delightful journey, I have had the great privilege to visit.

CHAPTER XIV

ST. REMIGIUS—THE CANOEIST

In the palmy days of a certain satirical review, there appeared an article entitled "St. Remigius." Commencing with the axiom, "To pretend to be better than one's neighbours is a fault which may possibly be pardoned in the next world, but which will certainly never obtain forgiveness in this," the article proceeded : "No people are generally more unpleasant than those whose virtue and piety are on all occasions prominent. To be full of good sayings, to preach in all societies, to point every topic with a moral, to have our eye always upon the immortal soul or the peccant nature of the listener—all this is, by universal consent, intolerable."

After hinting that "among persons who would be likely to offend their fellow creatures in this way, perhaps it would not be uncharitable to reckon the various and zealous correspondents of our excellent contemporary, the *Record*," the writer threw off all disguise and boldly announced its "St. Remigius" as "the very energetic philanthropist of Ragged School and Shoeblack reputation—Mr. Mac Gregor."

The article continued :

We do not know how many people he has converted, but he lets everybody know how many he has tried to convert. He represents thus far the tourist of the most terrible and portentous species—the tourist Evangelo-tractual. Nevertheless, it is acknowledged that this distributor of tracts, this preacher of discourses, this awakener of souls, is neither more nor less than a first-rate oarsman.

It is a curious freak no doubt for the correspondent of a religious paper to have taken to. The soul of their Protestant Defence, the champion of all their best movements, had taken to the water like a duckling brought up amongst the hens, and was splashing about over the Continent in a manner which, for gaiety and freedom, left the votaries of worldly pleasures an infinite distance behind. Curious as it may seem, there lies the journal in black and white, and the writer is as much at home in a boat as Lord Shaftesbury is on a platform. Full as he is of the souls of men, he is keenly alive to his day's enjoyment, and it comes as easy to him to mend a plank as to probe a conscience. Down the rapids of the Danube, over the lakes of Switzerland, along the canals of France, the Rhine, the Moselle, the Seine, he floats and steers and preaches. He finds books in the running brooks, sermons in stones, and a text in everything. From the canoe to religion, and from religion to the canoe, he flashes backwards and forwards with a genial relish which is so thorough that it can hardly be affected. At one moment the reader is lost in admiration of the devotee, and at the next he sees before him one who is every inch a waterman. The whole thing is absolutely and purely natural ; there is no straining for effect, no extraordinary unction in the language. It is hard to say exactly what it is that is so bewildering in the mixture we have attempted to describe. Is it really a half-humorous thing that a traveller should go over Europe with a paddle in one hand and a bundle of tracts in the other ? or is it merely that we look at the enterprise from a wrong point of view? The real truth is that it is seldom that one is brought face to face with a mind of such strange simplicity. The nearest approach to it is in reading the Pilgrim's Progress. If John Bunyan were alive now, he would beyond question be rowing down the Rhine, like Mr. MacGregor, and saving souls, almost, so to speak, at every stroke. There is nothing incongruous to such a character in a boyish eagerness after the water, and an apostolic zeal for the world to come. This is quite a different thing from the religion of the ordinary muscular school . . . .

One might describe Tartuffe to the life, and not include a single trait which can be reasonably ascribed to 'Rob Roy.' It is such a character as one does not often meet, and such as is well worth examining when one does meet it. Here we have a man who can steer a canoe with a paddle over a dangerous rapid in the Danube, and then give to a farmer's child 'that remarkable tract which contains Napoleon's testimony to the proofs of Scripture inspiration being sufficient for him at the least.' Strange then as the spectacle is—strange in the midst of the educated, busy, reticent, critical society of our time—it is one that must not be laughed at ; or, at all events, must be smiled at good-humouredly. Is it worth thinking how the matter appears from the other side? If we look with puzzled curiosity at 'Rob Roy' with what wonder must he return the look !

Of course we have no quarrel with the writer of this article, published nearly thirty years ago. We gladly adopt its title and reproduce a portion of the skit in order to show that there was a diversity of opinion as to the peculiarities of Rob Roy. It was his habit to make room on every voyage for a plentiful supply of tracts and leaflets with portions of Holy Scripture thereon, and as many New Testaments as he could carry.

As to the general utility of tract distribution we have no remarks to make. But MacGregor had many and here are some of his utterances :

Let me say once for all, that on this voyage [the Baltic], as on every other tour, I constantly gave tracts; feeling, too, that if the people around me were not available for this sort of communication, or if I was not ready to use it on their behalf, there must be some constraint on their side or on mine, which ought not to exist between the sons and daughters of Adam, pilgrims in a world together, and with great and deep and lofty things in common, which ought never to be very distant from our thoughts, and which one day must be near.

He says of this northern voyage :

The Norwegians and Swedes are able to read. More of them are so far educated than in the like number of any nation of Europe. They eagerly accept papers (call them tracts or not), and they do this more readily from Englishmen, and most readily when the man who gives them is otherwise enlisting their attention by his manner of life or travel.

Again :

Because many tracts are weak and badly written, and are given imprudently, therefore some people decry all tracts. As to the amount of good they may do, let those speak (yes, and only those) who have carefully given them and patiently watched the results.

Another peculiarity of Mac Gregor as a traveller— and it is a pity that it was a peculiarity—was that he kept holy the Sabbath day. He never rode in cab or train on Sunday except on two occasions, and he was no believer in the doubtful morality of "When at Rome do as Rome does." To his unsophisticated mind the claims of the Sabbath were equally binding everywhere, and he had no notion of observing it less strictly abroad than at home. But some travellers regarded it as a very eccentric thing that he should lose a steamboat, or break the continuity of a journey, or mar an expedition "just for the sake of a bit of Sunday travelling which could not do a jot of harm to any one." They forgot, however, that it would have done harm to *him ;* that a weakened conscience would have sapped the strength of his moral life, and that to whom a custom appears to be sin, it *is* sin. So St. Remigius snapped his fingers at all his critics and continued to do what, in his opinion, was right.

The third peculiarity, according to the view of his objectors was, that he *would* write and speak about "religion." But they forgot that it is "out of the fulness of the heart that the mouth speaketh," and while they would commend a politician for ventilating his politics, or a scientist his science, or a literary man his bookishness, they censured a religious man for talking about his religion. Of course these objectors were in a miserable minority—for the heart of the nation is Christian—but there were objectors, and it would not be well to ignore the fact.

As to his "talking religion," MacGregor wrote :

It seems strange and unfriendly to live with men for days, and not to impart one word to them about the great eternity in which they and we shall meet again most surely.

But this kind of writing sometimes offended not only the editors of the secular press, but also those of the religious newspapers. Some very good people, whose sole delight was in "other-worldliness," were shocked because on the same page he recorded that he read the *Times* newspaper containing an account of the formation of a Cabinet, with John Bright as one of its members, and at the same time had something to say about John the Baptist; and again, when on the Lake of Gennesareth, he moralised on the authenticity of Christian revelation, expatiated on the advantages a canoe had over a boat in stemming a high sea, traced the course of the boat in which the disciples had been rowing against a wind when Christ came walking on the water, looked for subaqueous ruins close to the shore, and dodged a swimming Arab!

But despite a few criticisms such as those to which we have referred, the whole English and foreign press were unanimous in this—that his writings were full of interest, amusement, and information, and that Rob Roy was a model traveller.   Throughout the whole of his canoeing days he won respect wherever he went and it was a noteworthy fact that all the steamers in the East carried the *Rob Roy* gratis.   England had set them the example when the " P. and O. Co." kindly took her from Southampton to Alexandria and brought her back again free of charge.   The French, Russian, and Austrian steamers did the same, showing not only kind feeling to the voyager, but an intelligent approval of his purpose.

He was an original traveller, striking out new methods for himself, taking his own views of men, progress, and things, and telling with boyish frankness what he thought and felt.

The mission of the traveller is a very important one and Mac Gregor sustained the honour of the national

character.   If every one who travels would do the
same we should not be branded as we are—"a nation of
hypocrites."   He did not think it was consistent
to do abroad what he would not do at home ; he
carried with him everywhere frankness and straight-
forwardness, respected the prejudices of others while
maintaining his own, adapted himself to circumstances
and so won golden opinions from all men in every
land he visited.   He says :

> It is a traveller's duty to think of others who may follow his route,
> and to remedy abuses, and to punish extortions, and to abstain from
> doubtful actions, lest others may suffer, even if he is not injured.
> No person can be more sensible of this duty than one who has been
> so much benefited by the good conduct of other travellers as I have
> been ; and it would not be from carelessness or a forgetful content
> with my own good fortune, that I should by weakness, or lavish
> giving, or by niggardly pay, or winking at wrong, do anything to
> spoil a good road for future tourists.

In his rapidly written letters to the newspaper press,
as in his more studied writings, there are no distorted
caricatures or personalities in describing the people he
met.   He might have read every line he had written
in the presence of the people he described without
feeling that he had wounded their self-respect or
affronted any of their national tastes.   It is not all
travellers who could do this.

Unfailing good-humour was another characteristic
of Rob Roy as a traveller.   Nothing ever seemed to
"put him out."   On rivers or canals, when the bargees
hailed him with, "Any room for another?" or "Got

your life insured, Gov'nor?" he smiled and nodded to every one and every one on river and lake was friendly to him. He wrote in one of his early works :

A man respectfully asked me to delay the start five minutes, as his aged father, who was bed-ridden, wished exceedingly to see the canoe. In all such cases it is a pleasure to give pleasure, and to sympathise with the boundless delight of the boys, remembering how as a boy a boat delighted me ; and then, again, these worthy mother-like wholesome-faced dames, how could one object to their prying gaze, mingled as it was with friendly smile and genuine interest?

Unselfishness is one of the ingredients that make up a model traveller, and Mac Gregor possessed the virtue :

It was not easy to enjoy my comfortable bed, piled up with blankets, and sheltered above from the dew, while some of my dependants were out the livelong night in a keen, cold, frosty winter blast lying upon the bare ground.

Hearing one of his attendants cough in the night gave rise to this reflection :

Thick walls in England separate us from the dark, wet, freezing misery of the poor amongst us, and deaden to our ears their cries of hunger and of pain. Life would be impracticable if we could realise one tithe of the wretchedness around us ; but his is a stony heart that does not think of this often, and get nerved by the sad thought to do his share in helping.

We may sum up Mac Gregor's remaining characteristics as a traveller as consisting of splendid courage, a dash of audacity now and then, a touch of recklessness here and there, admirable discretion, indomitable pluck, readiness of resource, and persistent determination.

Canoeing forwarded the development of these qualities. Skill, tact, and decision were needed at every turn.

You must choose, and that promptly, too, between, say, five channels opened suddenly before you. Three are probably safe, but which of these three is the shortest, deepest, and most practicable? In an instant if you hesitate, the boat is on a bank; and it is remarkable how speedily the exercise of this resolution becomes experienced into habit, but of course only after some severe lessons.

Especially was promptitude necessary in the exploration of the rivers of Palestine. Here is a striking illustration :

It was true luxury to be whirled in the swift eddies of the Abana and to speed at a river's gallop among rocks and forests, where the midriff is tickled in the paddler's breast by the sensation often felt on a high rope swing, and the mind expands into an exulting glee, always begotten by rapids encountered alone.

Many birds and animals were roused from their uninvaded haunts, and they splashed into the stream or scurried away rustling among the dusky brakes. The canoeist soon finds that it is impossible to note these pretty companions when he is in this sort of river, for the stream carries you suddenly to where a dozen prostrate trees are tangled in the water, while their straggling roots hold fast to the bank. . . . . A heavy treacherous rock overhangs on the left and the right shore is steep with soft mud. The whole picture of this is presented in an instant as you round a point, and the decision as to how you will deal with it must be instantly made or the current itself will decide.

Strong to the left hand, seize that bough with the right, swing round a greater circle, then duck the head for ten seconds under the thorn, and shoot across below the second tree, drift under the third and five strokes will free us surely ! After settling all this as the course to be pursued, at the first paddle stroke out splashes a shrieking bird, rattling the close thicket of canes as he plunges into the water.

Now in such a place, if you look at him even for an instant, the whole programme above is in confusion—the bough knocks your hat off, the rock catches your paddle, and the third tree gets hooked in your painter. This comes of mingling ornithology with canoe craft, and yet it is in such a place that strange birds are most likely to be flushed.*

Of the many hair-breadth 'scapes of Rob Roy in his canoeing expeditions we have no space to give an adequate record here; but in his published works many of these are detailed and we may see him clenching his teeth and clutching his paddle as the canoe dashes into the rapids of the Reuss; or battling in his frail craft in a fearful storm off Beachy Head, when a white dazzling gleam of forked lightning cleaves the darkness, disclosing close at hand a huge vessel hitherto unseen, lofty, full-sailed, for a moment black against the instant of light, then utterly lost again; or, in Syria and Palestine, amongst wolves and wild boars—"tuskers which might charge the *Rob Roy*, smash her to pieces, and leave me helpless on the concealed island;" or, worst of all, alone and at the mercy of the Arab brigands of the Hauran.

One of the most exciting and best known of all Rob Roy's adventures was when he found himself pursued by a mob of furious Hooleh Arabs, who followed him, running on the banks and waylaying him at various turns of the river, until one, more reckless than the

* "Rob Roy on the Jordan," chap. viii.

Y

rest, covered him with a gun and fired, but happily missed. This was the signal for all the pursuers to dash into the water, surround the canoe, and take Rob Roy captive, amid the yells of a savage crowd; the canoe and its occupant being lifted bodily out of the water, and carried into the presence of the sheikh. The sentence in open court, held in the sheikh's hut, was that Mac Gregor must forego his intention of visiting the lake (Hooleh) but, the court having been cleared, this punishment was bought off by a bribe of a gold Napoleon. It was not so easy to know how to "square" the rank and file, and unless Mac Gregor could secure the active co-operation of the sheikh, his position would still be a very serious one. So he resorted to a stratagem—a masterpiece of ready humour—which must be narrated in his own words:

No one had as yet offered me any food. This gross neglect (never without meaning among the Arabs) I determined now to expose, and so to test their real intentions. My cuisine was soon rigged up for cooking, and I asked for cold water. In two minutes afterwards the brave little lamp was steaming away at high pressure, with its merry hissing sound. Every one came to see this. I cut thin slices of the preserved beef soup, and, while they were boiling, I opened my salt-cellar. This is a snuff-box, and from it I offered a pinch to the sheikh. He had never before seen salt so white (the Arab salt is like our black pepper) and, therefore, thinking it was sugar, he willingly took some from my hand and put it to his tongue. Instantly I ate up the rest of the salt, and with a loud, laughing shout, I administered to the astonished, outwitted sheikh a manifest thump on the back.

'What is it?' all asked from him. 'Is it sukker?' He answered demurely: 'La! melah!' (No, it's salt!) Even his Home Secretary

CAPTURED BY ARABS

laughed at his chief. We had now eaten salt together, and in his own tent, and so he was bound by the strongest tie, and he knew it.*

There were two other aspects in which Mac Gregor was often regarded as an eccentric traveller. The first, his curious *penchant* for journeying alone; the second, his almost sentimental attachment to his canoe. With the exception of his first tour, when he was accompanied for some distance by Lord Aberdeen,† all his canoe and yawl journeys were made alone. His reasons have been given in many places but never more clearly than in his latest book when, describing his difficulties in making his way through an apparently inaccessible marsh, he says :

The thing must be done somehow, and plans for new projects of this kind cannot be hit off in a moment. Long consideration, and a resolve to leave nothing haphazard, are the true secrets of ensuring success, and here comes in one of the great advantages of travelling alone. You have time and silence to consider maturely. You do not mar your plans by feeble compromises. You see, hear, and think a great deal more than if a 'pleasant companion' is beside you all day, whose small talk (and your own) must be run dry in a month, and neither of you is free. In these solitary expeditions I have never a sensation of loneliness. Hard work, healthy exercise, plain food, and plenty of it, early hours, reading at night, and working, moving, noting, drawing, observing and considering all day, one's plans are quietly perfected, and there is no more of tedium or solitary dulness than is felt when you read or fish alone,

* "Rob Roy on the Jordan."

† Lord Aberdeen was drowned, and his brother, the Hon. James Gordon, was killed by the accidental discharge of his gun. For both of these brave and noble fellows Mac Gregor had a strong attachment. Both were associated with him in the London Scottish.

or paint, or write in a town—the place one can feel most lonely in after all.

It can scarcely be a matter of great wonder that the canoe, in which he had spent so much of his time, which had borne its part in all dangers and diffi-culties, pleasures and successes, should have been regarded by him with a feeling almost amounting to affection.   And this is how he vindicated himself to his critics :

Is it maudlin that one cannot help personifying a boat like this, the companion of many happy hours, the sharer too of anxious times? When we see even deal tables merrily turning round, and can fancy a smile on the face of a clock, are we quite sure that there is no feeling in the 'heart of oak,' no sentiment under bent birch ribs ; that a canoe, in fact, has no character? Let the landsman say so, yet will not I.   Like others of her sex, she has her fickle tempers. One day pleasant, and the next out of humour ; led like a lamb through this rapid, but cross and pouting under sail on that rough lake.   And, like her sex, she may be resisted, coerced, nay con-vinced, but, in the end, she will always somehow have her own way !

Many expressions somewhat similar to the follow-ing, appear from time to time in his books :

All the Bedouins of the desert could not catch us when afloat, nor could they reach me with their rifles, for, in two minutes I should be hidden in by the reeds.

At such a moment the *Rob Roy* seemed more than ever dear to me, if such an expression is ever permissible respecting an inanimate object.

In all the works written by Mac Gregor, the descriptions of scenery are graphic, and of men and

manners photographic. A reflective mind gives its
reflections naturally without striving for effect. A
keen sense of humour runs throughout, often combined with deep and sympathetic feeling. But above
all there is a joyous holiday spirit. The reader feels
that the writer is about as happy as any mortal can
be, and the happiness becomes contagious.

From a literary point of view some of the most
valuable parts of his earlier works appear to us to be
those in which he brings his keen powers of observation to bear, and in his quiet and unassuming way
"drops his good things as an ostrich lays her eggs."
Some of his descriptions of scenery, of the habits and
peculiarities of living creatures, of the passage of a
thunderstorm, or the varying aspects of sky and water,
are inimitable.

Let one example suffice :

When the scenery is tame, and the channel of the river is not made
interesting by dangers to be avoided, then we can always turn again
to the animals and birds, and in five minutes of watching will be sure
to see much that is curious.

Here, for instance, we have the little kingfisher again, who visits
us on the Danube and the Reuss, and whom we knew well in England
before ; but now we are on a visit to his domain, and we see him in
private character alone. There are several varieties of this bird, and
they differ in form and colour of plumage. This royal bird, the
Halcyon of antiquity, the Alcedo of classic tongue, is called in German
Eisvogel (Ice bird), perhaps because he fishes even in winter's frost,
or because his nest is like a bundle of icicles, being made of minnows'
bones most curiously wrought together. But now it is on a summer
day, and he is perched on a twig within two inches of the water, and
under the shade of a briar-leaf, his little parasol. He is looking for

fish, and is so steady that you may easily pass him without observing that brilliant back of azure or the breast of blushing red. When I desired to see these birds, I quietly rowed my boat till it grounded on a bank, and after it was stationary thus for a few minutes, the Halcyon fisher got quite unconcerned and plied his task as if unobserved.

He peers with knowing eye into the shallows below him, and now and then he dips his head a bit, to make quite sure he has marked a fish worth seizing; then he suddenly darts down with a splash and flies off with a little white minnow or a struggling stickleback nipped in his beak.

If it is caught thus crosswise, the winged fisherman tosses his prey into the air, so that it may be gulped down properly. Then he quivers and shakes with satisfaction, and quickly speeds to another perch, flitting by you with wonderful swiftness, as if a sapphire had been flung athwart the sunbeam, flashing beauteous colours in its flight.

Or, if bed-time has come, or if he is fetching home the family dinner, he flutters on, and then with a little sharp note of 'good-bye,' pops into a hole, the dark staircase to his tiny nest, and there he finds Mrs. Halcyon sitting in state, and thirteen baby kingfishers gaping for the dainty fish.*

Could White of Selborne, Wilson, McGillivray, J. Bertram, J. G. Wood, Frank Buckland, or any of the host of literary naturalists have brought the mysterious, brilliant and active fisher-bird more vividly before the mind's eye?

By universal consent, Mac Gregor's " Rob Roy on the Jordan " was, both as regards style and matter, a vast advance upon his former works.

He was no longer the *dilettante* wanderer but a serious explorer into the vexed question of the Upper

* " A Thousand Miles in the *Rob Roy*," chap. xiii.

Waters of Jordan and other matters to elucidate Old
Testament history.   No one was better fitted to the
task ; his intimate acquaintance with the history and
geography of Palestine ; his knowledge not only of
the Bible itself but also of the commentators, histo-
rians and travellers who had written on the Holy Land
in all the ages ; and above all, his intense enthusiasm,
which made him insensible to time, trouble, expense,
or fatigue — all these fitted him for his important
work.

Nor must the permanent value of his services as
an explorer be overlooked, for although Robinson,
Wilson, De Saulcy, Stanley, Porter, and a multitude
of others had written learned volumes ; although thousands of tourists had visited the Jordan at Jericho,
surveyed it from the heights of Tiberias, Kedesh and
Banias, yet John Mac Gregor was the first who really
discovered the course of the Jordan from Dan to the
sea of Tiberias—twenty miles of river as unknown as
the course of the Zambesi was at that time.   In like
manner the devious courses of the famous streams
Abana and Pharpar were laid down in his chart with
an accuracy never before attained.

So much as to St. Remigius the canoeist.   In our
next chapter we shall endeavour to detail the practical
uses to which he devoted the knowledge acquired,
the experience gained, and the intense enjoyment
realised in these feats of navigation.

CHAPTER XV.

ON THE CREST OF THE WAVE

JOHN MAC GREGOR returned from his Jordan tour in April 1869, and the occasion was one of great rejoicing among the members of "The Open-air Mission," who had prepared for him a pleasant surprise-gift consisting of a portrait of his father, Sir Duncan Mac Gregor, the English Hexapla, exhibiting the six important English translations of the New Testament Scriptures, and an address. In acknowledging it he said, "It is an assurance of what was often felt in lonely times of danger that, though I was far away and so long time gone, there were friends at home who did not forget to plead at the throne of Him who is the great Friend of us all."

In May he commenced the preparation of "Rob Roy on the Jordan," and in November passed the final sheets for press. It is only necessary to take up the book and glance cursorily through it to be assured that this was a surprising example of literary energy, but the surprise is increased when it is found that the work is one of critical research, giving the result of the reading of a lifetime, and abounding in references to learned authorities.

Before the day of publication two thousand copies were ordered, and within a fortnight nearly 5000 copies were sold. The book, published by John Murray, was dedicated to " H.R.H. the Commodore of the Royal Canoe Club."

In an early stage of his canoeing experiences, Mac Gregor had seriously asked himself the question what practical use he could make of them, and how could they assist the great philanthropic work in which he was engaged, and to which everything else, he felt, should be subsidiary.

He had found that by the invigoration of his strength he qualified himself for greater activities, and we have seen how he had devoted the whole of the proceeds of his literary labours to the betterment of deserving institutions—a princely gift we may imagine seeing how great was the success of his works.

His book on Palestine he rightly regarded as a part of his life-work. It gave him the opportunity of speaking directly to the hearts of tens of thousands on religious matters, enlivening some, and deepening the insight into holy things in others.

Like all his other books, it appealed straight to young men and won their admiration. They were accustomed to hear good men ridiculed, and sometimes deservedly so, as poor weak creatures who were so absorbed in their fears for the present and strivings for the future as to be unable to take part in the

practical work and rational enjoyment of life. Rob
Roy showed them that a religious profession and
marked activity in Christian work need not, and did
not in his case, diminish a love of manly sports or
quench the ardour of interest in all that concerns the
progress of true science and learning.

Grateful as he was that his books had a useful
influence among young men, he was anxious beyond
expression to come more immediately in contact with
his readers. It was not enough that he should be
read, he wished that he might be heard, so that he
might deepen by that means any impression he had
already made. Out of this wish there grew the
settled purpose to visit every city and town in the
kingdom and lecture on Palestine. But even this was
not enough for his ambition. He could not disguise
from himself that he was "the rage"; he felt fairly
certain that his lectures would "draw" and that
multitudes would come to hear him, especially if he
lectured gratuitously. This, however, was not his
intention. If he felt justified in giving up so much
time as this proposed lecturing campaign would
involve, would it not fare ill with many of the institutions with which his name was associated and to
whose interests he was pledged? It was true that
many new labourers had entered into the field, and
that institutions he had started were being successfully
carried on by others. What seemed to be the pressing need of that particular time was not so much
efficient labourers as sufficient funds to carry on the

multitudinous philanthropies. The times were bad : there was universal distress among the working classes ; good old institutions were being pressed out of the field by noisy and clamorous new ones ; there were tens of thousands who could only be reached by offering them the meat that perisheth, before present- ing them with that which endureth unto life ever- lasting ; and there were no funds for dealing with the initial difficulty. Meanwhile invitations were pouring in to Mac Gregor, begging him to lecture for this institution and that, here, there, and everywhere.

He resolved, therefore, that he would undertake a great lecturing campaign, but that he would not give a single lecture under £20, £50, or £100 ; that he would continue the enterprise—health and strength permitting—until he had earned ten thousand pounds ; that every farthing of this he would devote to charities, philanthropies, deserving causes, and that this should be net cash as he determined to pay all his own expenses. It was a noble and daring idea and he carried it out to the letter. Surely, when the philanthropic history of this country is written, this fact should stand out as a lasting memorial to Mac Gregor. Many have written cheques for thousands of pounds to be distributed among the poor ; few have given up time, strength, and convenience and endured the exhausting fatigue, the personal exposure and the wear and tear of life to accomplish so earnest a purpose.

His plan of action was on this wise. The head of

a struggling institution would write, beseeching him to lecture on behalf of its funds. Mac Gregor would thoroughly investigate the *bona fides* of the appeal and if he were satisfied, he would promise to lecture on condition that his fee, of say fifty pounds in a small town or one hundred in a larger one, were raised by sale of tickets or by special subscription. In due course he would arrive with bag and baggage, scenery, curiosities and paraphernalia; deliver his lecture to a crowded audience, and hand over his cheque for the benefit of the institution.

A few notes from his diary may be given here:

1870.

Jan. 9.—Excellent sermon, Vaughan, 'Whom shall I send?' Good for me to feel a missionary spirit in the twenty-five lectures and other engagements I am now bound by. Temptation to like life and health too much. Second temptation, scarcely less insidious, to be too much troubled that I *do* like life and health so much. Troubled about many things instead of that 'good part.'

Jan. 12.—First lecture on the 'Rob Roy on the Jordan,' at Edgware Road Working Men's Institute. Rev. H. Allon presided. Crowded, and all went off well.

Henceforth for several years the diary is full of records of constant flittings from place to place with perpetual and exciting work. The last entry for the first year of the lecturing campaign is a record of extraordinary success.

Dec. 31, 1870.—From Jan. 1 to Dec. 31 lectured or presided or spoke at public meetings 128 times besides all minor occasions. Of these I gave 'Rob Roy' Lecture 56 times, earning sum of £4160, and have six more lectures engaged for, each at £100.

JOHN MACGREGOR IN HIS LECTURING COSTUME

It will be readily surmised that a man who could command such terms and audiences as Mac Gregor did for some years, must have been no ordinary lecturer. Nor was he. The lectures were always delivered in a free, unaffected, and highly amusing style, and were what Max O'Rell would call "comedy lectures." On the platform were arrayed a full-sized model of the *Rob Roy*, with the identical sails and masts, together with the cooking apparatus, miniature lamp, bed, and other fittings used during the voyage, with diagrams and maps *ad lib.*

Soon after appearing before the audience and making his introductory speech, he would retire for a moment or two and re-appear in his canoeing dress, including a red serge Norfolk jacket (to be changed for a grey one when in an enemy's country) and light helmet with flowing puggaree, to protect head and neck from the heat.

In giving an amusing description of a long desert ride on camel-back, he would assume a scarlet tunic and turban, and mounting a chair which represented the camel's back, and holding an umbrella of many colours, would depict the movements of a camel rider to the life, and at the same time imitate the noises made by camels to express various emotions or moods—such as anger at being loaded, or pleasure when drinking water. Then, when describing the remote parts of the Nile about the hour of sunset, he would imitate the noises of lions and the general chorus of animals of many different kinds. When discoursing on mummies, he would burn before the audience a small portion of mummy dust, to demonstrate how largely creosote entered into the embalming material.

In giving an example of eastern music, he would promise to fetch from behind the screen a petulant Arab boy, and running to the back of the stage, would in a moment or two re-appear—a tall slim figure dressed in long flowing white Arab costume! Then, sitting tailor-fashion, he would light a chibouk and smoke a whiff or two; or, seizing a musical instrument not unlike a biscuit box, give forth the Arab's guttural notes as from a bagpipe, or break into a sweeter song, beating time upon a box; at the same time assuming the postures and gestures of a Bedouin desert ranger.

He was wont to conclude his lecture on the Jordan with the famous "crocodile story;" then tying his bed on his back, putting on a Greek cap, and arranging his mosquito screen and oil cloth, he would light his lamp and lie down comfortably in the canoe, reading a copy of the *Times.* Suddenly the howl of a jackal would ring across the room, and MacGregor would spring up, tell in an excited way of a dreadful dream about an encounter with a crocodile, when forthwith the animal would appear on canvas at the back of the platform, with MacGregor riding triumphantly on its back, and "God save the Queen" and "Success to the —— Institute" inscribed above and below the head and tail!

These lectures added greatly to his popularity, and the flattering things that were said of him were enough to turn the head of any man with less ballast.

His buoyant spirits, his joyousness, his fund of anecdote and experience, made him a welcome guest wherever he went, and he went from the palace to the hovel, passing through the various strata of society that divide the one from the other, with equal serenity.

A glance at some correspondence about this time will emphasise what we have written, and we select three specimens representing society, literature, and art.

The (Late) Duchess of Sutherland *to* John Mac Gregor.

Stoke-upon-Trent, *Thursday.*

My Dear Mr. Mac Gregor,

Thank you so very much for your kind trouble in choosing such a beautiful little canoe for me. I think it is the prettiest I ever saw, and I am longing for to-morrow morning to try it. I daresay I shall have a ducking the first time, but I will try implicitly to follow your directions, for which I am much obliged. She is lying in the water with two hundredweight on board as you desired. How I hope I may learn to use her. I hope you will come to see me when I go to London, and tell me of all your good works. That last you sent me the pamphlet about is, I am sure, a very blessed one. The poor little children! I should be so glad sometimes to help you a little when it is needed.

Yours most sincerely,

A. Sutherland.

Next day Mac Gregor received another letter, which began :

I have had my first lesson in the dear little canoe which is perfect.

CHARLES DICKENS *to* JOHN MAC GREGOR.

GAD'S HILL PLACE, HIGHAM BY ROCHESTER, KENT,
Tuesday, June 15, 1869.

. . . . By this post I write to my publishers, begging them to send a set of my books to the Inns of Court Lending Library. I hope I need not add that I most readily respond to your request and I shall feel most obliged to you if you will give me the first opportunity the Athenæum affords of becoming personally known to you. I am so very well acquainted with the *Rob Roy* canoe, and have taken passage in her with so much pleasure, that I have a special interest in her Captain. . . . .

This letter led to an interesting personal acquaintance, in the course of which Mac Gregor introduced to the great novelist a splendid specimen of the London street Arab, who became one of Dickens' "characters."

SIR JOHN E. MILLAIS *to* JOHN MAC GREGOR.

7 CROMWELL PLACE,
November 25, 1871.

DEAR MAC GREGOR,

I have just returned from the North and hasten to tell you I have read your book with great pleasure. I wish I could anchor a raft at the spot which you give an illustration of, and paint a careful picture of it, the lane of water coming into the lake, banks of papyrus on either side, and two mountain peaks just breaking the line of papyrus forest. . . . .

Very truly yours,

J. E. MILLAIS.

Although the lecture season continued all the year round so far as Mac Gregor was concerned, it had its limitations, and the summer was much freer for him than the winter.

But with his indomitable—or shall we say restless—
energy, he did not avail himself of any lengthened
period of rest. So we find that in the "off season"
of 1869 he was "much occupied about the Exhibition
of Palestine Exploration Fund at Dudley Gallery,"
and was canvassing, lecturing, and speaking on
behalf of the Martyrs' Memorial church at Smithfield,
entering on a new crusade against the current
literature for boys, going heart and soul into the
formation of new canoe clubs, superintending races,
yachting matches, and such like, keeping up at high
pressure his outdoor preaching, and at the same time
not indifferent to the claims of social life. But we
will let a few disjointed extracts from his private
diary speak for him again :

Nov. 23, 1869.—Lunch Vaughan. Met Jenny Lind.
1870.
March 10.—This day I was elected a member of the Oxford and
Cambridge Club.
March 13, *Sunday.*—Noble sermon from Vaughan—but my life is
too happy to feel properly anxious to leave it.

Why should he have felt anxious to leave it?
It is only morbid and unhealthy life that wishes to
die, despite hymns and sermons to the contrary.

March 20, *Sunday.*—Vaughan's sermon on 'jesting.' Bold and
useful, but too difficult to preach unless each hearer interprets for
himself the words 'not convenient.'

This is good, for no man loved a joke better
than he.

April 10.—Fear I am quite proud of my book, lectures, speeches, and self generally—health and happiness. To pore over the thought that I have so few trials may be itself a temptation.

Here is a large Christian heart struggling against a narrow creed. Why should not a man be as happy as his capacity will admit? Is not this presupposed as one of the elements of Christianity, "in Christ to have all things and abound?"

May 22, *Sunday*.—Battersea Suspension Bridge. Found a man with crowd to whom he read 'The Creed of a Fop' in nineteen clauses and half an hour in expounding it. Near him a teetotaler and beyond a Mr. Kaspary preaching 'the religion of God,' a Buddhist-Deism with transmigration of souls. He used a Tischendorf New Testament. After some time I began and a great crowd came and I held up Christ and discomfited the Jew present much to his confusion. This was one of the most curious Sundays I ever had. Dined at the Club with Tyndall, Laurence Oliphant, and Gibbs, and heard Oliphant's faith. Walked with them afterwards.

May 27.—Dined Lord Lawrence. Lectured 'Rob Roy' forty-fifth time; Vestry Hall, Kensington, for Y.W.C.A.

May 29, *Sunday*.—Meant to preach at Battersea, but drawn to converse with C. about Chunder Sen, the Hindoo Deist, Unitarian, who had lectured. C. logical and calm in his religious views. He has much altered. He is much nearer Christ than many Christians. I look to answers to many prayers for him. Read Newman's 'Grammar of Assent.' Struck with plain good sense when he says Assumption or Axioms are needed in all arguments for demonstration. In mathematics this is so, and also in Revelation. He declines to argue with those who do not grant a God, conscience, as foundations.

In the summer of this year Mac Gregor spent much of his time with the Canoe Club and not a little with his own canoe. We find him at Cowes and Southsea, at Plymouth, Falmouth, and the Scilly Isles. One curious entry in the diary at this time shows a strange development of the canoe idea.

Sep. 8.—Crossed from Tresco in *Rob Roy*. Rev. H. Mayo in his canoe. He visits the sick in her and carries communion plate. Good lines, very clumsy above. Squalls too heavy, he had to be towed back. The evening chapel full, chiefly of men. Told them about Jordan cruise with black board in pulpit, clergyman there also and all much pleased.

The Rev. H. Mayo was not the only disciple of Rob Roy who used a canoe for religious purposes. In the far south the Rev. C. R. Fairey "paddled his own canoe," the *Evangelist*, along the coasts and rivers of Australia. His little craft (weighing with sails and all fittings only eighty pounds, carried a light mast and a lug sail which enabled him to make seven or eight knots in a fair wind) was built in London under Mac Gregor's direction. The cargo, like that of the *Rob Roy*, consisted chiefly of tracts and Testaments, and on her first voyage of 300 miles round the iron-bound north and east coasts of Tasmania, Mr. Fairey held services and distributed books at many places where the sound of the Gospel was rarely, if ever, heard.

The main object of Mac Gregor's coasting tours was to visit sailors, the coastguards, lifeboat crews, lighthousemen, fishers and shrimpers, bargees and yachtsmen, and all and sundry who live by the water and can be approached by a boat.

We cannot resist the temptation of giving one brief, but very vividly descriptive, note from a letter headed St. Mary's, Scilly Islands, September 10, 1870.

By our side are the pilchard boats, each lightly anchored and with crew aboard ready at a moment to rush out upon 'a school of fish' and to surround it with speedy snares and gather the rich glittering harvest of the sea. Meanwhile they must watch for the fish on the high cliff. Above is a 'Huer,' the man who scans the wide sea, and by its roughened surface can discern the fish long miles away. For hours, for days, for weeks the boats must be thus instant in readiness, and the Huer gazing far. At last he sees the well-known, welcome flutter on the waves, and, seizing a long horn, blows the signal loud and hoarse when away go a score of boats eagerly straining their oars. The Huer seizes two round light balls of gorse in his hands and by motions like a telegraph he directs the crews to their prey. He waves forward and they advance; he swings left and they turn; he circles and they bend round; he lifts both balls aloft and the boats stop; and while his arms give the last signal of 'cast the nets the fishers pour out the great seine and compass the teeming millions of fish, then close them nearer and gather them into their boats. The take may be long delayed, the chance may come seldom; but the prize of even one good shoal may win a thousand pounds.

On his return, the formation of the first London School Board was the all-absorbing topic of the day— a topic in which he took an exceptional interest as it was one that he foresaw must affect, for good or for ill, many of the institutions in which he had taken a lifelong interest.

His action in the matter and his own part as a member of the Board will be told hereafter.

In the meantime he was prosecuting his labours as

a lecturer with unflagging zeal, and at the close of the season of 1870–1 he was able to write :

1871.

May 1.—R. R. Lecture, No. 65, and last lecture of the season realising in all £5062. The first lecture was given Jan. 12, 1870. Perfect health and happiness and all this gain to charities in fifteen months and a half, being an average of just one lecture a week on the canoe all that time.

May 17.—Royal Literary Fund. Spoke responding to toast of Travellers.

June 9.—At Stafford House with Dr. Birch and H. Wright and opened mummy brought by Duke. Got some grains of corn and resolved to plant them.

The wooden sarcophagus, and mummy encased, were brought from the Khedive of Egypt by the Duke of Sutherland. The lid of the mummy case seemed to have been unopened before, as the clay luting was in the joint nearly all round. From the hieroglyphics outside, Dr. Birch pronounced the mummy to be that of a priest sacred to Osiris, and about 2600 years old, and he predicted there would be found inside several articles, a blue glass net, images, &c., and such were duly found. Among the loose débris inside the case were four grains of corn, two of these Mac Gregor planted a few days afterwards in a small flower-pot filled with sifted mould from the Temple Gardens ; the other two grains were sent to Mr. Sowerby at the Royal Botanic Society, Regent's Park : the pot from the Temple was also sent to Mr. Sowerby later on, with one of the grains grown up about eight inches high. This was returned in December 1871, as a stalk four feet long, with twelve grains of oats, growing on it as represented in the photograph held in Rob Roy's hand in the illustration facing page 350. The other two grains grew up into several stalks, but without fruit, as shown in the flower-pot beside the sitting figure.

In August 1871, MacGregor started on one of the most interesting of all his many cruises—the coast and canals of Holland and the Zuyder Zee. It is unfortunate it was not undertaken sooner ; it should have been one of his first voyages and he would have gathered the subject-matter of an exceptionally novel and entertaining book. As it was it came after the Egypt and Palestine cruise, and MacGregor, wisely, did not care to lessen the fame he had acquired by his *magnum opus*, by telling the minor story of this voyage in book form.

In all the journeys in Europe, Asia, Africa and America that he had made, never were so many and such persistent starers found as in Holland. On his first night afloat in Dutch waters, a crowd stood for hours gazing and whispering until it was pitch dark. Rain fell but the gazers stood in rain and darkness. He put out his reading-lamp and the people gradually dispersed ; he re-lighted it and they came back to stare. Burgomasters and aldermen, schoolmasters and their schools, peaceful inhabitants and stolid Dutch workmen turned out day by day to see the new wonder and to comment thereon. Even the lowing herds came to stare, to toss their heads and tails, and

then to gambol a mad dance round the field—"those
worthy kine which will come to London by thousands
alive in steamers, and we shall eat them, exclaiming:
'Oh, the roast beef of Old England.'"

At the island of Urk the whole population appeared
to turn out, hundreds of people wading round and

THE *ROB ROY* ARRIVING AT THE ISLE OF URK, ZUYDER ZEE

round and standing in thick groups on the piers, the
shore and the housetops.

Even on this Dutch cruise he had some stirring
adventures. One day the captain of a huge steamer
hailed him and he tacked for a "tow astern," while he
dined on the deck of the canoe. At the bend of the
canal the *Rob Roy* somehow got under the steamer's
"quarter," and so into the terrible suction wake of the
immense revolving screw-blades. The draught into

this awkward current was sudden, strong, and irresistible, and only at the last moment when within an inch of the plashing propeller was he saved. Another moment and one stroke of the sharp-edged blade would have crushed his frail craft to atoms and not improbably have given him his quietus.

One curious experience was in sailing from Helder to the Texel. Mac Gregor chose for his night quarters a smooth bay near Eierland, the eastern end of the Texel and the "land of eggs," where sea-birds innumerable have their haunts, and no man intrudes. All went well until the moon rose. Then the sea-birds of a hundred kinds, and thousands in number, quickly assembled, screaming, yelling like jackals, twittering, darting swiftly hither and thither, flashing white wings in the moonlight, splashing the dreamy waves, and causing Mac Gregor's dog Rob to dance with Highland rage at their impudence.

All sleep was dissipated for the night, and at sunrise he sped away southward.

We must not linger over any more of Rob Roy's tours. New and widening experiences in other spheres were opening up before him, and we have yet to see him in other lights than those in which he has hitherto been introduced to us.

On returning from his Dutch tour, he found the work of the London School Board and his lecturing campaign all-absorbing. But he nevertheless made time to visit and to keep up the brief daily notes in his diary.

It is a thousand pities that he had not time to·
record more fully his opinion of the distinguished
persons he met, and the good things they said; it
would have made a volume of unusual interest. We
can only give here, however, some bald indications
of his movements.

THE *ROB ROY* ON THE TEXEL AT MOONRISE

1871.

Aug. 6.—Dined with Millais at Athenæum.

Aug. 13.—Sold my yawl, dingy and stores for 100 guineas to a
man at Melbourne, Australia.

Sep. 30.—Visited Exhibition, last day. Dined Sir Harry Parkes.
W—— told me the Queen had four hours downright good work
every day. His own box sometimes gave her two hours. She
sometimes altered the proposals for Parliament from Cabinet
Councils. Professor Owen lunched here and said skull from
Holland was fair average man and my camel's tooth from the
Temple is not a camel's but an ox's, and perhaps one sacrificed at
beginning of Temple.

Oct. 2.—Huxley lunched with me and smoked and examined the skull.

Nov. 21.—Read paper Society of Arts on 'Street Folks.'

Dec. 20.—Dined B. Powell. Met Lady Franklin, Leslie Stephen, Browning the poet.

Dec. 23.—To Farmer of Harrow about School Music. My letter in *Times* about Refuges.

Dec. 31, *Sunday.*—Splendid sermon Vaughan. 'Set thy house in order.' A year of health and happiness and hard work. The disciplinary sorrow and sickness, if yet in store, will come from the same physician and be for the same life of the soul.

1872.

Jan. 6.—Saw Liddell, Home Office, about the clause for Streets Bill as to licensing sellers.

Jan. 7.—Lord A. Churchill told me the name of a friend of his who had a loan from a crossing-sweeper of £1000. A barrister friend of mine told me that his own father had been asked to dinner by a crossing-sweeper and went and dined well.

Jan. 24.—Birthday, 47 years old. Nobody has had a happier life.

Jan. 31.—Heard grand accounts of arrival of dear old yawl at Melbourne.

Feb. 13.—Wrote to Prince of Wales and Prince Imperial about Canoe Club.

June 21.—Good sermon, Lawrence of St. Albans. He put duty and pleasure in opposition and at night I felt two months' vacation to the Crimea was no longer a duty because being quite well I did not need it for health, so must give it up and take only one month elsewhere.

June 22.—Resolved as last night, and sent to countermand all and gave up Russian steamer, &c.

So instead of a long looked-for visit to the Crimea —full of interest to him in its glorious as well as painful associations—he contented himself with a quiet cruise in the Shetland Isles. On his return from many of his tours, Mac Gregor was in the habit of sending an interesting general account of them to the *Times*; and after he had given a good description of people and places, he had the happy knack of inserting an appeal for aid to some good work. Thus on his return from Shetland, after telling of the progress of the people owing to better postal arrangements and the introduction of the electric telegraph, of the state of old and new industries, and of the dangers of their coast, he contrived to weave into his story an account of a projected Seamen's Home and Institute at Lerwick; but as the sum it would cost "was quite beyond the resources of this outer end of Britain," he called upon all interested in sailors and fishermen to lend their aid, and so gave a splendid advertisement which led to good results.

We cull here a few extracts from the diary for 1873:

1873.

Feb. 2, *Sunday*.—Planted two grains of mummy corn from stalk grown in my rooms. [On March 2 the corn stood two inches high in the flower pot.]

March 16.—My dearest Father was 86 years old to-day and in full possession of his faculties.

March 22.—Dinner to Tyndall and Hurst, Athenæum; present also Roupell, Sir W. Boxall, Spottiswoode, Busk, Rev. Pullen, Herbert Spencer, J. Fergusson, A. C. Ramsay, Self, Huxley in the chair. This was a success, but one felt 'in partibus infidelium.' Played pool afterwards and killed four lives of balls.

July 6.—What with splendid weather, perfect health, constant useful work and frequent success and praise, the life on earth to which one ought to set lightly gets undue claims of the heart and these must be loosened or some description of illness or suffering or even shame may be necessary in the wisdom of the great Physician. I record the thought because the thought itself was put into my mind to warn in mercy.

July 18.—Stafford House. Music. Lord Lorne introduced me to Princess Louise, who chatted very amusingly and kindly.

The diary has now brought us up to what we may perhaps regard as the most interesting episode in the life of John Mac Gregor.

He had planned a trip to the Azores with his canoe, but, at the last moment, on the eve of starting, he decided not to take the canoe having been told that his father was very anxious about him. He left London on the 7th of August promising himself a restful tour, after the manner of the old days before the *Rob Roy* was in existence, and sailed to Lisbon, thence to the Azores, and on the 25th reached Grazioza. While walking the deck on the evening of that day, he formed a resolution of such importance that he posted back to England full speed to put it into execution.

In a letter to his very particular friend, the genial Sir John Burns, of Castle Wemyss, he tells what that resolution was :

1 MITRE COURT BUILDINGS, TEMPLE,
September 15, 1873.

MY DEAR J. B.

      Annie Caffin to be my bride. I loved eight years in silence. I did not like to entangle her unless I could give a suitable home.

＊   ＊   ＊   ＊   ＊

At Terceira in the Azores some days ago, I resolved to come home and propose, and after 1700 miles of steaming this came off last Saturday (Sept. 13).   Probably you have seen Annie . . . . still I cannot be trusted to describe her.

Let me bring her to see Mrs. B., and judge if she is not a darling. . . . . My father and Elizabeth are quite delighted, as Annie was the favourite of one and the ally of the other in all good works.

Yours,
J. Mac.

The news was received by some of his intimate friends with incredulity, by others with merriment. Professor Tyndall wrote :

My dear Mac,

What have you been doing? Stealing a march upon me! Oh you sly rascal! Giving me to understand that marriage had innumerable drawbacks, influencing thus my conduct, and going in the teeth of your own maxims.   I will never forgive you!

Yours inexorably,
J. Tyndall.

Not a few of Mac Gregor's special friends were so taken aback when they heard the startling news that he was engaged to be married, that they had afterwards to apologise for the manner in which they received it; the Rev. J. W. Bardsley, to wit, the present Bishop of Sodor and Man, who wrote :

My dear Mac Gregor,

You must have thought me slightly insane yesterday, but the grotesque side of the fact stated (forgive the word) came into view first, and it was not until after you had gone that the good and earnest side of the thing came into full view, and not without many deep aspirations in my mind for your happiness.   I use the word 'grotesque' because I looked upon you as an inveterate bachelor and if I had enumerated the things in last week's *Punch* 'Not seen—An archbishop on a bicycle, &c.,' 'John Mac Gregor in the act of being married,' should have been added.

I am truly glad that you have come to a right state of mind at last. I congratulate you on your choice and heartily pray that you may long be spared to each other.

You must look upon this letter as a sort of apology. I hope your other friends met you more in the right spirit than I did apparently. Sentences in your speeches about 'bachelor life,' and 'the ladies,' naturally came to the front. I shall not be the only one who receives the announcement with a grin !

Yours ever truly,

J. W. BARDSLEY.

Busy and happy days followed Mac Gregor's return to town. He chose for his residence No. 7, Vanbrugh Park Road East, Blackheath, close by the house of the father of his bride, Admiral Sir Crawford Caffin, K.C.B., on the one hand, and of his beloved father, Sir Duncan Mac Gregor, on the other.

The diary which had been faithfully kept since 1848 dwindled away to a mere word or two, until at length the following amusing entries are reached:

1873.

Dec. 1.—Preparing for execution.
Dec. 2.—   Do.   do.
Dec. 3.—   Do.   do.
Dec. 4.—Wedding Day !

The marriage was celebrated at St. John's Church, Blackheath, by the Rev. G. B. Caffin (uncle of the bride), the Rev. Canon Miller, D.D., Vicar of Greenwich, and the Rev. Ernest Cowan, Vicar of St. John's,

Blackheath. A thousand people were in the church and a crowd outside. Fifty boys of the *Chichester* training ship formed a guard of honour, flanked by a detachment from the Shoeblack Brigade, who came to testify their love and gratitude. Sir Crawford Caffin was there and his family; Sir Duncan Mac Gregor and his family, besides hosts of old friends and fellow workers. The School Board, the Royal Canoe Club, the Argonaut Rowing Club, the Ragged School Shoeblack Society, and many other associations were there with their gifts, or had been, and addresses of congratulation flowed in from all quarters. Never were they more heartily given, or more genuinely deserved. For, up to this time

> He is the half-part of a blessed man,
> Left to be finished by such as she:
> And she, a fair divided excellence,
> Whose fulness of perfection lies in him.

And if on that happy day he had quoted to her the now familiar lines :

> Beloved ! let us love so well
> Our work shall still be better for our love,
> And still our love be sweeter for our work
> And both commended for the sake of each
> By all true workers and true lovers born,—

he would have quoted a prophecy which was to be fulfilled to the letter.

CHAPTER XVI

LONDON AND THE LONDON SCHOOL BOARD

WE must now go back a few years in our story. The passage of the Elementary Schools Bill through the House of Commons, the public interest in the question, the new life that seemed to be in store for many societies to which he was pledged, gave intense satisfaction to John Mac Gregor, and when in October 1870, steps were taken to elect members for the first London School Board — ever memorable for the number of eminent men it contained—his labours were unceasing. For eighteen consecutive nights, Sunday only excepted, he delivered speeches in Greenwich and its neighbourhood—speeches which in those days of strong political and religious feeling and discussion needed most careful preparation—while on the day of the elections he laboured in the neighbourhood of the polling places, from day-dawn to sunset. Here is his brief and modest account of the proceedings :

1870.

Dec. 1.—Bristow, returning officer, told me the pleasing news of my Election—No. 2 in the four members.

Dec. 2.—Many congratulations.

Dec. 4, *Sunday*.—This month has culminated in interest and thankful gladness.

We have elsewhere spoken of Mac Gregor's *nous*, his business capabilities, and his sound judgment of men and things. Here is his account of the first meeting of the Board :

Dec. 21.—First meeting of L. S. B., Lord Lawrence evidently not up to rules of chairman and meetings. Minutes of former meeting incorrect and incomplete. Report of committee incorrect, and not presented with explanation. As they had not notified to me my appointment on it, or their meeting, or their report, I had to dissent from it on the Board. This made me speak too often, which was a blunder. I hope my augury not true that Lord L. is not fit for his post, and will leave and that future secretary will easily rule the Board.

We know of no better commentary on this prophecy of Mac Gregor than the words of Sir Charles Aitcheson, one of the biographers of Lord Lawrence. He says :

In the autumn of 1870, Lord Lawrence allowed himself to be nominated for election to the London School Board under the Elementary Education Act, which had just come into force. It was not work for which he was naturally suited. He hated Boards, and considered himself constitutionally ill-fitted to be member, even of a Council of Three. He was no speaker and the practical training of an Indian career, in which there is much writing and little talk, was not such as to cultivate the gifts required for the conduct of affairs in a large board of fluent debaters. For three years he acted as Chairman of the Board. The term of office came to an end in November 1873, and he declined to stand again on the ground of failing health.

Almost immediately after his first attendance at
the meetings of the School Board, Mac Gregor commenced an agitation.   In his profession he felt it
incumbent upon him to call together right-minded
men to pray that right judgment might be given
them ; as a volunteer it seemed to him that drills and
firings, reviews and parades, were useless unless the
men engaged in them prayed for Queen and country,
for wise counsels among the rulers of the nations and
for peace in the hearts of citizens, and so the Lawyers'
Prayer Union and the Volunteers' Prayer Union were
instituted.   But how much more need was there for
prayer in an organisation which would deal with the
moral, mental, and spiritual welfare of millions upon
millions of school children ?   So we find from his
diary that on January 28, he called together some
friends to meet "at Smithies' to consider what to do
about prayer question on the School Board."   T. B.
Smithies, a man whose life of labour deserves to be
written in letters of gold, was one of those earnest,
quiet men who, while standing himself in the back-
ground, gave leverage to some of the finest movements of his time.

Three days after that meeting Mac Gregor wrote :
"Lord Sandon suggested requisition to chairman for
room for prayer—excellent proposal, to which we got
38 signatories, including Huxley."

These are the well-known names of some of those
who attended the prayer meeting of the London
School Board in 1873 :—Samuel Morley, M.P.,

Canon Cromwell, Lord Lawrence, R. Freeman, Rev. J. Rodgers, John Mac Gregor, Sir Charles Reed, M.P., T. B. Smithies, Rev. J. A. Picton, J. Stiff, J. E. Tresidder, A. McArthur, Prebendary Thorold (the present Bishop of Winchester), Dr. Joseph Angus, J. Watson, Very Rev. J. Mee, A. Lafone, J. B. Ingle, E. H. Currie, T. Scrutton, E. N. Buxton, W. H. Smith, M.P., Prebendary Barry, C. E. Mudie, H. S. Gover.

The form of prayer used at the first and second Boards, and it may be later, was as follows, and we heartily commend its perusal to all those who are interested in the present "religious difficulties," and irreligious discussions, on Bible Teaching in Board Schools :

Almighty and Everlasting God, who knowest the hearts of all men, and understandest all their ways, without whom nothing is strong, nothing is holy; Hear us, Thine unworthy servants, who now draw near to Thee, beseeching Thee to guide and prosper the work of our hands. May the dew of Thy blessing continually rest upon the whole of the wide field in which we are called to labour. As Thou hast taught us in everything, by prayer and supplication, with thanksgiving, to make known our requests unto Thee, do Thou impress upon us a sense of the solemn responsibility which rests upon us, and increase our faith in the assurance that Thou wilt direct those who in all their ways acknowledge Thee. Grant that we, and all associated with us in the great work of teaching and train- ing the young and ignorant, may be so guided and overruled by Thee, in all our thoughts, words, and works, that the children entrusted to our care may learn in their early days to know Thee, the only true God, and Jesus Christ whom Thou hast sent.

Be present amid the deliberations of this day. Give us a constant sense of Thy presence.   Vouchsafe to us the grace, the wisdom, the courage we may need.   Direct and control all hearts, so that all things may be ordered and settled upon the best and surest foundations, and the children of this generation may become a people fearing Thee and working righteousness.

Guide with Thy counsels those who may be called to select teachers, and grant that there may never be wanting able and godly persons to carry forward the education of the children of this country.   Bless the religious instruction given in the schools.   May those who teach never be weary, amid the many discouragements of their work, in giving line upon line, precept upon precept; and may those who are taught have their hearts so opened by the Holy Spirit as to attend to the things spoken in Thy name from Thy Word.

With these our prayers for future help and blessing, we join our praises and thanksgiving for what has been already done.   We thank Thee that many, by means of the schools hitherto established, have been taught in childhood those Holy Scriptures which are able to make wise unto salvation through faith which is in Christ Jesus. Vouchsafe the continuance of Thy blessing to those who may come under instruction, granting them in this world knowledge of Thy truth, and in the world to come life everlasting, through Jesus Christ our Lord.   Our Father, &c.

Just before the Elementary Education Act came into operation, there was much searching of heart among the various philanthropic societies as to how they would be affected by it.   Mac Gregor's concern was chiefly for the street-sellers and street-workers of London, and it was a curious fact that their case could not be effectually dealt with by the new Act.

Young criminals were provided for by the Reformatory Acts, wandering children were the subjects of the Industrial Schools Act, workhouse children were cared for under the Local Government Act,

children of outdoor paupers could be educated under
Denison's Act, children in factories or workshops
came under the Factory Acts and the Workshop
Acts, children working as shoeblacks or messengers
were specially dealt with under the Street Traffic
Acts, children of the wage-earning poor would soon
be sent to school under the Education Act; orphans,
idiots, blind, cripples, foundlings, deaf mutes, all had
special asylums, but the ten thousand little folks who
sold and worked in the streets had so far no law to
protect, regulate, or discipline them.

Mac Gregor's constant plea was that begging should
be made an offence; that street vendors should be under
regulation, and especially that newsboys, matchsellers,
and crossing-sweepers should be organised, disciplined,
and licensed.   He had no love for the professional
crossing-sweeper, "the privileged beggars of the
chief city of the world, every one of them a standing
monument of gross parochial neglect and misused
private sentiment;" he felt it to be a disgrace to our
national life that naked shivering children should be
sent out by the parish to rack sympathy by their rags
and dirt; taken in fact from the schoolroom to be
thoroughly instructed in the art of mendicancy,
sometimes under the guidance of hulking men who
could menace as well as whine, and poor haggard,
tottering widows, pleading by their very feebleness,
without even a semblance of work.

Many of the abuses of which he then complained
have been abolished or rectified, but some remain, and

we still need—perhaps more than ever—philanthropists to inquire into the street population, and to agitate for the regulated control of the outcast, and the downfall of the professional idler and impostor. What Mac Gregor wrote about crossing-sweepers, for example, in 1872, needs to be re-written again to-day.

> Tolerated by the police, and petted by the public, they are the envy of all other beggars, the astonishment of honest workers on their way to school or business, and most of all a puzzle to the man who lights the street lamps, the man who waters the road, and the man who scrapes it all day for a shilling, close beside the self-appointed functionary who is ten times better paid than himself for merely wielding a besom.

He went into this matter thoroughly, and the result of a careful inspection of the work of a man, a woman, and a boy, each on a crossing, gave this result: the boy received 2s. 6d. for less than two hours' work, the woman 3s. 6d. for less than an hour, and the man 5s. for under two hours' labour. No wonder therefore that Mac Gregor waxed wroth and wrote strongly of the absurd position of the British philanthropist who insists upon feeing impostors and does not stir hand or foot to force them out of their false claims.

There is development in the art of imposture, as in every other art, and only within quite a recent date a case came under the observation of the present writer, in which a man, ostensibly a beggar and a cripple, acted as "farmer" of the crossings of a whole district. His plan of action was to send a strong labourer to make the crossings clean, and then to plant at his various stations the best assorted collection of cripples and monstrosities he could hire so as to extort pity. The returns were large, and they went, not to benefit the poor wretches who worked for him, but to pay for his own luxuries, dissipations, and extravagances when the evening shadows fell.

The question which Mac Gregor so often asked still remains unanswered. "If the 'Streets Act' enables the police to regulate messengers, shoeblacks, and others, assigning to each of them a proper stand, why cannot the whole army of street vendors, crossing-sweepers, and other beggars be similarly dealt with and properly licensed?"

Perhaps a word or two from Mac Gregor's pen may stir up some one—for all great reforms come from the individual in the first instance—to take this matter up. He says:

Let every man and woman of us who loves children, and who would pour out tears if *his* children were to be degraded by the doles of false sentiment, and not raised by the help of true sympathy, desist from, and denounce, the cruel selfishness of haphazard alms-giving—that skin-deep charity which costs no trouble and confers no good: and let all of us pray God to give us wisdom as well as love, so that our feeble but right efforts may have His blessing, and we may *rescue* the lost ones for whom Christ died.

To carry out the principle of compulsory attendance at school, as a new and comprehensive means of good for the people, taxed all the energies of the Board, and Mac Gregor rendered signal service from the fact that

he had visited other lands where the compulsory system had been long applied and was working admirably,
and from personal knowledge he could speak with
authority of the schools of Germany, Holland, Sweden,
and America.

He soon found that it was impossible for him to
give full attention to the ever increasing duties of the
School Board and to labour at another calling, and
therefore he abandoned his profession that he might
devote himself more fully to that great work—the education of the people. At one time he wrote to a
friend, "I give eight hours a day for five days a week
to this School Board."

He held the office of chairman in the "School
Management Committee"—an office involving a large
amount of correspondence and personal interviews
with prospective teachers—and he was also chairman
of the "Industrial Schools Committee." Seeing that
for twenty years past he had been familiar with the
latter kind of work, dealing exclusively with the
vagrant children and those who were destitute or going
to ruin by incipient crime, there was no doubt he
was the right man in the right place.

In the course of three years he *personally* investigated
2000 cases of such children brought before him by
five officers of the Board, with the result that 1000 of
these were sent to Industrial Schools by the action of
his committee.

No better man could have been selected for this
task. His love of children was marvellous—not only

the nicely dressed and well-behaved "society" children, but the poor and neglected waifs and strays of the streets and alleys.

One scheme for the welfare of young lads which Mac Gregor brought prominently forward on several public occasions was for training boys for soldiers. Other boys were trained for the navy, why not train them for the army? At that time 6000 boys were under training for the navy; they were entered from fifteen and a half to sixteen years of age, and were usually transferred as first class boys to a sea-going ship, and at eighteen years old they were rated as able seamen. The cost of each boy's training for the navy was £60 which was willingly paid by the nation because the boys thus trained became splendid seamen. Why not in like manner train boys for the Army? There were many sources of supply—notably from reformatories, industrial schools, workhouse and elementary schools, and Mac Gregor worked up statistics with regard to these and showed that certainly 5000 lads could be obtained every year, fit and willing to be trained and to enlist. He combated the restrictions against boys from reformatories not being allowed to enlist; however good they were, if they came straight from a reformatory they were refused, although many of these same lads were readily accepted after a week or two spent in the wretched and demoralising life outside. His idea was to establish, as an experiment, an institution to maintain, instruct, and train for the army lads from fifteen to seventeen years old, when they should enter, selected as fit and willing to become soldiers, and that none should leave until they were eighteen. They should be educated in ordinary secular and religious knowledge, drill and gymnastics, industrial work indoors and out, drawing and music; pocket-money should be given in proportion to industrial earnings, and prizes for shooting, progress, and good conduct. Mac Gregor was of opinion that £25 a year would be ample to pay for all that was required in the training of a lad. But the scheme did not meet with success.

On the School Board he revived and revised it, but, still failing, he took a very active part in the establishment of drill competitions between Board schools. On one occasion there was a demonstration in Regent's Park, when 10,000 children were put through various drill exercises, so admirably executed that an agitation was got up by the Workmen's Peace Association, and a deputation from that body was sent to the Board to express their disapprobation of such demonstrations on the ground that they tended to foster a military spirit in the minds of the young! These views found sympathy from some members of the Board, drill competitions began to be looked upon with suspicion, and within three years from this incident, only about 400 boys competed for the challenge banner awarded by the Society of Arts.

Mac Gregor's interest in boys' training ships never ceased, and the boys of the *Chichester* and *Arethusa*

at Greenhithe were the objects of his special care.   He
never missed the "annual prize day " if he could possibly help it, and the boys never flagged in trying to
obtain one of the Rob Roy prizes, derived from the
profits of one of his books of travel.   Nor did he ever
forget the interests of the boys when it was in his
power to help or defend them.   At one time many
foreigners were crowded into our merchant navy.   " By
all means give foreigners fair play," wrote Mac Gregor,
" but only after English boys are cared for.   Charity
begins at home, and our home is England; English
boys make far better sailors than any foreigners, when
it comes to rough work on stormy seas."   On another
occasion he made an appeal in the *Times* on behalf of
the boys of the *Chichester*.

Many a young lad has been rescued from a life of sorrow and
want, and they are sent out as trained sailor-boys.   But although
these boys are approved by the ship's captains, it is found that until
the boys can be taught how to steer a vessel, as well as the other
duties of a seaman, they cannot be well received by the rest of a
ship's crew.   Steering is not to be taught by book or precept only,
or in a ship at moorings : the boys should be taught to handle the
tiller by voyages to the Nore.   They would learn also the use of
buoys, beacons, and lights.   A cutter of twenty tons would be of
immense service in their training.

The result of this appeal was the gift by a clergyman, the Rev. C. Harrington, Rector of Bromyard,
of a strong well-built sea-going yacht, the *Dolphin*.

Among the subjects that Mac Gregor took up with

great vigour on the School Board were cooking and plain sewing for girls, and drilling, swimming, and athletics for boys.   Upon the subject of swimming he was particularly keen.   He used to tell a story of a philosopher who came to a ferry and got into the boat which was to take him across a Highland lake.   The talk between him and the boatman was pleasant at first in the calm, but as the boat went further the wind increased and the waves splashed, yet the philosopher heeded not.   Nay, worse, he said : " Boatman, do you know ontology ? " and the answer was "No!"   "Well," said the wiseacre, "you have lost half your existence." And the wind blew stronger and the waves splashed wetter, and the boat tossed higher, until the boatman said to the wiseacre, "Will you let me ask *you* one question—can you swim ? "   "No," said the philoso-pher.   "Then," the boatman cried, "you have lost the whole of your existence, for this boat is going to sink in five minutes."

A very good plan, advocated and carried out largely by Mac Gregor, was to give a boy proficient in swim-ming a reward of two shillings for teaching another boy to swim.   The plan worked well and there was not any accident on record during his oversight of the scheme.

It greatly delighted him when the Royal Humane Society gave medals for swimming to competitors in the leading public schools, to prepare them for deeds of human kindness.

The Royal Humane Society was an institution in

which Mac Gregor maintained a constant interest. "Some good men and things," he was wont to say, "are vigorous in their youth, but slow and stagnant as they grow older; or they even become fossilised. The Royal Humane Society has the experience of a hundred years and more of noble work, but in activity and practical means for its great purpose this society adapts, improves and invents new ways of saving life and new incentives for devoted exertion." He regarded this society and the Royal National Lifeboat Institution not merely as good and useful philanthropic associations but as distinctly Christian in their tendency. "Did not the Highest," he said on one occasion, "come down from Heaven to seek and to save that which was lost. Let us, with deep reverence, follow in His footsteps."

A firm believer in swimming as a Christian duty—on the ground that it gave opportunity to help and save other lives—Mac Gregor was ever the advocate of caution and the discourager of rashness. Moreover he took the sensible view that every one who went in for swimming, or, in fact, anything in which there was an element of hazard, should master all the conditions and possibilities of any critical circumstances in which they might be placed. As captain of the Royal Canoe Club he discountenanced canoeing by persons who were not swimmers, and as swimmers he urged them to study their responsibilities in that capacity. The following is an illustration, given in a speech to the prize medallists (swimming) of the Royal Humane Society:

Another caution may be well enforced, by an example which occurred a short time ago. The Royal Canoe Club has existed for sixteen years with more than 600 members scattered over the world. In the hundreds of canoe voyages during all that time, only one man has been drowned from his canoe (so far as we know) while a member of the Club. This was a son of Sir Charles Reed, who was both a good swimmer and canoeist, and who had accomplished a long cruise in Norway and Sweden safely enough. He lost his life while canoeing in Ireland, on a lake full of bog water, which is an astringent and contracts the body. Therefore let swimmers beware of bathing in bog water.

It is perhaps unnecessary to say that on the question of the Bible in schools, Mac Gregor's trumpet gave no uncertain sound. He held that the Bible should be read by everybody, everywhere, and at all times and seasons, and that the first duty of parents and teachers was to "drive home" its sacred, guiding, and sustaining truths into the minds of the young. It would not be of interest to any one to revive the old discussions or even to indicate the line of Mac Gregor's arguments in connection with them. One extract from the diary will show the spirit which animated him.

July 10, 1873.—Settled the tenders for 15,000 desks, and at four had a meeting in my rooms to establish examinations of Board children and pupil-teachers in Bible Knowledge. Present, Barry, Rigg, Tressider and three members of S. School Institute Committee. After prayer and much consideration it was agreed that my proposal should be carried out. I consider this the most important meeting held in these rooms, where many other interesting movements have begun.

Next to the study of the Bible Mac Gregor had

hope in pure literature for boys, and he took advantage of his position on the London School Board to air his views on this subject on every fitting occasion.

It was his great ambition to see a boys' newspaper established which should be read with as much avidity as the "gutter press" and the "penny dreadfuls."

So early as 1869 he called into his counsels such men as Dr. Macaulay, the editor of the *Leisure Hour* and *Sunday at Home*; Mr. T. B. Smithies, of the *British Workman*; W. H. G. Kingston, and R. M. Ballantyne—princes in the realm of boys' literature, and men who year after year satisfied the craving for adventure and romance, but never penned a line that could bring a blush on the cheek of man, woman, or child, or lost an opportunity to enforce a good sterling moral. The Boys' Newspaper, as he wished to see it, never saw the light, and for the nearest approach to his ideal, the *Boys' Own Paper*, he had to wait for ten weary years.

To this magazine, as to many others, Mac Gregor wrote a number of spirited papers, and to all his terms were "£0 0s. 0d."

If space permitted we might well devote a chapter to his correspondence with young lads in whom he took an interest and who admired him. It is both curious and interesting, but we can only give one specimen.

When Rob Roy's canoe books came out they were largely read by public school boys, and many of them

dreamt ambitious dreams, or saw magnificent visions, of
their own exploits modelled upon his.   But there was
a fascination in the style of Rob Roy's books which
won the hearts alike of athletic and contemplative
youth, it appealed to their noblest manhood, and many
answers to the appeal came in the shape of confidential
letters.   Some of these lie before us, carefully docketed,
and in one or two instances, a rough draft of the reply
sent is appended.

   It will be no breach of confidence to give an extract
from a letter written by a Westminster boy—it gives a
fine and characteristic touch of pure English and
Christian boyhood.

A Westminster Schoolboy *to* John Mac Gregor.

   Ever since I read the 'Voyage Alone,' I have longed to make
your acquaintance, for, fond of boats, a lover of the sea and sailors
I was captivated by the little *Rob Roy* and always hoped to meet
the Captain and crew. . . . .

   But you are ignorant from whom this letter comes.   It comes
from one who in his holiday lives most of the day in a sailing-boat
on the Cornish coast, or in one of the fine Cornish luggers ; who in
a gale of wind is ever anxious for the dear fellows in the offing, who
at school has had many a breeze to weather, for, till lately, those who
showed the true colours have been in rough water, but thanks to the
Great Captain for the last two years, Westminster is another place,
refitted from 'stem to stern.'

   And now sir, having gone so far, may I ask whether the *Rob Roy*
still wears her burgee and is still afloat? for having accompanied her
over many hundred miles it is only natural that one should feel a
strong interest in such an old friend more especially when I have
planned and plotted a little craft, after her model, one day to help

me, I trust, in leaving many a vessel side lightened of some of a
cargo of Testaments.   Such is one of my hopes. . . . .

If Rob Roy won the heart of the Westminster boy,
in no less degree did the Westminster boy win the
heart of Rob Roy, and a cheery, genial letter went off
at once to beg the scholar to make an appointment to
overhaul the canoe and see the collection of curiosities.
No wonder he answered, " I appreciate your kindness
fully in so good-naturedly answering, with such a jolly
letter, one whom you never met."

CHAPTER XVII

FAMILY, SOCIAL AND CITIZEN LIFE

In 1874, when Mac Gregor settled down in his home at Blackheath, he did not begin his family life, as many do, by giving up all outside work. On the contrary, he added to the labour of the London School Board, Cookery School Committees, Palestine Exploration Fund and Exhibition, Canoe Club, and a dozen other engrossing matters; new enterprises in the neighbourhood of his own home, such as a Bible meeting in the Royal Naval College at Greenwich; a prayer meeting at Blackheath, drawing-room meetings in his own house for various societies, such as the British Syrian Schools, Medical Mission, Miss de Broen, and the M'Call Mission in Paris; periodical visits to the workhouse, and other local charities, besides the entertainment of many guests, for he was in the midst of relatives and an ever widening circle of friends.

For nearly two years after his marriage he abstained from the arduous work of lecturing. He resumed it, however, in December 1875, and continued it at intervals until he successfully finished the stupendous task he had set himself.　Then he wrote :

March 8, 1878.—Last lecture for the sum of £10,000 aimed at some years ago as possible to be got from people by offering information and advice for money.　Gave the lecture at Eyre Arms, St. John's Wood, where I had twice been before on a similar errand, once to found, again to build up, and now to finish Trinity Schools, St. John's Wood. The place was full and the audience very appreciative.　At the end a boy and girl came on the platform and presented me with a splendid bouquet of camellias.　These children had (as also the stewards) scarves of Mac Gregor tartan with wands, &c.　This is lecture No. 126 of this numbered list.　The amount obtained over all expenses is £100.　Therefore, the number of lectures is 126 and the sum gained over and above expenses has been £10,042.　Only one lecture in all these had to be put off on account of illness, and this was given afterwards for the same object.

Mac Gregor did not entirely abandon public lecturing after this, although he greatly decreased his engagements, and from time to time the proceeds of a lecture came as a boon and a blessing to some specially deserving causes.　But as the years went on he cared less and less for being away from home, and became conscious of fatigue and anxiety in their delivery, sometimes almost approaching nervousness.　In the following letter to his wife he records his last great effort in that direction.

Queen's Hotel, Leeds
November 21, 1884

My Own Darling,

Everything has prospered completely, and I am so very much pleased and thankful.　I was anxious, but I don't know why, and now I retire from my profession as a lecturer. . . . . The platform was wide and roomy, and I went nearly an hour beforehand to begin arrangements. Just before starting from the hotel, a young man called on me there, saying he saw my name on the bills, and that he came to tell me he was 'Johnny Reynolds,' the son of Constable Reynolds who was our lodge-keeper at Drumcondra! He went out to the Crimea (the father) with darling Douglas as an 'orderly,' and was invaluable as a staunch, brave, and godly servant till he put the sod over his dear master's grave. How very strange all this ! . . . .

To-morrow I hope to be with my sweeties safe and sound.

Yours,

J.

Always a lover of children, it was a source of no little joy when in October 1875 Mac Gregor welcomed his firstborn, who was named Annie Elizabeth Frances, and again in 1881, when in his diary he wrote of his second daughter, Helen Douglas ; "March 19, 1881 : Blessing, praise and glory to the Father of Heaven who gave us this day a darling baby girl."

His diary abounds in touching and beautiful references to his wife and children, and in frequent thanksgiving for his overflowing cup of happiness. "No man was ever so happy I think as I am," is the constant burden of his song. He watched the growth and development of his children with intense solicitude, and we think it will not be out of place to give just a passing specimen of his fatherly pride and joy.

Oct. 21, 1877.—A few days ago Ina was heard saying to herself, very softly, 'Nice God!' her only way of expressing love. The experiment of having her at morning prayers is made too soon in her little history. She sits all right at reading, but climbs upon the back of each servant at prayers !

Feb. 23, 1879 —Address to S. School of St. John's on a very remarkable subject. Last week little Ina had said 'Mama, *who* is God?' I never heard this simple question put before, and I endeavoured to answer it at this Sunday service which was very largely attended by teachers and children, who were unusually attentive from beginning to end. Ina, after this 'Who is God?' asked her nurse, 'Did God make Hisself?' These precocious indications of thought often dangerous to be incited. Well do I recollect Mrs. Bevan's little girl, whose creed was the essence of the Gospel and in these words : ' Jesus died astead of me.'

Jan. 6, 1881.—Ina, looking at picture Bible illustration of Mary and Child, said : 'There's the little Baby that made his mother.'

Jan. 2, 1882.—Delightful tea party of Ina's dolls.

He used to write comical little letters to his children. In those days they were very fond of playing at "keeping shop " in their nursery, and they let down over the bannisters, by means of a small bucket and string, groceries and other articles, close to their father's study door ; he thoroughly enjoyed their play, and bought the contents of the bucket, returning it with the payment, and on one occasion the following letter accompanied the penny :—

7 VANBRUGH PARK ROAD EAST,
March 3, 1886.

MADAM,

    I am very much pleased with the 'plumes,' and I hope they will match your new bonnet. The biscuits are too too delicious, and I hunger for a hamper of them. But most of all I *do* love the sago.

    You will please return the bill receipted.

MR. PAP.

Some of the letters were illustrated with comical sketches, some with the consecutive letters of the alphabet commencing each line, and all were merry and loving.

MacGregor was very fond of dogs, and for many years was wont to take one, bearing the name of "Rob," on his canoe trips. He was remarkably considerate for all animals, but especially for dogs, and would never keep Rob waiting for food until it could be given without inconvenience—he thought the dog should come first. "If you love a dog at all (and the man who does not love one I don't envy)," he said, "one of the pleasantest things is to see him well fed, and one of the least pleasant things is to see him patiently waiting until you are fed first."

We could tell many good stories of dogs in connection with Rob Roy, but we will let one suffice, given in his own words:

Behind the banks of the Thames near Greenwich, are wide plains below the river's level. Into these, millions of tons of slimy mud dredged from the river and brought by barges are poured by steam engines, and the half liquid mass flows sluggishly on the plains till it dries at last into firm soil. In 1876 I was walking by the river and climbed up the bank and looked on the huge mud basin—vast, silent, ugly, and deep !

It was far more dangerous, too, than any pool of water, because in mud you cannot swim, and, once sinking there, your eyes and mouth and nose are filled with slime : and so there is certain death. After one look and almost a shudder, I turned away, carefully stepping on the slippery edge, but a moment after there came a cry from my boy-companion : * 'Oh, Uncle John, Rob has jumped in !' 'Rob' is my faithful little canoe dog, the fourth dog of the name, which has been my sole companion in voyages over lakes, rivers, and seas. I rushed back up the bank and was horrified to see only the nose and

---

* Graham Wilmot Brooke, who went afterwards to the River Niger as a C.M.S. Missionary, and died of fever in March 1892.

eyes of my pet dog, while all the rest of him was covered by the blue-black slimy mud.

He was motionless, utterly unable to save himself, but his eyes looked up, faintly pleading for help. My heart beat fast as I cautiously glided along a slippery plank to save him, and reached to him with an umbrella, at great peril, too, of certain death to myself, for no help was near if I fell in. 'Twas useless! At last I stooped on the treacherous board (in greater peril still) and dived my hand and firmly grasped the dog—heavy and clotted with disgusting slime.

The story sounds egotistical as it stands, it was used as an illustration in a discourse, and the moral was to show how sinners were saved from " the horrible pit and the miry clay."

It was a great joy to Mac Gregor to have his grand old father, Sir Duncan, as a near neighbour and frequent visitor. There are many entries in the diary concerning him :

1876.

Jan. 23, *Sunday.*—Sir Duncan came here. He told me mother had a Testament in the *Kent.* Soldier was found to have it when all saved at Falmouth. Said a Roman Catholic had taken it 'because it might have luck,' and this same Testament was afterwards in the hand of the soldier of the 43rd Regiment who had to be shot under Sir D.'s orders. Sir D. of course visited him in his cell and there gave him this Testament.

March 16.—Dined with Sir D. (his birthday, 89 years old). He gave us short address after. He was at twelve commisioned officer in Mac Gregor regiment of Fencibles. At thirteen changed 55th.

Aug.—Sir D.'s fall and illness at Eastbourne. Found Sir D. in perfect possession of mental faculties, calm, pleasant, after eight hours' sleep, reading *Times* and Lord Albemarle's book with deep interest. As day went on his arm began to swing, and hand to clutch, and this with more violence causing some uneasiness and pain. Dr. Bell visited him and prescribed with judgment. Sir D. said how merciful in God to send him this warning. Scarcely ill once for seventy years. Never fully realised death coming. At same time thankful, realised entirely presence of God, faith in the blood of Christ, joy in the Holy Ghost, and peace. Also felt entirely convinced that he 'when absent from the body' would be 'present with the Lord.' He still read the *Times* fully and the *Daily News*. Strove hard to rise and walk without help, though staggering from weakness.

March 16, 1879.—My father's birthday, ninety-two years old. Annie and I dined with him, and R., E., P. and D. During dinner he was very bright and collected. At prayers I read Psalm xci., after which Sir D. sitting, prayed. He soon showed great weakness and rambled in ideas, and in words for a considerable time. He said in his prayer (always till now so very beautiful, eloquent, powerful and simple) that he 'felt he could not pray,' could not express what he wanted, but, 'Thou knowest better than we do what we need. Oh give us what we *need*.'

June 8, 1881, *Wednesday*.—A time never to be forgotten in my life. On my way to the Bible Society Committee (exceptionally held on Wednesday) I called as usual to see my loved and honoured father who was apparently in better health than for the last ten days. As I came in he said, 'Oh my darling darling first-born,' and seemed cheerful and peaceful but weak. At the Bible Society two foreign agents spoke, and I went to the Club and then came out home. At my own door, dear Annie met me with the awful intelligence that my precious father had died peacefully, painlessly, at ten minutes past one o'clock. The rest of the day was so full of thought, prayer, work, that I cannot record it.

As years advance sorrows must of necessity increase. In 1883 his beloved sister Elizabeth passed away, and in that same year, "our well-beloved father," Sir Crawford Caffin.

It would have been well for Mac Gregor if, when he settled down into home life, or even when he left the London School Board, he could have given up at least two-thirds of his public engagements. But it would have been impossible, even had he wished to do so. Standing at the head of so many growing movements, he was thrust forward by the multitudes behind, and feeling himself still to be in possession of all his old physical and mental strength, it was not in his nature to seek rest while so much good work was at hand to be done. We cannot tell of a tithe of his labours, but we select a few samples.

The Open-air Mission still claimed his services, and in addition, he preached and lectured to large audiences in many places on the Christian Evidences, and on Science and the Book. One such lecture was given at Woolwich, and being badly reported, he wrote to the editor of one of the papers and asked to be allowed to state what he really said on that occasion. Here is a portion of his letter :

After allusions to Art, and to mixed science and pure science, I said that, besides in these ways of inquiry, the man of science searches for other knowledge, in four directions : (1) outwards, to the illimitable space about us ; (2) inwards, asking, 'What is this "Me," "Myself,"?' (3) forwards, 'What is there to come?' (4) backwards, 'Whence and when did things begin?' Take only the last —'Each of us,' I said, 'would like to know whence and how came I?' Various are the answers. Take again only the last of these as Darwin, Tyndall and Huxley, those splendid thinkers, try to answer. This is not the time or place to discuss their theories, except from one point, and upon that I will say a few words. No doubt—as a

question of pure science it is quite possible, nay probable, that
mankind was developed from something else—say from a quadruped
on land; and that that was developed from one in the water, say a
crocodile! [some one laughed]. No one should laugh at what is
feasible enough; but no one can stop at this point. The crocodile
must have come from a lower form, say a fish with fins; and that
from a jelly fish, moving by its own action; and that from a jelly
fish, fast to a rock; and that from a jelly (not fish); and that from a
substance of millions of atoms, loose in liquid, say like pea-soup.
Go back ages more, and that turbid liquid came from pure liquid;
that again—going back—from gas; and that must have been developed from a rare 'something.' Let us call the very farthest you can
fancy by the name 'Ether,' as the origin of all.

Well, let us take breath. Now, while we look at this unimagin-
able 'first thing,' let us clearly understand and agree that it must
have possessed the following properties :—

1.—It (the 'something') must have existed from all eternity; for
if anything came before it, then that previous thing is what we
are to look to, and, at any rate, one thing must have existed from all
eternity, else something would have come out of nothing.

2.—We must next believe that our 'Ether' was always and in
every point of space, unless we have reasons why it was 'here' and
not 'there.'

3.—This wide-spread Ether must have had in it (and that from
all past eternity) the property, energy or elements, or cause for
developing into (successively) gas, liquid, fish, &c. &c., down to the
specimens now in this room, you and me, men with muscle, thought,
and moral sense.

Now, I ask you, if the difficulties of understanding—nay, of even
faintly conceiving—a thing such as described—(and which is the
latest answer from pure science) are not precisely of like kind, and of
the same degree, as the difficulties of conceiving or understanding
the idea of a personal God, in the three attributes of—(1) His existence from all eternity: (2) His existence in every point of space;
(3) His power of originating man?

But until these difficulties are removed, or acknowledged to be inherent and necessary, thousands of reflecting people will not look at Revelation, because they cannot conceive how a God to reveal can exist, and my one point (now) has been to show that the difficulties are inherent in any conception of a first cause.

The difficulties, then, of believing with understanding what some men of science lately suggest are the same in kind, and, at least, as great in degree as the difficulties for believing what Revelation from the first asserts.

Students will go but a little way with science before they are pulled up by something they cannot fathom. What, then, is that power which could endure from all eternity, could operate universally, producing, controlling, evolving, and developing all nature, unless it was an all-powerful and everlasting God? The moral is that students need have no special difficulty in believing a revealed religion, although their brains are too small to understand the source in its essence. They must not make their incapacity to understand such matters the ground for unbelief.

So far as to my assertion at the meeting that 'Science' does not in the least reduce the difficulties of belief as to our origin, either in amount or in kind, by substituting Ether, or a 'thing,' or a principle, for a living God, the occasion was not one for discussing the claims of the Book, as a revelation, but perhaps you will allow me to state some of my convictions on this subject, the result of many years of reading, thought, and converse with able men of all opinions and grades of life, and in many lands.

Convinced that a Being made me and governs me, I expect Him to communicate something about His nature, and something for my mind and heart. The Bible asserts itself to be such a communication. It is believed to be so by vast numbers of intelligent people; and this surely justifies, at least, further inquiry. The Old Testament is vouched for by Jesus Christ, and His history is in the New Testament. The whole issue seems to turn upon the character of Christ who is at once the subject of the Book and its voucher.

I acknowledge that, if Christ was a knave or a fool, His testimony to the Book is worthless; but, if He was a knave, then a deceiver has done more, and willingly suffered more, unselfishly, for humanity, than any true man; or, if he was a fool, then a fool has said and done wiser things, every day of His life, than all the sages before or since.

The difficulties of not believing in His integrity and intelligence are greater than those of accepting both. No place can be found in history and among mankind for Christ, that is not speedily seen to be preposterous—except the position which He himself assumes. Prince, teacher, healer—each of these titles a designing man could assume; but who of the noblest of heroes could say, to enemies and inmost friends, 'Look at my life and conduct, absolutely without flaw?' Plato would have been laughed at by his disciples had he done this, and Aristotle would have been rightly called mad.

The Book, in both Testaments, is also unique in all its features and its fortunes. The text of the older part is vouched in antiquity, and guarded in genuineness by the jealousy between Jew and Samaritan; each for ages past the best watch on the other against any alteration of the charter of both.

Greek Church, Roman Catholic, and Protestant have, in a similar way, by their very antagonism wonderfully guarded the New Testament canon; so that there are more variations now in a single play of Shakespeare (printed too in his lifetime) than in the MS. of a Gospel. I accept the 'Book,' then, for careful examination and test, as containing God's revelation to me; necessarily subject to the human defects of language, transmission, and understanding; for it is a message to erring men not to perfect seraphs.

Looking around on the hostile critics, I notice the slavish bondage to each other's opinion among infidels and sceptics of the highest mental powers—and intimately known to me—while they wave the banner of 'Free-Thought.' But I remark the universal acknowledgment, even among these, that if men really did live up to Christ's example and doctrine, and the precepts of the Book, every one would be happier and wiser than under any other code.

I see the joyous change in life of brave soldiers, hardy sailors, great lawyers and statesmen, the leaders of mankind, who were once unbelievers but now accept the Book and the Saviour. Also, I see the weary vacant life of the gayest, most successful, political, witty, and sarcastic, when pain or loss, or failure comes, and the present is unhappy, and the prospect beyond is utter gloom.

These are enough reasons for me to examine, with all diligence and humility, and to the very best of my ability, the evidences for the Book within my comprehension. I find its prophecy fulfilled often before my eyes and in far-off lands. I find its miracles quite a part of God's regular laws; as the striking of a clock, at long intervals, was arranged by its maker, as well as its constant pendulum tick.

Deeper still, I find precious promises made in the Book, each faithfully kept in my heart when it claims them, and thus, even if I do doubt His truth sometimes, it is when the bad part of me wishes me to be still bad. I have tried in vain to conceive what the world would be, or even London, if the Book were taken away and all its teaching. Those who disregard it now would find a strange cosmos of confusion round them then to live in. Their ill-success is their best protection against such a disaster.

If God were such as I could comprehend, in His essence or in His ways, He would not be infinite. What he has revealed in His Son, I can know and understand sufficiently to have Him for a Saviour; and what he teaches me by the Spirit, I can learn enough to know my own feebleness and His power, my own sin and His mercy, my own short span of life now, and how it can still be sanctified and prepared for a joyful resurrection to an immortality of blessedness and glory.

I believe the Book with all my mind, and seek to love its truths with all my heart.

This letter was re-printed, and a copy was sent to Professor Tyndall who acknowledged it thus:

ROYAL INSTITUTION OF GREAT BRITAIN,
November 23, 1875.

MY DEAR MAC GREGOR,

I have read your letter through from beginning to end. It is very able intellectually, and full of spiritual vigour. More I need not say.

Yours ever,

JOHN TYNDALL.

C C

Of his miscellaneous work, his general movements, and the people he met, the diary furnishes such ample material that we may select almost at random. Day by day, year by year, there are entries of attendances at committees, addresses, public meetings, writing reports, contributions to the press, starting new schemes—such as cookery classes, public gymnasiums, School Board Drill Competitions—or aiding old ones.

Notes from John MacGregor's Diary.

1877.

July 18.—Bible Society Committee Deputation to Chinese Ambassador. Four members with me. Ambassador with three attendants and Dr. Macartney. Made us sit. I was spokesman, and told of Bible at Coronation and every day in Parliament and in 216 languages. Found, when read and believed, men more moral and happy, more ready for death and eternity. *Daily* issue of Bible Society, if piled up one on another, higher column than St. Paul's Cross by one half. The copy we gave was one printed in China for the Society, but bound in London. He asked us to explain constitution of Society. I said it was all over Dominion of Canada, larger area than U. States of America, all over India, nearly as populous, with the others, as China itself. He asked interesting questions, and said he would like to visit the Bible Society House. This is one of the few very important matters I have engaged in.

Jan. 26.—Dined Burns, 29 Queen's Gate. Twenty there. Sat next Admiral Sir Houston Stewart and Cameron, African traveller. Opposite me was Stanley, the other hero of Africa. He recognised me as last seeing him in 1869 at Suez—a man with calm sensible air. The American Minister was there, and Lord Kinnaird with his new title.

April 29.—Capital meeting of Open-air Mission to celebrate our first quarter of a century. I read my summary of twenty-five years' work.

May 6.—Ragged School Union prizes to children in Exeter Hall, Lord Shaftesbury presided, and I addressed the children who crowded the gallery.

Nov. 25, 1878.—Met Laurence Oliphant at Athenæum. He had been a third or fourth time with Lord Salisbury at Hatfield concerning the scheme for the colonisation of Palestine which we had anxiously considered. He was to go with Lord W. to Egypt and would at once proceed in the business. I consider this to be the beginning of a very important effort.

The story of Laurence Oliphant's scheme for the colonisation of Palestine is too well known to need repetition here, but we give a few notes as to Mac Gregor's intimacy with this strange and wonderful man.

1880.

May 27–29.—Met L. Oliphant at Athenæum and heard his wonderful tale.

June 15.—Palestine Exploration . Fund. Oliphant there, and we resolved to survey Eastern Palestine.

1882.

Feb. 6.—Took Laurence Oliphant to see Besant. Oliphant at the Athenæum told me his design for restoration of Jews had been formed in 1878 in the smoking-room of the Club in conversation with me in corner opposite. We went to Palestine Exploration Fund.

May 19.—To Lord Mount-Temple by his request to meet Lord Shaftesbury and Lord Folkestone about Jews for Palestine. We all agreed it was not now ripe for action.

April 14.—D. of Sutherland invited me and four others to consider Jordan Canal from Haifa to the Hooley Lake and Dead Sea and out at Akaba. Most curious chapters in Ezekiel and Isaiah bearing on this. Mr. Mackinnon, a great steamboat man, a valuable helper. Something will come of this. Remarkable passages as to Jordan, Zech. xiv., Ezek. 47.

The scheme was to construct a navigable channel between the Mediterranean and the Gulf of Akaba, which constitutes the north-eastern arm of the Red Sea. The channel was to pass from Haifa, a point immediately north of Mount Carmel, through the plain of Esdraelon to the Jordan, and thence to follow the course of that river to the Dead Sea. From the Dead Sea it was to proceed southwards through the Wady El Araba until it effected a junction with the Red Sea at Akaba, the ancient Elath, the port where Solomon is supposed to have kept a fleet.

Neither the colonisation scheme nor the scheme for a canal ever came to anything, but we insert here one of many letters written to Mac Gregor by Oliphant with regard to the former enterprise :

From LAURENCE OLIPHANT *to* JOHN MAC GREGOR.

DAMASCUS, *April* 29.

MY DEAR MAC GREGOR,

You will be interested in hearing how I have been progressing. I did not delay in Egypt owing to quarantine delays but pushed on at once for Beyrout, saw Midhat Pasha who told me to go and make my examinations and come back and report. From information I received, I determined to strike from Sidon for Banias, and from there struck south-east, keeping on an average from fifteen to twenty miles east of the Jordan, and so traversing the whole length of Jordan, Ajlun, and the Belka. The latter I found to be a perfectly magnificent tract, thirty miles by twenty. A plateau 3000 feet above the sea, with well-wooded and watered mountain ranges of from 4000 to 5000 feet—and not a private proprietor in it. The whole crown property, and far finer than anything to be found west of the Jordan. I took neither tents nor dragoman, nor paid a farthing for Arab escort. Fortunately I had as a companion an Englishman who spoke Arabic and was ready to rough it with the Arabs, and we went in such an impecunious style that we were not worth robbing. We crossed by Jericho to Jerusalem, and rode back by Nazareth and Tyre, the whole lasting over a month and only costing for the two of us £40. I have put the whole scheme before Midhat Pasha, who approves, and is now engaged in so modifying it as to make it acceptable to the Porte. As for guarantees of protection from Arabs and from Turkish officials, I see plainly that this can easily be provided for by the colonists themselves. If they are sufficiently numerous, and are backed by a strong European board of directors, neither Arab nor Turkish authority will dare to interfere with them. Such Jews as I have confidentially spoken to, say they will readily emigrate when they can become landholders in their own country. The whole affair is very much simplified by my finding so much land *en bloc* belonging to the Government. On the western side so much is already in private hands that the State lands are too poor and scattered to be desirable. The tribes of Gad and Reuben certainly had the cream of the thing, and it is here I would propose to commence now. Midhat Pasha is placing troops all along the Hadj Road which would form the eastern boundary, and the best proof that the Arabs are pretty well cowed lies in the fact that I was able to ride all through them without being robbed or paying them blackmail. It is very different now from what it was when you were laid hold of in the Huleh, as I found when I was over the same ground. I am going over the scheme with Midhat Pasha, clause by clause, in a few days, and hope to leave Beyrout for Constantinople on the 12th May. It is there that I expect my real difficulties will begin, but events have been so wonderfully ordered for me, so far, that I do not despair. Please keep all this very quiet as I am afraid of publicly creating difficulties at Constantinople, and I am keeping my object most secret here. If we can once get hold of the Belka, it will be the small end of the wedge and the rest will follow. The entire financial collapse of the Porte makes the moment favourable. . . . . .

Yours affectionately,

L. OLIPHANT.

Notes from MacGregor's Diary continued.

1879.

Feb. 9.—Sent off first article to Waugh for *Sunday Magazine* upon Palestine, past, present and future, with some misgiving as to embarking on so important a work.

Feb. 12.—Lord Elcho's Testimonial Committee. I was made Chairman.

March 7.—Curious letter from an old woman to me, addressed, 'Dr. MacGregor Roy. C/o Postmaster-General,' who kindly sent it to me.

1881.

August 19.—Dined at Castle Wemyss with Lord Shaftesbury and Lady Edith Ashley, &c.

August 22-3.—Duke of Edinburgh, Lord S., and large number of people on *Cumberland* training-ship to distribute prizes.

1883.

June 23.—To Buxton's, where School Board boys and girls were drilled. A very beautiful sight in lovely weather. Prince of Wales, Princess and three daughters lunched with us.

July 13.—At Fisheries acting as one of jury for small boats for seven hours.

May 11.—To Totland Bay.

1884.

May 19.—In this week had deeply interesting meeting with Tennyson on his invitation. He was finishing a strange Irish story with all the odd words and phrases, and I was able to give him help from knowledge of the Irish-English. Then in a long walk with him and his niece to the cliffs, and the beacon—full of information, repartee, and original thought.

May 27, 28, 29, 30.—Tennyson, four long walks with me.

June 1.—Once more to Tennyson's. Seven or eight others, and the dogs.

June 14.—In a pleasant letter from Miss Weld, she told us that my remonstrance with Lord Tennyson as to the light use of the name of the Devil,* had been considered in writing the Irish story, which he read part of to me at our first meeting, and she said, 'You will be pleased to hear that my uncle has omitted the word you took exception to from his Irish poem.'

Feb. 23.—Mr. Moody (and his daughter) gave us the delight and honour of a visit to our house where we had him for more than two hours. It was a season not to be forgotten all our lives. His restless interest in my curiosities was eager and delightful. I shall never forget Feb. 23.

Dec. 23.—China Inland Mission, a remarkable meeting in the Rink when I presided. Some noble young Cambridge men who have volunteered to go out, spoke admirably. Stanley Smith, C. T. Studd, one the Captain of the Cambridge Cricket Club, and the other stroke of the Cambridge University Boat Club. The Hall was full and the Spirit of God was there. The China Inland Mission is on different lines from any I know. I have always been interested about China since my visit to the fair at Nijni Novgorod on the Volga, where there were 25,000 Chinese. And then the six Chinese officers at the Royal Naval College here.

1885.

March 1.—To-day is sixty years since the *Kent* was lost. I had Scripture Class at King's Street, Mr. Bacons, and Penifer who was a boy on the *Kent* was present. My cousin, David Pringle was there too—he also was in the *Kent*.

March 16.—The Royal Naval College Bible Class was begun on March 15, 1874, and it was stopped on Monday, 16 March, 1885 (eleven years).

So early as 1855 Mac Gregor was strong upon the question of erecting monuments to martyrs. He wrote at that date :

---

* Mac Gregor believed in a personal devil, and objected strongly to the name of the devil being used lightly. He was greatly pleased when the clause in the Lord's Prayer was altered in the Revised Version of the New Testament to " Deliver us from the Evil One."

We had the first of a series of ladies' meetings last night for a shilling subscription for the Martyrs' Memorial. We are appointing trustees to collect in America, Canada, India, and Australia, and money is pouring in in England. This is indeed a noble work and we had a grand assembly. I told of the 180 martyrs burned in Smithfield, and that the ground is just free and a pillar to be put up on the blackened embers of those 'of whom the world was not worthy,' and read the account of John Rogers, the first martyr—it all told admirably . . . . This is a work strictly scriptural, for God with his very mouth told the Jews thus to commemorate their examples of faith.

For some years Mac Gregor worked hard in this cause, and in 1870, he had the satisfaction of noting in his diary :

March 11, 1870.—Martyrs' Memorial in Smithfield was opened to-day—an important and striking ceremony. I have longed for this fulfilment.

One day, not long after this, as he was walking alone on the level sands of an Eastern seaport, a stranger joined him in his stroll, and conversation turned upon Bibles and martyrs.

In parting, the stranger said, " Sir, you are a man that ought to promote a suitable memorial to William Tyndale ; good-bye." The incident passed into oblivion for a time, but when, in 1878, public interest was stirred in the matter, the voice of the stranger came back to Mac Gregor as a call to action.

To be instrumental in the erection of a statue may not be considered by some a very important work, and certainly not sufficiently so to call for permanent record as a notable event in the career of a popular public man, but the story of Tyndale's statue on the Thames Embankment is, we think, worth telling, more especially as it brings out prominently one feature in the character of Mac Gregor—his perseverance in the face of difficulties.

Mac Gregor had said, and heard it said hundreds of times, that the greatness of England was due, in a very large degree, to the translation of the Bible into the common tongue, so that it could be "understanded of the people," and its precepts taken home to their hearts, thence to issue in renewed life and vigorous enterprise.

Not only did Tyndale give England and the world this great boon, but he helped to make the English language what it is. Mr. Froude, in his History, says: "Of the translation itself, though since that time it has been many times revised and altered, we may say that it is substantially the Bible with which we are all familiar. The peculiar genius—if such a word may be permitted—which breathes through it, the mingled tenderness and majesty, the Saxon simplicity, the preternatural grandeur, unequalled, unapproached in the attempted improvements of modern scholars, all are here, and bear the impress of the mind of one man —William Tyndale."

On these and other grounds, Mac Gregor thought that a memorial to Tyndale would form a common rallying ground on which all sects of Christians could meet, and that there was no name which simple Christians of all churches and schools would more readily agree to honour.

The publication of the Revised Version of the New Testament gave a strong impetus to the scheme of the memorial from the fact that the preface called attention to Tyndale's work as "the true primary version."

There was much in the character of Tyndale that appealed to the sympathies of Mac Gregor. "Tyndale achieved the reputation of a scholar, the work of a benefactor, the glory of a confessor, and the supreme honour of martyrdom at the early age of thirty-six He was in the prison which he was only to leave for the stake, before the date of the English Reformation. . . . . He had actually done his great work, the translation of the New Testament, at the age of twenty-six, and from that age to his martyrdom was fleeing from city to city, or in prison, and still labouring to perfect his original work and to add to it a translation of the Old Testament."

The splendid doggedness in the purpose of Tyndale won the admiration and was helpful to the character of Mac Gregor. Tyndale set his hand to one thing, and he never looked back. He published hardly anything besides his translation, and as fast as the book was circulated or destroyed, he published new and improved editions—thirty thousand copies altogether in one year.

Again, Rob Roy was a lover of the Bible apart from Church dogmatism. He was content to allow it to speak for itself and to do its own work; and although he was clearly of opinion that often it was better that instruction should go with the Book, he held that it

THE TYNDALE MONUMENT

was not indispensable there should always be some
one at hand to say what it meant and what it did not
mean.

The whole movement was to do honour to the Bible
by honouring the man who made it accessible to the
people, and, reviewing the subject, the *Times*, in an
admirable article, hit upon a *motif* which was one of
the incentives to Rob Roy to continue his persistent
labours. "Immensely as the literature of the country
has increased this century, the Bible now occupies a
larger proportionate space in that literature than ever
it did. No book raises so many inquiries or touches
so many interests. The Bible sends the student to
libraries and archives. To the Bible we owe much of
the intense and spreading interest in languages, and in
the originals of customs and of peoples. It directs the
traveller to buried cities, to the tombs of kings, to the
records of States once great, and well-nigh forgotten.
Wherever the battle of opinion is now the liveliest,
wherever the race for discovery is the most eager,
wherever the earth at last reveals her buried history,
it is to add to our knowledge of the sacred story
and to our understanding of the sacred volume. So
far as the people are concerned—that is, so far as
all except a very few learned men are concerned
—all this literature dates from William Tyndale's
translation of the New Testament into our vernacular
tongue."

The statue, the work of Mr. J. E. (afterwards Sir
Edgar) Boehm, R.A., represents Tyndale in his

doctor's robes, his right hand on an open New Testament resting on a printing-press ; his left grasps his
cloak and holds a manuscript while he is supposed to
be uttering the memorable words, " If God spares my
life, ere many years I will cause a boy that driveth the
plough shall know more of the Scriptures than thou
doest."   On each of the two brass entablatures is an
inscription, the first is :   " William Tyndale, first translator of the New Testament into English from the
Greek.   Born A.D. 1484.   Died a martyr at Vilvorde
in Belgium, A.D. 1536.   ' Thy word is a lamp to my
feet and a light to my path.'   ' The entrance of Thy
word giveth light.' Ps. cxix. 105, 130."   And this is
the second, " ' That God has given us Eternal life and
this life is in His Son.'   1 John v. 11.   The last words
of William Tyndale were, ' Lord open the King of
England's eyes ! ' and within a year afterwards a
Bible was placed in every parish church by the King's
command."

A few incidents in connection with this work may
not be uninteresting.   The Tyndale Memorial Committee was formed in 1879, but its operations were
stopped for nearly two years, as a movement was on
foot to do honour to Robert Raikes, the founder of
Sunday Schools, and it would not be seemly for
two sets of philanthropists to be in apparent opposition.

The work was again fairly started in 1882, and the
spirit in which Sir Edgar Boehm did his part of it
may be gathered from the following letter :

SIR EDGAR BOEHM *to* JOHN MAC GREGOR.

KISSINGEN, *August* 2, 1882.

DEAR MAC GREGOR,

I came here a short time ago to strengthen myself for Tyndale and am going to Nuremberg to find a printing-press of the XV. century to introduce on the statue. If I am not successful there I shall go and stay at Antwerp, where, in the printers' museum, there is everything I shall require. It may seem of small importance, this adjunct to the statue, but I should rather leave it out altogether than not have it perfectly correct. . . . . .

J. E. BOEHM.

Opposition was, of course, raised in some quarters to so costly a memorial as was proposed, and Mac Gregor had a good many arguments—if such they may be called—put before him like this :

" Tyndale died for the name of Jesus. Multitudes are daily dying without the name of Jesus. Tyndale longed to give the Gospel to the people, and shall we erect a bronze statue to a man who gave up his life for the sake of his Master, who said carry the Gospel to every creature "—and so forth.

Happily approval outweighed opposition a thousand-fold. One enthusiastic supporter urged that monuments "higher than Nelson's" should be erected in all parts of the great Protestant city of the world. " Let Cranmer speak again," he wrote to Mac Gregor, ' And as for the Pope I refuse him with all his false doc- trines.' Let the noble Hooper speak again, ' Mr. Mayor, I am not come hither as one forced or com- pelled to die—for it is well known I might have had

my life with worldly gain—but I am come to confirm
the truth which I taught here with my blood, willing
to offer and give my life for the truth rather than consent to the wicked religion of the Bishop of Rome,
and I trust by God's grace to-morrow to die a faithful
subject to God and a true obedient subject to the
Queen.'   Latimer should speak once more and say,
' Be of good comfort Mr. Ridley and play the man ;
we shall this day light such a candle by God's grace
in England as I trust never shall go out." . . . . and
John Bradford of Pembroke Hall, Cambridge, should
again speak his great warning, 'O, England !
England ! beware of idolatry, beware of anti-Christ,
take heed that they do not deceive and destroy
thee.' "

From John MacGregor's Diary.

Nov. 26, 1879.—Tyndale Committee. Two nuns called at the
office asking to see, 'Mr. Tyndale' and were informed 'Mr. Tyndale
was burned 300 years ago for translating the Bible !'

May 7, 1884.—The day for a grand man to be brought into the
remembrance of millions. All passed off well.

From THE REV. CARR J. GLYNN *to* JOHN MAC GREGOR.

8, SUSSEX PLACE, HYDE PARK,
May 8, 1884.

MY DEAR MAC GREGOR,

    I am full of thankfulness to God for yesterday's
completion of seven years' anxious work as to W. Tyndale. It is a
noble figure and I do trust that many and many a soul will have first
impressions, or increasingly so, on looking at William Tyndale and
reading the texts. No one can say how important the statue is on
many counts, especially in these days when the Reformation and
Protestantism are so attacked.

As to yourself it will be a bright and happy reflection for you in all your future life and William Tyndale will be well remembered by your dear children,

Very truly yours,
Carr J. Glynn.

July 12, 1884.—Last meeting of Tyndale Memorial Committee—presented last audited account with a balance after all debts of £150. Thus God has most graciously allowed me to form and to continue, and to finish, one of the most blessed and interesting works I have had to conduct.

The ceremony of unveiling the Tyndale memorial was performed by Lord Shaftesbury. In the following year the "Good Earl" passed away to his reward.

On the day of his death the following letter was written:

Sir Edwin Chadwick *to* John Mac Gregor.

United Service Club, Pall Mall, S.W.,
Oct. 1, 1885.

Dear Mr. Mac Gregor,

In answer to some inquiries as to our illustrious friend, my former colleague and supporter in sanitation, I received, with description of his condition, the following from Lord Ashley:—'In spite of pains and discomfort, it is marvellous and beautiful to see the ineffable peace and faith and trust, which possess his mind and soul; a lesson and a picture on how to live, and how to die.' I apprehend the release to him is near. Knowing your regard for him I send this notice to you, that it may be considered what steps may be taken for paying due regard publicly on the occasion, in which I should be glad to have an opportunity of consulting you, at any time here, that you might appoint.

Yours faithfully,
Edwin Chadwick.

D D

We have seen from time to time in the course of this narrative how closely Mac Gregor was associated in important philanthropic works with the Earl of Shaftesbury. It could not be otherwise, therefore, than that the death of so noble a coadjutor should fill him with the deepest sorrow. He was a man who, from the morning of his life to its evening, was incessantly engaged in works of benevolence and mercy, intended to alleviate the sufferings and elevate the moral and physical condition of his fellows ; a man who lived a public life for sixty years almost without an enemy, who died amid the universal blessings of the people, and on whose whole career there rested not the shadow of a single stain.

The memory of such a man, John Mac Gregor felt, must be perpetuated through all generations not only in the hearts of the people but by outward and visible signs, and when a National Memorial was proposed— to comprise a statue in Westminster Abbey, a drinking fountain in Shaftesbury Avenue, and a National Con- valescent Home for poor children—Mac Gregor became the Chairman of the Executive Committee, and devoted to the work much of the old energy he had displayed on the Tyndale Memorial.

In March of the same year, 1885, the " Gordon Memorial Fund for the Benefit of poor Children," was originated at a united meeting of members of the Ragged School Union and the Reformatory and Refuge Union. It was decided to raise a fund for the benefit of boys and girls in need of temporary help, by reason of poverty or their friendless condition, by sending them to country homes for a visit when in need of change, or to the seaside or to hospitals in sickness; to give outfits for their emigration, to minister to their safety and comfort, or to help in any way that might be devised.

Mac Gregor became one of the treasurers of the fund, and the labour that it entailed is only known to members of his own household and to those with whom he worked in the good cause. But the final shape taken for the Gordon Memorial he did not live to see. It was, however, a cause of great thanksgiving to him that he was able to be present in Westminster Abbey on the memorable occasion when the fine statue of his old friend and colleague, Lord Shaftesbury, was unveiled.

It is a fact beyond contradiction that Mac Gregor was not a good correspondent. Even his most intimate friends lament that they have no memorial of him in the shape of a really good letter. This is not to be wondered at considering the enormous amount of work he had in hand, and, in consequence, the mechanical way in which he had to deal with it when it involved correspondence. And this habit grew, until his letters dwindled down from sheets to half-sheets, and from half-sheets to lines. But those who wrote to him were generous, and his short note, "Pray tell me what is being done with regard to so-and-so," would often bring out a long letter in reply. From a mass of letters which he treasured, we have selected a few for insertion here, and have endeavoured to choose those which bring out points in Mac Gregor's character as well as idiosyncrasies in the writers.

He had appeals for help from many quarters and for many objects. He took an intense interest in the work of other workers, and always helped them if he could. For none did he feel greater sympathy than the late Miss Whateley, of Cairo, in her splendid efforts for Egypt. She appealed to him to tell her how she could best approach the Great City Companies for help. During the Arabi war she had been the victim of robbery, her school-house had been turned into a refuge for the destitute, and needed repairing and enlarging, the school meantime increasing too rapidly for the funds. Here is an extract from one of her letters :

From Miss M. A. Whateley (*Cairo*) *to* John Mac Gregor.

In all the dark views we have of this poor country, in all the mistakes made about it, in all the different opinions about these mistakes, all Christians, I might say all men of sense (only *can* a man of real sense *not* be a Christian ?), agree that education is the best of *all* good. May I remark that of the hundreds of lads trained in my school not one has been found a rebel ; and that the wonderful way in which the railways and telegraphs worked on in the midst of the (Arabi) war may not unfairly be—in part at least—attributed to the fact that a large proportion of the young men working in these Departments come from the 'Madress El Inglese.' I dread so appearing to put the secular part forward too much that I have never before put this on paper, but possibly it is as well to show that, even for this world's good, Christian teaching is the best. Don't we deserve a helping hand from wealthy English companies? 700

children being taught to walk the right way as far as can be taught, and all with civilisation and Scripture instead of fanaticism and the Koran. . . . .

Yours sincerely,

M. A. WHATELEY.

From MARTIN TUPPER *to* JOHN MAC GREGOR.

ALBANY HOUSE, NEAR GUILDFORD,
March 9, 1868:

DEAR SIR,

I suppose myself to be beholden to you for sundry Protestant Alliance papers ; also I am told that you are the Rob Roy Mac Gregor of canoe celebrity. Let me thank you—hypothetically—on both grounds. But the chief errand of this note is to state why I have not hitherto (and probably shall not still, without cause found) joined either the Church Association or the Protestant Alliance in these difficult days. It seems to me I should be getting out of a large field into a little one—sinking from a national and universal greatness to a self-imposed partisanship on a small scale. In this Protestant country and with our constitution of Church and State, I may fairly assume that by birthright I belong irrevocably to the Church Association and to the Protestant Alliance ; one would hardly care to join— as if de novo—the Human Club or the Sane Society. I am, and have been all my life, a moderate Churchman and a free Protestant, and I need not join any private companies to prove these.

There ! and I know how you will reply : that the enemy associates in E.C.U. and Catholic Alliance, &c. &c., and so we must, too. I don't know that ; we have the vantage ground of a Protestant Crown and a Reformed Church, and need not condescend to lower platforms. That I am heartily with you and against Rome, Puseyism, and Colensoism is most true. You read me in the *Rock*, *e.g.*, and I send you now (ill-printed and inaccurate) one of my old Directoria, as another—*e.g.* next week—a neat new edition will be ready at the *Rock* office. Let me hear from you : my daughter will keep your autograph.

Truly yours,

MARTIN F. TUPPER.

From FRANK BUCKLAND *to* JOHN MAC GREGOR.

4, OLD PALACE YARD,
Nov. 13, 1869.

DEAR MAC GREGOR,

I quite approve of your idea. 'The boys' of 1869 will be 'the men' of future years, and when we are dead and gone will represent our nation. It is therefore the duty of those who are now 'at work' to pass on some of their experiences to those who will come after them.

There is so much rascality, 'half truth telling,' nay, positive lying for self-interested purposes, that the boys ought to be told what I have found out for myself, 'Experientia does it.' I hope, therefore, that your paper will succeed. Mind you, I do not think it will pay unless it be A 1, and then it will have a large circulation.

Do not try to amuse the boys too much. Young English minds only want to have 'the right road' pointed out and they will follow it. I will support your new journal in every way I can.

Yours ever,

F. BUCKLAND.

BISHOP OF MANCHESTER (DR. FRASER) *to* JOHN MAC GREGOR.

July 21, 1870.

MY DEAR SIR,

I am much obliged by your letter, which deeply interested me. Certainly one's prayer for Christianity ought to be like Dido's— *Exoriare aliquis!* But the cumulative evidence of Christianity is a feature which, while it constitutes its strength in every mind competent to weigh evidence, constitutes its weakness also before an untrained and unlettered audience, and I should be sorry to stake the faith of hearers upon the result of a combat, in which to raise objections is so much easier than to answer them. At the same time, I feel with you that the efforts of atheists and secularists are too much ignored by the Clergy, and that too many of the advocates of Christianity are intellectually incompetent to deal with its opponents. We want a more educated, better-grounded, clergy : we want, still more perhaps, a higher standard of Christian life wherewith to reply to the gainsayers. I am very ignorant myself of the extent to which secularism and atheism prevail among the masses. But I do not think they are deeply or widely lodged in the mind of Lancashire, which, 'au fond, is too religious to welcome them. But it is time for the Church to gird on her armour for a real fight, instead of wasting her strength upon miserable internal controversies.

Yours very truly,
J. Manchester

Sir George Grove *to* John Mac Gregor.

Lower Sydenham,
Feb. 16, 11 P.M.

My dear Mac Gregor,

    I am immensely grateful to you for your note and for the corrections which I am sure I shall find most valuable, pray continue them throughout the book. I see that many of your remarks concern the colloquial style, of this I have already been made aware on reading the book myself. I am unable to write unless I fancy an auditor before me, and I can truly say that I never wrote a line of this book without having in imagination a boy or a grown person by my side to whom I was talking. Hence many of the colloquations. But such scaffolding ought to disappear, and shall disappear. Please let me have the rest. Such hints are invaluable, especially when conveyed with such kindness and sympathy as animates, and has always animated all our intercourse.

I am just going to bed and shall take your little address there with me.

Yours ever truly,
G. Grove.

From Matthew Arnold *to* John Mac Gregor.

Athenæum Club,
June 16, 1875.

My dear Mac Gregor,

    I make it a rule not to bother the School Board with

recommendations, but I am going to break my rule in favour of an Irishman called O'Conor, whom I have never seen.

He sent me his poems some time ago—he had scraped together money enough to publish them, though only a working man down at Deptford. I opened them with a feeling of *bore* with which one does open the volumes of poetry that one receives, but I found real gaiety, tune, and pathos—something that made me think of Burns, but a Burns infinitely less educated, without the training of Presbyterian Scotland. I find O'Conor is applying for a place of School Board visitor in your district. I am sure he would be humane and sympathetic and I am told that he has an excellent character for sobriety and steadiness. I tell you fairly that his letters are often not spelt correctly and have mistakes in grammar, but he has a real dash of genius and it is sad to think how often this merely makes a man's misery for want of any chance for it in his circumstances. That is why I write to you. Do try and interest Mr. Legge and Mr. Waugh in the case, if I have succeeded in interesting you.

Ever sincerely yours,
MATTHEW ARNOLD.

REV. BENJAMIN WAUGH *to* JOHN MACGREGOR.

HAXTED COTTAGE, EDENBRIDGE, KENT,
March 13, 1879.

MY DEAR MR. MACGREGOR,

You may be interested to read what my good old father says about you, and your paper of last month. Having referred to another paper as pleasing him, he continues: But more so in the paper, 'What we found in Palestine.' There are few contributors to the *Sunday Magazine*, whose productions, whether for young or old, I love to read and think about so much as those of Mr. MacGregor. He throws so much intelligent and generous sympathy into what he does, and he always honours the Bible, no doubt because the Book has honoured him. He gives it a first place in everything. Alike to old things discovered and new things created, it is the light that lighteth, and to civilised and barbarian the giver of heaven-born liberty. He is making Pales-

tine to live again, pointing out its place in the world, and in its
future history. When ready, and after reading the paper, I was
prompted to pray that the Lord would long spare his life and bless
him with good health and happiness in the exceeding great and
precious promises that he may continue to be a servant of God, and
a blessing to mankind.

Yours truly,

BENJAMIN WAUGH.

From REV. C. H. SPURGEON *to* JOHN MAC GREGOR.

[A Mr. Mac Gregor, a member of Mr. Spurgeon's
church, brought a pair of huge horns from South Africa
as a present to his pastor. Spurgeon wrote a letter of
glowing thanks which was sent by his secretary in
mistake to " Rob Roy " Mac Gregor :]

NIGHTINGALE LANE, BALHAM,

Feb. 25, 1880.

MY DEAR FRIEND,

This is real fun. The letter was not for Rob Roy at
all, but for quite another Mac Gregor altogether. Pray forgive my
Secretary's blunder. It is your own fault for being so famous. He
knows only *one* Mac Gregor. I should not have thought of your
carrying horns to Blackheath. The right Mac Gregor is a member
of my church and is often in these regions.

Yours, and no mistake,

C. H. SPURGEON.

DR. SAMUEL SMILES *to* JOHN MAC GREGOR.

8, PEMBROKE GARDENS, KENSINGTON, W.

Dec. 9, 1884.

DEAR SIR,

I am glad that you found my little book interesting.
Now that I am getting old, it is my recreation and amusement to put
together many of the things I have been searching into ; and it is a

pleasure to me to know that others find my books pleasant and interesting. I had already mentioned the subject of Blasco de Garay's paddlewheel boat in my lives of Bolton and Watt. I was indebted to Mr. Bergewroth, for his account of the papers at Siman-cas, when, like you, he found no mention of steam being used. I had a letter from him on the subject, obtained through Mrs. Bennett, a cousin of Mr. Gladstone. I also added that 'this statement is confirmed by the independent examination of J. Mac Gregor, Esq., of the Temple, who gives the result in a letter to Bennet Woodcroft, Esq., inscribed in a note to the "Abridgments of the Specifications relating to Steam Propulsion."' I did not, however, know that the writer of that letter was the famous Rob Roy Mac Gregor. The late Charles Gilpin told me of a very singular circumstance about you—of having been placed in the arms of one of his aunts at Plymouth (I think) after your rescue from the *Kent* East Indiaman, one of the burning (?) recitals heard in my boyhood. Like me, you must be getting pretty well on in years. I think I must have read all you have written and published and I have also read many of your speeches on public questions. I am very pleased to hear from you now, and I will send your letter to my daughter to put among her collection of autographs.

Believe me, Dear Sir,
Yours very faithfully,
S. SMILES.

From the BISHOP OF EXETER *to* JOHN MAC GREGOR.

CHRIST CHURCH VICARAGE, HAMPSTEAD,
Jan. 23, 1885.

DEAREST MAC GREGOR,

. . . . Warmest thanks for your congratulations, but my heart bleeds to leave my flock after thirty years' ministry here. Breathe a prayer for me and them. It is delightful to hear from you of all the loving labours in which the Master is using you. He is worthy for whom you do this.

I have not a photograph of Tyndale's Statue. If you kindly send it, only view it as a pledge that you will come with Mrs. Mac Gregor and see it in the Deanery Library, Gloucester.

> Your ever affectionate Friend,
> E. H. BICKERSTETH.

REV. J. N. DALTON (*tutor to the late* DUKE OF CLARENCE) *to* JOHN MAC GREGOR.

> TRINITY COLLEGE, CAMBRIDGE,
> *Feb.* 25, 1880.

DEAR SIR,

I thank you very much for sending some of the papers relating to the London Shoeblack Societies. Prince Edward has read them with great interest. It must be a great satisfaction to yourself, as the founder of the movement, to see what excellent fruits it has, under God's blessing, brought forth. That it may continue so to do is Prince Edward's earnest prayer.

> Yours very sincerely,
> J. N. DALTON.

LORD KINNAIRD *to* JOHN MAC GREGOR.

> 50 SOUTH AUDLEY STREET, W.,
> *May* 11, 1887.

MY DEAR MAC GREGOR,

I felt sure you would be grieved to hear of my father's death. I gave my mother your message. It is a comfort to us all to know we have the prayers of many friends. What a difference, thank God, there is in London work since Lord Shaftesbury, my father, you, Judge Payne, and others 'put your shoulders to the wheel,'—what really marvellous progress! With heartfelt thanks to you for all your past kindness ever since I can remember,

> Ever yours affectionarely,
> ARTHUR KINNAIRD.

CHAPTER XVIII

BY THE STILL WATERS

Few men could have borne the strain of so active and hard-working a life as Mac Gregor had led without succumbing to sickness. But in his case, until he was sixty-three years of age, he never had any illness, except in 1849 when he fell a victim to malarial fever contracted during his first tour in the East. On the contrary, his health was so uniformly robust and his spirits so buoyant that when he was verging on sixty an old friend said of him, " He never grows older, never relinquishes anything, and is as much a youth as a man."

Nevertheless, he had occasional "warnings" and sometimes there seems to have been on his mind an apprehension of evil days in the future. The first really serious warning was within a few months of his retirement from the School Board :

Feb. 11, 1877, *Sunday.*—Soon after the sermon began I felt drowsy and went off into a slight faint and unconsciousness lasting only a few seconds, but with clutching of hands and nervous action.

Walked out of church with Col. Field.* Burton came and prescribed rest.† My work last week particularly exhausting.

A very short rest seemed all that was needed and as we have seen in the previous chapter he was soon in the full stream of new and old activities. We may supplement the narrative in that chapter by a few notes from his diary :

1885.

April 12, *Sunday.*—Visited Arthur Mac Gregor, ‡ ill of rheumatic fever. I had to go in by train. The only other occasion of my using Sunday thus was when I came back from Holland very wet from the steamer at 4 A.M. Went to the Athenæum for luncheon. Only about ten members there, not one in the smoking-room, and the billiard-room closed up. A very great difference this from some Sundays when I had to get lunch there after four or five hours of open-air preaching thirty years ago.

April 17.—Arthur Mac Gregor buried in Brompton Cemetery. A most impressive scene. Persons attended from the Y.M.C.A., the Open-air Mission, the Ragged School, Shoeblack Society, and the Polytechnic. Arthur had been active on each of these committees. Several of the young men going out to China were there. Arthur himself was preparing to be a missionary.

April 25.—With Williams, Kirk, and Maddison to the Lord Mayor who received us cordially and acceded to the request to join the Gordon Memorial Committee.

From that day forth for many months he was every day at work on " Gordon business," throwing himself

* Now General Sir John Field, K.C.B.

† Mr. John M. Burton, of Lee, the medical attendant and valued friend for many years of both Sir Duncan Mac Gregor's and Sir Crawford Caffin's families.

‡ The eldest son of Colonel H. G. Mac Gregor, C.B., John Mac Gregor's youngest brother.

into it with the enthusiasm of a youth and as if it were the only one thing that claimed his attention

1885.

Oct. 1.—Lord Shaftesbury died.

Oct. 9.—Was one of the pall-bearers at Lord S.'s funeral.

Oct. 16.—Meeting at Mansion House for memorial to Lord S. Excellent speeches from Lord Granville and Lord Mount-Temple.

Then for many months occur such entries as this: "Working hard at Lord S.'s Memorial."

1886.

Jan. 16.—Another delightful visit to old Pennifer who was in the *Kent* (aged 77), a true Christian sailor.

Feb. 27.—Settled with Boehm that he would erect the marble statue of Lord S. for the Abbey, and Mr. Gilbert would make the bronze statue for Shaftesbury Avenue.

April 23.—Wrote to Chamberlain as to Home Rule.

April 30.—Splendid meeting at the Rink on Home Rule. I was chairman.

The politics of Mac Gregor were not very pronounced. He was anything but a lover of party and voted for principles rather than for men. He was described as a "philanthropic liberal"—the embodied expression of disinterested patriotism—"a Liberal so far as he has any party politics at all." When, therefore, Greenwich, and the regions round about, wished to express disapprobation on the question of Home Rule and held a monster meeting at the Rink to that end, Mac Gregor, as chairman, fitly represented the principle of non-party unity prevailing in that crisis between patriotic Liberals and Conservatives " who were determined to maintain the union between Great Britain and Ireland and the integrity of the Empire."

It was MacGregor's practice habitually to stand aloof from political strife. But in the present instance, he considered that loyalty to his country and old association with Ireland alike demanded an expression of opinion.

1886.

June 5.—London Scottish R. V. opening large building for the corps and muster of the corps which has nine hundred men.

July and August were spent at Braemar with his family; this he much enjoyed, and his Rob Roy Lecture in the Free Church was largely attended by residents and visitors.

Sept. 6.—Twenty boys playing football without shoes on the sand (at Portobello, near Edinburgh) with a small hand-ball splendidly. I asked the name of the club. 'The Bare-Foot Rangers.'

Dec. 29.—To the Seamen's Hospital where I sang Eastern music.

Up to this time there was but little perceptible difference in MacGregor, except that perhaps he appeared to live more in the past than in the present and had lost somewhat of his old mental and physical vigour. Still his interest in everything that worked for good was keen, and many new schemes were in his mind. He lent substantial aid in promoting the erection of a Presbyterian church in Blackheath where he and his family worshipped. He was a constant attendant at the church, and greatly valued the minis-

trations of the Rev. J. Head Thompson, the pastor ;
he still loved to visit the Naval School at Greenwich,
the workhouse, and other local institutions ; and he
enjoyed his visits to London to mingle among his old
associates.   Every institution with which he had been
connected seemed to have for him even more than the
old attraction.   Schemes for the betterment of young
men came in from all quarters, and wherever he could
help he helped.   He greatly sympathised with Canon
Farrar in his attempt to establish a large gymnasium,
with cricket and football clubs, boat clubs, a cadet rifle
corps, singing classes, swimming baths—anything that
would bring London youths together for physical recreation and in contact with muscular Christian laymen
and clergymen who would enter heartily into the work.
He followed every movement of the Palestine Exploration Fund, and was a constant reader of the *Jewish
Chronicle*, to which in former days he had been a not
infrequent contributor.   The Shoeblack Brigade, the
Pure Literature Society, the British and Foreign Bible
Society, of which for many years he had been an
active member, and especially the Open-air Mission
still engaged his time, thought and sympathy.   " Mac
Gregor and I often got a Sunday afternoon walk
together," writes his well-beloved friend and brother-
in-law, Major E. Owen Hay—"a much-valued time
to me.   One day we were crossing Blackheath and
came upon a preacher standing inside the railings
on the Heath while his audience, a small crowd,
were gathered outside the rails.   Mac Gregor's only

remark to me was : ' Owen, that man is on the wrong side of the railings.' "

In 1888 it was evident to all that a serious change was taking place in Mac Gregor, and the diary bears painful testimony to the fact. From time to time many days elapse without any entry. Each event recorded, however, tells of the clinging interest he still had in his life-work. Thus :

1888.

May 6.—Committee meeting of Lord S. (Shaftesbury Memorial) with Mr. Billing, Williams, and myself. The inscription finally ordered. But next day I wrote to Williams that it ought to be improved as it had no relation to God.

Among the last entries is one of touching interest. To understand it we must go back eighteen months in the diary to quote the following :

1886.

Dec. 23.—John Thompson committed a burglary in this house. He was well known to me for about a year, and I assisted him at various times. In the afternoon of the day I gave away dolls, &c., to the workhouse children, and a delightful duty it was. At night, when I was in bed after 11 P.M., the police roused us up by throwing gravel at the windows. Three very brave young men of the police met the thieves and they searched their pockets. Next day they were tried at the Greenwich Police Court and remanded.

1887.

Jan. 7–10.—I went four times to the Court before our case of the burglar was brought on, and in the end he was sentenced to a year and a half in prison with hard labour.

This man Thompson was one who had been be-friended by Mac Gregor over and over again, not only with monetary help, but by many acts of personal kindness and sympathy. Surely for such ingratitude there could be nothing left but the bitterest indignation. Such, however, was not the spirit of Mac Gregor. He had prayed too often the prayer : " Forgive us our trespasses as we forgive them that trespass against us," to cherish animosity, even against one who had so treacherously wronged him. And we find on the last folio of his last diary this short but eloquent sermon which needs no comment.

July 5, 1888.—The man Thompson released. Came here, and I got him emigrated by the good man Wheatley.

Only occasionally was the diary now in use, and on the last two pages are these significant entries, showing how his heart was in full touch with the past.

Oct. 1.—Went to Westminster Abbey with Annie (Mrs. Mac Gregor).

The occasion was the unveiling of the statue of his old and well-beloved friend and fellow-labourer for so many years, Lord Shaftesbury.

1889.

June.—The Committee of the Bible Society elected me as one of their Honorary Governors for life. This I prize much.

June 16, *Sunday*.—On a very hot day went to some O. A. M. (open-air missions).

July 17.—Wimbledon. Queen's Prize by a Scotsman.

There the Journals end. A few days later he wrote to Mr. Walter Besant, then the secretary of the

Palestine Exploration Fund, saying he would be unable to attend the Committee meeting. To which Mr. Besant replied :

July 29, 1889.

. . . . That any ordinary man should be ill is a matter of course, but that you should be ill is a surprise to anybody. I thought you were built of iron. I trust, however, that your illness is only temporary.

But it was, alas, an illness from which he never could recover. Already he was in the doctor's hands, and in 1889 a sea voyage was recommended. At once Mac Gregor, with his wife and eldest daughter, Ina, set forth northwards, intending to go to the North Cape. But the strong sea air increased the weakness of the patient, and he was very ill on board. It was a time of intense anxiety to Mrs. Mac Gregor, and she had a consultation with three medical men who were passengers on the boat. They advised landing at Trondhjeim, the nearest port, and returning home by the next steamer to Hull. The voyage was accomplished with great difficulty, and it was the last the gallant sailor ever took.

But the end was not yet. Four years of illness, with gradual loss of strength, lay before him—years of hoping against hope.

The old home at Blackheath was broken up, and he removed with his family to Boscombe, near Bournemouth. He would not believe that the days of active work were over ; he was ready, patiently to follow any recommendation that might tend to improve his health,

and he could say, " God will make clear His purpose,
I, at least, can wait in silence."

It is not the province of a biographer to intrude
into that sacred silence. But it is meet that those
who tended him and watched the flickering spark of
mortal life, and the steady ever-brightening light of
Christian faith, should tell the story of the inner life,
that grew while the outward life was perishing, and
the narrative that follows has been given on our
earnest plea.

In the spring of 1890 Mrs. Mac Gregor was very
tired with long watching and nursing, and the doctor
insisted on her leaving home for ten days. During
that time daily bulletins were sent by her eldest
daughter :

> BOSCOMBE, BOURNEMOUTH,
> *May* 7, 1890.

We have just come in from a delightful walk with Pappie. It is a
beautiful evening so we went on the pier. The sea was simply lovely,
and Pappie seemed to enjoy it very much and was quite interested
watching the ships and fishing-smacks. He seems better to-night
than he has been for a long time. He took prayers this morning
and read the Twenty-third Psalm. . . . .

We had such a happy evening together last night. I played to
Pappie a little, and before I went to bed read him the evening portion
from 'The Cheque Book of the Bank of Faith,' and he said a few
words of prayer.

> *May* 9, 1890.

. . . . Pappie thought it was best not to go out as it was damp
after the rain. He has been wonderfully bright to-day considering
he has been kept indoors. The last two evenings I have been reading
to Pappie Stanley's Lecture ; he enjoyed it very much, especially
about the ' pygmies.'

May 10, 1890.

Pappie told me last night that he had felt better the last three or four days than he had for a long time.   He seems so happy to think you are having a change and is quite cheerful.

May 15, 1890.

. . . . I read Pappie some of Livingstone's Life from the book Uncle Robert gave me.   He is very bright indeed, and Dr. Scott* said his general health is excellent.

We make no apology for lifting the veil which hid him from the public eye to take this glimpse of him in the seclusion of his home in the days of weakness and suffering.   Surely it is good to see him thus and to see the ruling passion strong in death ; prayer and praise, Livingstone's and Stanley's stirring adventures —ships, sails, and sea—the struggle to keep well and cheerful in order that his loving wife might have a brief respite for rest and change—peace and companion- ship in the love of his children.

During these last years Mrs. Mac Gregor and her eldest daughter were in the habit of noting in their diaries some of his sayings, and we are privileged to give a few extracts here :

From Mrs. Mac Gregor's Diary.

1891.

Aug. 23.—J. spoke of the return of the Lord Jesus Christ.   J. said, ' We are allowed to be ready, and we ought to delight to tell others of Him. When He comes there will be many doing some things very nice, very good, but they haven't got the real thing, and they will be just too late. We ought to look to it and to make sure of having the love of Christ ; unless a man has this he is not happy.'

* Dr. T. B. Scott of Bournemouth, the medical attendant and kind friend of John Mac Gregor during his last illness.

Half an hour later he spoke most beautifully upon the nearness of the Lord to him; and said, '*I feel him nearer and nearer to me.*'

Sept. 6, *Sunday* evening.—'We must do our work for the King. It is *most delightful* to work for God. . . . . God knows our position. He is going to do great things. It is delightful to tell of the love of Jesus. Just to go and tell a poor man or woman of the love of God, and to help them, and the boys too. Oh! yes, the sailor boys and the ragged school children —that's delicious!' After this, he gave me a full account of his method of open-air preaching, and spoke of the King's Cross days, and his arguments with infidels.

Dec. 29.—J. said, with great earnestness, and with his old determined way of speaking, while sitting by the fire in the drawing-room, 'We ought to be preaching, preaching, we are far too comfortable here'!!

1892

Jan. 10.—'*He* never makes mistakes you know, other people do, but He *never.*' 'It is nice having you with me my darling, but oh! soon I shall be with Him, in the glory.'

'Our Lord God is very near us. He is waiting for us. He does not tell us the exact day, but it is sure.' 'We shall see Him, and His hands that were nailed for us, and His side pierced.'

'People wil' run, and call upon the rocks to hide them—but He is coming and all His people will come with Him. He says so, and He will reign for ever and ever, and *my delight is that I am getting nearer and nearer to Him.*'

March 14.—'Whether I go, or whether I stay, *He* is with me, and He is with you too my darling.' And then he spoke of our dear girls.

March 22.—On returning home from one of Mr. Selwyn's * services, I told J. about it and Mr. Selwyn's address—he looked at me very earnestly, and said, '*Does he bring souls to Christ?*' 'Yes,' I replied, 'this is his one desire.' J. added with great vigour, '*Help him on, help him on.*'

In June (only a few weeks before he went Home) he said to me

---

* Rev. S. A. Selwyn, vicar of St. John's, Boscombe.

one day, when we were speaking of the Lord Jesus : '*I see him every day.*"

From Ina Mac Gregor's Diary.

1891.

April 2.—I had been reading the portion of Spurgeon's 'Chequebook of the Bank of Faith,' and Pappie spoke of our working and living for God; and added, 'When at last He shall call us, may we be ready.'

September.—He was speaking of Christ's coming soon, and then began to speak of his life, and said, 'I am an old man now,' and spoke of the opportunities he had missed for God. With the tears in his eyes he said, 'And you too will have some work to do for God.'

1892.

July 15.—2.15 P.M. He had been unconscious for some hours— a gleam of consciousness came back at this time, and he smiled so sweetly on us, and when mother spoke of his going to the Lord he said quite distinctly, '*I'll go to see Him.*'

Early in the evening of the following day, July 16, the call of the Master came, and John Mac Gregor passed away to his reward.

A few days later all that was mortal of him was laid to rest in Bournemouth Cemetery beside the graves of his old friend Canon Carus and his fellow worker Earl Cairns, and ere the mourners left the sacred spot they sang together the touching hymn beginning "The sands of Time are sinking"—one of his favourite hymns in which are the following lines :

> I shall sleep sound in Jesus,
> Fill'd with his likeness rise
> To live and to adore him.
> To see him with these eyes.
> My kingly King in Zion
> My presence doth command
> Where glory, glory dwelleth
> In Emmanuel's land.

Of testimony to the life and character of John Mac Gregor there is more than abundance, and only one or two extracts from letters innumerable will be given here.

From Mr. Nathaniel Bridges *to* Mrs. Mac Gregor.

I cast my eye back to the year 1851, when I first made his acquaintance and joined him in his most interesting and successful Shoeblack Movement of which he was the life and soul. I felt at once I was in touch with a most uncommon character, calculated to influence all more or less who came in contact with him. It was the power of a man who possessed, believed and enjoyed the religion of the Lord Jesus Christ and was ever anxious to impart the same blessing to others. His life, his activity for good, even more than his words, were the sermon which I know influenced the lives of young men of his own age and who, in the day when the secrets of the hearts shall be revealed, will rise up and call him blessed. His work amongst the ragged children, his efforts with the infidel, his sympathy with all who in whatever way were seeking to hasten the coming Kingdom, and, in the meantime, to ameliorate mankind and mitigate the sorrows of human existence, rise up to the memory of those who knew him while one feels that not the half has been known or told. . . . .

From the Rev. Ernest Cowan *to* Mrs. Mac Gregor.

. . . . I can never forget that I held your clasped hands on that day when you both knelt at the Communion rails of St. John's, Blackheath, and pledged your troth either to other. Neither can I forget all your dear husband's kindness to me when he was a member of the congregation and a resident in the parish. . . . .

It has indeed been a long and weary illness, but I doubt not accompanied by many gracious alleviations and the ever soothing consciousness that you were ministering to one who loved you and who loved you best on earth. Oh, blessed rest for that soul, so human in its sensibilities and yet so different from others—cast in an uncommon mould and doubtless fashioned for special employment in the coming Kingdom.

From Lord Bangor *to* Mrs. Mac Gregor.

It was not three years ago that I stood on the platform of Exeter Hall with Lord Aberdeen who called on me to move a resolution, and when I mentioned the name of dear John Mac Gregor, the whole meeting rose to their feet and for the moment you could hear nothing but the deafening applause, testifying to the love and affection they had for one who, in connection with Lord Shaftesbury, had been the means of rescuing so many waifs and strays from the purlieus of London. I well recollect now more than forty years ago, hearing him preach the Gospel on Sunday morning in one of the streets off the Strand, when a man came up to him and asked, 'What's the use of preaching here? When I want to hear that kind of thing I go to Church.' He talked much in reply to him, and said, 'When were you last in Church?' The man was dumbfounded and did not reply, when Mac Gregor said, 'You would not have heard the Gospel to-day if it had not been preached in this street by me.' The man seemed quite touched, and was an attentive listener afterwards. John Mac Gregor showed wonderful tact and earnestness in everything he did.

There are many lessons to be learned from the life of John Mac Gregor. He being dead yet speaketh, and the main burden of his message is to young men.

He was a firm believer in " enduring hardness," and had an honest contempt for a life of listlessness. He despised all short cuts to knowledge, and thought that if anything was worth knowing it was worth knowing thoroughly. He maintained that no life could be kept

in a healthy state unless the habit were acquired of
forcing oneself every day to do something heartily dis-
liked but which it is one's duty to do.   The man at
ease, without plan or purpose demanding energy and
zeal ; the listless man who cares for nothing ; the poor
meaningless " butterflies," who flit from so-called pleasure to so-called pleasure for lack of knowledge as to
what real pleasure is ; the deluded young man who
seeks all his enjoyment in theatres, music-halls, billiards,
and such like—it was to these that John Mac Gregor
spoke some of his most burning words, and for these
that he had a consuming anxiety.   Apostle as he
was of muscular Christianity, in all his words and
actions he showed that athleticism was only a good
thing when it "girded up the loins of the mind" for
those moral possibilities and activities which belong
to every useful life.   And he carried this theory on to a
higher platform ; a life of spiritual ease, of contentment
in being "a hearer of the word and not a doer," of
gaining good more than of doing good, of preaching,
or "talking" Christ, and not "living" Christ—this he
conceived was the great bane of religious life, and he
contended that the need of the Church was that its
members should be men who would "endure hardness
as good soldiers," and thus become strong, courageous,
invincible Christians.

He believed in pressing everything into the highest
service ; a musical voice, a volunteer's uniform, a canoe
paddle, the power of entertaining, a man's professional
calling, the gift of utterance, the winning manner, the

art of social ice-breaking, good-fellowship, sympathy—
no matter what the gift might be, he believed that
it came from God, and was ready for His using.
Probably nothing in all his life pained him more
than to see young men with splendid qualifications
squandering them upon selfish indulgences and
meaningless pleasures. He felt that if a tittle of
this wasted power were only utilised in direct effort
to make the world better there would be a social
and religious reformation such as never yet has been
known.

Perhaps the most influential part of his own work
was that unpretentious, quiet, helpful aid he gave to
obscure boys in obscure places, and at all times. There
was no applause to be gained, no recognition to be
given; nobody knew of the work or shared it with
him, it was simply quiet, continuous, self-sacrificing
work, having for its sole reward the opportunity of
saying a word that should bring perchance new hope
and aspiration to a weary life drifting away with the
strong current of evil. Self is unhappily so much the
trade-mark of religious labour; it is so much the
fashion to put our philanthropic goods in the front
window; so general to depend for a good name in
the Churches, to find reward in advertisements and
newspaper paragraphs; so easy to overlook the
naturalness and simplicity of the goodness of Christ;
that it is pleasant to find a man who loved society,
music, and literature, who was courted, fêted, and
sought out, stealing away into courts and alleys

where everything was repulsive, to try and seek and
help and save some poor ignorant, unfriended street-
boy by holding up before him an ideal life. And
in this field of usefulness never was there a greater
need of labourers than now, when evil is daily growing subtler, and the " old paths " are being " improved " off the face of the earth.

One who knew Mac Gregor well has given this
testimony :

To some his manner may have appeared a little abrupt and self-
asserting; it was really a consciousness of power and purpose, which
was not arrogance, and to those who knew him well he would often
make it plain that he was the humble-minded Christian, alive to his
own shortcomings, and ever ready to recognise and appreciate the good
that existed in others. His influence with young men of all classes was
remarkable. His ready sympathy with their difficulties attracted
them, and his own manly character and pursuits won their admiration. His aim seemed ever to be to show them that Christianity is
meant to encourage and elevate the best feelings of our nature, by
setting its stamp on every innocent and beautiful recreation, with an
ultimate view to their own best good, and the glory of God. His
canoe and other expeditions were the outcome more of a strong and
aspiring nature than, as has been mistakenly suggested, of a restless
disposition; and they gave him a large acquaintance with life and
manners, increasing thereby his usefulness in intercourse with
others.

He was a believer in the plain Gospel of Christ, in
prayer and in the power of faith. Of religious difficulties he had to encounter many—for no man can
study the "evidences" and keep abreast of current
literature without finding them bristling around him ;

but of doubts he had few. If ever they arose—"these spectres of the mind"—he faced and laid them by the single charm, "It is written." Miracles, the stumbling-block of thousands, were aids to faith with him. Here is his artless argument:

"Some people feel it difficult to believe that any miracle has ever occurred, because they say, 'It would be a breach of the laws of nature!' I do not believe that any breach of the laws of nature has ever occurred, but that these laws have been always observed, and that one of the laws He ordained (though we did not know it—being ignorant) is that He can do, has done, and will do, whatever is His will and pleasure at all times, in all places."

The popular cry for social reform never for a moment drew him away from his conviction that there was "one thing needful" for each individual—the salvation of his own soul—and that this was a far higher mission than to wash, clothe, and feed the poor, or to provide education and amusement. At the same time he did not leave this undone, but took a persistent and consistent part in gladdening, elevating, and reforming the lives of the poor—work which he regarded as an outgrowth of the Christian spirit, but not Christianity itself.

We think that all who have followed the narrative contained in these pages must have come, with us, to the conclusion that John Mac Gregor was a man of no ordinary type, but a unique and remarkable personality, a brave, honest, and gifted man, who lived a life of patient well-doing and left the world better than he found it.

In many lands the interest attaching to his name and fame still lingers, and, as with his historic name-sake, so with him :

> Far and near, through vale and hill
> Are faces that attest the same,
> And kindle like a fire new-stirred
> At sound of Rob Roy's name.

INDEX

Printed by BALLANTYNE, HANSON, & CO.
London and Edinburgh

EARLY IN OCTOBER.

Demy 8vo, cloth, about 400 pages, price 6s.

THE WOMEN OF SHAKESPEARE

By LOUIS LEWES, Ph.D.

TRANSLATED FROM THE GERMAN BY
HELEN ZIMMERN

SYNOPSIS OF CONTENTS.—Translator's Preface—Author's Preface—Shakespeare's Times—The English Stage before Shakespeare—Shakespeare's Life——Shakespeare's Narrative Poems—The Female Characters in the Plays belonging to Shakespeare's "First Period": *Lavinia—Marina—Margaret of Anjou—Adriana—Katherina, &c.*—"Second Period": *Julia—Helena—Hermia—Juliet—Portia—Princess Anne—Duchess of Gloster—Constance—Mistress Ford—Rosalind—Viola—Beatrice, &c.*—"Third Period": *Volumnia—Portia—Cleopatra—Lady Macbeth—Ophelia—Desdemona—Cordelia—Isabella—Hermione—Imogen—Miranda—Queen Catherine, &c.*—Index.

EXTRACT FROM THE TEXT.

"We have ended. They have all passed before our vision, these female figures a mighty genius created, inspiring them with warm fresh life, and filling them with the breath of his spirit. We seem to have lived and suffered in their company. They have passed before us, powerful and terrible criminals, and noble women diffusing happiness, joy, and blessing, the strong and the weak, the happy and the wretched. We have looked into their eyes, we have heard their voices. They have spoken of all the bliss and woe of earth, of all the riddles of man's breast, of virtue and vice, of love and hate, of heaven and hell. We have felt all springs that move the soul of mankind. The poet's magic wand has laid open the depths of woman's nature, wherein, beside lovely and exquisite emotions, terrible passions play their dangerous and fatal part. We take leave of the poet with thankfulness and wonder. But not for ever. We turn back to him continually, with constant new delight. We always thirst to drink at the fresh and inexhaustible fountain of his poetry ; we lose ourselves in the beauty and eternal youth of his creations."

· HODDER BROTHERS
18 NEW BRIDGE STREET, LONDON, E.C.

IN PREPARATION.

Crown 8vo, cloth, price 3s. 6d.

ONE OF LIFE'S SLAVES

(LIVSSLAVEN)

By JONAS LIE

AUTHOR OF "THE VISIONARY," ETC. ETC.

AUTHORISED TRANSLATION

By JESSIE MUIR

"'The Visionary' is the best translation from the Danish that we have met with for some time; it is a real pleasure to read it; and we venture to express the hope that Miss Muir will follow it up by giving us an English version of LIE's 'LIVSSLAVEN,' THAT INTENSELY TRAGIC AND PATHETIC STORY OF SUFFERING AND WRONG."—*Athenæum.*

―――――

HODDER BROTHERS

18 NEW BRIDGE STREET, LONDON, E.C.

Imperial 4to, in wrapper. Price 5s. each part.

Complete in Six Parts, each containing Five Plates, making Thirty Plates in all, also issued bound in cloth gilt. Price 32s.

ANIMALS IN ORNAMENT

BY PROFESSOR G. STURM

The Plates have been reproduced by the finest collotype process, each Plate consisting of several designs with especial reference to their use by Art Workers. These designs may be copied, amplified, or enlarged as required.

The *BUILDING NEWS* says :—" A well drawn folio . . . . beautifully rendering the crisp and spirited delineations of the Author. Considerable ingenuity of balance, coupled with a degree of conventionality of application, is obtained by most of the designs, none of which are careless, and all are clever."

Imperial 4to, with 200 Plates, price £4 4s.

CHIPPENDALE'S
GENTLEMAN AND CABINET-MAKER'S DIRECTOR

BEING A LARGE COLLECTION OF THE MOST ELEGANT AND USEFUL DESIGNS OF HOUSEHOLD FURNITURE, IN THE MOST FASHIONABLE TASTE

BY THOMAS CHIPPENDALE

FACSIMILE OF THE THIRD EDITION
MDCCLXII.

HODDER BROTHERS
18 NEW BRIDGE STREET, LONDON, E.C.

JUST PUBLISHED, demy 8vo, pp. 462, cloth, price 14s.
At all Libraries and Booksellers.

THE NEW PARTY

DESCRIBED BY SOME OF ITS MEMBERS

AND EDITED BY

ANDREW REID

With a Frontispiece, " The New Era," by Walter Crane.

CONTENTS AND CONTRIBUTORS:

DAILY NEWS.—"This handsome, luxuriously-printed, and very striking volume."

DAILY CHRONICLE.—"It contains a number of thoughtful discussions of the most vital topics of our time; it is filled with inspiring suggestions; it positively reeks of independence and courage; it is characterised by the most contagious enthusiasm."

NEW YORK RECORDER.—"One of the most remarkable books, not of the year only, but of the decade."

METHODIST TIMES.—"Every intelligent Christian should buy, beg, or borrow this book. . . . It is the first attempt to crystallise the Social Movement which is fermenting in English society . . . . and which is certainly destined to have a tremendous effect upon the organised churches of the country. . . . This book is one of the most significant and characteristic signs of the times in which we live."

HODDER BROTHERS
18 NEW BRIDGE STREET, LONDON, E.C.